MOSCOW MAGICIAN

MOSCOW MAGICIAN

a thriller

John Moody

St. Martin's Press
New York

Library of Congress Cataloging-in-Publication Data

Moody, John.
    Moscow magician / John Moody.
      p.   cm.
    "A Thomas Dunne book."
    ISBN 0-312-05473-4
    I. Title.
  PS3563.0553M67   1991
  813'.54—dc20   90-48999
                                               CIP

First published in Great Britain by Victor Gollancz Ltd.

First U.S. Edition: January 1991
10 9 8 7 6 5 4 3 2 1

To my darling Alexandra
who felt the warmth of Viktor's story
when I saw only cold ashes

I

The flashing red lights sent exactly the right message: we are important and dangerous, out of our way! Like an angry hornet, the militia patrol car zipped through stop lights, shattered the speed limit of fifty kilometers an hour, and generally made a spectacle as it left Gagarin Square and the titanium statue of the canonized cosmonaut behind. The fact that no pedestrians were forced to dive for cover and no cars found it necessary to swerve into snowbanks did nothing to diminish the authority of the siren. After all, it was way past ten o'clock. What would anyone of decent intent be doing outside at this hour?

Inside the car, a battle raged. Levinsky had only just managed to tune the crackly car radio to the opera when Sudarov, without taking his eyes off the road, killed it with a counter-clockwise twist of the dial.

"Turdkicker!" said the younger man. "Do you know how seldom they play *The Valkyrie*?"

"Just about as often as is necessary, I imagine," said Sudarov. "They can play it at your funeral after they find out you've turned off the service band."

"They've just given us an assignment, haven't they? They're not going to call again, they're waiting to hear from us." A pause. "Who the hell would rob a flower shop?"

"I've been to this shop," the graying driver said. "Do you know it's the only one in Moscow open at this hour?"

"I'm not surprised, if people keep robbing them." The *non sequitur* worked somehow, and they shared a forced laugh.

Levinsky said, "It's here for Mischa, in case he forgets his wedding anniversary and needs to get something for the Tsarina."

"I still say you're too tough on him. He's the first one with brains that we've had since Lenin."

"What? Stalin wasn't intelligent?" asked Levinsky.

Sudarov gave him a hard look. "You're too young to know what it was like then. Do me a favor. Don't mention that name."

Leninsky Prospekt stretched on for ever; they veered left on to Profsoyuznaya. Because it had been categorized a division two boulevard, the amber lights were spaced every half kilometer. It made driving seem like a constant series of tunnels with short patches of blinding illumination between them. A block to their right was the Moscow Department Store; nowhere near as famous as overpriced, understaffed GUM, but stocked with exactly the same misassortment.

Aside from its unusual hours, the flower store was in fact different from others: it had a name, not a number. "The Petal" it styled itself, ignoring its official designation as Flower Store No 221. Customers, in their turn, seldom referred to it as anything but "the flower shop that stays open late". As Levinsky had suggested, it was beloved of absent-minded swains and errant husbands, trying to veil their true characters for anywhere from 50 kopeks (one wild flower without cellophane wrapping) to 15 rubles (a dozen pouting roses gathered by a length of red thread). For twelve years, it had been presided over by a rough-skinned woman of indeterminate age whose distaste for rising early had been the seed of a quiet revolution. By the time the proprietress arrived at her shop at noon, the glass door was blocked by a waist-high mound of blooms. By the time she had taken them inside and arranged them in vases or plunked them in buckets of water, her suppliers were staggering back from lunch at the bar on Vavilova Street. Business began to pick up at four, when the students from Patrice Lumumba University ambled over and, ashamed of their linguistic incompetence, pointed out their selections silently. Black hands held out clutches of black market rubles, trusting her to take the right amount. By eight at night, the late-rising florist's was the only light still burning in the area and would remain so until midnight. The routine had remained unchanged all this time. But after Gorbachev took over, it was held up as an example of bold new thinking.

The store, according to the radio report, had been robbed on March 23rd at 11.48 p.m., twelve minutes before closing time. The proprietress, whose only experience with crime had been customers who tried to filch extra flowers, used the aggressive tactics that had served her throughout her life. For her trouble, she was pushed headfirst into a corner of the shop, and her wrists were bound behind her with a meter and a half of her red ribbon. Her assailants she described as dark but not Russian, probably Georgian or Armenian. After they left with the day's till – 87 rubles, 40 kopeks – it took her twenty curse-filled minutes to free herself. And the ribbon was ruined.

For a crime site, it was strangely tranquil when the patrol car eased off Zalinskovo Proyezd. Levinsky was ready to jump out, when his partner leaned over, touched his shoulder, and said, "Remember, you're representing the Soviet Union when you walk in there. Act like it."

The first stone caromed off the windshield before Sudarov had cut the motor. Though they both heard the "thwack", neither could identify its source. The second missile was a paving brick. It battered its way through the driver's window and came to a halt against Sudarov's temple, preceding by a tenth of a second the meteor shower of fragmented glass. The older cop made a noise that sounded like an old man sitting down. Levinsky realized his partner's head was lying on his lap. For no real reason, he looked into the rear-view mirror mounted outside the passenger's window.

The woman had been right; they were dark, but there were more than two of them. They approached casually, as if window-shopping. In the mirror, he caught the reversed slice of a grin. It occurred to him that he should not be able to see their faces so clearly at one in the morning. That was when he noticed the torches. His brain was suddenly littered with random thoughts: no wonder the streets are in such terrible condition if people tear up the paving stones, Sudarov's head was very heavy, it would be expensive to have the bloodstains cleaned from his uniform, it is illegal to carry torches in Moscow without a permit. He was wondering idly if he would be able to climb over Sudarov's jack-knifed form and start the car when the back windshield imploded. He felt the air rush in, and on its wings, a sharp sweet smell that he associated with the garage where his father had fussed endlessly over the family's first car.

"Pour it on." "Be careful, not so near the flame! Do you want to join them at this barbecue?" "Toss a can inside so it soaks the seats." Levinsky clawed the right-side door open and was trying to get out when someone's thigh blocked him. "Do you know what you're doing?" A liter-sized can landed on Sudarov's back and began drooling out its contents. "Please," he said, "he's my friend." ("Pozhalostye. On moy droog.") He picked up the can and, for a second, looked around for some place else to put it. The gasoline stung as it touched a cut on the back of his hand, and, flooded with sudden understanding of what was going to happen, Levinsky put the canister back where it had fallen.

Reality became voices. "Lift up the hood and sprinkle some juice on the engine." "Open all the doors." "Okay, bring our friend up here."

There was a collective shout of fear as the car's outline was sketched against the darkness.

*

9

A passing motorist, a Party member, called the Central Complaint number, when he got home, to report a bonfire, which he said he assumed was the work of the monkeys from Lumumba. The special number was one of the first innovations Muscovites noticed after Gorbachev took over. It was supposed to bring citizens closer to the authorities, help them understand the problems in running a behemoth like Moscow, and give them an anonymous way to air their dissatisfaction. Of course, everyone assumed the line was tapped.

When the call came in, the dispatcher checked the service grid to see which car was nearest the area. He was not surprised when Sudarov and Levinsky did not answer the call. The dispatcher had spent twenty years on patrol, much of it the graveyard shift, most of it with his radio switched off. Besides, there was a fire department for jobs like this. Police in Moscow had more important things to do.

2

He blew on his hands, not because they were cold, but from habit. Vsevolod Poshtats thought it steadied his nerves and made him look and act more like the hero he knew he was. Dave had called him that and Dave knew.

As he stood by the southernmost entrance to the inner courtyard of the US Embassy, Poshtats wondered if he would ever see the rest of Moscow again. For most of his twenty-four years, Poshtats had been an outsider in his own land. His family came from Moldavia by way of Byelorussia, where he was born. Vsevolod was not a common name there. Too Russian, jeering friends said. So when his father left them, and his mother received permission to come to Moscow to work in a factory, Poshtats thought his name problems were over.

They were not. The Vsevolod was fine. But to ever-vigilant Muscovite ears, Poshtats sounded slightly, though not definitively, Jewish. The boy, by then a teenager, was subjected to periodic nose measurements with calipers by classmates who thought it hilarious. Once he was held down by several rough boys, who convinced a notorious hussy to inspect Poshtats by hand and determine whether or not he had been circumcised. He had, a common enough practise in Moldavia, but it only added to the evidence against him.

He had shown them. A stainless Komsomol record and high marks in Soviet history and German had made him prime material for the Foreign Ministry's youth recruiters. At eighteen, he saw himself as a future ambassador, a guiding light in the Soviet constellation. He attended the ministry's Institute of International Diplomacy, the spawning ground of new Gromykos. For eighteen months, he perfected his German, learned about the real Soviet view of world troublespots, listened to returning diplomats lecture on the opportunities for those willing to work hard.

One day he was called to the office of the sub-rector, a nearsighted man who was generally despised by the students. "Your family came from where?" he wanted to know. Poshtats wearily went through his familial itinerary. Would it never end?

The sub-rector made notes as he spoke, squinting and saying nothing. At the end, he said simply: "Thank you", and began working on something else. Poshtats backed out of the office.

There was never another meeting, no formal notice. It was just that from then on, Poshtats's progress at the Institute stopped. He was rejected for the advanced German course, told there was no room in the prestigious Foreign Policy seminar, and when he showed up for the first day of Western Cultures, his name did not appear on the seating roster. When he was blocked from taking second-year English, he knew the dream was dead.

The sub-rector, and those he represented, could not prove that Poshtats was Jewish, but did not believe that he was not. At the end of his second year, he was told that he had been drafted by the Army. He could enlist as an ordinary private, or he could report the next day to a yellow building that sat behind a high fence just beyond the third ring road in the far southern corner of Moscow.

KGB Personnel.

He could not be trusted to be a diplomat, but his facility with language made him acceptable to be a spy. Or so he thought. But, after a week of filling out forms that asked his views on pornography, the names of all past lovers, and the form of death he most feared, he was given a gray uniform and told to report for duty the next day to the American Embassy.

He was going to be a militiaman, a guard.

He could not believe it. All his hard work, his blameless conduct, his devotion – all wasted because his name did not sound Russian enough and his foreskin had been snipped as an infant.

His training for his new position would be on the job. He was put under the command of Morozov, as fierce a Jew-hater as Libya or Syria has yet produced. He ignored Vsevolod's explanation of his origins. "Look, kike," he said, "I can't figure out why they trust the likes of you for work like this. Or why they don't send you all to Israel in liter jars. I'm not in charge of those questions. I am in charge of guarding this embassy, and you will do as you are told, or you'll pray for a fate as kind as crucifixion."

"Guarding" was, of course, a euphemism. The twenty-four Soviet militiamen assigned to the US Embassy were all enlisted in the KGB, and their primary function was to gather information about what went on inside its walls. It was taken for granted that all American diplomats stationed in Moscow were spies, and since they could reasonably be

12

regarded as enemies of the Soviet state, the state had the right to protect itself.

The notion of a hapless state under attack insulted Poshtats's intelligence. He had seen at first hand its immense power, cruel selectivity and idiotic prejudice. Poshtats was no traitor, but neither was he easily duped. He regarded Morozov as the latest impediment to his success as a new Soviet man. And he had decided that, this time, he would defend himself.

The tactics themselves were numbingly predictable. The KGB had taxis parked about half a block from the embassy. When a Soviet tried to enter the embassy, he was intercepted and his reasons for going inside established. Once he left, he was usually picked up, and taken off for a brief interrogation/debriefing. It was amazing how slipshod the Americans were about security: office doors left open, conversations about classified topics carried on in hallways. Once this was discovered, the KGB began sending in its own polylingual people under cover of being a farmer from the Ukraine interested in American agricultural techniques.

When an American drove out of the embassy compound (they all seemed to have cars), the guard rang the taxi kiosk from the gray guard box set up near the main entrance. The taxi followed and reported where it went. After a while patterns began to develop: some of them visited known dissidents, some were having affairs with other foreigners, a few were boring enough to go straight home from work (though Morozov was sure that, once there, they pored over spy cables while their wives and children languished unnoticed). For a week Poshtats stood in the guard box and alerted the taxis.

To Poshtats it all seemed ridiculous. We know who our dissidents are, and people around the world screwed with partners to whom they were not married. Penny-ante blackmail fluff, that was all it was. What serious diplomat would rather betray his country than confess an indiscretion to his wife?

As the newest and lowest-ranking guard, Poshtats was soon put on the miserable one to eight a.m. shift. It was awful trying to turn his sleeping pattern around, to slumber at noontime and stay awake at three-thirty in the morning. He paced the sidewalks, envying the Marine Guards their warm comfortable niche behind bulletproof glass, inside the main portico.

At first he felt contempt for his colleagues. There was Borislav Nemetz, a gray little man under his little gray uniform. The cigarettes he smoked constantly stank up the guard box, even if they were, as Nemetz was proud to point out, foreign.

"Nothing better than Marlboro," Nemetz would wheeze.

"Not even emphysema?" Poshtats asked once.

"Not even a Jew's blood," was the little man's reply. Poshtats avoided him after that, although he quickly learned the source of Nemetz's Marlboros.

Vassily Ignativich Petrov was younger, better educated and just as impossible. He let Poshtats know their first day together that he considered the newcomer suspect. "Just keep your eyes open, Moishe, and don't forget which side you're on."

"Which side is that Vassily Ignativich? The side of uninformed prejudice?"

"Don't talk to me like that, Hooknose, or I'll report you for anti-State slander."

"Even if there hasn't been any?"

"And who do you think they'll believe? You or me?"

The answer was clear enough, as was the reference to "they". He kept his opinions from Petrov as well, but he was better prepared for what he was sure would be an inevitable face-off. He saw him squirreling a package away one night in the guards' room, located at the corner of the embassy. Guards' room was not exactly an apt description. It was an underground bunker, really, where the odd Soviet lunatic was dragged and beaten bloody after trying to rush into the embassy.

"What have you there, Petrov?" he asked, causing the young man to spin around as if thrown from a centrifuge.

"Nothing, nothing at all." Petrov actually tried to hide it behind his back, like a little boy caught with forbidden sweets.

"Oh let me see, I'll bet it's the plan for the new spy satellite to be launched next month." This was pure jokery on his part, of course, but Petrov took it seriously.

"How dare you mention that!" he roared. His hands appeared, still clutching the package. "I'll show you, you piece of shit. It's a girlie mag, nothing more. At least I don't betray state secrets."

The tits exposed on the cover were bigger than Poshtats ever imagined could be hung on a human frame. But he saw something even more alluring: a chance to put Petrov on ice.

"So I see. But that's American pornography, is it not?"

"American? I don't think so?" Petrov was cagy now. He did not speak any foreign languages, and saw his disadvantage.

"Oh yes, Vassily I'm afraid it is. *Penthouse*, it's called. I'm afraid I'll have to let our superiors know about this."

"You do and I'll tell them you're talking loosely about the spy satellite to be launched next month."

Poshtats bestowed what would later be called his "scheming kike" smile and said: "You ignorant clod. There is no spy satellite being launched then. You know less about your own country than you do female plumbing. Those tits are fake."

"They are not. Viktor gave me last month's issue and there's a girl with even bigger ones." There was a kind of victorious smirk in the comment. But Poshtats was the winner. He knew who Viktor was. He was the Marlboro man, the Moscow magician, and the porn pawner too, it seemed.

Four months into his assignment Poshtats was put on the evening shift, a welcome change from the constant darkness. He saw the embassy empty out between five and six o'clock, then repopulate as diplomats, journalists, businessmen, and off-duty marines began to fill up a cramped room off the main courtyard that at midday was used as a cafeteria. At night, it suddenly became "Uncle Sam's", a bar and pickup strip that titillated Petrov beyond endurance.

"Look at the ass on that one," he would hiss as a secretary in the American political section ambled down the road, both arms wrapped around the newly arrived French cultural attaché.

Poshtats was not unaware of the sexual appeal of the women, but what interested him most was their mindless complacence and their willingness to leave with different partners on each trip. Surely this could be put to use?

Morozov was grudgingly impressed. "I don't imagine you've ever caught the scent of it before. How would you know what normal is? Still, you're right. If we catch someone in a triangle, it could pay off."

Morozov passed on the observation and recommendation as his own. This did not surprise Poshtats. In fact he was grateful when Morozov, obviously pleased with himself, instructed the young man to keep a close eye on who was going home with whom.

This proved less pleasant work than it might seem. Trying to remember between fifty and seventy faces, outfits and partners on the way in, and matching them up again on the way out is roughly as challenging as memorizing each hand of cards in a poker match. Poshtats put his good mind to work and soon developed a system: it broke down men versus women, nationalities, and visible characteristics: hair color, flashy jewelry, average state of inebriation at the end of the evening.

Morozov grunted, but Poshtats could tell he had scored again.

As his reward, he was put back on the graveyard shift.

Morozov placated. "What are you complaining about, Hymie? It shows how much we trust you, putting you here alone. You're the only layer of Soviet security attached to the embassy at that time of night."

Poshtats knew that was not true. True he was the only KGB man outside the embassy, but there is always a motor patrol making rounds through the city, checking on every sensitive post. The American Embassy is considered sensitive indeed.

Poshtats decided not to complain, to settle into the job. For one week, two weeks, a month, he plodded lonely long hours. Uncle Sam's was closed by the time he came to work, but since he had no personal life to speak of, he got into the habit of coming early and watching the couples leave from the window of the guardhouse.

"Who is the blonde?" he asked Petrov one night.

"Aha, finally found one you fancy. Well, at least we know now you're not both a Yid and a homo!"

He was not interested in the blonde's body. He was interested in her clothes. He was also curious because she arrived alone every night, and always left alone, well after Uncle Sam's was closed, sometimes as late as two and three o'clock. And because of whom he saw let her out of the side door.

Russians make a show of racial tolerance, but it is a sham. They regard black people as coiffed monkeys with developed prehensile ability. African students who come to Patrice Lumumba University or who are lucky enough to gain acceptance to Moscow University are invariably hazed, insulted, and finally, ignored. "Too dark, didn't see you," a motorist will say if he knocks a black down with his car, and the militiaman dispatched to the scene will unswervingly agree: "People can't see in the dark. Wear a reflector around your neck. Or better yet a noose." And he and the driver will share a Russian laugh.

Poshtats, himself a victim of prejudice, was less bigoted than most. He did not care that the tart leaving the embassy was kissed on her snowy cheek by a strapping black American Marine. Nor that the young man had in his eyes that slightly dazed wetness that bespeaks recent intercourse. Poshtats did not see a nigger; he saw an opportunity. He would have made an excellent diplomat.

He began to arrive earlier each night, to see the woman leave. He followed her from as close a distance as he thought prudent. And he was rewarded. Despite the late hour, she marched to the metro and passed through its turnstiles with the sureness of rote. He saw her walk, saw her waiting for her train. Saw her turn and exchange a quick, meaningless comment with an old woman. She blended into the thin pack of passengers perfectly. She was Russian.

He decided to approach her on a Monday night, about an hour before he reported for duty. He had considered and rejected telling Morozov about her. This was to be his own coup and he wanted full credit for it. By ten p.m. he was across the street. He saw Petrov slither off to the guard's room, no doubt for a quick peek at his glossy pages. Amazing. That twerp has left the front of the US Embassy untended. He would store that away for future use. But, for the moment, his concern was the woman.

"She's not coming." The voice was so controlled that it might have come from a pocket radio tuned low. Poshtats did not jump, or scream or exhibit any other signs of surprise. But his insides felt as if they had been neatly melted with a blowtorch. He turned.

"She couldn't make it tonight," said a tall man in a black coat. Poshtats wondered if he also had "spy" written on his business cards, so hokey was the costume. But this was no smiling matter. Where had he come from? Was he, too, waiting? People don't come from nowhere, but Poshtats was sure the street had been empty of pedestrians a second ago. His Russian was perfect: inflection, idiom, accent. But this was no native. His face was unlined, but not handsome. He was tall and built differently from a Slav: naturally wide shoulders that helped him carry his frame straight, chest out. Russians are inclined, from historical experience as well as physiognomy, to bend and stoop.

"What are you talking about?" Reflexively he took half a step back. I feel weak, he thought. I want to run across the street, share Petrov's silly magazine, work eight useless hours and go to my miserable home.

"The girl, who calls herself Barbara when she's inside the embassy over there screwing soldiers and trying to worm information out of them. Relax, Vsevolod, you didn't make any mistakes."

Hearing his own name spoken by this stranger belied the last statement. How long has he known, how much does he know, how can he harm me? Poshtats was doing what he always knew he could; thinking fast, using his mind. This was not for his country, but for his survival.

"Take a walk with me, Vsevolod. You have an hour before you're due at work, and that idiot Petrov is inside whacking off again."

"You know a lot about us." He said it in English, though he was fairly certain he was right.

They walked wordlessly down Tchaikovsky Boulevard, away from the embassy, and turned left on Kalinin Prospekt. The American led him to the front window of Dom Melodia, and stiff with fear and some strange element of excitement, Poshtats pretended to scan records behind darkened glass.

"Look, we've had you spotted as odd from the beginning. You're a diplomatic dropout, aren't you?"

"Not so much dropped as bounced." Why was he answering the question? Why was he here?

"If we'd wanted to stop you from shadowing our lusty whore and making trouble, we'd have found some way to compromise you," said the black coat. "As it is, I think we can help each other, with you getting more than you give."

"That sounds extremely un-American."

The man smiled, briefly, then turned it off. "Not at all, when what we want is sufficiently valuable. We think you're that valuable."

"Who is we?"

The stranger pulled back. Though Poshtats did not look at him, he was sure he was being given a cold stare.

"Look, Vsevolod, how many people outside the KGB know as much about you as I do? Your mother? That idiot Petrov? Morozov? We don't have much time before you're due at the gate. You're at a dead end here, and nothing you do – nothing – is going to rescue you from what they see when they hear your name. They're always going to think of you as a scheming, smart-ass anti-Russian Jew. And maybe you are. In America, that would make you just like everyone else." He laughed to show this was a joke.

Our lives come down to minutes, seconds sometimes, of decision. Years of instinct, training, preparation are put on exhibit and tested. What we know, we know. Things new and unfamiliar must be analyzed, and weighted on merit. Poshtats heard the stranger's words, held them against the profile of his life so far, and judged them true. He let go of his inner tension. This could not be treason. The decision had been made for him, years ago, in the sub-rector's office.

"What do I call you?" he asked.

"Call me Dave."

Six weeks later, Poshtats stood in the southern courtyard entrance, blowing on his hands. No, not a traitor. Not yet. Six weeks, he thought, was how long it had taken the system to tell him he was no longer a candidate diplomat. Five weeks ago, he and Dave did their first "exchange". Meaning he explained what the KGB guards really did outside the embassy, and Dave told him what the Americans would be willing to do for him. He could continue to work under cover, and pass information along, all the while collecting $1,000 a month in any bank in the world. Including the Moscow Vneshtorg bank, Dave had said, smilingly, if he was feeling suicidal. Alternately, after completing his work, he could count on a warm reception in the West. What appealed to

Poshtats – even while recognizing that it was meant to appeal to him – was Dave's promise that he could teach a course of CIA operatives specializing in Soviet counter-intelligence.

The first job was to break up the Marines' romancing of Russian sluts. The Americans could have done this themselves, but that would have set off alarm bells within the KGB. The embassy spooks already knew who "Barbara" was and where she lived. Poshtats paid her a visit one afternoon; she still in her dirty polyester robe, he without having slept since his overnight shift. Poshtats did not identify himself, he simply told her to let him in, and she knew with what kind of person she was dealing.

"We're very pleased with your work," he said, smiling in what he hoped was a gentle, reassuring way. "But the Americans have grown suspicious. How many reports have you made? Six?"

"Nine! Did Voroshilov tell you only six? I imagine he'll try to pay me less. Or maybe it's because I wouldn't sleep with him, that lizard."

The name meant nothing to Poshtats but it would to Dave. He had accomplished his mission in less than a minute, but he had to put on a good show. He handed her rubles.

"We want you to leave town, take a vacation. Maybe the Crimea. Once back, tell no one, absolutely no one, where you've been. Not even Voroshilov. He won't be running you any more."

"Oh? Will it be you then? You're not a lizard." She ran her tongue over her lips as she took the money.

He did not tell Dave what happened then.

He worked at his relations with Petrov and Nemetz. Let it be known that he had learned his lesson and wanted to be one of the boys. Petrov was easier. He had never seen such a hard-core magazine as Poshtats gave him. "They're Israeli girls," Vsevolod confided blushingly, as if selling his sister.

I knew it, Petrov had said. Always knew. But, he added, you're not a totally bad sort. For a Yid.

They had taken him two weeks ago. "Listen," said Poshtats. "Since we've become friends and all, I'm letting you know. Do you have any idea what kind of movies they show inside the embassy at night? Orgies. Women with women. Women with horses. Taking one after the other. I got so hot I had to go take care of myself."

First, Petrov was horrified. "You've been inside?" "Sure," said Poshtats. "One of the marines is Jewish. He'd do anything for me."

This *non sequitur* worked in Petrov's unkeen mind. Two nights later, throat engorged with expectant lust, he let Poshtats lead the way into the embassy portcullis. The marine behind the bulletproof glass booth gave him a hard stare, then a smile. The electric lock on the gate buzzed open. Petrov hesitated for just a second. He grabbed Poshtats's arm, and the young man tensed for the blade or bullet he was sure was coming.

"With horses?" Petrov asked.

"Horses," he confirmed and they went in.

Overhead, a video camera's blinking red light recorded it all.

Petrov's disappearance caused a furore. As the relief man, Poshtats was grilled thoroughly about what he had seen, and not seen, when he arrived for work. Once he thought he might snap.

"Did Petrov have any weaknesses?" asked the interrogator, whose name was never offered.

"He was . . . weak," Poshtats replied, beginning to shake.

"He liked tits and bum, didn't he?"

Poshtats noticed the past tense. "I think he liked thinking about them, yes."

The interrogator's back was turned but he may have smiled. A second later he told Poshtats he could go.

A week ago, Poshtats walked into the embassy, becoming number two. While it officially ended his life as a Soviet, it also removed suspicion from him. For him to report another missing militiaman when he came to work would be too much now, Dave said.

"I'm a traitor," Poshtats sighed an hour later.

"You're a hero," Dave assured him.

One preyed on the next. Friendships, rivalries, the chance to even old scores, a possibility of promotion. Petrov brought in Vasiliyev. Nemetz, a rank lower, envied Vasiliyev so much that he took the bait when he appeared at the guard box.

"Fuck your mother, you traitor! I'll shoot you," he shouted, groping for his gun.

"No you won't. Not when you hear what I've been doing. It's a cover operation. We're going to find out who the CIA chief is at the embassy. I'm supposed to recruit one more man. We don't like each other, I know that, Nemetz. But you're the best. I choose you."

Now, a week later, they argue.

"You said if I brought the first one in, plus myself, it would be enough."

"You're the only one who can take Morozov," Dave said, as if complimenting him on his cologne.

It is the cheapest kind of bunkum and Poshtats recognizes it as such.

But he also knows that he has traded one kind of misery for another. There will always be one more request, one more job. He knows this already but cannot protest.

Ready? they ask him.

"Morozov!" He is on one side of the embassy's thick southern wall. He can see Morozov on the TV monitor, heading towards the guard box. It is a screamed whisper, he thinks to himself. He has practiced it all day, all the time trying to convince Dave that he should have to do no more.

Morozov stops, looks around, continues walking.

"Morozov, it's me, Poshtats!"

This time he stops and looks at the wall, trying to understand.

"Where? Poshtats? Is it you?"

"Help! I've been taken prisoner. The Americans have me. Help me get out!"

"Where are you?"

"I'm in the embassy. They're coming for me. Help!"

On the TV monitor, it looked as if Morozov was having a discussion with someone inside the embassy. But, without the sound, the logical conclusion to be drawn was that he was trying to get in. And the scene on the monitor was also being recorded.

Dave congratulated him. Dave promised him a happy life. Told him he had performed an enormous service that would be remembered for years to come. Poshtats sat in the Marine Guards' changing room, thinking how much cleaner it looked and smelled than the one in which he had previously worked. He was no longer a guard. He was no longer a KGB agent. He was probably no longer even a Soviet.

He was a traitor. And he wanted to make sure that he was not the only one who suffered.

"Tomorrow we'll talk about where you want to resettle," Dave said. He looked, thought Poshtats, like a man anxious to leave his mistress's boudoir.

"I want to tell you one other thing," said the young man. "Something you may find interesting. All the guards at the embassy take bribes, presents, you know, not to make trouble for Soviets who need to get inside. There's this one fellow who seems to have a gift list of everyone who works here."

"Who's that?" Dave was no longer in a hurry to leave.

"His name is Viktor. Viktor Nikolaich. A driver. He has them all eating out of his hand. He's a real pro. A magician."

"Is he now?" Dave asked.

21

3

Viktor eyed the bottle. He desired it as much as any man looks forward to a first one after eight hours on the job. Perhaps he craved it twice as much, for he had worked for the past fifteen hours. He sank into the comfort of his chair as the little electric clock from Switzerland struck thirteen. This was due to a mechanical problem and not overzealousness or impatience. Having become used to it, Viktor knew that thirteen meant eleven and fourteen meant twelve. Somehow the mechanism righted itself during the next hour and began again with only one chime. It was one of the many mysteries of life that Viktor found more convenient to accept than to consider.

The desire for the bottle was something else. To accept that meant submission. Vodka steals the soul and turns the tongue into a trigger. There had been different days. In some ways better, for when he had been young and unmarried (had there really been such a time?) he had often awoken the next morning in a strange room, feeling pity for the person trapped inside him. But they had also been days when he ate less often and less well – his bulging French sweater, still sticky with the day's perspiration, was evidence. No, his bottle, like his bachelorhood, he had put on the shelf. And though either could be retrieved easily, the attendant cost he rated as too high. He had grown used to the pleasures of a home life and was unwilling to surrender them for mere excitement.

Marya came into the room. The clock finished striking thirteen. Like her husband, Marya had learned to live with the extra chimes. If was infinitely easier than trying to get the clock fixed, especially one made in a foreign country. Gorbachev talked about strengthening the economy by integrating it with the rest of the world, but what happened when this imported example of integrated strength went ka-fluzz? Just answering questions about where and how and from whom it had been obtained would take the better part of a day. And it was unlikely that a piece of such sophistication would come back in any working order at all.

Complaints were always useless and most often dangerous. They had both chuckled when the Central Complaint number was published. "Complaints come from people who are looking for problems," Viktor had said. They could, for instance, lead to further research into the origins of ownership. And no one wanted that. Better to listen to six extra chimes a day. Better yet to be asleep most nights at this time so the fourteen chimes would cause no irritation.

"Soup's up." She knew he was hungry.

"Hmm." He pushed himself out of his chair, took three steps and was in the dining room. The two areas were separated only in the mind of the beholder. Throw rugs of different styles and colors might have represented a psychological border, but there were different rugs in the sitting room and the dining room contained one and a half; the other half of the second extended into the kitchen where Marya stood while cooking.

What greeted Viktor at the end of the table was a reddish-brown fluid with vague hints of meat. The same sight would have been visible had he arrived when he was expected, five hours earlier. His tardiness merely required reheating the borscht to rearrange the distribution of the fat flecks. To heat borscht too much damages the flavor of the beets if it is properly made. To heat it too little fails to dissolve the fat that accumulates from the pieces of pork, chicken or beef that comprise the stock. Marya, an adequate cook, knew about the first danger, and regarded the second as less serious. Slices of thick black bread sat stacked on a chipped plate in the center of the table. He took two and tore them, let them fall in the soup. Viktor took a steel spoon – the one he had been issued twenty-two years earlier in the army – and scooped up a piece of sodden bread.

The contrasting tastes, the sour doughiness, the sweetness of the beets, the odor of the meat, made him wince in appreciation. It was the first thing he had eaten for twelve hours. In that time, draughts of steaming black instant coffee had turned his stomach into a growling acid pit. He hummed slightly as he swallowed and Marya knew he was satisfied.

"What kept you?" It was her first complete sentence since he arrived home and the first allusion to the hour.

"A turkey – " Viktor said as more soup went down, " – needed a home."

Marya would have accepted any answer. She had come to understand that her husband's whereabouts were really none of her business. But this explanation demanded elaboration.

"Where", she asked slowly, "did you get a turkey?"

Viktor looked at her as one might a cloying child who asks again and again where lightning comes from, then patiently, as Marya was not privileged like him to work among foreigners, said gently, reprovingly, "Tamoshna, of course."

Yes, of course, where else but at the customs warehouse would one see the wealth of the outside world? Who had seen a turkey in Moscow, the jewel of Soviet society? And, the joke went, if he had seen it, who dared show it to him?

"But Tamoshna closes at six o'clock."

"Yes, and waiting till then was the only way I could give Fedirov his cigarettes and get the damn thing. Even then I had to argue for an hour."

That explained it. Marya long ago stopped testing her husband's answers for veracity; she now merely tried to probe to understand the depths of his genius. It was not recognizable as such: Viktor Nikolaich Melanov laughed an idiot's laugh. He made a riotous fool of himself in public, and looked like a jolly butcher at the local market. That, perhaps, accounted for his success at what he did, which was to wind, wheedle and worm through the stifling bureaucracy of the Soviet Union as well as anyone in the country, and far better than those who ran it.

Beneath the laughter and buffoonery, he was a machine, calculating, adding, certainly subtracting and hoping to find a lower price, a shorter line, another egg, or in this case, a turkey that had been flown in from Helsinki. This job was easier than most in terms of frustration. He knew the bird was in the customs warehouse – the tuchina – and he knew that Fedirov was the only man who could release it. Knew through months, years really, of listening seriously to pathetic petty officials give orders followed by hints at what might make them happy and thus make them agreeable. Having followed the orders and gotten nowhere, Viktor came to understand that only the hints were worth listening to, not the rules.

Now as he swallowed soup, he was allowing the guile that guided him through the day to slip away. An air of tired honesty took its place. He never needed to act with Marya. She was not one of the "mafia", as he called the collective irritations of his day. What he meant, though he would have had difficulty verbalizing it, was that she was not a part of the system, but, like most Russians, its victim. With her he could shed pretenses, discuss problems of the flat – there were many – and the frustrations of her factory job. She had been working at it when he met her nine years ago, stubbornly refused to quit it though it galled her to rise every day and face eight hours of attaching the arms of eyeglasses to their frames.

Still, because of it, they lived comfortably, if not well. To Viktor there was a qualitative difference between the two that he had a difficult time reconciling with the gray doggerel that filled his newspaper each day. What difference whether the workers in the Volgograd auto-plant overfilled their October production quota if Marya was unable to find meat in the store? But such questions spoken aloud were dangerous, and he was too canny to make such a mistake. So he accepted the good things that came from their combined incomes and sought the things that they needed from other sources. The meat in the borscht, for instance, was provided in exchange for having the flat tire of the butcher fixed. The garage mechanic had been persuaded to repair the tire on an hour's notice by the gift of a bottle of his favorite Armenian cognac. Viktor kept a running list of personal preferences, revising it as tastes, and important people, changed. The cognac had come from the special grocery store – the Gastronome – reserved for foreigners. So had the cigarettes for the customs man, who preferred Marlboro 100's. And entry to the Gastronome was made possible because Viktor knew that there was an unclaimed turkey at the customs warehouse, and had obtained it for the manager of the store.

Viktor was, according to his job specifications, a chauffeur for the Moscow bureau of an American news agency. That did not mean he was uneducated. He knew his Russian classics, especially beloved Pushkin, and whatever poems of Pasternak he had been able to read, before such things became completely legal under Gorbachev. Viktor's schooling had been sufficient to teach him the world's geography, a Soviet version of its ancient and modern history, and of course, the contributions of the motherland. His job was a matter of convenience, not training.

Certainly, he was often behind the wheel of a car. But usually it was en route to finding something in short supply, or to make arrangements for future suspected shortages, or to deliver gifts of gratitude, rather than delivering people. His salary was guaranteed, as were annual raises, proof perhaps that Communism and not capitalism is the chief cause of inflation. Viktor was technically "on loan" from the division of the government that provided Soviet employees to foreign companies doing business in Moscow. His salary in rubles was paid faithfully, whether or not the company had actually transferred money to the Moscow bank account assigned to it on time. If the money was not there, the Soviet employment agency simply withdrew the necessary amount from a collateral fund that the company was required to set up in order to be admitted for business to the Soviet Union. Each year, the amount required of new companies to be registered was increased one per cent over the previous year's figure. If a company's collateral fund at any time fell below the amount required the year it was registered, it was obliged to start a new account – at the new year's price. Most firms, seeing the extortion for what it was, found it more economical to keep up its payments to Soviet employees.

Viktor had devised the system.

It had been a natural enough suggestion. At least it seemed so at the time, six years earlier. He was working as a janitor in the office of the employment agency, and as he was emptying waste cans – to be systematically emptied into a closely supervised oven, lest any top-level doodling fall into the wrong hands – he had overheard two officials cursing the unreliability of foreign employers. It was costing them thousands of rubles a month to advance the salaries of the Soviet workers they provided, then chase down the various offending foreigners for compensating payment. In the meantime, money that could have gone to rocket research or vodka was lost and the cost of badgering the businesses was further eating away at the profit edge.

Had Viktor's mind been more theoretical, he might have pointed out that profit does not have a place in a land of Communism. Instead, he emptied another of the huge green metal waste cans and said, more to himself it seemed than to the executives, "Probably they should have to pay first to hire Soviet workers, then be punished if they fall behind."

"Dos vedonya," he said, and wheeled out his cart of refuse slowly.

The next day, he went into the same office and cleaned the wastebasket of its contents, noticing it was uncommonly full. Though it was forbidden to inspect such papers, Viktor stole a look at some of the sheets that had not been crumpled up, and saw it contained columns headed : "Initial investment", "Escalating fee?", "Penalty provisions". Outside the office, he took a risk and opened more sheets of paper. One was full of handwriting. It began: "A proposal for establishing a contingency fund for advance payment by foreign companies that employ Soviet citizens." Blood ran to his face and if not for the inner regulator that checked his temper many times at crucial moments, he would have bellowed in rage.

He had contributed an idea free of charge to the state. The next day he was told he had become a chauffeur.

The borscht lost some of its taste and he pushed his chair back from the table slightly, munching on a piece of brown bread, heavily laden with butter.

"What?" said Marya, knowing his hunger was not that easily disposed of.

"Another militia car was attacked, I heard."

"When?" She appeared only mildly interested, but he knew better. She rarely commented, but kept tight track of the ragged-edged esoterica he brought home. So there was no need to introduce subjects of conversation

26

with anything more than peripheral references. Few Soviet citizens actually believe their homes are bugged, but they ask, what is the use of speaking loosely until they are proven wrong?

"Last night, they say."

"Were they specials like the last ones?"

"Ummm." He swallowed again. "One was a Jew. The other one comes from Semipalatinsk, and has a wife who's a research scientist." There was, again, no need to go into specifics. Semipalatinsk is the closest population center to the country's main nuclear testing site.

He looked at her for several seconds, debating whether to say more. Knowing what he was doing, she also knew he would continue. Alone, together, they held back nothing.

"Was it like the one last week?"

"Worse. This time they got both of them. Out on Profsoyuznaya near the African playground. Set the car on fire and left them to burn in it."

Marya was interested but not shocked. "What can it all mean?"

"It means I'm not going to pick up any strangers on Profsoyuznaya."

"Daddy!"

The sound broke the silence like the unexpected ring of the telephone. Viktor turned and saw his daughter, tiny in sleeping shirt of red and gold that said "Trojans – No 1", standing in the arch that led to the bedrooms.

"What, my mulchik?"

"I thought I heard you." The voice was sleep-filled but still sweeter sounding than anything else he had heard that day.

"And you were right," he answered, and as he did she ran to him and he scooped her up in his arms and lifted her over the back of the chair to sit in the vast expanse of his lap. She snuggled against the leather jacket he wore until winter forced him to don heavier clothes and said, "Where were you? I love you," and was halfway asleep in his embrace, needing no answer but his presence.

Marya smiled. She was jealous of the bond between father and daughter that did not include her, but knew also that in the next few years that would change. Anna was eight and the joy of her father. She adored him as only children can adore, rapt with attention whenever he spoke. To her he seemed so wise, so powerful, the perfect arbiter for any problem. But Marya was content to bide her time. What Solomon-like wisdom will he come up with when she first tells him she is in love?

And with that comfort she went to the kitchen and unwrapped a whole slice of the ice-cream that Viktor had brought home as he always did. Made only of pure cream and sugar, it was one of the national treasures of the Russians that even Communism could not kill, though there were those who said it had tasted better before the revolution. But anyone who lived before the revolution was old and the old coloured all their memories in favor of the past. What could life have been like then, Marya wondered as she stripped off the silver and red paper, unconsciously licking her fingers and tasting the gooey sweetness. Carefully she washed off the foil and put it above the drainboard on the sink. It would be used to wrap a piece of fish, or meat, or – wonder of wonders – the remainder of a slice of ice-cream. If there ever was a remainder.

"Mama, can we have some ice-cream?" The two voices joined together – one high and slightly lisping, expectant, unsure. The other deep, playing along, knowing full well that ice-cream was being peeled out of its silver skin before the cry was raised.

"May I have some?" Marya called back as always, and as always she was met by the mingled giggling that accompanied her grammar lessons.

"Sure, go ahead." More giggling. She wondered when the joke would grow old. Until it did she would go over the lines with them again and again, like Bolshoi dancers rehearsing a *pas de deux* until their muscles cramped and their wills crumpled and they did it right.

Marya returned with the ice-cream and saw there was no sleepiness in her daughter's eyes now. Like her countrymen, Anna was serious about food. She watched the bowl lowered to the table, fantasizing as always that the bottom would never be reached, that somehow her father had stumbled on to an ice-cream trough as deep and rich as the oilwells in Siberia that she heard about in school.

"Mmmmmm," she said, smelling its sweetness already, feeling its frostiness waft up to her like under-the-blankets warmth.

"Ann-schka. Let's make it like yoghurt."

"You do it, it's too hard for me."

"Oh, come on, you."

And like deranged cooks whipping a batter, they thrust in their spoons and stirred the ice-cream, and as it always did half the hard white block slopped out of the dish and on to the table and they competed to get it to their spoons and back into the bowl, howling at its coldness against their fingers and rushing those fingers to their mouths just as Marya had.

She watched them forgivingly, wondering again how her husband could take such an unexciting event and turn it into a magical act. The beneficiary was not always Anna, although she knew he would rather please her than anyone on earth. Any stranger or worse, enemy, could be lulled by Viktor's smile, charmed by his actions. It made her uneasily proud. Was he, as her mother had said, cursed with charm? "Anyone who can smile that openly has something to hide." But was that not also what drew her to him in the first place? That and the need of youth to defy advice. But mostly what had attracted her was his way with people: how in a time and a land where wise men kept silent and looked away, Viktor had a hearty "Strasvuyte" for anyone and a moment to listen to their problems, their joys.

"Mmmmm," he said now, holding the ice-cream an arm's length out of reach of Anna, miming swallowing it, rubbing his stomach with a free hand.

"Oh you!" came the little voice, but it was only part of the elaborate charade that constituted a game with her father. She knew that at least her share, and probably more, of the ice-cream would be there when he lowered his arm. She had never known it to be otherwise, and if the world were made of ice-cream she would be a princess.

"Ahhhh, here little birdie, eat it," he said and his hand, holding the spoon heaped with a slushy mountain of white, came shooting down toward her parted lips.

She gobbled it with an innocence that knew no suffering, and a joy that knew no guilt.

It was part of being Russian, part of being one of the successors to the tsars, one of God's damned and chosen.

The Moscow night became darker. Morning was a moment of sleep away.

4

The Moscow subway is world-famed for its chandeliered stations, its steep escalators that carry most of the city above and below ground at some time during the day, and its overall efficiency. All this is chronicled in any number of Moscow guide-books, one of which says, "The Moscow metro truly must be experienced to be fully appreciated." What the guide-book does not mention, but also must be personally experienced to be credited, is the smell in the Moscow metro. It is not the smell of chugging cars burning fuel, or of the famed chandeliers gleaming with brass polish.

It is the smell of people. People waiting.

Viktor waited. Viktor smelled. That is to say, Viktor smelled like any Russian waiting at the platform of Shchbakovskaya Station. Although spring had come and the trees were in leaf, it was still cold, and so many commuters were more prudently dressed than they had been the day before. Leather jackets abounded and women were wearing their fake-fur-collared coats. Shchbakovskaya was the next to last station in the northern line on the road to Sheremetyevo Airport. Those who worked in the center of the city had a long and hot ride ahead of them. This, along with the suffocation imposed by heavy coats, and the defensive suffocation proposed by their nasal passages as a method of protection from olfactory martyrdom, made them a craggy lot this morning. But Viktor was placid. He stood up at the front of the throng, nearest to where the train would swoosh by, and smiled absently. He was thinking of Anna, and of how she had curled up on his lap the night before, asleep even before the last of the ice-cream was gone. Of how he carried her, gently as a china doll, to her bed, tucked her in and nuzzled her, receiving for his extra loving gesture a purr of enjoyment.

His reverie was interrupted by the sound of a quarrel nearby, and as he focused his attention, he immediately was confronted by a choice. Two old women tugged at opposite ends of a rug, filthy with age and pedestrian abuse.

Almost without meaning to, Viktor became involved, as he caught snatches of their argument and realized they were debating the best place to have the item cleaned. Both options being proposed offended his sense of intelligence.

"Strasvuyte, ladies," he said easily, his smile an automatic buffer zone. He heard the subway approaching.

"May I recommend a shop on Prospekt Mira. Fast service and good results." Quickly he imparted the name of the shop and turned, saying "Tell them Viktor Melanov was your introduction."

This was his way. The name Melanov seemed to float from one shop to the next in Moscow, ushering in new customers. It was more effective than advertisements, which Russian newspapers lacked anyway, and was more personal. And Viktor took care not to endorse a shop unless it was of the highest quality, or at least the highest quality available. Though he would never have said it, he felt his recommendation spoke tellingly of his own character, and he would have been terribly ashamed to be told that someone who took his advice was cheated or disappointed.

In a word, it was a matter of honor. And it was about to be tested.

"What is your name?" It was not that the woman had not heard him. Patronymics are as natural to a Russian as black bread.

"Viktor Nikolaich."

"All right, Viktor Nikolaich Melanov," said the other. "I will try this shop on Prospekt Mira. And if they ruin my rug I'll bring it to you and you can buy me a new one." But she smiled as she said it, showing stainless steel front teeth.

"My pleasure, comrade."

Viktor turned and darted into the metro a second before its doors whooshed shut. There was not a seat to be had in the car. There never was at this hour. The inheritors of the class revolution sit glumly on the uncushioned seats, some reading *Pravda*, others chatting in a low voice, still others swaying from the effects of the morning's first vodka or Armenian cognac, which plays a role in most Russians' breakfasts.

Viktor enjoyed the rush hour, whether or not he was standing. To him, the crowds, and their bustling, meant going somewhere, more than the deserted cars chugging along at midday or midnight. He had heard stories of the unbelievable crush of people that forced their way in and out of the New York subways and the London Underground between eight and nine in the morning and five and six at night. This, he knew, was not the same. But he would settle. He settled back comfortably against the door, removed *Pravda* from his pants' pocket and creased it lengthwise into quarters.

"We will live up to the ideals of Lenin," said the headline above the main article.

To himself, he wondered if there were any ideals of Lenin and if there were if they were truly being fulfilled. What would the founder of the Soviet state think of Mikhail Sergeyvich Gorbachev and of what he was doing? Putting people out of work by closing unprofitable factories was not Leninism, it sounded more like the despairing streets of New York featured regularly on television. The smell of cabbage breath and unwashed bodies filled the car. Was this what a New York subway smelled like?

He heard a rythmic thumping on his right and saw an old man kicking the heel of his shoe against the floor. Almost without thinking, Viktor was moving toward him.

"Strasvuyte, comrade." The last word was formed more with his smile than his tongue.

"Strasvuyte."

"You seem to have a problem there, or are you just like a horse, counting your age with your hoof?" It was said quietly enough that it could be shared just between them.

But the old one laughed aloud. "Oh my, like a horse. Did you hear that comrade? He asked if I am like a horse, counting my age."

And the man next to the old one chuckled and so did the man sitting next to him, and the woman behind them, and soon the back half of the car was sniggering, tittering, guffawing.

It was a good morning joke.

"No, comrade, I'm just trying to make this cursed heel stay put. It seems to want to go the opposite direction that I ask it to."

It was Viktor's turn to laugh, and he did, easily and without strain.

"Perhaps it's trying to get to the United States and needs to be nailed down."

"If it were, I'd follow it."

But this last was said much more quietly.

"Have you tried Arkady's shop on Gorkova? He uses real nails, the kind they used to use all the time, not the pitiful thumbtacks you see nowadays."

The old one surveyed him carefully. "You're not old enough to know how it used to be."

"Thank you, but I wear my age well, that's all."

"I think you have seen fewer winters than most on this car," said the ancient one. "But you act like a wise man. I will try Arkady's shop today."

"Good, tell him Viktor Nikolaich bids him well. Perhaps I will see you on this train tonight coming home and you can tell me if I was right about the nails."

"I'll see you again," said the old man. "I feel certain of it."

"Take the day as it comes," Viktor advised in reply, and deftly maneuvered through the crowd and out of the train door.

A rude wind met him as he got to the top of the 250-foot escalator, and he involuntarily reached for the scarf he should have had around his neck. But it was bare, for he had left it near Anna's coat with a note that said, "Wear this and think of me today." Under other circumstances she might have refused, seeing through his concern for her, but if it was to help her think of him . . .

Viktor smiled and dared the wind to attack his neck. At least Anna would be warm today.

The walk to the compound took him about seven minutes, but today he lingered. Why, he asked himself. What are you doing? The answer was clear. He was looking for an entrance line. Mysteriously, he could think of none. An entrance line was as much a part of his job as driving, and he hated to fail. He dragged along like a man on his way to a party where he knows he will be turned away. And then halfway over the bridge that spans the Moscow River he picked up his pace.

He hastened down Dorogomilskaya Boulevard, past a shop where he sent people in need of household tools. Just next to the bakery was a green double door with no name. Inside, on most days and many nights, was a small untidy madman who called himself Napoleon and insisted he was descended from the family of the French emperor.

Viktor had first gone into Napoleon's shop by mistake, thinking it was the bakery, but he had immediately noticed an electric drill lying on a shelf. "Is that for sale?"

"Ha," said Napoleon. "Have you ever seen an electric drill being sold in this city?"

"That's why I was asking."

"That's why he was asking, messieurs et mesdames." Napoleon used French words constantly, Viktor later learned. "No, youngster, they're not for sale. But I might part with them for a day or two, if someone nice asked me nicely."

And so it was. Napoleon had collected through a lifetime of wheeling and dealing an unrivalled set of tools, some Russian-made, most not, which he rented to nice people. His business was never inspected, taxed or even known to the authorities because officially it did not exist. He used space that was listed as a kitchen of the bakery. A succession of bakery managers had agreed to the arrangement, and in so doing had been able to carry out home repairs with quality equipment. Viktor almost never recommended Napoleon's shop to first-time acquaintances, as he had the shoe shop or the dry cleaners. The tool trove was very much like everyone's favorite small restaurant: too good to share. And Napoleon was, after all, singular.

The office in which Viktor worked was a caricature either of foreigners trying to adapt to conditions in the Soviet Union, or of Russians managing to bedevil outsiders who presumed themselves to be equal to the task of existing in this society. The office of the news agency was located on the sixth floor of a building not so much decrepit as desecrated. The building was one of a dozen built within the confines of a concrete and mesh-wire perimeter that cut if off from a broad boulevard along which hustled tens of thousands of people each day. But very few of them loitered near, let alone approached the compound; this was a foreigners' ghetto, even in these enlightened times off-limits to anyone except those who lived and worked in the buildings. The word on the street was that the hallways of the foreigners' buildings were carpeted with sheepskin that was changed each month; that on the walls of the foyers were priceless icons looted from Orthodox cathedrals and presented to the foreigners as permanent gifts.

Wire baskets with signs reading "In" and "Out" sat on top of the desks that could have been attractive were it not for the three coats of paint on them and the array of scratches that made them look like an evil carpenter's bench. The rugs were not sheepskin, nor derivatives of anything else that had ever been alive. They were a tacky synthetic by-product of petroleum in an orange-yellow and green swirling pattern. The rug had not been replaced for ten years, nor cleaned in half that time. It was hard to tell if the wavy black pattern that swept through the swirls was the intent of the designer or the result of a carpetlayer who had forgotten to wipe his feet.

Viktor loved it.

"Strasvuyte," he boomed before he was halfway in the door, and half a dozen faces lifted from their morning coffee, tea, cognac.

"Have you heard? They're bringing back Khrushchev," he said, wondering why the air over the bridge made him think better.

"It's true," he answered to their expressions of shock and nervousness. "They found he was responsible for last year's bad harvest."

They all laughed, but it was a tittering thing, not an outburst. Viktor knew they would all retell the joke when they went home that night and claim it as their own.

34

He looked at them now as they pushed out their final "tee-hee". There was Vladimir the maintenance man. Anything that was nailed down, he could screw up, Viktor always told him. His most intricate tools were a hammer and a curse, but in the Soviet Union that made him as well equipped as most technicians. He was usually drunk and preferred his vodka room temperature because cold drinks hurt his throat.

There was Ludmilla, the librarian, charged with keeping track of the voluminous piles of newspapers, magazines, information periodicals and letters that passed through the office. She was quiet, efficient, and capable of handling a more important job. Viktor knew that feeling well, and always made an effort to be kind to her. Ludmilla was a big-boned woman with an open laugh and a drunken husband. Viktor knew she kept some of her weekly pay hidden among the shelves of books in the library room, in case her husband took her purse from her one day for a drinking spree. It had happened before and Viktor found out only because he was courteous. He insisted on holding the door for Ludmilla the day after the incident and then noticed as she walked ahead of him that she was limping badly.

In relieving her of her purse, her husband had kicked her and broken a bone in her ankle. She still limped.

The cleaning woman, Galya, Viktor did not address. Once, when working for a low-ranking American diplomat stationed at the US Embassy, Galya reported to the authorities that he had brought her back a bottle of hand cream from England, where he and his wife went on vacation. The crime was so petty that even the KGB watchdogs assigned to bedevil diplomats were unwilling to do anything about it. But one investigator, anxious to show his resourcefulness, showed his superiors how the infraction could be viewed as a violation of Soviet importing law.

The diplomat was forced to leave.

Galina, the teletype operator, sat at her machine glumly leafing through the same issue of *Pravda* that Viktor was carrying.

Viktor sidled up to her. "Reading Gorbachev's speech?" She nodded. He whispered, "Did you read between the lines?" loudly enough that everyone could hear.

She looked startled at first, then said, "I don't know. I didn't see anything important."

"Ah, so you did get the message!"

More laughter. More giggling.

"Viktor Nikolaich!"

Viktor pulled out of his reverie and stared at Nina, possibly the most beautiful Slav ever made. She sat, as always, erect behind the receptionist's desk, her creamy blonde hair in a tight bun, a disobedient wisp trailing down the side of her face just in front of her ear. Every man, thought Viktor, should know a Nina once in his life, even if it is only to talk about her. Otherwise he would have to make her up.

"Da, Ninuchka?"

"Stop clowning. There's a lot to do today."

He danced up to her in sweeping circles, one arm cradling air, the other cocked rakishly outward, and blew kisses to her.

"Then why, beautiful lady, are you holding me back, asking me for just one more dance?"

Galina stared harder at *Pravda*. Surely whatever the General Secretary said was important?

The rest of the office – the very desks it seemed – stared harder at the actors in this comedy.

"Stop it," Nina said as he waltzed around her, crooning loudly enough only for two. But the words held no edge. Like a knife that must be pushed through soft bread, scattering crumbs of suggestion.

What do clowns do when the greasepaint comes off? Do they drink and make love and raise a family, or do they continue to juggle balls and pull ludicrous pranks, victims of their chosen profession? Often Viktor looked at Nina and felt like he had swallowed a too-large chunk of good-tasting meat: a wonderful thing to be enjoyed until it impeded breathing. Like a schoolboy awaiting pronouncement of his punishment, he watched Nina consult her agenda for the day.

"First, there is almost no computer paper left and I have heard there is none to be found. You'll have to . . ."

"I've gotten it already."

"Where?"

"Where do you buy your dresses?" As always, she was dressed with a stylishness unknown to Russian women.

"That's my business. Where did you get the paper?"

"That's my business." He smiled as he said it, and she had to too.

"There's some mail for the American Embassy box."

"Davai." He intentionally used the rougher more direct expression, knowing it always got a reaction from her. But this time she ignored it, merely handed him a bunch of envelopes, all with the agency's logo stamped on them, all unsealed.

"And what else, my taskmistress?"

"I'm sure there'll be something more later." But there was little conviction in what she said. She'd been had again.

"So it's not such a busy day after all?"

By the time she could think of something to say, he was dancing out the door, allowing his airy partner to lead.

The American Embassy in Moscow both befitted and contradicted the country for which it stood proxy. A former apartment house on Tchaikovsky Street, its canary yellow stucco exterior is as incongruous to the rest of gray downtown Moscow as the flashy Cadillacs, Plymouths and Mustangs that dart in and out of its two porticos. The American compound was once just across the street from the Kremlin, near the historic National Hotel where Lenin made some of his fieriest speeches, once political conditions made it possible for him to return from exile. But Josef Stalin, who slept in the Kremlin just down the hall from his office, objected to seeing the Stars and Stripes waving at him when he woke and smoked in his bedroom behind the Red walls. Stalin told the Americans they would have to move. He similarly complained to the British, who flew the Union Jack directly across the Moscow River, on the Maurice Thorez Embankment, which could be seen from the same bedroom.

The British told Stalin, politely, that if he disliked seeing their flag, he should look the other way when he drank his sugary morning tea.

The British Embassy is still there.

The Americans moved obediently to the less spacious, less conspicuous apartment house that Stalin procured and bugged for them.

The Embassy epitomized the state of relations between the countries. There were water fountains in the hallways: the only building in all the Soviet Union that could make that claim. When the plumbing failed and Soviet plumbers were called in to fix the pipes, only cold warriors in Washington were heard to grumble that Americans should service the American Embassy. Afterwards, when the water gave off high readings on a Geiger counter or when the new faucets were found to contain radio transmitters, senior diplomats temporized. After all, it is their country, and we are their guests.

Viktor usually enjoyed making trips to the embassy even on such dull errands as dropping mail into a diplomatic mailbox. Technically, there was no reason for news agencies to have access to this privilege. But grumbling correspondents reminded the ambassador they were as American as he, and fearful of being accused of practising democracy only when it was convenient, the ambassador opened the mailbag to all the American community in Moscow. It was an action he regretted immediately since correspondents, no less than diplomats, used the service to sneak in forbidden materials – some as harmless as *Playboy*, some as patently illegal as cocaine – and to sneak out Russian icons and tapestries. This did not improve relations with the Foreign Ministry. Occasionally its police pounced upon the outgoing mailbag and insisted on inspecting its contents. Outraged at first by this breach of etiquette, the ambassador finally gave in on the theory that the Soviets were protecting their national treasures. The larger issue of mail piracy and diplomatic immunity was skirted.

Soviet citizens were not particularly welcome within the confines of the American compound, especially since the day when seven rabid Pentacostalists determined to become American citizens had barged past the two Soviet militiamen who kept twenty-four hour watch outside the main portico.

The Siberian Seven, as they became known, were convinced that if only they could reach the embassy grounds, they could be smuggled to the United States. The family patriarch assured them that a tunnel had been dug under the embassy grounds that led under the ocean and directly to America. His wife knew this was poppycock. Why should the Americans dig a tunnel when they had a rocket pad inside the embassy courtyard, which launched satellites bound for Washington? When, on the day of their uninvited arrival, they asked the Americans to settle the debate, they were told that neither a tunnel nor a launching pad existed. The Siberians immediately accused their unwilling hosts of religious prejudice and fascism.

The Americans were in an impossible position. The Soviet government insisted, quite rightly, that the Siberians had no right to leave the country because they had no exit visas, and that they had illegally entered a diplomatic compound. They categorically refused to grant the family permission to leave, lest other citizens get the idea that Soviet power could be challenged. If the Americans forced them to leave, they would be the object of unthinkable retribution. On the other hand, if they were granted asylum, could they eventually be helped to leave the country? Finally, the decision from Washington was handed down: find room for them. And so, a ten-foot by seven-foot storage closet was cleared out and fitted with beds, a stove, and little else. For four years, the embassy had seven more or less permanent guests, until they left in the mid-Eighties. To discourage other such visitors, more US marine guards were posted at the doors, standing shoulder to shoulder with Soviet militiamen. It was not the kind of cooperation either country enjoyed.

Viktor, as always, was a special case. One of the Soviet militiamen on duty knew him and let him pass, overruling a querulous objection from a second, newer officer on the job. The more experienced one was taking a chance, especially with things as they were. The risk was made worth while because he knew that each Friday Viktor would accidentally drop a carton of Marlboro's near their post.

Embassy personnel were usually glad to see him, because he was their most reliable supplier of the painted lacquer boxes from Palekh and other hard-to-find merchandise made in cities that were closed to foreigners. His prices were always lower than the hard currency shops which catered to and milked tourists. Viktor, though, was a man who could be counted on to keep a deal.

He sauntered into the mailroom, made an intentionally clumsy effort to relieve the guard of his holstered gun (the first time he did it, it had not been interpreted as a joke, but Viktor was willing to teach them slowly his ways) and mimed a kiss at the secretary. As it did each time he visited, the cleanliness of the room struck him — newly painted walls, shampooed rugs, upholstery with not too many cigarette burns. The people, too, appeared to have bathed within the last week. Viktor thought of the metro car in which he rode each morning. He wondered how these people got to work in their own country.

"Strasvuy – I mean, 'Howdy, everyone.'"

Laughter. From another room: "Viktor must be here." Even in times of pressure, especially then, a clown was a welcome visitor.

"I would like to send these envelopes to the United States, but I don't seem to be able to fit in any of them."

Ann Snyder, in charge of the mailroom, had heard the jokes before. "Well, Viktor, if you ate fewer potatoes at night . . ." She had worked on that line for just this occasion.

Viktor knitted his eyebrows. "But then I could not make love so much, Annie." He lifted one eyebrow. "Or so well, eh?"

An explosion of guffaws. Miss Snyder decided not to prepare any future responses for Viktor.

He dropped the envelopes in the mailbox as carefully as he would have released a child he was teaching to dive. He wondered which of those fine Americans censored the mail and what they looked for. The letters that were sent through the embassy pouch had to be handed in unsealed. Security, they said. Viktor failed to make the connection between the land of the free and the home of the brave and snooping through everyone's correspondence. But then, as he would have admitted, he was an ignorant man.

He left the room to laughter, cringing against the wall opposite the armed guard, eyes wide with fright, and waved easily as he turned down the hall. Nice people, Americans.

"Viktor."

The voice caught his ear, but the word was said softly enough that he might have missed it. So he knew it was important. A tall man in a white shirt and black tie (Viktor immediately thought of Velodya the unlicenced undertaker who would host wakes in the old Orthodox tradition for a fee – Viktor sometimes discreetly recommended him) approached from behind, stopped just a half step away, too close for an American to stand to someone else. Viktor saw him pull out an envelope and was relieved. Only another customer for icons.

"Take this please," said the man. The Russian had a lifelong Muscovite accent.

"Moy droog," Viktor began to say, "My friend . . ."

"I just wondered if you'd give this to Ludmilla" – he winked confidentially – "she's a friend of mine."

"Oh, well, yes, I suppose . . ." He was startled, caught off guard. Why did he know Ludmilla? Too much data, too fast. He reached out and took the envelope.

Already the man had swung round and was walking along the other side of the corridor, the opposite way. He turned a corner and was gone.

Viktor pocketed the envelope and walked slowly to the door, out into the courtyard. He slapped the militiaman respectfully on the shoulder.

"Dos vedonya, tovarich."

"Dos vedonya, Viktor. Friday, eh?"

"If you're still here." His face must have shown how much he regretted saying that. His attempt at recovery was at best feeble. "By then, you might be a general."

The militiaman was not even pretending to smile.

He got into the car, a green Zhiguli station wagon that was registered to the news agency. Not for years had he said such a stupid thing aloud. Probably it was the time a Party recruiter showed up at his door, with an invitation to attend the next Agitprop gathering. Viktor said he preferred jets. Within a month he was working as a janitor.

This was more serious. A militiaman assigned to the front gate of the American Embassy was never just that. Which, of course, was what made the whole situation so extraordinarily sensitive. And why no comment, even the most innocuous, would be overlooked.

He started the car and carefully pulled away. On the way back to the office, he drove well below the speed limit. The last thing he wanted now was more trouble.

5

Left turns are illegal in Moscow. U-turns are not. Drivers whose destination is on the opposite side of the street must continue until they come to a traffic island that has a sign with an arrow curving back on itself. The trip back from the embassy had only one U-turn, or razvorotno. Viktor had calculated that he drove an extra one hundred and fifty miles a year because of the ban on left turns. We shall maximize the people's resources, stamping out waste wherever it is found! He had actually seen that one once on a poster, black letters on white, framed in the blazing red of socialism and punctuated with an exclamation mark. So what would happen if he made a quick left turn into the compound's parking lot one day, and when the inevitable militiaman swooped down on him, quoted from the poster and reminded him of Mr Gorbachev's policy of openness? He would be charged not only with reckless driving, but also with making an anti-Soviet statement. A statement that had been displayed by the same crowd that decided what was anti-Soviet. It did not bear deep scrutiny.

After lunch, he sorted the mail. Three personal letters for the boss, two from the company's head office in New York, two bills that Nina would pay directly, two more that would have to be approved before payment was made. Viktor had not looked into any of the envelopes. He did not need to. He knew their contents from their color, from the return addresses, and the postmarks.

He went back to the library. Vladimir was slouched in one of the chairs, eyes closed, breathing shallowly, his hands fastened tightly over the chair arms. Viktor wondered where he had gotten enough money to get this drunk by mid-afternoon.

The most popular method was to stand outside a liquor store, pointing two or three fingers straight down, while waiting for another alcoholic to stumble along. Two fingers meant you had enough money to buy half a bottle, three fingers meant you had a third of the price. Even in the city of nine million, where perhaps ten per cent of the population are drunk each day, Vladimir rated special attention. Once, on an errand, Viktor had passed by the liquor store nearest the office and heard two hopeful investors joking. "No really, I saw him yesterday. He had eight fingers down."

"My God, what does he do with the money he makes from those Americans?"

"You know Vladimir. No money is enough. No fuel packs enough punch."

Fuel was slang for any kind of cheap liquor. It derived from the fact that, several years ago, a dozen or so alcoholics had been found crumpled together, dead in an alleyway. In the center of their silent circle was a large bottle of clear liquid. It turned out to be jet fuel of the kind used in military planes. The tramps had bought it from a Georgian army private who was a mechanic at Vnukovo Airport just south of Moscow. The private's execution was reported in the press as an object lesson.

He considered for a moment destroying the envelope he had been given for Ludmilla. He could always deny having been given anything. Given his recent idiocy, it would probably be safer. Then again, Ludmilla was a good woman. He would not treat her like one of the mafia. He flipped the white envelope on to her desk. He went back out to the main office with a new joke for Nina. As he passed the toilet, he heard a flush. That would be Ludmilla.

Nina laughed at the first joke and the next six he told. There was really no work to be done, she admitted, especially with the boss away. He would return from Leningrad in two days, and then it would become busy again. Slowly, Viktor let himself forget his stupidity at the embassy. He had nearly finished the cup of coffee he had poured himself. A mistake he knew, he would not sleep tonight. But as long as he was drinking coffee, he felt he had a reason to sit on Nina's desk and talk to her. Could beauty be musical?

"Okay," he said in slow, ponderous English. "Time to go."

"Very good," Nina said. "You really are trying. But don't go. Stay a while."

Then his life changed.

There was a loud noise from the library, like a chair being dropped on the floor, then a sharp wail. They had all seen Vladimir emerge from stupor and they all tried to help him endure the pain. Viktor always assumed a loud noise would shatter his skull. But the scream was undeniably Vladimir's. He shrieked into the main office. "She jumped. She jumped!"

"Easy, comrade." Viktor was searching for soothing words, perhaps humor.

"She just jumped. I looked up, she was choking and she jumped."

"Who? Tell us, Vladimir."

"Ludmilla! She jumped out the window."

Militiamen removed first the body, then the fragments, and finally the stains. One of them told Galina that none of them were to leave the compound. He did not need to tell anyone else – it was expected that Galina would pass the word. If anyone wasn't there when they were being sought, there would be enough trouble to go around for all of them.

They milled about miserably, in plain view of the two militiamen posted at the entrance to the compound parking lot. It was not enough that the militiamen knew they would never dream of disobeying an order; they were also expected to remain within an easy line of vision. Even their trustworthiness was mistrusted.

At seven-thirty, after they had been waiting there for over four hours, a black Volga pulled up, its back window curtained in red. KGB.

"Get in," said the driver.

Nina, holding back tears, made a sound in the back of her throat. Without thinking, Viktor clutched her right hand, squeezed it gently, closed his eyes, wrinkled his nose and shook his head a fraction of an inch. He whispered: "Don't let them know." Nina drew a deep breath, got into the center of the back seat.

Vladimir, nauseous from vodka and fear, vomited on the concrete in front of the car.

"Clean it up," said the driver, eyes dull with promised cruelty.

"I didn't – get any – on the car," Vladimir protested.

"If you had, I'd make you eat it," replied the driver. "This is state land, citizen. You've befouled it. Now clean up after yourself. Don't let the foreigners think Soviet citizens do such things."

They were all in the car now except Vladimir. All silent.

"There's nothing to clean it up with," he said weakly.

"You have a handkerchief?"

"Yes."

"Well?"

Vladimir removed his handkerchief – one of only two he owned – from his pocket, and bent over the puddle of vomit.

Slowly he bent over it, looking up as though expecting the driver to tell him the joke was over. The dull eyes stared back.

He palmed the handkerchief, tried to scoop some of the vomit over to the sidewalk.

"Not there, pig. Put it in a trash can."

The nearest was twenty yards away.

Hands dripping, Vladimir walked to it, let the sodden handkerchief hang over the opening and dropped it in.

The expression on his face when he came back was one of carefully controlled agony. He looked at the driver.

"Get in the back."

Vladimir's hand squooshed as he put it around the door handle, but the driver chose not to notice. It was a state car, not his.

The KGB headquarters at Dzerzhinsky Square have been romanticized. Before the revolution, it was the Rossiya Insurance company building. There are no deeply carpeted, wood-panelled offices upstairs for its ranking officers. Nor are there sophisticated torture caverns below. There is a soundproofed room beneath street level, where Stalin's KGB chief, Lavrenti Beria, was executed in 1953 for trying to seize absolute power after his boss's death. Yuri Andropov, one of Beria's successors who briefly gained control of the Party, had kept an office suite in the Dzerzhinsky building, but it was mainly used for ceremonial greetings of security chiefs from fraternal countries. The square itself, named for the Polish revolutionary Felix Dzerzhinsky who helped Lenin establish the Cheka, is as much a cliché now as Langley or the Circus. Important matters that require secrecy or security are usually taken up at the agency's building outside the three Ring roads, a beltway system that circumscribes Moscow.

Viktor knew, or thought he knew, most of these facts, through the normal Soviet learning procedure of listening to rumor and hearsay, dividing it by two, and factoring in enough uncertainty and nefariousness to ensure that he himself never discussed the KGB with anyone, ever. So he was more than surprised to see that the Volga was heading straight for the Square. He unconsciously admired the driver's skill as they flashed down Kalinin Prospekt, using the inside lane closest to the center line that is reserved for official cars. The driver was very confident. They reached the Alexandra Gardens on the south end of the Kremlin, and the driver pulled into the intersection, although there was a red light. A traffic policeman noticed him, and Viktor saw him raise his whistle to his lips, puff out his cheeks and take a tentative step toward the Volga. Then the cop read the license plate. The whistle, attached to a cord, dropped back to his chest. He expelled air.

The Volga shot past the Armory, where the tsar's jewels and Fabergé's egg collection are kept, and made another tight left turn in front of the Metropole Hotel. Directly ahead of them stood the Bolshoi Ballet Theater, where Viktor had taken Anna for the first time the previous summer.

As the Volga turned right, Viktor wished mightily that he was being summoned for nothing more sinister than a lecture about line-jumping and fooling honest Soviet culture lovers.

They passed his favorite bathhouse, the Centralnaya, before he could summon up memories of his last visit to it. The bathhouses of Moscow, unlike those in the West that cater to quick anonymous sex, are dens of comradeship in the purest use of the word. There, men who have worked too hard without thanks amble in warm nakedness through steamy rooms, nodding to acquaintances. They savor the mingled odors of clean sweat rushing through pores, the chlorine that keeps the wading pools sanitary, and, most of all, the pungency of bay leaf twigs that are tied in bunches and used to flog each other in the incredible heat of the steamrooms. The sting of the branches as they rake across the skin, mixed with the dizzying effect of the steam, and the constant buzz of conversations from all around creates a dreamlike atmosphere. It was an honest, simple pleasure.

The brakes of the Volga needed work. The engine was shut off before the car had settled into its parked position. Viktor had not paid attention to the final hundred meters of the trip, past the toy store Dyetski Mir, around the statue of Dzerzhinsky and through the small gate that led into the KGB complex. There were no signs restricting entrance. No Soviet motorist, no matter how drunk or how much an out-of-towner, would intentionally drive through that gate. Viktor, Nina, Vladimir and Galina were seeing a part of their country that very few citizens had seen. It was not what they expected. Two uniformed KGB guards stood inside the gate, smoking, their AK-47s leaning against a wall. A few civilian laborers, or yard rats as they are known, walked without much vigor across the courtyard. At the far end was a wooden double door in need of new paint.

The driver's work was done. He reached into his jacket pocket, pulled out a red packet of Sparta cigarettes, tapped one on to his palm, licked it, lit it.

"Do we get out?" Galina hated vagueness, preferred clear instructions. The driver inhaled smoke.

Nina spoke, as if to a lunatic with a gun. "What do you want us to do?" The smoke was released.

Directly behind the driver in the back seat, Vladimir coughed uncertainly. The driver crashed against the door, and jumped clear of the car, losing his cigarette in the process.

"Out! All of you lepers, out."

45

They were happy enough to leave the car but, once outside, the courtyard looked huge. Viktor felt like a tourist.

The peeling doors hid a hallway that startled first-time visitors because of its brightness. No electricity conservation here. But it was just as grimy, and as shabby-looking as the halls of the building where they worked. The driver made a show of looking at ease in this place, nodding to two men who passed. In response, he got two stern frowns. Their faces told Viktor that the driver was nobody.

The nobody was in good shape. He took two flights of stairs two at a time. Viktor was as winded as the others. Still sucking air, they obeyed the driver's finger that pointed them into the first room on the right.

Against the far wall were four metal folding chairs. On the second from the right sat an older-than-middle-aged man in a baggy gray suit with no tie. He had been reading a newspaper, but when he saw the newcomers, tossed it aside as though he had been caught with pornography. The driver stayed in the hall, and pulled the door shut behind him. The man remained seated but they had his full attention. His glasses had steel frames and fitted his thin face. Perhaps Marya had constructed them. Viktor thought he looked more like a victim than an oppressor.

Ten, twenty seconds of silence. Either someone had to speak or the tension would become unbearable. Evidently, the stranger felt it too. "Who are you?" he asked.

Nina, Vladimir and Galina had all turned toward Viktor to hear what he would say. He was their leader, that was clear.

"At the risk of sounding imitative, comrade . . ."

"Yes, of course. You all know who you are. It would enlighten more people if I were to introduce myself. My name is Karushkin, Alexander Alfredovich."

Viktor and his colleagues murmured their names. At each Karushkin bowed his head. "Although I am quite certain that we are not the only ones listening," – he raised his face for a second to the ceiling – "may I ask why we are meeting in these circumstances? I myself am here for questioning."

Viktor liked him. He spoke with an irony that denied fear its due.

"We don't really know why we're here, Alexander Alfredovich. One of our colleagues at work committed suicide. We were brought down here. Like you, we are waiting."

"Actually, waiting is the hardest part. The questions are usually easy enough."

"You sound like you have been through this before." In the back of his mind. Viktor remembered that he was not here to chat with a stranger. But it helped whittle away time.

"I have, more times than I care to remember. This organization takes an interest in me."

"Why? Are you disloyal to the Soviet Union?" said Vladimir. "If so, don't talk to me. I love my country." He said the last words clearly for the microphones. He was pathetic.

"No, I wouldn't say I'm disloyal. Some might." Karushkin sounded mild, but steely underneath. "It is a shame about your colleague. Why did he commit suicide?"

"It was Ludmilla, our librarian. She was unhappy at home." Viktor realized that he too was speaking for unseen listeners. But it was the truth.

"Hmm, bad business. These people don't like events that take place in full view of foreigners. I imagine they will be disappointed in your answer." Karshkin spoke like a doctor diagnosing cancer.

"Would you ladies like to sit down?" he said suddenly. "It might be a long wait for you."

Galina heaved, and a sigh rippled out ahead of a snort of fear. "How long do you think? I don't want to stay here much longer. I haven't done anything. I hardly knew Ludmilla."

Karushkin wrinkled his forehead. "Hardly knew her? But you worked with her. Colleagues at work generally know many things about each other that they're not aware of. Things that have no apparent value until they are fit into the right slot requiring an answer. Then those little things become the linchpin of a mystery."

The door opened and a drab green uniform entered, wrapped around a smart-stepping young man.

"Comrade Colonel Karushkin. We have the results of the autopsy." The old man rose slowly from his chair, his face creased with a mixture of sadness and fatigue.

The others looked at him. Viktor's mouth was suddenly very dry. He remembered, for some reason, the first time Anna had deliberately disobeyed him. She had been two and they were walking along a semi-wooded path outside Moscow. Anna, excited, had run ahead. Viktor called out: "Anna, not too far." He saw her turn, look at him, and then decide. She bolted ahead. He watched her move away from him, and thought he would cry. She stopped soon enough, came back shamefacedly. He could not think of anything to say. They walked the rest of the way in silence.

"Tell me about the autopsy." Karushkin's voice had the same level tone to it as before. But it carried an edge of command.

"Death caused by the fall. But the coroner took the added precaution of inspecting the contents of the stomach."

"Let me guess. Fatty meat, cabbage and potatoes."

"No meat, comrade colonel, but potatoes and cabbage all right. Also this." He produced a small transparent sack, of the size Viktor had seen the Americans at the embassy store their lunch in.

"She was on a diet of plastic?" Karushkin's question was general. Anyone might have answered.

"I meant the contents of the bag." The young man held it out now. The inside was covered with a gray-green film, punctuated by the occasional air bubble. Beneath the slime was something that might once have been white. It was flattened out and had irregular edges. Viktor could not take his eyes off it. To one side, he heard Vladimir begin to belch.

"Just tell me, lieutenant."

"It is a piece of paper, Comrade Colonel. The victim swallowed it before jumping."

Karushkin sighed. "Obviously not after jumping."

The young agent tried to save face. "The paper had been written on."

"That is often the case, don't you think, with paper? Did the writing say anything?"

"It's too decomposed to read. But the ink is distinctive. It is the type used by the Americans at their embassy."

And now it was Viktor's turn to feel the rising sickness, to wonder if his legs would support him, or if the mist floating across his line of sight was visible to everyone else as well. He stared at thin frail Karushkin, with whom minutes ago he was trading irreverences. He showed no emotion now as he walked away from them. At the door, he turned, and looked at them.

"I'm sorry for the subterfuge, comrades, but it was necessary to see if we could avoid what's known here at our establishment as deep research. Unfortunately, you all appear unwilling to cooperate. That means that we will be spending a bit more time together, but separately. Lieutenant, give them each a room. And him" – he nodded idly at Viktor – "we'll save for last." Karushkin stepped into the hallway and was gone.

The lieutenant's eyes shone like streetlights. "Pity you lot," he said flatly. "All right, you heard the colonel. Move. All except you, funny man."

Galina walked out without looking back. Vladimir had his hand over his mouth and was heaving. Nina moved quickly toward Viktor, squeezed his hand. She really was lovely. "It will be over soon, Viktor. As soon as they realize we had nothing to do with Ludmilla's death. That there is nothing we can tell them."

Viktor thought about the letter. Why had he accepted it? What could it have said? Why, above all, was the KGB interested in a poor woman's death? And when would they find out about the letter?

"Yes, Ninuchka. I know. We'll just have to wait."

Karushkin had been to university, he was no leg-breaker. He whittled down wills, chipped at confidence, scraped away security. In the few minutes he had spent with them, Karushkin had decided how to deal with each of his prisoners. Waiting, in various doses, was the first step. He bit a sugar cube in half, held it between his teeth, and lifted a clear glass with no handle. He sucked steaming acidy tea so that the sugar dissolved and was digested along with the rest. The metaphor was apt. One of the keys to controlling people is to rob them of their individuality, make them feel and act as special as ants. It seemed to Karushkin that he had always known those facts, from his earliest years in the rat's nest of primary school, through the mandatory absorption into the Young Pioneers, then Party membership. He saw it in every facet of Soviet life: the notion that individual freedom was subordinate to common welfare, that an invisible entity called "state" had the authority to arrange and direct lives. The young Karushkin was repelled. He was, at heart, a humanist. Thirty years and a continent removed, he might have led a chant like "Power to the people".

Instead, he determined quickly that, to survive in his homeland, he needed to become a part of the system that reserved such audacious power for itself. The Committee for State Security was a logical stopping place. Karushkin spent the Second World War wearing a blue epaulet on his Red Army uniform and shooting Russian infantrymen who tried to retreat from the front line. Surviving Stalin's black madness was more difficult. He made men admit things they had not known a minute earlier. The KGB was not overstocked with brains: he prospered. And then Gorbachev came along . . .

Now sixty-nine years old, Karushkin was the chief interrogator for the Moscow district, although that was not known publicly. He felt a bit insulted to be working on this group. He put down the tea glass, walked through the hall, the lapdog lieutenant at his heels. He paused outside a swinging door, like the kind leading from a restaurant kitchen, that had neither a number or a knob. He took a deep breath and nodded once to the punk, who kicked the door, catapulting it against the room wall and making an echoing sonic boom.

Vladimir, who had been sick on the concrete floor of the room, screamed when the door exploded, and fell to his knees. He had been standing against the wall furthest from the entrance. There was no furniture anywhere in the room.

The lieutenant ran straight at Vladimir, snapped him to his feet by the collar of his shirt, and planted a knee smoothly between his legs. Vladimir screamed again. Karushkin walked in slowly, gave the door a slight push so that it swung back closed. Staring directly at Vladimir, Karushkin said to the lieutenant: "Beat him senseless."

The screeching "Nyet" stretched out for five seconds. Karushkin nearly winced from its volume. It was a good start.

"Then you had better tell me everything." His voice was a caress and a last hope.

"I will, I will. Just tell me what you want."

A disappointment. The willingness was as real as the fear. It probably meant he knew nothing. He turned to the lieutenant.

"Kick him around until you break a sweat. Wipe up that puddle of puke with his hair. Then throw him out." Vladimir was nothing more than he appeared, a drunken blob. Karushkin was anxious to get to Viktor.

Contrary to his orders, Galina and Nina had been put together in another bare room. Karushkin kicked in the door himself, heard them gasp. He looked at Galina and saw a female Vladimir.

"Get out," he said.

She never once looked back at Nina.

He walked up to Nina, put his face an inch from hers. Quietly: "If I think for even a second you are holding anything back, or lying, you will spend the night here. Understand?"

A wide-eyed nod.

"Why did she jump?"

"I have no idea, comrade."

"What did she do at the office?"

"Clipped newspapers, kept files, folders." The voice trickled off.

"What did she do with her spare time?"

"I don't know."

"What do you know about her family?"

"Nothing."

"Did you know her husband is a drunk?"

Nina's lips curled unintentionally into a typically Russian and very attractive moue. "Yes, I knew that."

"Did you know she had a relative who has applied to emigrate?"

"Yes."

"You see, it is as I said. Small snippets of knowledge must be fitted carefully into large patterns. Describe everything that happened today."

With time for liberal questioning, Nina talked for two hours. When he left her, she was sobbing with exhaustion.

He walked, fast, down the hall, noticing again the grimy paint job. Did the CIA work under these conditions? To his left he heard Vladimir's punishment still in progress. The lieutenant was probably exceeding his orders. Well, the drunk would have a good story the next time he shared a bottle. But who would stay long enough to hear it? Wise Soviet citizens — and this includes most of the alcoholic ones — will not linger near someone who has been pummelled by the KGB.

When he was within kicking distance of the door, he stopped, thought it over, brought his breathing under control. He pushed the door open gently, and was startled when there was a metallic crash on the other side. Karushkin had to use body force to get into the room. Within one second he knew what had happened.

Viktor was sitting against the far wall. The metal chairs that had been in the room lay flattened a foot from the door.

Karushkin forced composure on to his face. "What is this?"

Viktor made a palms-up gesture. "Tidying up?"

"You stacked the chairs against the door so they would make noise when I came in. You were sleeping." It was true. Fear made Viktor drowsy, an escapist's defense. He had spent the last forty minutes dozing on the floor.

Karushkin was miffed. Fatigue weakened wills, made his job easier. Now that edge was lost. "You're in a pack of trouble, comrade."

"Yes, comrade?"

"Yes, comrade. The paper in her stomach came from the American Embassy."

"And this puts me in jeopardy?" Viktor wondered when he would start shaking. Inside, he was chilly. His blood was not reaching his fingertips.

"It contained a message, written with a pen produced in the United States."

"I am beginning to feel better, Comrade Karushkin. None of this can have anything to do with me. American paper, pens . . ."

"Where did you go this morning?"

"To pick up the mail."

"Where?"

A pause. "At the American Embassy. As you know."

"Exactly. As I know. I haven't been sleeping. And I also know that you suggested to a guard at the embassy that he might somehow disappear. Friend, you've tumbled into hell."

"I've heard this building described in that way."

51

"Whoever said it was right. Now try to stay awake. I have some official questions, which will be recorded."

"This hasn't been?"

Karushkin opened the door, said what sounded to Viktor like a single syllable. It produced a slender man in a gray suit with steel-rimmed glasses like Karushkin's. He carried a clipboard with about a hundred sheets of paper.

"Do you know how hard it is to find paper in this city?" Viktor tried to keep up the banter.

Karushkin's tone of voice told him that was over. "Citizen Melanov, Viktor Nikolaich?"

"Da."

"You have been detained by the Committee for State Security for questioning. You are suspected of criminal actions. You can be held under arrest for up to ten days without any official charges being lodged. Or you can be released, provided you promise to return for further questioning at the agency's discretion. Do you understand?"

"Da."

"Do you know what has been happening at the US Embassy recently?"

Viktor was actually relieved by the bluntness of the question. "I have heard rumors, nothing more."

"And what do those rumors say?"

"That in the past two months seven militiamen stationed outside the embassy have disappeared."

Karushkin gave him an odd stare. "How the truth can be distorted. The correct number is twelve. In six weeks. The most recent incident being two days ago. And from whom did you hear these rumors?"

Viktor was prepared for the question. They were not friends, they were not family. He had decided he owed allegiance to none of them. "I heard about the most recent disappearance from a customs agent named Fedirov. Before that, I was talking with . . ."

"Never mind. I can see you have decided to speak openly. And that is wise. Did you also know that four militia patrol cars have been attacked in the past month, and that, at last count, five officers have been killed?"

"I did not know it was that many."

"Well, it is. You know, Melanov, these officers, both the ones killed on patrol and the ones at the embassy — they all share some common characteristics. For instance, all of them, while they wear the uniform of the citizens' militia, are actually employed by this organization. No, don't bother to pretend ignorance. Of course you knew that, or had a very strong suspicion. But, there is something else that makes it hard to believe

52

they would willingly drop out of sight in a way that would bring official displeasure. Can you think of what that link might be?"

"That they all have families?"

"You are as perceptive as I had imagined. Yes, they all have families. As do you. Wife: Marya, factory drudge. Daughter: Anna, above average intelligence, with the prospect of higher education. The prospect, I said. Do we understand each other?"

Hearing Karushkin speak those names made him dizzy. "I understand perfectly."

"I know you do. Comrade Melanov, you may go. You will be notified when you are required for further questioning."

He stood still. Another fear took over. They were going to turn him into a zombie.

6

"Zombie" was as accurate a term as any in describing the KGB's playtoys. People who had been picked up once, either on suspicion of involvement in, or because they might have some tangential information about, a crime. Many, of course, were political activists: Jews yearning for Israel, starry-eyed students who wanted the American experiment to be given a chance in their country, Ukrainians who thought bombs made a nice noise, bumpkins who took the Party propaganda about freedom at face value. Others were mere victims of bad timing: a dog-walk that led past a Western embassy ("Why do you go that way? Who do you know there?"), a nod of assent when a provocateur on the trolley complains about crush-hour overcrowding ("So you know better than our transportation specialists, do you?"), taking a vodka with a co-worker whose kid brother had tried to evade military service in Afghanistan ("And how do you feel about the fraternal aid we rendered?").

The questions were always broad enough for any answer to be construed as incriminating. For most, the interrogations, once begun, became permanent fixtures. A case officer assigned the hour and the day. Tardiness was proof of guilt. The KGB provided official excuses for absence from work. The buff-colored cards were the same as those provided by doctors. But no one who hoped to advance professionally would make the mistake of using it. Better to be docked pay than branded a risky citizen.

Some people said the questioning had become less abusive since Gorbachev, and perhaps it had. But the effect was the same, and it was something Gorbachev, for all his charm and promises, did not control. To be of interest to the KGB was the end of normal life, in a country where it was considered not only stupid but unpatriotic to arouse official interest in oneself. Those who presented the cards to their superiors often found themselves out of work the next week. Marriages deteriorated under the mental strain. Children heard in school that their parents were traitors. Their futures were shattered completely. Alcohol became the only unwavering friend. Suicide sounded like salvation. Living entombment. Zombies.

When Viktor had first spoken to Karushkin, he thought he might be a zombie. He had talked about being there often, about the special interest the KGB took in him, about how some might think him unpatriotic. That had been the colonel's intention, of course. Zombies were reviled by everyone except those who shared their situation. Would it happen to him, Viktor wondered. Was this how he would spend his final days?

He was walking along Chernyshevskogo Perioulek. No use looking for a cab at this hour. He wondered about Vladimir and Galina. Had they been released? Had Nina told them that he went to the embassy? Or could Karushkin summon that kind of information with a punch of a button, one crisp order to a minion? The embassy guard had obviously reported his flippant remark; could he explain that to them, make them understand it was only a joke? Viktor knew almost nothing about how the KGB really worked. It might have been all-powerful, the force that kept the Earth from crashing into the moon, or it might have been peopled by the same kind of drunken bunglers that he saw everywhere, every day. Karushkin was clever and dangerous, but the rest of the flunkies whom he had seen had not impressed him.

He could not call Marya. They had no telephone in the apartment although, according to the waiting list, they were only six years from getting one. And he dared not rouse neighbors. What would he do: call, apologize for waking them and ask them to get dressed, go across the street, knock until Marya answered the door, and deliver a message that he had been unavoidably detained by the secret police? He was not even sure he would tell Marya when he saw her. Zombie mentality was setting in.

Chernyshevskogo led to Sverchkov. It was not exactly a road, but alleyway made it sound too charming. It was a passage, lined with dirty, paint-flaked doors that did not manage to contain the smells that circulated throughout halls and foyers.

Viktor could distinguish odors like a florist can tell blooms. A keen sense of smell can save time. Viktor never waited in line at the bakery unless he detected the yeasty smell of new bread. Without seeing it, he could identify a new car battery and an old one (new batteries have no pungent acid on them). And, he was almost certain, if he had been transported here while fast asleep, then suddenly roused, but not allowed to look around, he could have told that he was on or near Sverchkov. He could still remember walking along the street as a boy, and sniffing the odors that came from the synagogue a quarter-mile away. It floated along the narrow passageway, out of the houses, which, if any section of Moscow could be called it, was the Jewish Quarter. He had no idea of the components: some comforting blend of old clothes, cooking oil, full beards and dust.

It was the only working synagogue in Moscow, a city where Jews had as much religious freedom as anyone, which is to say they had better know their place. Viktor had nothing against Jews. He thought it strange that a people that had been persecuted for centuries on end had also managed to acquire a universal reputation for being deceptive and cunning. He wondered whether the people on this street considered themselves first to be Jews, or Russians. It was easy to convince this country that nothing could supplant loyalty to motherland. The roots of chauvinism reached deep, they required only occasional nurturing. Any pretext would do. In these confused days, no one wanted to stand out.

Except Shishkin. Foolish, fearless, wild, wise. Viktor had never been to the address that Shishkin had once given him to memorize. Writing down someone's address in a book is no act of kindness.

Walking into the foyer was like entering a fish shop. Could people live here? By law, every multiple residence building must have the names of all occupants on mailboxes on the ground floor. Shishkin's was there, printed beneath the no 6, in the black ink script that the post office used. Underneath, in pencil, a helpful neighbor had added: "Kike." Shishkin would have liked that, might even have scrawled it himself.

Room 6 was on the third floor and there were no lights in the stairwell. Why should there be? Why would good citizens be walking around at this hour? And if they were, why should the state pay for them to see? Let them grope in darkness.

Three of the wooden steps were missing completely, victims of rot. Two others groaned so pitiously under Viktor's weight that he expected someone to come charging out on to the stairwell to challenge him.

He moved like a man coming home late from a binge. Why was he here and not plodding along the street to his own home? He thought of several possible answers, but they made his eyes sting with fear.

The door swung open, quickly, not the way one greets a friend. Viktor, used to the dark, was at a disadvantage. The light from the room was surprisingly strong; the odor too.

"What do you want?" The voice was husky, prepared for confrontation.

"You, Yevgeny Moisovich." The advantage was back with him, where it belonged.

"Who is it then?" Shishkin's voice was different now, already adapting to the fact that his name was known to an intruder. It was the way that Viktor liked to think that he would react.

"Yevgeny Moisovich, it is Viktor Melanov."

There was a noise like a mouse's squeak. It was a gasp in preparation for laughter, which followed. "Well, well. So you finally find time to come see me. And what a convenient hour. Welcome Viktor." A door across the hall flew open and a massive form filled it.

"You filthy shit-eating Jew, shut up, and let decent Russians sleep."

"They've been sleeping since 1917. It's time a few were roused." Shishkin's voice rose in volume. "But by all means, Vera Radoviana, bury your bovine face in the pillow. It looks much better there." The woman muttered something about bastardy, and banged back into angry solitude.

Shishkin was laughing again. "The first time she saw me, when she first moved in six years ago, she said she would have me arrested for looking as I do. Then one night about a year later, she was very drunk, and came knocking on my door. She said she wanted to shave me, then sleep with me. I told her I might recover from the shave, but I would die of shame from the other. Most cordial, don't you think?"

It was a good story, but the woman had a point. Shishkin was no model for the new Soviet man. He might have been anywhere between forty and sixty. His brown beard began high on his cheeks and disappeared into his shirt collar. His hair was turning gray, but there were still patches of darkness on the crown of his head. The back was straggly, like hairy raindrops on a window. His eyes were inset above two cheeks as hard and small as marbles. The nose was a classic Semitic scimitar. The mouth was the grin of a fox, in constant search of rabbits.

It was not until the door shut behind him that Viktor realized Shishkin was fully dressed. "Are you expecting someone?"

"Oh, Mischa said he might stop by for a drink and we'd listen to the Voice of America. But now he's missed his chance. Viktor Nikolaich honors me, and my neighbors, with his skulking presence."

"Meaning you'd like to know what I'm doing here."

"Mi casa es su casa."

"Yevgeny Moisovich, I have just spent the last twelve hours in the presence of the caretakers." No one used KGB in conversation. Why add unnecessary risk to an all too uncertain life? Everyone knew exactly what was meant, just as everyone knew that Mischa was a not entirely respectful reference to Gorbachev.

Shishkin did not hesitate. "Excellent hosts. They insist on nothing but the best. Won't take no for an answer from their guests."

"I am scared."

"I always assumed you were endowed with good common sense."

"And I don't know what to do next."

"Said the actress to the bishop: 'What has this to do with me?'"

"I don't even know why I came. It was stupid and it could endanger you."

"Viktor, do you remember when I was in trouble?" For the first time, Shishkin's face softened, the very hairs of his wild beard seemed to lie smoother.

It was before Gorbachev. The police had been given orders that day to make an example of the demonstrators. They knew there would be little sympathy at home for a bunch of Jews trying to cause a disturbance in the middle of Moscow. The Refuseniks had even had the effrontery to call up foreign reporters the night before to announce that the protest would take place in Pushkin Square at ten a.m. Viktor had driven his American boss to the site, parked the car fifty yards down the road to ensure that it would not be included in any police film footage. Then he had gone into the ground floor café of the Centralnaya Hotel, ordered a cup of coffee which never arrived, and waited.

All of the Jews that day had been trying to emigrate for at least five years; all were caught in the cycle of delays and reprisals that inevitably follow the filing of a request to emigrate. At five minutes to ten, the protesters began to slink into the square, making little effort to conceal the banners and posters they were carrying. The first to raise a sign was a tall thin hairball with a crooked mouth that Viktor could see even across the street. He wore a snap-brim hat and a long black raincoat that made him look even more ridiculous. Viktor had never actually seen the police close in on "politicals" before. He had watched some fat uniformed fakers bluster around Lenin Stadium once in pursuit of a dozen or so football hooligans. This group, known as specials, never hesitated. A short pug-nosed tough walked up to the bearded Jew and stuck the end of his collapsible black umbrella into the other man's groin. Viktor saw the victim double over, already out of commission. That was the signal for three more plain-clothes men to surround him. Pedestrians on the street that passes the square were totally unaware of the punishment being inflicted. For each of the fifteen or so protesters that day, there were at least four KGB. A blue and white panel truck marked "Ambulance" pulled up and three uniformed men with truncheons jumped out. The felled Jews were loaded into the truck like sandbags. The Western correspondents meanwhile had their cameras stripped of film or broken by apprentice KGB hoods. Several, including Viktor's boss, had been intelligent enough to leave camera and tape-recorders back at their offices. Unmolested, they chased after the ambulance on foot. Viktor's boss would not be needing a ride back.

Viktor ignored the orders of the waiter that he sit still until his coffee came. He crossed the street to the car, melted into the crowd walking toward Pushkin Square. The statue of the fablist rose gaunt and green from a pedestal of poured concrete. Near the statue, Viktor now saw a long, lean form stretched on the ground. It was the first Jew who had raised a banner. He had been left behind for some reason. Viktor knew what he should do: avert his eyes and move past, quickly. He never doubted the wisdom of that action, even as he bent over the man, lifted him by one arm, and propped him up against the concrete pedestal. Viktor was surprised that the face was not bloodied, the nose not broken, no gashes, no visible proof of violence. He looked again at the face, and found himself being stared at by two fox eyes.

"No blood, you're thinking, this bastard must be faking," said Shishkin with painful effort. "And once a doctor hears who I am and how I was injured, he'll say the same thing on any official diagnostic form. But I can feel one of my kidneys has been ruptured, and that comrade with the umbrella was trying to make sure that I never contribute to the next generation of this country."

"Stop talking. You don't even know who I am," said Viktor.

"Oh, right. Wouldn't want to get in any trouble, would I?"

"Can you move?"

"Well, my speciality is falling down while being pummelled. But I'm willing to try other directions. Where did you have in mind?"

Yefrim Yankovsky made Shishkin happy by contradicting him. "No rupture, but some very artistic bruise-work. You'll never take peeing for granted again, once it heals. But where are my manners? Would you care for four liters of water?"

"I feel like four liters of water," said Shishkin.

"Viktor, your friend here has not been taking care of himself," said Yankovsky. "I think you should take him home and let Anna jump on his ribs for an hour or two. He'll be a new man. Or woman."

"So, who is he?" Shishkin stared straight ahead as Viktor drove the car along Leninsky Prospekt.

"Yankovsky? Probably one of the best doctors in this country. At least that's what I've been told. But he complained a bit too loudly about the condition of our hospitals, and about the uses to which some of our psychiatric wards are put. So he underwent a professional conversion."

"Meaning?"

"He's now a night watchman, which is how I knew he'd be home at this hour. Occasionally I send friends to him, when the doctors at the clinics are too busy, or too drunk to do decent work."

"I'm not your friend," said Shishkin.

"We'll see."

*

Viktor stood in the doorway of the flat.

"Yes, Shishkin, I remember."

"So it's not as though you don't have a claim on my time."

"I need help."

"Obviously, if you could think of no one better than me to consult."

"Are you going to ask me in?"

"I would, but I have a great fear of rejection. Ever since childhood."

"Shishkin, you never left childhood."

The flat smelled awful. Viktor was no purist, but he could not stop from sneezing in self-defense. Shishkin pretended to be oblivious, but a smile split his face. Two steps into the apartment Viktor stopped short, let his mouth drop. Both walls of the entrance foyer were covered, completely, with cigarette packets. The ceiling was about one third concealed in the same manner.

Shishkin came up behind him. "I'd offer you a cigarette but I don't smoke."

"What in the name of . . ."

"Don't say 'God' and don't say 'Lenin'. One would be blasphemous in the Communist state; the other ridiculous in my home. You decide which is which."

"Explanation please, Shishkin, even though I am a guest and newly arrived."

The bearded man smiled. "Sit Viktor, sit and relax. From the looks of you it's something you haven't been doing a lot of either lately."

Viktor sat on a lumpy divan, declined a drink of vodka, accepted tea which Shishkin assured him, accurately, would be awful.

"So you're impressed with my decorating scheme. I have so few visitors I forget to warn newcomers in advance. Well, it's like this: Do you know, Viktor, how much money the state liquor monopoly makes each year?"

"Not really. A lot I suppose."

"A lot? How about 15 billion rubles' profit. Just profit! And that's what they admit to, after Gorbachev's efforts to cut down on our national pastime. Viktor, it's a tenth of the civilian gross annual product. They take advantage of our weakness, of our national deficiency, of our traditional thirst, to milk us while they drown us in an ocean of alcoholic filth."

"So, don't drink. I don't any more."

"I know, I remember. I don't either, although I dearly love the taste. I won't give them the pleasure of profiting from me. Do you smoke, Viktor?"

"Not any more. But I still do the final thing that most men like, before you get around to asking."

Shishkin laughed. "Ah, yes, but for most men, married ones anyway, that's free. And freely given. But let me finish. You know that the state controls tobacco growing, harvesting, drying, cutting, the production of cigarettes and their sale."

"Shishkin, is this a midnight economics seminar?"

"No, and it's not a lung cancer hotline either. The tobacco business is the same as drinking. The bastards that run the country prey on the craving for nicotine. But a long time ago, they made a mistake. They set a low price for cigarettes and promised not to increase it. How much did cigarettes cost when you stopped smoking Viktor?"

"Fifteen kopeks."

"They still do. Despite higher planting, harvesting and production costs, the price has stayed the same. It's one of those things they thought they could safely promise, since they thought they'd never fall victim to inflation."

"Just explain why . . ."

"I just have. Only you're too obtuse to see it. The tobacco monopoly loses millions of rubles a year. It's a loss-maker. That's not a well-known fact, but it's true. Each day, every day, the state loses money making and selling cigarettes. Every time someone buys a packet of Spartas, or Boredinos, or Kievs, they're hurting the economy, weakening the control of these turds."

"And you . . ."

"I buy a packet every day, even though I don't smoke, and glue it to the wall. I've had to start on the ceiling. Before I leave here I plan to start a fire and charge admission. Every chain-smoker in Moscow will pay to inhale the flames."

A laugh, the first good one in many hours, escaped Viktor. "And I was coming to you for help."

"Don't worry. I've got no matches."

Telling his trouble took less than an hour, probably because neither of them was drinking. Shishkin did not speak until the inevitable ". . . and here I am" signalled an end to the tale.

"Wow! No halfway measures for you, Melanov. The American Embassy, missing guards, suicide. You might as well become a Jew. You've got nothing to lose."

The first rays of false dawn battled through the grime of the flat's one window. Viktor heaved to his feet. "I can get a bus home now. Thank you for listening."

"Has one night without sleep left you stupid, Viktor? You think you can jump into bed for an hour and wake up in the Age of Enlightenment?

The minute you go home and try to pick up your life, your family will suffer too."

A chill sickness spread through Viktor. "Shishkin, don't tell me to abandon my family."

"Viktor, it's been years since you pulled me out of Pushkin Square, took me to that off-license voodoo artist and then to your home to recover. I saw the look in your wife's eyes when you told her who I was. And I heard her ream you out when you left me on the couch to sleep. The next day I met your daughter and I saw the kind of sparks that fly between the two of you. Later, it turns out we know a few of the same people. You know them because they are brilliant connivers, I because they are Jews longing to go home. In three years, we've met, what? Six, eight times? And usually because I want to ask you a favor. Pushy, dirty, hairy Shishkin. Viktor, where can I get some paper, Viktor, do you know how to get hold of an English dictionary for a few hours? You don't ask why, but even you can figure I'm printing nasty little dissident leaflets, for the nosy Western reporters to send home.

"Now for the first time you've stumbled on to real trouble. The KGB doesn't bother with suicides unless they're assisting in them. The remark to the guard wasn't a brilliant action. And it's hard to explain why you were delivering billets-doux to someone who then jumps out a window. But there are ways around even these kinds of problems. Know why I was fully dressed when you, uh, arrived? You have to promise never to repeat what I'm going to tell you."

"I don't see how my bargaining position is such that I'm making promises to you. But go ahead."

"I was waiting to see someone who would pass on to me a most wonderful thing."

"A million dollars?"

"Better. A Romanian passport."

Viktor nodded heavily. "Oh yes, I see. Truly worth its weight in plutonium."

"Think Viktor. What does Romania have that none of our fraternal allies has?"

"Widespread malnutrition. Scurvy."

"Diplomatic relations with Israel."

"And I've broken up your meeting? Perhaps if I told Karushkin, he would not only forget my little indiscretion but arrange for a medal."

"No. I don't think he'd be too happy to learn about it. One of the reasons you came to me tonight was because you think anyone who has been in trouble with the police as often as I must be slightly unsavoury, and therefore able to help you solve your own problem. Which, by the way, is more serious than you think." He paused to let the impact of his words sink in. "And you're right. According to this country's values, I'm little more than a traitor."

"Shishkin, I don't . . ."

"Your views on the subject do not matter. What's important is that you believe me when I say you must not involve your family. You've been told to report back for another interrogation, right?"

"Tomorrow. One o'clock."

"If you go, you will be inducted into a world so sickeningly perverted, and made to live an existence so inhuman, that I predict you will commit suicide within six months."

No one had ever said that to him before. He was suitably depressed.

"There could only be one thing worse than showing up for that interrogation, Viktor. Not showing up. For whatever reason, if you stay away, they'll hunt you down and punish you with the kind of vigor they lack for everything else. And when they find you, they'll send you to a gulag, or to a psychiatric ward: they may even force you to make the choice.

"They'd enjoy that. Each has its own unique terror: the constant cold, hunger, and pain of prison without end, the beatings, the special isolation, the nights of special punishment in the refrigerator. The way your teeth fall out, your hair molts, your skin turns yellow, then gray. Then, after all that has happened, being forced – forced, Viktor – to confront your wife and daughter, who will have been told that you're being released. Of course, you'll never be released, and you'll watch them, first as they lay eyes on you, then as they're being told the release has been rescinded, because you were caught in a homosexual liaison with another prisoner. And you'll see them as they walk away, crying uncontrollably.

"Or perhaps you'll choose the loony bin. Just seeing the others there and knowing that you'll soon be like them would cost most sane people their minds. The shrieks all through the night, the shit everywhere on the floor, the stench of unwashed bodies and uncleansable brains. Then, after a few days, the injections. First sulphazine, which makes you feel like your blood is burning holes through your veins. Your brain tissue literally swells against the cranium. Of course it's damaged immediately, irreparably. But that's only the first course. A week later, they'll administer a hallucinogenic, together with more sulphazine, to see what you do. You won't have any memory of it, until you and all the others see yourself on the videotape. That's called 'movie night'. Then there's the electric shock therapy, and the wet canvas wraps around your chest, and your throat and your eyeballs."

"Shishkin, stop it!"

A smile poked through the beard. "Yes, something wrong? Oh, I've upset you. Well, comrade, let me assure you I know people who've experienced each of the delights I just described. None of them is alive now, at least not in a way we would recognize. And not all of them are Jews. Some were just patriotic Russians, like you, certain that they could never get into such deep trouble."

"Shishkin, what about my family?"

"I know, I know. It's impossible to think of life without them. We'll talk about it more, after. For now, trust me a bit. It's good that you came here. I may be the only man in Moscow who knows how to help you. But, of course, you're known for being able to find just the right man for complicated jobs. For now, Viktor, sleep. I can only offer you the couch. I'll take the floor. I doubt that you were followed here. They assume that no one who has just been released from their embrace has the brains to do anything but what they tell him. The trouble will begin when you miss the interrogation today."

"Miss it? But you just said . . ."

"And it was all true. Now sleep. I can offer you this much: sometime today, you'll see your wife and daughter."

A whimper came from nowhere within him. "I have to. I have to see them."

"Yes, Viktor. First, though, an hour or so of sleep."

The hour or two became five and when he startled himself to consciousness by rolling off the couch, it was nearing noon. He knew where he was, the smell was even worse than it had been. Tobacco, dirt, years of neglect. "Shishkin?" No answer. He got up, spotted a piece of paper tacked to the door. "Some people have an easy life, don't they? Lenin Library Metro, 1.10. Near the newspaper kiosk. P.S. Don't strike any matches."

It was a logical meeting place for scholars, spies and sweethearts. The metro at Lenin Library connects to three of the city's main lines. Just above is one of the most copious reading facilities in the world, as long as one's taste for knowledge runs to the officially sanctioned. Computers hum, ready to locate one of the 10 million volumes stored in the main library. But they are seldom used by ordinary readers. No one, not even a diligent researcher of Marx and Engels, wants his name included on any more official lists than absolutely necessary.

Viktor had come to the library often when he was younger and still believed its contorted promise, paraphrased from Ezra Cornell: "In this room, any comrade can find the answers that he seeks to any question."

64

How hopeful he had been on those first visits: "May I borrow a book by Boris Pasternak please?" "That criminal is not published in this country, comrade." "Is there a text of the speech made by the West German chancellor last year, on the subject of arms control?" "There most certainly is. The highlights were published in *Pravda* the day after. You may read it there." "Is the American almanac called *Information, Please* in the library system?" "Why should we stock that? What is wrong with the *Great Soviet Encyclopedia*? Let me see your identity papers, comrade."

So even though he had ample time, Viktor decided not to make the trip upstairs from the metro stop to see that selective storehouse of fact. Instead, he trudged through the Alexandra Gardens of the Kremlin, reminded, as he so frequently was, of times when he had walked the same paths, holding Anna's hand. He wondered how his absence from work was being interpreted, if the KGB knew of it, if the agency had already sent people looking for him. He felt no danger of arrest, even as he passed within one hundred feet of the Kremlin's southeast tower. This was his city. They would have a job finding him if he avoided his normal routine. The bells in the Spassky Tower, facing the Moscow River, whirred into action. Like everyone else in the garden, Viktor stood still, as though by reflex, while the hour was struck. An angry old Bolshevik had snapped his answer without hesitation when Viktor once asked him about the unacknowledged tradition. "Why do we stand still when the belltower rings? To see if those stupid bastards can get the time right, at least." Viktor turned back, walked slowly down the steps that led to the metro below the library, and muttered, "Ah, friend, but the things that those bastards can do well . . ."

At both ends of each metro platform, just where the trains roar into or out of the dark tunnels, there is a digital clock that counts down from three minutes to zero. Trains are guaranteed to arrive no more than three minutes apart, and the clocks give passengers a feeling, entirely unjustified, that they are holding the government to its word. Two zeros and a six were showing when the first carriage whooshed into the station, pulling seven others like it. "Lenin Library," said a prerecorded female voice with all the warmth of a crime report. "Change here for the Circle Line, the Southern Line, and the Central Line. Watch the doors." Viktor always rode the next to last car. He had heard the rumors about the head-on crashes in the tunnels. In one, in 1980, more than two hundred people died in a collision between two trains headed in opposite directions on the same track. The crash caused a fire that closed nearly half the subway system for a week. Not a word appeared in the press, however, except a short notice in a small circulation Moscow weekly announcing that repairs were being conducted. Viktor had heard that on each of the trains, there had been no casualties in the next to last car.

Shishkin evidently had heard the story too. He slipped out of the seventh car wearing the same clothes in which he had received Viktor the night before. His hair was still a dishevelled lump of grey and brown attached to a scalp. What was different was his expression. He had none. The same man who at three in the morning could light his home with a smile and warm it with an ironic chuckle, now kept his eyes blank. His head was tilted slightly downward, so that his field of vision hardly extended above the metro platform. Viktor stood still in front of the kiosk and watched Shishkin sleepwalk with the rest of the passengers. For all the irregularity of his appearance, he was doing a fine job of blending into the crowd. Shishkin walked a straight line on the edge of the platform closest to the train, which was slowly pulling out of the station. He was six feet from Viktor but kept walking away. Viktor was ready to move after him; there was no chance that Shishkin could have missed him, he was standing right where instructed. A hand fell on his shoulder and whiskery cheeks brushed his face. "My friend, my friend," said a jovial voice that sounded as though it belonged at a drinking party. "How have you been?" Viktor felt his shoulders enfolded by two fat arms. Had he been discovered so quickly? Had Shishkin betrayed him? "Come with me, Viktor," said the bearded man who had now draped his arm over Viktor's shoulder. "I am with Shishkin."

The very words, "Come with me," force Russians to make a momentous choice when they are spoken in the way Viktor heard them. They can lead to solitary confinement in one of the faceless gulags of the East, or to a warm reception at a party in progress. The identity of the speaker makes the difference; does he wear a uniform and have dead eyes, or is he a twenty years' acquaintance, with a taste for good times? This voice was strange, and the command left no time for delay. Accede or run? In that moment of motionless anticipation, Viktor understood that the life he had known was over. Because someone had chosen to hand him a piece of paper, he had forfeited his right to a normal existence. He put on the smile he wore when recommending a particularly talented tailor: "Of course, my friend, delighted to see you."

The metro ride made Viktor feel he had been away for months instead of a day and a night. As each stop brought him nearer his home, he felt less a part of the scene. The disembodied metallic voice that announced the stations sounded threatening. His companion simply would not speak, even when Viktor asked pleasantly, "Since you know my name, what's yours?" The fellow showed no recognition that he was travelling with someone else.

But, at Shcherbakovskaya Station, he rose and said matter of factly: "Come on, Viktor." It was the same neutral tone of command with which he had approached Viktor. The station was so familiar; he even recognized the woman who made change for passengers who did not have the correct five kopeks' fare. She had once broken into sobs when Viktor was at the window of her kiosk. Her washing-machine had overflowed in her apartment and ruined a new carpet for which she had saved for years. Viktor had helped her to have the carpet cleaned and dried properly at a discount. He hoped she would not see him passing by. The man with a thousand good deeds in his past now craved anonymity.

He had always been pleased that there were no shops or cafés near his apartment. He cherished the notion that this part of Moscow was meant for living, not for commercial activities. His companion touched his elbow: "Down this side street."

"But I live further along this main road."

The man nodded as though he had just heard the score of last night's football game. They went in the back entrance of the building on the corner. "Third floor," said the man, and when Viktor took a step toward the lift, tugged delicately at his arm, and gestured toward the staircase.

They were both puffing when they reached the landing, and Viktor thought for a second of how the Americans called the ground level the first floor. Another proof of how much easier their life was, he reflected.

The door of the flat straight ahead of them was open. Shishkin was staring out the window. Viktor walked in. He was learning to accept the strange as commonplace, the unexpected as routine. When Shishkin turned from the window, Viktor saw he was holding a pair of Sputnik binoculars.

The foxy smile was back. "Not bad for Soviet-made," Shishkin said, waving the field glasses as though weighing them. "Copied from the East Germans, who supply the KGB with theirs. Still, they're adequate for our puny efforts."

"And a good day to you too, Yevgeny Moisovich."

"Strasvuyte, Viktor. Care to take a look?"

"Voyeurism at your age?"

"And at yours. Come. Look."

As soon as he stepped to the window, Viktor realized the flat overlooked his own. Although they take long country walks in order to be able to discuss politics, Russians seldom think of the ease with which residents of high-rise blocks can snoop on their neighbors. Even looking into his own home, Viktor felt something akin to guilt as he put the lenses to his eyes. He turned the knobs to bring the scene into focus. He had never realized before that the apartment directly above his was decorated with exactly the same furniture. He saw a man standing in the window on which he was focused, with a gray box held near his face. A woman who had borrowed one of Marya's dresses was seated in the far corner, her hands folded. Evidently Marya had also lent the woman her face. He moved the binoculars up, down, and saw the neighbors who had always lived above and below him.

Miserably, he returned his gaze to the window in between. Marya sat, hands folded. The man stood with the gray box poised.

"They arrived half an hour after you failed to show up at work." Shishkin was sitting down, his voice was flat. "Whatever they think you've done, comrade, they're very anxious to have another discussion about it."

Viktor's head seemed to be inundated with irrelevancies. "Whose flat are we in?"

"What does it matter?"

"How did you know?"

"I'm a Jew. I always expect persecution, at best."

Then the real question. "Will they hurt Marya? Anna?"

"I don't see why they should. It would certainly be out of character. Of course, if they should think you can be pressured into giving up, they'll use them as pawns. But if they don't know how to contact you, their pressure is ineffective."

Viktor stared through the binoculars again, but the scene had not changed. "You make it sound like a military operation, Shishkin."

"You think it's any different? What is war except a competition for control? What is this government except a vast conspiracy for controlling us all?"

"Enough philosophy. What do I do?"

"You've already made your choice. You made it when you came to see me. The only questions now involve tactics." Shishkin stood up, went out of the room. Viktor heard water creaking from a rusty tap. Shishkin returned with two glasses.

"Here Viktor, drink a toast of purification. You're a free man."

"Free?"

"Certainly. You have broken the rules, irrevocably, permanently. You have gone overnight from being a nobody who's fallen into a hole, to being a desperado, with all the freedom of a man making his life over. You lack only two things."

"And they are?"

"A choice about what to do next and time in which to decide."

"Shishkin, what are you saying?"

"Lucky devil. Send me a postcard when you get to New York."

7

Viktor could not stop thinking of the sun. There had been times when, leaning against the hood of his car, alongside the bank of the Moscow River on a summer day, the heat and the tingle of his skin made him feel as though he had died and been reborn. And, inevitably, he remembered times with Anna, once especially when Marya could not convince the factory to give her holiday time that was owed her, and just the two of them had spent a week in the Crimea. Their room was an odor-filled converted garage that Viktor had rented, sight-unseen, from a crone in Simferopol. The miserable hag had given him directions to what she assured him was an airy, light wing of a Black Sea villa. When they arrived, Viktor saw what she meant. The garage room leaked and was painted yellow. He had known that he was out of his element in the south, but Anna had enjoyed herself thoroughly from the moment she saw the room, and claimed it as "ours". They ate at cheap restaurants every night, skipped lunch, swam in the sea for hours, and watched each other's hair become lighter under the sun.

"Enough, I have to come out!" At first, he wondered if anything would happen. A minute – he counted to sixty – passed. There was a scraping sound, and then a God-like voice from somewhere above said, "Lazurus wasn't so impatient."

"Out, now!" Victor kicked his feet out for the inch or two available to him, making pitiful thumps against pinewood.

God's voice said, "Turn off the gas. Get him out, dammit."

The hissing stopped. Then, like the final cataclysm, a shaft of light broke through solid darkness, and descended. The pain made him realize that his eyes had been open. He closed them.

"Nap time is over, comrade. You can get out now and have a stretch."

Slowly, Viktor was working out his vengeance against the owner of that voice. He would have to do something particularly witty and exceptionally cruel, not his speciality. But the barbs and taunts were becoming too much. He lifted one leg – it might have been filled with concrete, it hurt so much to move – over the edge, then the other.

"God alive," he said. It was a mild profanity from the tsarist era, when such assumptions were taken for granted.

"If he's not then we've squandered two thousand beautiful years," said Bessmyrtinkh. He was a tiny man, with a frog's face, and the humor of a carpenter in a forest fire. He always had something to say, whether or not it was called for or welcome.

"I, Velodya Jerusalemovich, have not been wasting that amount of time."

"No, I can see from your latest performance, you don't like spending much time on anything. This, for instance, took you only six and three-quarters hours, dammit."

Viktor reddened. "I needed to stretch. You said that would happen at first."

"At first, at first, yes, but this is your fifth day here. How long do you think this is going to go on? We're not running a winter seminar for moles."

"You could have fooled me." Viktor felt the edge of his anger seeping over, like boiling milk out of a pan. "Is Shishkin coming today?"

Bessmyrtinkh fixed Viktor with a stare, trying but failing to rechannel the heat that he knew was inside him. "Yes, I believe he is coming, Viktor. That was the last word I had."

"And that means . . ."

"I don't know, dammit, man. I've told you at least a hundred times in the last five days. I'm not privy to all the information that Shishkin has."

"You've told me a lot of other things too, that proved to be untrue," Viktor said. He so seldom uncorked the feelings inside him. But that was in another life. "You promised me yesterday that I could see Anna today. You promised."

Bessmyrtinkh smiled broadly, and raised his eyebrows at the two men sitting with their backs to the wooden door of the apartment.

"Did you hear that, comrades? He thinks it was just yesterday that we talked about his daughter. It is progress of a kind, eh?"

He turned back. "Viktor, that was the day before yesterday. Remember, you slept for twelve hours. Our great triumph."

There was nothing to say. He had no rights, no memory, no consciousness of time. There was only a vague appreciation of its passing, fuelled by promises of seeing Anna. There had been two, neither fulfilled. It made him hate them.

Them? He did not even know who they were.

There was Bessmyrtinkh, whom he had come to regard as an evil dwarf. He was not much more than five feet tall, ugly in unprecedented proportion to his height. Bessmyrtinkh had outfitted Viktor, taught him about breathing with a tube, instructed him in meditation, an art that Viktor, like most of his countrymen, had always assumed was irrelevant north of the Punjab. Russians do not meditate. It has as much meaning for them as box top coupons. But it was amazing what it did for him, the concentration, the trick of thinking about a flat, black lake, with himself at its edge. Bessmyrtinkh never commented, never congratulated, never reviled. He taught a craft; there was neither merit nor failure, only degrees of competence. Viktor feared that given enough exposure, he might like Bessmyrtinkh.

There was no danger of his liking The Blob. No other name seemed to fit. To call him fat was the same as noting that Communist candidates always seem to win elections. His shirt, the seat of his pants, his bulging socks, all reached away from his gross body as if running in self-defense. His bifurcated chest jiggled like a slut's. His chin was slavishly obedient to the law of gravity. His arms were chunks of meat awaiting a judicious butcher. The Blob had never spoken to Viktor, never acknowledged his presence except to nod once when Bessmyrtinkh said they would be training someone new for a few weeks. Viktor had tried a courteous smile, an extended hand, and had been met with the straight-lipped dullness of inborn stupidity. The Blob was never addressed by name. Instead he seemed to know what orders were directed at him. He never smiled, or commented on Bessmyrtinkh's endless flow of commentary. He was a one-man island of dullness in the sea of chatter that Bessmyrtinkh fed, drop by drop.

Viktor had recognized Pronsky immediately, which pleased neither of them. For ten years Pronsky had been the driver at an African embassy in Moscow. He and Viktor had a nodding acquaintance, the kind of relationship suburban commuters might develop after years of waiting together. Then, one day, shortly after the arrival of a new ambassador, Pronsky appeared no more. Finally the story emerged: the African country had always been too poor to school its diplomats in Russian before sending them to Moscow. At no time had any of the previous three ambassadors who had served in Moscow during that decade realized that Pronsky was addressing them as "Boy". Viktor had always assumed that Pronsky was Jewish because of his name. Now it was confirmed. He was amid Jews, and, like it or not, was in their hands.

For five days he had repeated the same routine with Bessmyrtinkh, The Blob and Pronsky. Since the second day he had been promised that he would see his daughter. Shishkin had never explained why he was taking

Viktor to the southern suburbs of Moscow; or why it was necessary that he learn to remain motionless for twenty-four hours at a time. By the time Bessmyrtinkh had told him what he would be doing in the sunless basement of the house, Shishkin had already left.

He rebelled the first time Bessmyrtinkh ordered him into the box. "Fuck your mother," he said, standard Russian street talk, but far beyond his normal protests. In the darkness, he came to the conclusion that he had not used the phrase since Anna's birth. Bessmyrtinkh had shrugged, left him in the house, guarded by The Blob, who watched him as if he was a steaming meal. When Bessmyrtinkh returned he said merely, "Do what we ask and you will see your daughter tomorrow." Viktor got in the box, and stayed for forty-five minutes.

They had lied, of course. There was no Anna the next day or the day after. He demanded to see her the fourth day, and was assured he would. Again, they lied. Bessmyrtinkh seemed to be elsewhere much of the time. Viktor assumed he was getting directions and instructions on what lie to tell next.

This time, he made up his mind. He would not go in the box again until they kept their promise. The Blob settled his heavy eyes on the ground. Pronsky listened to the radio. Bessmyrtinkh disappeared.

"I mean it," Viktor growled. "No more of the craziness. I'm not a criminal. I can go back and set things right." Each word convinced him more that he could not. The Blob and Pronsky were neutral, he concluded. They did not care whether he died, became a zombie, joined the Party, or ran for President of the United States. But they would not allow him to do any of those things while they were watching him. Neither was cordial but, Viktor thought, neither had any reason to be. He was a stranger thrust upon them, in a country where strangers can bring trouble. He abided the long appraising stares, the nods that substituted for conversation, the uncertainty.

"May I go outside?" He had learned to ask. The first time he flung open the door, The Blob lunged at him. That was how he learned that he was more a prisoner than a guest. He walked outside the rough wooden house that was his refuge. It was set on a hill, overlooking the village. So little had changed on this hill, or that village, for two hundred years. Water was drawn from ground wells, horses hauled bunches of faggots down dirt paths to cottages that looked incapable of supporting human life. Yet the dwellings had, with few exceptions, been well broken-in before the word Communism was added to the language. That was Russia's strength, he thought. Its backward peasant ways could survive foreign invasion or internal corrosion. Whether Stalin came back to life or a conglomerate

72

bought the entire country, that well would be the life-blood of the hundred people who were within the sound of his voice.

He breathed in fresh Russian air, but saw his breath released. He had forgotten that it was spring; the room and the box erased the textures and edges of life. Far down the road he saw a figure walking, arms slashing air, head bobbing like a rooster's, feet in competition to get ahead of each other. He had heard that Lenin was identifiable to his followers from a mile away. Now he believed it. Shishkin waved as he mounted the hill, plopped himself on the sloping ground outside the house.

"Don't you love this country life? Feel like you've left all your problems behind?"

He was finding it hard to maintain his composure. "Did you walk out here?"

"You expected my sleek black Zil would deposit me at the doorstep? Actually, I took the metro as far as it came. I've only been walking for an hour."

"Fuck your mother, you're weird, Shishkin." The expression was becoming second nature to him. He would have to stop using it or Anna would pick it up . . . The pain of realization shot through him and he could control himself no longer. "What game are you playing with me? I've been locked in a box, watched like a germ under a microscope, treated like a traitor . . ."

"Viktor, have you noticed that our conversational standards have dipped to unacceptable levels? Like a couple of old marrieds, we seem to have nothing to say to each other, except occasional threats, placation, and reconciliation."

"And lies."

"When necessary. That time, happily, has passed. How are your legs?"

"Joined, I think."

"Good. Then you are capable of exploring this beautiful land with me. Come along."

Shishkin waved weakly at The Blob and Pronsky, on the other side of the window. Viktor understood that without that wave he would not have been allowed to leave the grounds. It was like being transferred from one KGB to another.

"Is the prisoner allowed to walk now?"

"Definitely. It keeps the spirit up."

"Why not tell that to The Blob?" He used the name without thinking. "Who?"

"The big ugly one."

"Ah, Rudolph. It's true, he is not the sort to make a woman swoon. But he is good."

Viktor did not think he could learn to call The Blob Rudolph.

Instead of descending to the village that could be seen from the house, Shishkin led him over the hill. Within minutes they were wandering among lush conifers, whose green only began to shine with cold weather. Here, amid primeval splendor that awed tsars and commissars alike roamed an ill-kept, eccentric misfit and an average citizen who until a week before had believed his wits could help him avoid conflict with a system he knew was neither fair nor functional.

Shishkin fumbled in his back pants' pocket, extracted a dirty and much folded newspaper. "You might as well see this now. That way, when you bellow, no one will hear you."

The paper was the previous day's edition of the *Moscow Evening News*. It was folded open at page 6, which carried one and two sentence items. The page was widely read because the stories often contained oblique references to events not generally known or elsewhere published. It had been on page 6 that the 1980 subway fire was first, and exclusively, alluded to. There was no need for words. Shishkin handed the paper over. Viktor saw, almost immediately, his name in the story in the fifth column, just above the middle fold. "At the request of his family, the Moscow militia are seeking V. N. Melanov. Those who know about him are advised to contact the authorities."

"Don't feel slighted. Khrushchev's obituary only got one line."

"What does it mean?"

"Since we are walking here, instead of in the exercise yard at Lubyanka, it means they cannot find you. I'm beginning to think I overrated them."

"It's a strange beginning: 'At the request of his family . . .'"

"They're hoping you read it and get worried about your wife and child."

"They've got their wish."

"Come along. I want to show you something." For twenty minutes they trudged along needle-covered paths, climbed over felled trees, slushed through puddles that had been camouflaged by leaves. One instant, they were lost in nature. The next, an onion-shaped spire dominated their vision.

"We're in . . ."

"Yes, Peredelkino."

"Why not straight to Dzerzhinsky Square, Shishkin? There are fewer Party members per square foot there."

Peredelkino is an evergreen-shaded colony of cottages and lanes reserved for the use of state-approved writers. Yevtushenko can usually be seen pushing his way to the head of the line at the bakery on Saturdays. Sholokov sits on a porch, trying to recapture the magic he created with *And Quiet Flows the Don*. Other writers, true to the cause of the Party, and they think, the pen, vie for the choicest dachas. It is pleasant country land that farmers in the surrounding towns believe could be put to better use.

Viktor and Shishkin walked to one end of the village. Running off the main road was a dirt-covered path along which only the most careless drivers would intentionally take their own cars. The fourth house on the lane, a chocolate-colored, three-story behemoth, betrayed the lack of care it had been given in recent years. Both men looked at it with reverence.

Shishkin shook his head. "Short of being a Jew, I think Pasternak suffered as much as any Russian possibly could."

"You know about his house?" Viktor asked. "The family asked permission to convert it into a museum with their own funds, then turn it over to the state to run. They were told that because Pasternak had been expelled from the Writers' Union, he could not be honored with a museum."

"Didn't the family try to move into the house last year?" Shishkin's interest was sincere.

"Yes, but then they were told that Pasternak had obtained the house because he was a writer."

"So what?"

"So, they say, his actions during the time he lived here proved that he was not a writer but an anti-Soviet influence."

"There's a certain beauty to their logic, isn't there?"

"Why are we here, Shishkin?"

"We're waiting."

"For what? For who?"

"Someone good. Someone you'll like."

"That's what you said about that bunch up the hill. The fat one is really a loser."

Shishkin stopped walking, jabbed an angry finger. "I've heard about enough from you on that topic, my friend. There's something you should know about Rudolph. Until I took an interest in your problem, it was he who was practicing in the box. He would have been our first test case."

Viktor said nothing.

The putt-putt of a weak motor from far down the road gradually became a choking growl. Viktor stretched his neck toward the sound. "Your friend?"

"Possibly mine. Certainly yours."

The car was dirty; the driver was a risk-taker. The Moscow police stop unwashed cars and level immediate fines. It is against the law to give foreigners the idea that Russian cars, especially those in the capital, might be dirty. The windshield was fogged over, indicating that its inside heater was on. Its headlights blinked once and it pulled to the right side of the path, about fifty yards from Shishkin and Viktor. The motor was stilled. The left front door half-opened, a black boot touched the ground, a hand curled over the top of the door, and the driver slipped out and began walking toward them.

"Go to the car, Viktor. Get in."

"Why? Where am I going?"

"To hell on angel's wings, with me supplying the gas. It's a bit late not to trust me."

"I also trusted you when you said I would see my daughter."

"Viktor, I'm trying to be patient. Please go to the car."

The windshield was not just fogged, it was as dirty as the rest of the car. He opened the door on the passenger's side, saw a bulky blanket in the back seat.

"What is this?" he muttered.

The blanket moved.

"Daddy?"

He had her in his arms so quickly, so tightly, that he nearly crushed her against the seat separating them. She squeaked, so he released her, and, unwilling to get out of the car for even a second, scrambled clumsily over the seat, scraping his foot along the roof.

"Anna, Anyishka, oh my little birdie." He thought it impossible that she had changed so much in a week. She looked more mature, poised, sadder. Too many emotions competed for his voice. Each was replaced by another, so he said, "You're not cold, are you?"

"How could I be cold? Look what I'm wearing." It was, of course, his scarf. He had not been home since he left it with her. "I've worn it every day, and I take it to bed at night. It still smells like you, a little."

"And what do I smell like?"

"A bit like this scarf." Giggles. It was as natural for them to lapse into banter as for him to squeeze her too tightly. "Daddy, I don't like you being away." She said it with no more expression than she might use to ask when dinner would be ready. Viktor disintegrated into a spasm of sobs that made it impossible to inhale. He began to choke, finally drew in some air, and laid his head on her shoulder.

"There now, Daddy, don't cry." She rubbed her index finger on the back of his neck at the bottom of his hairline. It was something he had done years ago when he rocked her to sleep. The memory brought more tears.

"Daddy, stop now. We have to talk."

Viktor stared wide-eyed at his eight-year-old daughter. It was she who was comforting him, giving him just enough time to empty his eyes before reinstating reason. Matured? She had grown wise in a week. Like a wind shifting course, he spoke differently to her when he regained control a second time.

"Yes, Anna, we must talk. First, how is your mother?"

"Sad, of course. How else could she be? She cries every night, and I hold her and she holds me, and then we both go to sleep. But sometimes not for a long time. Daddy? Do I have to do what they tell me?"

"What who tells you? No, whoever it is, except your mother."

"The woman who brought me here."

"Woman? That was a woman who drove you here? When did she meet you? How?" The questions he wanted answered seemed endless, but he could not put an order to them.

Anna's smile radiated patience and Viktor wondered: Is this how she will look after me in my old age? He was becoming completely fuddled. Fool, you might not reach old age.

"Daddy, listen. When I got out of school this afternoon, there was a woman at the gate. She told me that Mama wanted me to go with her."

"Anna, you must never . . ."

"Go with a stranger. I know. I told her I couldn't. And she said I was right, and said I was very clever, but in this case it was important. Then she showed me your picture."

"She had my picture?"

"You were asleep, and there was a newspaper on your chest. You know, the newspaper you always make fun of at home."

"*Pravda?*"

"Yes, and I could see the date was only two days ago, so I knew she knew where you were. At first I was scared, I thought the picture meant you were dead, but the woman said no, you were asleep and, oh, anyway, I was so glad you weren't dead and that she knew where you were that I went with her. It was all right, wasn't it? I mean, I found you, didn't I?"

And, for that moment, it truly was all right, and Viktor would not have cared if the woman was Karushkin's sister.

"Yes, it's all right, little one." His wits were beginning to hone themselves again. A week's disuse and darkness were being replaced with a combativeness that, until now, he had wasted on jumping queues and finding scarce goods.

"Listen, Anna. I want to ask you a few questions. And I just want you to answer me as simply as you can. Use as few words as possible. Understand?"

She nodded her head, down, once.

He laughed. "Well, you can talk a little more than that. Does your mother know I'm here?"

"Even I don't know you're here. Where are we? The lady told me to stay under the blanket. And I can't see through the windows. We're in the forest though, aren't we?"

Stupid, stupid, he cursed himself. He almost drew her into this. Shishkin's woman, whoever she was, had been persuasive, cautious, and competent. He must not undo the careful work. But neither did he want to lie. He chose his words like tomatoes at an Azerbaijani market stall.

"It doesn't matter where we are. We're together. That's what's important. Anna, I'm away from home because there are some things that happened that I have to fix. It's harder than my normal work, you know, driving. And worst of all, I have to be away from you and your mother."

"I know. Mama told me."

"What did she tell you?"

"About the lady who died at work. I remember meeting her once, but I don't remember her name. She seemed nice. And Mama says that now you have to work hard, to make sure that no one else gets hurt like that. And that we should be very proud of you. Didn't you think I knew all that, Daddy?"

It sounded like Marya. They would have thought along the same lines in trying to explain to Anna something about which they knew nothing.

"How did Mama know about the lady who died?"

"The man who's staying in my room told her. I don't think he feels very well."

Alarm bells. He kept his voice even. "Which man is that?"

"The one who came to stay while you're gone. He's small, and in the morning, when I go past him into the kitchen, he smells bad. Like when I got sick when I was little. That's why I think he doesn't feel well."

"And is he always at home?"

"Always. Once I told him about the path where we take walks. I thought he might like to get out and get some air. But he said no. Mostly he writes in a little book and talks on the radio."

"And he sleeps in your room?"

"Well, first he slept on the floor near the dining room. Then Mama told me I should sleep with her, and she told him he could sleep in my bed."

"And is he always nice to you?"

78

"Oh yes, but only nice like people are nice when they don't really know you. You know, they smile when they say yes, and they said 'Excuse me,' and they watch you a lot."

Whoever Karushkin had put into the house did not sound like a brute. That could change, of course, if the KGB decided to switch tactics. But for the moment, Marya and Anna were safe.

There was a tap on the window, not startling but neither was it tentative. Viktor rolled down the window an inch. A black-gloved hand came through the space, and a finger wagged reprovingly. The finger crooked and straightened, crooked and straightened.

"Anna, I'll be right back. Don't move."

He got out. Shishkin, now wearing gloves, was at the back end of the car. The woman stood well down the road, her face indiscernible.

"Shut the door. Now, about promises kept, Viktor Nikolaich."

"Shishkin, have you endangered her?"

The dissident's face lost its smile. His mouth was straight. "Would you have cared if we had? If I had told you it was dangerous for her if she saw you, would you have released me from my promise? No, you kept on day after day, 'Shishkin broke his word, I'll never trust Shishkin again.' You weren't thinking about your daughter's welfare. You just wanted to see her."

It was true. He had no cause for grievance. "All right. Have I endangered her?"

"How? In case you don't know, she was supposed to be trying out for a part in the class play this afternoon. So she won't try out. Will anyone notice? She'll have to mislead her mother a bit, but not lie to her. All the girl has to say is she didn't get the part."

Viktor remembered. The play was going to be a tractor special, one of those no-plot tales that glorified the clean life of collective farms and the dignity of giving everything to the Party. It was probably written in a room somewhere within a mile of where they stood by a hack who had pried a dacha out of the Writers' Union. Viktor hadn't encouraged Anna to try out, but he knew she understood his skepticism. Marya would not be surprised if the girl was not chosen for the cast.

"All right. Who is the woman who brought her here?"

"Oh, a bored Politburo wife who hates idle afternoons. What does it matter?"

Everything Shishkin said was right. Everything Anna said was right. Even the trite comments of Pronsky had the ring of truth. Viktor wondered whether he was losing his discernment, or if Shishkin was playing a mind game with him.

79

"If anything happens to my wife and daughter, Shishkin, I won't care about myself any more."

Again he saw the smile disappear like a jet plane's vapor trail.

"Demands, threats, conditions. I am getting tired of it. You want to leave, please, Moscow is due north. Take the car and your daughter, drive as far as your courage or your passport will take you. But don't come back here saying you made a mistake, and don't mention to the gentlemen who will stop you where you've spent the past week."

"Okay, okay, sorry. You want rational thought? With my wife playing hostess to a KGB thug and my daughter asking me when I'm coming home?"

"You have every right to be confused, friend. All the more reason to put some trust in me. I've earned it, I think. Now I'm sorry to cut this reunion short. But Anna must get back. And you have some important sleeping to do."

"Not more time in the box?" He saw Shishkin begin to draw a deep breath. "All right, I'll do it. How can I be sure Anna will be safely returned to her mother? Where will the woman drop her off?"

"The comrade, who may or may not be a woman, will drop your daughter a block away from the hall where the tryouts for the play are being held. Anna will not have to go to the hall. She can take a metro home from Reznikov Square. She does take the metro alone, doesn't she?"

"And why should she not? Not only is the Moscow metro the cleanest and most reliable, it is also the safest in the world." Viktor smiled. They were friends again.

Shishkin mimed vomiting. "You should have joined the Tourist bureau. Now, Viktor, I think you should let Anna tell your wife she's seen you."

"No way!"

"That's my comrade. Always an open mind to new ideas. It will be too much of a strain on the kid to keep that a secret. And your wife deserves to know."

"Shishkin, I . . ."

"Stop arguing. I'm telling you, do it. You have two minutes more with her. Then she must go."

And you, my friend, are sounding more like a hostage-taker. But he did not say this. Instead, he got back in the car, made sure the window was rolled up tightly. Anna looked at him as she often did, when waiting for him to call an end to some practical joke. I, too, am waiting, darling Anna. They spoke for four minutes and Viktor felt he had won a victory.

As a boy, Viktor made a point of never looking at cars or buses carrying friends or relations as they left him. Nor did he look back when it was he who was leaving. The habit held, but he could not help listening to the car wheezing down the dirt path.

"So what will she tell her mother?"

"Just enough to keep her spirits up."

"This is the worst part, Viktor. Being so close but unable to reach out. It will get better. Sunrise is just around the corner."

"What's that?"

"A friend who managed to get out. He sent a message to me – I remember it by heart – he said: 'It is sniffing the air and knowing, as we Russians do, that snow is on the way. It is that which I find impossible to forget, or replace. But then we convince ourselves: sunrise is just around the corner.' Which is funny, because if he had stayed in this country much longer, he'd be in a place where the snow never leaves and the sun never comes."

They took the long way back to the house on the hill. Shishkin seemed to want to say something, but was biding his time. Viktor revelled in the freedom of walking, the spring air, the tingle that contact with Anna had left. Life was awful? Where's the proof? Each day that he was not arrested, he came to believe more firmly that the sense of freedom he felt was deserved, not a filched thrill. Shishkin's amiable defiance was treason, nothing less; he had no right to call himself a citizen. Viktor had known that from the beginning. What was changing, more rapidly each day, was Viktor's attitude toward that treason. Russia was his motherland, and he would never renounce her. But if one's mother is being held captive by madmen, is the more loving son he who does whatever he is told in order to assure her safety, or the one who strikes back at his mother's abusers, risking her life for the chance to free her? Viktor had never asked himself these questions. He doubted that Shishkin saw the struggle in patriotic terms. To Shishkin, Russia was no mother, just another oppressor of his extended family. Shishkin had his faith. Now that he had seen Anna, Viktor once again had hope, the outer edge of faith.

"Some conversationalist," Shishkin said. "The subtlety of your observations. The irresistible logic of your points." It had been minutes since either spoke.

"Shishkin, why are you doing all this?"

"Oh, I don't know. To show that the bastards can be outwitted, I suppose. Does it matter?"

"No." That had not been the question. He had meant to ask why

Shishkin was what he was, if it was necessary to fight the way he did – every minute, never a waking moment without bitterness – to feel free.

As they came within view of the house, Viktor had an urge to bolt, run flat out until someone, or something – a police bullet, a speeding car, a wild Jewish extremist – stopped him and gave him the luxury of having no choice. The notion made him smile. He had that already. "I should have picked some wild flowers for The Blob," he said. "I don't think he eats enough greens."

"Where are they?" Shishkin began lifting his feet higher, stepping more deliberately. His psychic antennae bristled.

Finally, Viktor saw. The front door of the house was open an inch. The entire time he had been with The Blob, Pronsky and Bessmyrtinkh, they had never left the door open longer than it took them to pass through it. Shishkin must have seen it a minute earlier. The door lock had been ripped out of the jamb.

They went in like visitors to a hospital ward. The front room was empty, except for the overturned furniture. Shishkin went into the room where the box was kept. Viktor followed. The box was gone from its normal place, atop two sawhorses. It stood, instead, on its end in the corner of the room. Viktor pulled the door open. One of The Blob's jackets hung inside, food from a meal still adorning it. Some crumpled shirts lay on the bottom.

Shishkin had moved quickly to the room that had served as a kitchen. He came back, put his hand on Viktor's shoulder, a finger to his lips. They went outside and retraced their path through the woods.

"They did everything just right," the dissident said quietly. Viktor, who was thoroughly frightened, thought Shishkin sounded more tired than alarmed. "Amazing that they should come while you were away. You're in the path of a lucky star, friend. Better not make any unscheduled turns."

Viktor could think of only one detail. "The box . . ."

"Looks pretty convincing as a wardrobe, doesn't it? Not like they built before the Revolution, but functional."

"So they must have had some warning."

"A car engine, loud footsteps, a look through the window. A knock before they broke the door lock. They knew they were taking a chance."

"If I had been there . . ." He had no idea of how to finish the sentence.

"What? Your brawn would have scared them away? You'd have convinced a KGB officer that he had the wrong house full of desperate-looking men? The only difference if you had been there then is that you wouldn't be here now. For all we know, they weren't even looking for you."

That thought had not occurred to Viktor. Shishkin saw it in the expression on his face.

"Remember the night you came to see me? I told you I was waiting for someone who would give me a Romanian passport. Your being there meant I had to postpone the transaction. I finally got it two nights ago. Anyway, the deal called for him to doctor the passport, phony name, picture, the works. The passport had Rudolph's name on it. He was supposed to use it to get out. Keep walking, Viktor."

He found it hard to pick up his feet. "And this house?"

"It's registered as belonging to Rudolph's grandfather. He was some kind of Jewish poet, back when being Jewish was acceptable."

"But why would they come here?"

"Because our last job was sloppy." He looked at Viktor, waiting for the question.

"All right. Tell me everything."

"Everything? Now that, I assure you, is more than you want to know. Let's just say that certain militiamen could justifiably hold certain grievances against us."

It came together so quickly he was ashamed of not suspecting before. "The attacks. Shishkin, you're telling me you're involved in these murders?"

"Murders? Hardly. Murder is a crime."

"That you find a militia patrol car, attack the men inside, beat them unconscious, then set the car on fire so they can burn to death?"

"To start with, it's only our KGB friends in the militia. One was a woman, a fat, nasty job named Vishnevskaya. She must have taken a long time to melt. Secondly, we don't have to find them. They come to us. Someone calls the emergency number, and they radio instructions to a patrol car to check it out."

"How do you know where the patrol cars are sent?"

"That, Viktor, is something you don't want to know."

Shishkin began walking again, waited until Viktor had come abreast of him on the path. "We're fighting a war. Those people are the enemy's front line. You? You've been drafted. I suppose that could account for your squeamishness. But I'm a volunteer, with all the enthusiasm of one. I'm fighting to drive that sickness out of our country, so we can be Russians again. It's not just for Jews. It's also for all the people like you, the victims, who fell into a hellhole and have no map to get out. Well, this is one way of slowing them down; to keep hurting them until they let us alone or let us leave. I've stopped caring which. I'd rather stay. It's like my friend said: sunrise around the corner. But I won't let them hurt me any more without hurting them back."

Viktor heard and understood. How could he not? Shishkin was speaking for him too. "And the missing guards – the militiamen from outside the American Embassy? Have you killed them too?"

"No. But I was happy when you told me about it. I don't know anything about that. I can only wish luck to whoever is behind it."

They had cut off the main path. Now they were coming out of the woods, near the road that led to Moscow. Shishkin stopped, kicked at the soft dirt once, twice, until he had made a bowl-shaped indentation three inches deep. He fished a brown plastic wallet from his back pocket. He pulled a few rubles from one section. Then he took one end of the wallet in each hand and gave a sharp tug. The cheap plastic gave easily, exposing a hidden storage pocket. From it, Shishkin pulled more rubles. Viktor could not tell how many there were, but he saw at least two blue notes, which were fifties, and a few salmon-colored tens. These he pocketed. Shishkin withdrew his identity card, which listed his nationality as "Jew". He also took out a police registration card, a small printed page that appeared to be in Hebrew, and two pieces of white paper, each folded several times. He put them all in the trough he had made with his foot. They both kicked dirt over the documents and Shishkin trampled them down with his foot.

"Today we bury Yevgeny Moisovich's identity," he said. "I imagine that soon enough, the rest of him will end up the same way."

They hurried to the road and began waving their arms. The seventh car that passed slowed down and the driver gave Viktor a lift into Moscow. Shishkin walked along the road for an hour before someone picked him up.

The next day, one of the Soviet militiamen assigned to stand in front of the US Embassy disappeared. He was the thirteenth.

8

Karushkin disliked movies in general. So predictable, limited in scope and vision. The ones he made, he thought much more original and effective. He was especially curious to observe the effect on the fat one. Rudolph, he called himself. Karushkin had expected Rudolph to show fear. It was natural enough for someone who had been arrested in a manner rough even by KGB standards. But during the initial interrogations – name, address, Party member or not – Karushkin had seen instead a hesitance, wide-open eyes and agonizing indecision before committing to an answer. Where fear was found there was usually bullish defiance. He decided almost immediately that Rudolph would be the best pressure point. Because either Rudolph was stupid, or he was trying to conceal something. Karushkin had dealt with both kinds of prisoners before.

Karushkin watched it all, sitting only a few feet from the obese captive and his two chums. Bessmyrtinkh was scared, as he should be. But there was a resilience about him that Karushkin concluded would take too long to break down. Pronsky already had a record. His dismissal as the African Ambassador's chauffeur meant that while he was not under active surveillance, he would never again be considered a trustworthy citizen. And, Karushkin knew, such citizens take a perverse pride in their status. "Heretics burn slowly and glow with spite." He had never forgotten that sentence since reading it in a very limited circulation book that described the interrogation methods used during the Spanish Inquisition. Even he had trouble prying the book out of the Lenin Library. He detested censorship in general, not only when it deprived him of knowledge. As he neared seventy years of age, Karushkin knew he was not a perfect Communist, only a successful, long-lived one.

He was playing his familiar role of browbeaten fellow prisoner, cringing in the corner as the lieutenant threatened first him, then Rudolph, then Bessmyrtinkh and Pronsky with disfigurement. "You think I can't strip the skin off your face, fry it in oil and make you eat it?

85

You'll see. Sasha! Get a frying pan." This and other threats were selected for the vivid images they summoned. Karushkin was not even sure it was possible to fry facial skin. But then, neither was the prisoner.

Karushkin sometimes felt himself to be a victim of his employer's success in image-making. Each year, free-lance technology smugglers offered the latest tools of persuasion being used in Chile, South Africa, Iran. The prices were always high. Was it reasonable to believe a country that had to import 120 million tons of grain to feed its people would spend the lavish sums required to perfect the art of discomfiture? He had once been asked how large a budget he wanted for interrogation facilities. He had enjoyed the ruffles he caused by responding one hundred rubles a year, unhindered use of a room, and a video cassette recorder. There were, he had heard, some sniggers. "Karushkin's going to drive them to the brink by running nonstop Ronald Reagan movies." "He's going to put on porno and make his prisoners wear mittens."

The laughter dried up when the first visitor to the room was brought out. People in the hallway complained about the smell. Karushkin was never asked to explain or justify what went on in the room. He let his one hundred per cent rate of success in extracting confessions speak for him.

"You, old man. What's your name again?" The lieutenant liked his role, perhaps too much.

"Karushkin, Alexander Alfredovich."

"You want to see what happens to those who defy Soviet power?"

"I have never defied Soviet power." At least not directly.

"Don't hand me that crap. You're going to see one of our specialists in memory rejuvenation down the hall. Just wait until I get back." The lieutenant slammed out of the room.

Karashkin looked earnestly at fat Rudolph. He hoped he would sound piteous enough.

"It's true. I'm not the defiant type. All I did was sign a petition that was circulating in my apartment building. It supported the United Nations declaration on human rights. I couldn't imagine there was anything wrong with that. The Soviet delegation voted in favour of it."

Rudolph ignored him.

"It was a favour, you know. To a friend, right? He's helped me out from time to time. He wants to leave, it's as simple as that. Date trees, the Wailing Wall, sunny climate, fresh fruit. Who can blame him? So, Alexander, do me a service and we'll be for ever squared. Sign a statement applauding the fact that the United Nations has adopted a motion calling for human rights and asking all countries to respect those rights. Next thing I know, I'm being charged with anti-Soviet slander. It's not fair, is it?"

Rudolph might have been deaf. He heaved deeply.

Bessmyrtinkh spoke up. "It's all right, grandpa. Tell them the truth, and no harm will come to you."

"So, friend, what are you here for?"

Bessmyrtinkh went mute. The silence built between them. Without warning, Rudolph's stomach rumbled. Both men looked embarrassed.

Pronsky picked up the patter. "The police came this morning, to a cabin where we were staying, out in Peredelkino. They broke down the door, beat us up, and dragged us here. We have done nothing, comrade. Nothing!"

So, Pronsky, who called black ambassadors "Boy" and thought it funny, who attended synagogue services, had finally gotten his come-uppance, as his still-bloody face attested. Karushkin was disappointed. Howlers seldom made good, or accurate informants.

He turned back to Rudolph. "It's hard enough, isn't it, to put up with the fear. But then they don't even feed you. Don't they have appetites, these people?"

Rudolph heaved again. He appeared to be having trouble breathing.

The door opened. Two men, one in uniform, another wearing dark pants and a white laboratory smock, came in. The uniformed man pushed a metal two-tier stand on which sat a television and a VCR. There was also a green mechanical device attached to several wires.

"All right, old man," said the uniformed one. "Take a good last look at your face. The next time you see it, it will be between two slices of bread, on your dinner plate."

Karushkin wondered how this sounded to real prisoners. Even he, who had virtually authored it, felt a chill when he considered the words and their meaning. He rose, turned to the other three and said, in what he hoped approximated martyred resignation: "I wish you all the best."

Once the door had been shut, he walked ahead of the uniformed man, down the hall, to his office. The lieutenant was drinking tea, watching the closed circuit monitor of the room where the white-coated man was addressing Bessmyrtinkh, Rudolph and Pronsky.

"Since you have transgressed Soviet law" – he stared a warning at Pronsky, who had been on the verge of protesting – "you should be aware of the penalty that must be paid. The old man who was just here is now learning first-hand the price of defiance. You can each look forward to this, before the day is out." He switched off the overhead light.

Watching on the closed-circuit monitor, Karushkin congratulated himself on his choice. The man with the prisoners was an army doctor, who had been decorated in Afghanistan and brought to Moscow. His speciality had been in questioning Soviet soldiers whose commitment to the war effort was under suspicion. The doctor had demonstrated a fine-honed ability to raise the anxiety levels in those about to be interrogated without actually harming them.

The doctor plugged in the TV, switched it on. The screen crackled with giant particles of gray dust. He turned on the VCR. There was no trailer film, no countdown. Instantly, the screen showed a dark-haired man whose arms were strapped to a wooden chair. A pair of hands appeared from offscreen on the left, holding a syringe. Without much care, the syringe was jabbed into the man's right arm. Before the needle had been removed, the man had thrown his head back violently, and emitted a howling scream. The chair jerked, the man's chin jabbed forcefully into his breastbone. Within two seconds, his face had become greenish-black, contrasting luridly against his bared yellowed teeth. His eyeballs seemed to grow white and rounder, until a gout of blood popped out of each. He became still.

The screen immediately dissolved to a new picture. A different man, bound to the same wooden chair, was stripped to the waist. Again, hands appeared from offscreen left, this time holding a liter bottle, whose contents were poured over the man's head. As the liquid coursed down his face, neck and chest, steam rose from the body. Where the liquid had touched, only black streaks were left. There was no soundtrack, but what was left of the man's mouth was twisted into a tooth-and-gum mosaic of a death wish.

The doctor stopped the VCR. "Now you see that you are not here to pay a traffic fine. This is the vengeance exacted in the name of the Soviet people against those who have betrayed the motherland. This will happen to each of you, today, within hours. You have only one possible way to avoid this, or something even worse." He switched on the light. Pronsky was swallowing hard, fighting down vomit. Bessmyrtinkh looked down at the floor, and made whimpering noises without control or shame. Rudolph had slid out of his chair and was sprawled on the floor, quite obviously dead.

"Dammit, get a doctor," shouted the doctor. He bent over the fleshy mound, hooked his finger over the eyelid, inspected the motionless pupils, and cursed again. He tore open Rudolph's shirt, put his left hand over the sternum, and slammed his right fist on to it. The impact sounded like the all-out punch it was. The body beneath the doctor's hands contorted for a second, then was still. He turned around, and shouted at the other two men: "One of you, blow air into this Jew's mouth. Maybe we can revive him." Pronsky made as if to drop to the floor, but Bessmyrtinkh put a restraining hand on his shoulder.

"Why would we do that, comrade. It was his heart, wasn't it?"

"Yes!"

"I thought I saw it happening. The heavy breathing, the redness in his face. No, I won't try to bring him back. Rudolph has escaped." Bessmyrtinkh made it sound as if the fat man was in Paris.

The door slammed open and Karushkin was over the body. He was clearly angry, but kept his voice controlled. "A bad job, doctor. You might have anticipated infarction, someone in his condition. Ah, well." He had the resignation of one who has backed a losing football team. "At least comrades, we know that your hearts are healthy."

"And that yours is diseased." Bessmyrtinkh seemed to have forgotten where he was. "A man, a good man, just died in this room because of you. You pretended to share our predicament. You talked about what was fair. You're just a blight on our people, you and your kind. You . . ." The words petered out. His face reddened. He looked at Rudolph's corpse and remembered his situation.

Karushkin spoke gently. "Never mind, little Bessmyrtinkh. You will have your turn." Both men watched the guilty glow of relief flood Pronsky's thin face. "And you, Pronsky, you don't know why you're here, do you? After all, you're not a spy. That's what the KGB does, isn't it? Chases spies. Well," he stroked his chin, as if having trouble finding the words, "you may be surprised to learn that people who work in this business take it very personally, and very hard, when their colleagues are ambushed and set on fire."

Pronsky was quaking. "I didn't want to do it. I told them it was a bad idea."

Karushkin spoke like a teacher. "You were right, Pronsky. A horrible notion. But tell me: who was 'them'?"

"Pronsky, keep your mouth shut!" The volume of Bessmyrtinkh's voice in the small room made Karushkin wince.

"Certainly, Pronsky. Keep your mouth shut if you choose. You wouldn't be the first person here to take that attitude. For instance, the second man on the film clip you just saw told us he would never talk to us. So we decided that he had no further need of his lips. Want to end up like that? Fine."

Pronsky looked at Bessmyrtinkh, who knew his outburst was going to cost him.

"I'm not as strong as the rest of you. I don't want my face eaten away by acid." He told Karushkin. "It was for the Jews who want to emigrate. Shishkin's idea was that two could play that game. But it was Shishkin who said that, not me."

"Shishkin?"

"Yes, Shishkin. Yevgeny Moisovich. He's . . ."

Karushkin walked out of the room, as if he had been called to the phone. The door shut behind him.

Karushkin was not particularly anti-Semitic. He merely shared with others of his generation a resentment of the blood that had been lost to save the Jews from extinction. He thought that Russians, no matter what their ethnic background or spiritual inclination, should give their best efforts to making the country strong and rich. Those who whined about their human rights he found easy to scorn.

The first time Shishkin had been brought before him for interrogation, Karushkin thought he saw a bleater. After ten minutes of exchanged insults, Karushkin had to leave the room to regain his self-control. When he returned, Shishkin was sitting with his feet on the table. "So, what else shall we discuss?" Their relationship became like that of Judah Ben-Hur and Messala.

As he came to the end of a nearly flawless career, Karushkin was thoughtful. The first guard at the American Embassy to disappear, Petrov, had been in the post for about three years, and had directed two major eavesdropping operations against diplomats. The uniform he wore identified him as a sergeant of the Moscow militia; in truth he was a KGB lieutenant and his loss was not taken lightly. His wife had not seen him since the evening before his last shift. That was normal, since the lieutenant was in the habit of writing up reports of his intelligence-gathering at the KGB office off the Ring Road, then spending the night in one of the sparse bedrooms at the compound. The reports were reviewed periodically by Section 2, which controlled Moscow-based operations. When Petrov's disappearance was reported, his last report entry was immediately requisitioned. It was brief: "Fuck you."

Of course, security was tightened. Of course, the background of each guard at the embassy was rechecked. But before the process was even completed, there was another disappearance. This time, it was a novice named Poshtats. The KGB assumed that just as they monitored every movement of the embassy staff, so the Americans kept track of the identities of the various guard-spies.

There were more meetings, more warnings, more background checks. In the next three weeks there were also six more disappearances. In each case, the families were interrogated. Wives wailed for their husbands, children showed their Party cards or their Young Pioneer kerchiefs and asked how they could be of help. These families were the bedrock of Soviet society. The idea that they should be punished because a husband or a father was missing without explanation was too drastic even for the KGB. Word got around: the bosses had no idea of what was happening or how to stop it. Three Moscow-based members of the Party Central Committee paid a call on the KGB Chairman, who was later reported to have left his office early, looking pale and shaken.

Karushkin knew there was opposition to bringing him into the case. His reputation had been won mainly in internal political dissent. When the Chairman called him in and gave him the case folder, Karushkin understood two things: that this would be his last assignment, and that his success or failure would determine how comfortably he spent his retirement years. It was a bind.

The day after he took the case, a militia patrol car was attacked. Also, another guard disappeared. Karushkin immediately demanded, and got, jurisdiction over the militia attack. He was appalled at how little information was gathered. Time, place, type of gasoline, nothing more. No descriptions of suspects, no useful evidence left behind, no motive.

Three days later, another car was attacked and set afire. No motive, no eyewitness accounts, no anonymous tips. And another guard vanished between the end of his shift and the time he was expected home for dinner. The Chairman asked for a progress report.

The next attack on a militia car came a week later, but it produced a witness. An elderly woman who called the police said she lived nearby the road in which the car was found smoldering.

Karushkin met with the head of Section 2 and ordered – did not ask but ordered – him to change the entire rotation of the guards outside the embassy. He was told such a drastic action would compromise delicate intelligence operations. He persisted. The team usually assigned to the Belgian Embassy was transferred instead to the American compound. At the end of its first week on duty, its senior officer disappeared.

The attack on the militia car near Lumumba University produced another witness. A motorist driving past the scene said he saw two men, one very small and another very large, near the car. Without consulting Karushkin, an enterprising captain who worked under him ordered a computer check of every resident of Moscow with a criminal record whose height was above six feet and below five feet two. The output was surprisingly small, about six hundred names. The same officer ordered surveillance of every one of them. Because Bessmyrtinkh was such an odd physical type, he was relatively easy to identify. When it was learned he was making regular trips to and from a cabin in Peredelkino, he was followed. When Karushkin learned about the computer check and the surveillance, he flew into a rage and had the captain transferred out of Moscow.

Karushkin flipped through the report of the officer who had arrested Rudolph, Pronsky and Bessmyrtinkh. The three had been taken completely by surprise, it said. The cabin was scarcely furnished; they had been eating out of cans. Thirty-two empty tins were found scattered around outside. A lot for three people? Not if one of them was the size of Rudolph. No printing materials, no anti-Soviet literature, no radio receiver or transmitter. Four cheap chairs, two carpenter's sawhorses, on which was balanced a piece of pressed construction board. Obviously, a makeshift table. A pine wood wardrobe standing in the corner. Some dirty clothes.

Karushkin filled out and signed an arrest warrant for Yevgeny Moisovich Shishkin. Most people thought the KGB could trawl the streets, picking up anyone at any time. It was not so. The Party leadership is always suspicious of the secret police, never wanted them to amass too much power. So it put up operational tripwires to ensure that the Party always knew what was happening at Dzerzhinsky Square. Karushkin did not object. In this case, any arrest he made, the Party would approve.

The meditation had been beneficial; he decided what to do. It wasn't as easy as outsiders thought. Give and take, take and give, finally, take and take.

Rudolph's only living relations were in Israel. A telegram was sent to the head rabbi of Moscow, who, not surprisingly, was also a Party member, to come and collect the body of a Soviet citizen of Jewish nationality. A call was made to OVIR, the passport and visa office, to have export papers issued. The corpse, now stiff, was hoisted on to a squeaky gurney while Bessmyrtinkh and Pronsky watched fearfully. Karushkin went down to the room.

"All right, Bessmyrtinkh, time grows short. Tell me how you carried out the attacks."

"We followed the self-defense instructions in the Young Pioneers manual."

The doctor, still in his white coat, appeared in the doorway pushing the TV and the VCR.

"Entertain the mouthy midget, doctor. Pronsky, you go with the lieutenant. You look in need of exercise."

The lieutenant dragged Pronsky down the hall, into the unmarked room that Karushkin had requested and been allocated. The first thing Pronsky saw was the chair featured in the video cassette. He turned as if to run away. His legs buckled and he fell to his knees. The lieutenant kicked him in the spine, hard. Pronsky sprawled on the floor. The lieutenant stepped on his left hand. Finger bones snapped. He screamed again.

"I liked doing that," the lieutenant said slowly. "If you're not in that chair by the time I count three, I'm going to give myself an early birthday present. One . . ."

Holding his left wrist in his right hand, Pronsky advanced toward the chair. He looked up. "What are you going to do?"

"Two."

Pronsky sat in the chair. When he looked straight ahead, he saw a portable camera, mounted on a tripod, aimed at him. He trembled so violently the lieutenant had trouble strapping his wrists to the arms of the chair.

A minute later, Karushkin entered the room.

"Well, well, Pronsky. No mirth? No wit? No racial epithets? I expect you're distraught by your new environment. You think this is where we torture people, reduce them to pulp? We think of it as intensive physical education. Something you can use. Even from here I can see that driver's gut of yours. Know what helps that? Leg lifts. A simple callisthenic. Have it focused?"

The lieutenant was fiddling behind the camera. "Yes, Comrade Colonel." A red light came on near the lens.

"Good, get over here and show Pronsky how to do a leg lift."

The lieutenant was taut as a greyhound. He sat on the floor, lifted both legs six inches off the ground, and grinned at Pronsky.

"You do it, Pronsky. Lift your legs."

"Colonel, I'll tell you anything you . . ."

"Yes, I'm convinced you would. But you see, I'm not interested in what you have to say. Now lift your legs."

Pronsky inhaled, lifted his right foot an inch, then his left. It hurt. His shoes hit the floor a second later.

Karushkin tut-tutted. "Even I can do better than that. I think you may need some incentive. Get the equipment."

The lieutenant dropped his legs and in one silky movement was on his feet. From behind him, Pronsky heard something heavy moving across the floor.

"Most people don't exercise because it hurts." said Karushkin. "That's true, don't you think? But what if the alternative was even more painful? Then a few muscle aches wouldn't seem so great a price to pay."

The lieutenant was pulling a metal box eighteen inches long, ten inches wide, and six inches tall, with a lip around its perimeter. Its top was covered with a metal grill. Thin rods were attached vertically to opposite ends of the box so that they stood straight up, about a foot. A single strand of copper wire was hung between the rods. An electrical cord trailed on the floor.

"The Japanese call it a Hibachi. It's an electric grill for cooking. Our country has imported some in return, I believe, for Matryuschka dolls. I've modified this one. When plugged in, the grill becomes quite hot. Leave your legs on top for long and they'll be as black as that ambassador's. Or as charred as the bodies of those men in their patrol cars."

The box was positioned in front of Pronsky. The lieutenant picked up the prisoner's legs, stretched them over the grill and under the copper wire.

"If I were you, I would learn to do this exercise quickly. If you stretch your legs straight out, parallel to the floor, you won't feel the heat too much. But don't put them any higher. That copper wire is also electrified. Plug it in, Lieutenant."

Pronsky heard the plug go into the socket. The grill made a tiny hissing noise. The copper wire buzzed. Within a few seconds Pronsky felt heat on the backs of his legs. He jerked them up instinctively. His right knee brushed the wire, and he felt as if his entire body had been sawn off, so sharp was the electric jolt. His legs fell back on to the grill. It was hotter now. He lifted them quickly, kept them just an inch beneath the wire. The muscles in the backs of his knees objected to the unusual position. His belt cut into his stomach. His calves hurt. He involuntarily lowered his legs, and the heat seared them.

"Oh, please, I can't hold them like this. Please turn it off. I'll tell you everything. I'll tell you about Shishkin. About Viktor Melanov."

"Yes," said Karushkin. "I knew you would."

The lieutenant said nothing, moved behind the camera, adjusted its position a fraction and, ignoring Pronsky's screams, walked out of the room and closed the door. The grill was already red hot.

9

"How can I let his relatives know the body is coming if you won't deliver
my message?" The Chief Rabbi of Moscow punctuated his question by
slugging back half a glass of sugar-laced lukewarm tea.

"That is your problem. Mine is to make certain that no unauthorized
communications leave this office." The Rabbi could tell he had no chance
of making progress with the dull mind powering the singsong voice on the
phone.

"May I speak with your superior, please?"

"My superior will tell you the same thing. You cannot place a call to
Israel and you cannot send a telegram. Israel is a criminal lackey of the
Western imperialists."

"Which does not mean that it is cut off from all forms of communication. What is your name?"

"You are wasting my time. I have explained the rules to you. I know
your telephone number and if you bother this office again I shall report
you. We all know about you Jews and where your loyalty lies." The dead
line made a purring noise. It was better than the voice.

Yet the taunting employee of the central telephone exchange had raised
a valid point, thought Rabbi Mark Davidovich Stiglitz. As he neared the
end of a long, exciting and complicated life, he was less certain now of
what he believed in than when he was twenty. He worked in a room that
he was permitted to call his office only because he was willing to eat all his
meals in the kitchen; otherwise it was just the dining room in his four-
room apartment next door to the synagogue. He was, indisputably, the
final voice on spiritual matters for nearly two million Soviet Jews. But his
title had been conferred only after he agreed to join the Party, and it had
been made eminently clear to him that he was first an employee of the
Soviet government and then a servant of God.

And yes, there were all the justifications: he had done much, perhaps
more than anyone else could have done, to make life more bearable for

the people he presumed to lead. He had not been totally compliant, he had argued and won more than they wanted to give him. Still, it was quicker and easier to remember all those times than the ones when he had bowed his head and carried out orders.

As he sat with the remainder of his tea, Rabbi Stiglitz genially reminded himself that he was a fool. This was a day to celebrate, not mope. It was unfortunate that the fellow, Rudolph was his name, had died, and even more regrettable that, at the time, he had been committing a crime (the police report that the Rabbi had seen was quite clear on that point). Yet out of misfortune sometimes came hope. Two days later, the deputy minister from the government office for Religious Affairs had called to say that Rudolph's long delayed application to emigrate had been approved on the same day that he had died. Pure coincidence. The emigration office, wishing to demonstrate its good faith in the matter, had decided that Rudolph's body could be sent to his relatives in Israel for burial. It was not an empty gesture. The Rabbi had been aware for years that the rate of emigration depended more on relations with the United States than on the puny efforts that people like himself could mount. So he tried a different approach. He understood that the government could not allow the departure of Jews who had once worked in sensitive jobs or who had no immediate relatives in foreign lands. He also conceded that those who asked to leave were in effect turning their backs on the fatherland, and should expect nothing but the contempt of true Russians. But could not those who had died be sent to Israel where they could be buried according to the custom of their faith? This received a better response than he had dared hope. The suggestion was taken under advisement and the Rabbi was awarded an Order of Lenin to mark his 75th birthday.

If the government was pleased, the same was not true of all the Rabbi's own people. As he talked to the hundred or so Jews of Moscow who openly and actively practiced their religion, he told them about his request and its encouraging reception, like a father spinning fantasies of elaborate gifts to his children. "And just think," he had concluded, "how much easier it will be to accept life's disappointments if we know that a plot is waiting for us in Israel."

The idea went over well enough with those who were nearly as old as the Rabbi, whose lives had been spent and had only death and the hereafter to anticipate. They found comfort in the thought of resting beneath Israeli soil. For Rabbi Stiglitz's generation, no Jew whose body rolled over gas jets could rest in peace.

The younger members of the community, however, found little cause to rejoice. One of the loudest voices of dissent (to no one's surprise) was that of Yevgeny Shishkin. His strange and varied affairs in the secular world did not take up so much of Shishkin's time that he could not also offer his opinions on every nuance of Jewish existence. Since he had nothing to lose in terms of civic respect, and no chance of ever leaving the land which so reviled him, he was, curiously, a freer man than those who still harbored hope. He was fond of saying that he attended synagogue functions religiously. His relations with Rabbi Stiglitz were, at best, irreverent.

"So all we have to do to merit this generous treatment is die? I'd call that a bargain considering how expensive long-distance travel can be. Perhaps you'll ask, Rabbi, whether the government might provide the bullets if we decide to take them up on this benevolent gesture? But what am I saying? Bullets are so costly and wasteful. One stout rope could be used again and again. The prospective emigrés could line up and each would kick out the chair from under the person in front of him. But Rabbi, better that some people shouldn't know how much happiness awaits them. We'll just say that those in line are waiting to take a bath before the trip begins. Clever, no?"

Honest man that he was, the Rabbi had to admit that he had gained very little. He found Shishkin abrasive (as who did not?) but accurate in his perceptions and passionate in his commitment. He sometimes reflected that if Moscow's Jews, like those in Egypt five millenia earlier, were told to select one man to lead them out of bondage and into the promised land, he would vote for Shishkin. He knew about Shishkin's many scrapes with the authorities, knew that he dabbled in the black market and associated with political criminals. Shishkin's affiliation with the synagogue was well known. The Rabbi had been called in by the KGB more than once and told that it was people like Shishkin who made Jews unpopular in the Soviet Union. As a young rabbi, Stiglitz might have replied that it was countries such as the Soviet Union that made Jews like Shishkin inevitable. Instead, he agreed humbly that Shishkin was an anti-Soviet element and promised that he would report anything that might be of interest.

It was not unreasonable to think that he might hear or see such things. To a large extent, Rabbi Stiglitz had abrogated the synagogue's function as a House of God. The splendor with which it was once endowed was little more than a musty recollection. Instead, he concentrated on preserving a sense of community. Jews who might be arrested for congregating on the street outside its front door could mingle and converse inside without fear. Formal prayer was frowned upon, and everyone knew that there was always at least one informer in their midst. But the tiny pleasure of being able to address each other in Hebrew or

Yiddish, and of discussing matters of specific interest to their faith was a comfort. And it was due to the Rabbi, who, through years of quiet diplomacy, had come to a subtle understanding with the authorities. He allowed the synagogue to be used for many purposes, some of which enraged Shishkin and the few other zealots. The year before, the Rabbi had agreed that all religious ornamentation would be removed for one month, so that the local chapter of the Union of Soviet Geologists could use the edifice as a lecture hall. In return for this self-abasement, the government permitted the Rabbi to send a telegram to the Chief Rabbi of Warsaw, congratulating him on the 25th anniversary of his rabbinate. His had been the only message from another Communist country. Shishkin had bitterly compared the deal to tossing a coin into the air with the understanding "heads you win, tails I lose". What only the Rabbi knew was that the geologists would have commandeered the synagogue anyway; the choice was between getting nothing or almost nothing in return.

Such were the minor stakes for which the Rabbi played; his successes were negligible, his failures inevitable. He quaffed the last of the tea and rose to go. He had been summoned to the office of the local procurator and told to bring any information he may have about the whereabouts of Yevgeny Moisovich Shishkin. It had happened before that, as putative elder of the community, the Rabbi was asked questions about the movements and habits of certain people. He had never been confronted before with such a demand about Shishkin, probably because the secret police were seldom in doubt. The Rabbi sighed. Once in, there was no way out of the nether world of complicity. Yet it had all seemed so different, so promising sixty years earlier. Fifteen-year-old Mark Davidovich Stiglitz had seen Communism sweeping through Russia and had rejoiced. He had no doubt that he was witnessing history and a happy progression it was. He knew, even as a rabbinical student, much of the history of persecution of Russian Jews. The deathgrip of the Orthodox Church on the throne of the tsar was unbreakable. Who could have foreseen the demise of the Imperial family? Who could have guessed that it would be replaced by an untried, prototypical government that proclaimed its complete independence from, and indifference to, any form of worship? Stiglitz had happily embraced the New Order. He was sure that under the rule of the councils, or soviets as they were called, Jews would be treated no differently from any other religious group. And he was right. But not in the way he had expected.

He began plodding down the street. The Rabbi walked everywhere. Once, a group of American Jews who had obtained tourist visas paid him an unofficial visit. They wanted to know the best way to smuggle Russian-language Torahs into the country for clandestine distribution. When they saw how he lived, they also promised to send money so that he could buy a car, hire a driver, and be chauffeured, as befitted his status. The Rabbi quickly declined their offer and showed them the door. Their departure from the Soviet Union was delayed for several hours while their luggage and clothing were meticulously torn apart. The Rabbi continued to walk the streets of Moscow. He pulled open the stubborn gray door of the procurator's office, went up the steps, announced himself to the glowering uniformed receptionist, and settled himself into one of the straight-backed chairs. He was Russian, he knew how to wait.

To his surprise, the deputy procurator came out of his office almost immediately, and summoned him inside. Sitting at the desk of the chief procurator was a man the Rabbi knew in theory, existed. Now he knew who it was.

"I'll get right to the point," Karushkin said. "I want Yevgeny Shishkin for questioning. He is missing, hasn't been seen in his apartment for more than a week. The longer he's unaccounted for, the more people we'll need to consult."

The Rabbi knew the code words; he recognized a warning when he heard one.

Karushkin was uneasy. "Now, there are two more things. First, the body of the criminal who died is ready to be released. Since he has no relatives here and since permission has been granted for a foreign burial, the body is being delivered to your custody. Pick it up on your way out."

"On my way out of here? But how am I to transport it?"

Karushkin did not bother to answer. He was fingering a yellow sheet of paper and spoke as though he was reading from a dictionary. "Last. I'm telling you this unofficially. But you can be sure I know what I'm talking about. The Chief Rabbi of Warsaw has replied to your telegram of congratulations. His response includes an invitation for you to make an official visit to Warsaw. I was informed of this communication, which I should tell you, came as something of a surprise here. The Polish Religious Affairs Office seems to be in a particularly generous mood. Nevertheless, considering your loyal service to the Party and our desire to promote good relations between ethnic groups of the various socialist countries, a visa has been issued for you to make the trip. Your telegram of acceptance has been sent. Here is a copy of it. Here is your authorization to exit the country. Arrange with the Polish Embassy to pick up your visa."

Rabbi Stiglitz had learned to accept disappointment with dignity. He was less experienced in handling astonishment. "I, I've never been out of the country before."

Karushkin was more at ease now that his messages were delivered. He was not so much younger than the Rabbi, so he used the familiar form of address: "Seeing Poland should make you glad to return. Call as soon as you find out about Shishkin."

In an existence calculated to frustrate, the claiming of a body is a singularly monstrous moment. The friend or relative is expected to identify the corpse, bring a corroborating piece of identification belonging to the departed, and prove his own identity and relationship. Rabbi Stiglitz anticipated a tiring afternoon, but knew he had to persevere.

It was his second surprise of the day. He signed one form, showed his identity card and within half an hour was told to go to the back door of the building where the procurator's office was located. A pinewood packing crate, six feet high and four feet wide, sat on the steps. A dirty-faced man leaned against it, smoking.

"You're the Jew? Here's your friend."

"Thank you. If you could just help me to lift . . ."

"Did any of you help Jesus Christ to lift his cross? Shoulder this wood yourself, murderer." He tossed his cigarette on to the street and went back into the building.

The Rabbi could not help smiling. How many Christian zealots could be left in this country? Who but he could have had such luck to run into one of them at precisely the moment he was in need of assistance? He went back inside the building and asked the guard if he could use a phone. The answer was no. Back outside, he left the crate sitting on the steps, walked around the corner and down half a block to a telephone kiosk. He put in two kopeks and dialled 225-0000, the radio taxi dispatch number. He was lucky, he got through after only sixteen tries.

"Taxi."

"I want to order a cargo taxi please, one that can carry a large box."

"What are its contents?"

"What does that matter?"

"What is your name?"

"What do you care?"

"Where are you going with this box?"

"I will tell that to the driver."

"Right. Where should he collect you?"

Accepting the body was one thing; delivering it was another. The Rabbi still had to arrange for the shipping, buy a ticket for the cargo, get it to the train station and somehow, he was still not sure how, notify the family. The taxi, about the size of a panel truck, arrived half an hour later and for an extra two rubles, the driver helped load the pine crate and carry it to the Rabbi's house. It would not fit through the door jamb. Embarrassed, and afraid of being left to handle the burden alone, the Rabbi asked the driver to help him get it into the synagogue next door. The driver was delighted to assist, and for only another two rubles.

The Rabbi had not known Rudolph well. He was not a regular visitor to the synagogue and, on the occasions when he came, he said nothing. But it was entirely appropriate that he should now find temporary shelter beneath its time-stained roof. They put the box in the back-left corner, near an extra prayer stand. The driver was still pleasant, though clearly in a hurry to leave. The Rabbi walked him to the door of the synagogue, then turned back on impulse. He wanted to say a short prayer of thanks, and, in the dank, quiet comfort of the synagogue, to ponder the day's strange events. He had a favorite spot for meditation, near the front, where he kept a chair. Anyone who spent as much time here as he did was entitled to sit. He lidded his eyes, and began to ease his body on to the cushioned seat.

"Trying to make new converts, Rabbi? Lure some workman in on the pretext of helping you, then tell him the story of Moses?" The voice echoed across the empty synagogue from the corner where the crated corpse lay. The Rabbi's eyes opened wide, his hands flew up in protective instinct. But his brain forgot to countermand the order to sit and his buttocks grazed the edge of the chair and plopped on to the floor. He did not know for a second whether to be more stunned by the fall or frightened by the ghostly visitation.

Hands pulled at his wrists, a shoulder bolstered and lifted him. Shishkin roared with laughter as he guided the Rabbi down on to the chair. "What, think you'd heard the voice of God? Is this how you plan to greet the Messiah?"

The old man's gape told Shishkin that a visit from the Savior could have been no less disturbing.

"We seem to have come at a bad time, Rabbi. I'd have called first, but I didn't want you going to any trouble, you know, killing the fatted calf." The wisecrack rang hollow; Shishkin could smell danger the way sailors sense a change of tide.

"Yevgeny Moisovich, what have you done? The police, the secret police, are looking for you." The Rabbi completely forgot the injunction against speaking aloud in temple.

"Your trusting nature never fails to warm my heart."

"Wait. You said, we've come at a bad time. We who?"

"We him. We me. We us." Shishkin pointed back to the corner farthest from them. "Viktor, come out."

"Strasvuyte, comrade." His words sounded as if they were swathed in gauze. "Anyone knocked to the ground by the sound of Shishkin's voice is a friend of mine. My name is Vik . . ."

"Say nothing more and we will both be happier! Shishkin, you must understand, it is not that I suspect you of wrongdoing, but I am under orders to tell the police if, when and where I see you."

Shishkin chuckled. "Well, I wouldn't want you blemishing your Party card by failing to do so. I have other friends . . ."

"Fewer than you think." He told them of Rudolph's death, of the arrests of Pronsky and Bessmyrtinkh. As he talked, he looked at them more closely. Both were unshaven, and had a sheen of dirt around their brows, chins and fingertips. They were men on the run. Shishkin's smile was gone. Viktor no longer wanted to call Rudolph The Blob.

"But you didn't see him, you don't know for sure they've given you Rudolph's body. It could be a macabre trick, Rabbi. Bags of sand to be sent to Israel. And they have enough of that there already I've heard."

"To what purpose, Shishkin? Dead is dead. The concession on their part is agreeing to let us send him to Israel."

"Yes, your dream come true."

"Don't bring that up now. Get away while you can. I will wait an hour before I call the police."

Shishkin's eyes were bullets. "I came to you for help, not a head start."

"But I've promised. And besides, Colonel Karushkin said . . ."

"Karushkin?" Viktor's voice shed its hoarseness. "What did he tell you?"

"You know Karushkin?" It was the first time the Rabbi addressed Viktor.

"Yes, yes," Shishkin cut in. "They've danced *Swan Lake* together many times. Rabbi, we won't impose, I don't want to be blamed if you're passed over for the next Central Committee vacancy. But I think you can afford to forget that you saw us here. I told Viktor that if we could make our way here, we'd find refuge. I must have been thinking of another church."

They live in different worlds, Viktor thought as he watched the two men stare into each other. They use the same religion to worship separate ideals.

"And one more thing. I'd like to pay my respects to my friend. I want to open the coffin and see Rudolph."

"What? Because you think the country is governed by body-snatchers? You might find this hard to believe, but take it from an old man: not every hardship on earth is targeted at you. Rudolph dies and Shishkin is insulted? A very arrogant form of paranoia. I think we will leave the box as it is."

They detest each other, Viktor was telling himself. They have nothing in common except a shared scar from a ritual incision, yet that is enough to bind them as tightly as thread holds cloth. Viktor had, for the moment, forgotten his own dangerous predicament. These two were as engrossing as well-directed theater.

"Rabbi, you can stay and watch or go and call the police. Tell them there are grave-robbers in the Synagogue of Moscow. They'll probably think that's a standard form of Jewish worship. But I don't think you can bring yourself to do that, can you? Turn me in for imprisonment, torture, then a stand-up performance at the Soviet version of the Wailing Wall, the one with all those holes in it. Besides, Rabbi, shouldn't someone respectable recite the Kaddish over Rudolph before he begins that long, lonely trip? You're not going to leave that job to me, the arrogant paranoid, and to Viktor, who's not even Jewish?"

The old survivor in him told the Rabbi to walk away, pick up a phone, and win enough official gratitude to see him through his final years. His pride shouted for him to give Shishkin what he had coming to him. Then he remembered the sneering voice of the telephone exchange employee, the look on the face of the deputy procurator when he summoned him into the office to see Karushkin, and the orange arc of the cigarette thrown by the dirty-faced man.

"I'll show you how to get into the cellar," he told Shishkin. "I think there's a crowbar down there."

Solid wood wraps itself around a straightly driven nail and holds it as though it was welded. The crate that the Rabbi had brought into his synagogue was a skeleton of spindly pine scrap shards fastened with snag-toothed, rusting tacks. Shishkin emerged, dusty and cobwebbed, from the seldom-visited basement, and started to beat the crate into submission. Viktor grabbed the tire-iron from him, and carefully prised away the framework so it could be used again. Under the outer crate was another wall of wood. He wondered if the body had been double-packed, but his common sense rebelled. Soviet workmen, especially those in a government ministry, would let the Fabergé eggs roll loose in a carton before they would expend such effort. He pulled away one more spine from the outer crate, and tugged at the inside box. It budged.

"Shishkin, help me slide it out. It's just a wooden box in the crate."

Shishkin pulled, but before it was halfway out he saw the problem. "They've put a seal over it." An inch-thick strip of red paper inlaid with an intricate pattern of hammers and sickles hugged the middle of the box like a belt.

From two feet behind them the Rabbi hissed: "If you break the seal, they'll know it has been opened."

Viktor, working on one knee, looked back over his shoulder. "Yes, that had occurred to me too, even without divine inspiration." He smiled at Shishkin. "Everyone knows that a rectangle has four sides, but lots of very smart people forget that a box has six." He began wedging the crowbar into the front end of the box that they had slid out of the crate first. The nails, driven in from the sides, groaned against the lateral pressure. Without using too much force on any one side, Viktor worked the end loose. He inverted the crowbar so its point was between the end and the side, and thumped it with his fist. The nail jumped halfway out of the wood. He repeated the process twice more, until the end was attached only by the nail from the side that was lying on the floor. He put the crowbar behind the end and levered gently. It popped off and fell away like a hubcap from a tire, which was the principle Viktor had in mind.

"It's all yours." he told Shishkin, and stood up.

In the musty corner of the synagogue, they could not see into the box. The dissident thrust his hand in, then retracted it quickly. "Something big and soft. Sure you wouldn't care to do the honors?" Viktor remained where he was.

"Rabbi?"

"Get it over with," snapped the old man.

"Right then." He reached in as far as his elbow, made contact with the unseen mass, and yanked. Half his forearm was visible. Shishkin tugged again, and they saw his hand come out, holding a piece of gray material.

"A blanket?" asked the Rabbi.

"A suit of clothes?" suggested Shishkin.

It was Viktor, the only one among them to have led anything like a normal life, who supplied the answer: "A body bag."

As Shishkin pulled it out, the zipper glinted along the side. Suddenly, Shishkin was on his feet, heaving. "My God, the smell."

Viktor had picked up a whiff of something unspeakable while he was prizing the casket loose. Now the stench wafted up again. He turned to the Rabbi and asked: "When did he die?"

"Three days ago."

Shishkin pulled the bag the rest of the way out of the box and, without pause, unzipped and spread it open.

"Fuck your mother," he said with ghastly reverence.

They all saw the face at about the same moment. Viktor wished he had not invaded this rude grave. "That's why it was so easy to pull him out," he whispered. The body in the bag was a foot shorter and fifty pounds lighter than Rudolph's.

Pronsky had died with his eyes open, and no one had bothered to close them. He was wearing the same shirt as when Shishkin had come to the cabin and invited Viktor for a stroll. Of course there were no pants. As they scanned his body involuntarily, they saw where the clothing ended, giving way to the ash-like remains of his lower legs. Viktor remembered a particularly grisly multiple-car collision, where drivers had been totally incinerated. The smell was the same, but he had failed to make the connection. Shishkin, of course, associated the smell with other circumstances.

Shishkin needed to take in each detail and, as he did, he gulped in more of the befouled air. He wanted to smell the pain, taste the last awful moments, hear the madness into which Pronsky must have descended as he waited for it to be over.

Only the Rabbi wept, deeply but silently, and probably not for the victim that lay before him. When his choked convulsions were over, he felt alone. He whispered: "They have made a fool of me before my God."

Viktor did not try to share their grief. His mind was already flying ahead, and he thought Pronsky would forgive him.

"Shishkin, I know this isn't the right moment . . ."

"You're right comrade, it isn't. Please don't interrupt me at a time like this. I'm trying to find the words, but it's difficult. Well, what the hell, here it is: I'm coming with you."

10

The Rabbi had no idea where the Polish Embassy was located, but when Viktor told him it was near the Tishinsky Outdoor Market, they immediately fell into an argument over which bus would get there quicker. Viktor found the old man to be obstinate, proud and sarcastic when challenged. He liked him, even if it took a parliamentary debate to drag agreement out of him. He had never seen a man undergo such a thorough change of character so quickly. He kept insisting that Viktor call him Mark Davidovich. "Yesterday I was a Rabbi and when this is over, perhaps I can be again. But, until then, I am a revolutionary."

"You're taking a good-sized risk, Mark Davidovich."

"Not nearly so big a risk as trying to get to the Gruzinskaya Bolshaya on the Number 64 bus. You must be a newcomer to Moscow." And so on.

At first Viktor wanted to do the job himself. "I've been there before. No one will think anything is out of place."

"And what about the militia guards out front? How do you know your name or your picture hasn't been sent around? You're a wanted man." Shishkin was acting and thinking like a general planning a battle. But he took no joy in the work. "Besides, the Rab—, uh, Mark Davidovich always does these errands himself, don't you? To suddenly have a lackey, and a non-Jewish one at that, would make no sense. No, he must go in person, and hope he can see this Gortowski fellow."

The Rabbi shook his head. "I still don't believe they would send someone to Moscow who does not speak Russian."

"I never said he couldn't speak Russian. But he can't read it at all."

"Ridiculous. The languages are very similar."

"Similar words, yes, but not alphabets. Ours is Cyrillic. The Poles use Latin. When my American boss wanted to take the train from Moscow to Warsaw, I took his visa request to the Polish Embassy. Gortowski asked me to read it to him, then stamped it on the spot. Then he joked about how long words in Russian all look alike to him. We both laughed but I don't think he was kidding."

"Then why hasn't this moron been discovered and sent back to Warsaw?" The Rabbi's nationalist streak was poking through.

"He's a second secretary, he's young, and likeable enough. He's not in charge of visas, just works in the section. I think he bluffed his way through the Foreign Service training. He probably hoped he'd be sent someplace like Paris or Washington. He does speak English well, I think."

"But Moscow is an important post too."

"Things haven't been right at the Polish Embassy since 1980," Viktor explained. It was in that year, when the Solidarity union was founded in Poland and its membership was growing with no apparent limits, that some Polish employees at the embassy – cooks, construction laborers, stenographers, telex operators and the like – announced to their stunned ambassador that they had formed a Solidarity branch in Moscow. The ambassador had been educated at Frunze Military academy and had a Lithuanian wife. He knew where his loyalties lay. Before informing his foreign ministry, he placed a call to a classmate who had graduated to the KGB. Within a few hours, a detachment of uniformed men, who looked like regular soldiers but for the blue epaulets they wore, had surrounded the embassy. The chairman of the twelve-hour-old local union walked outside and was taken away. There was no report of a trial, but his wife in Poland was told she could send one parcel a year to Chistopol prison. There was a noticeable decline in the number of Polish diplomats applying for Moscow thereafter.

"It doesn't matter if he composes poetry in Urdu, it's the only chance we've got." Shishkin's patience had eroded with his humor. "This has all got to be done on the same day, you know, Mark Davidovich."

The Rabbi was unpleasantly surprised when the bus he was riding turned off Gruzinskaya Bolshaya and began rumbling down a bumpy side street. He moved to the front and asked the driver why he had not gone straight.

"Because that's not my route. If that's where you wanted to go, you should have taken a Number 64." The half-mile that he had to retrace on foot was made more tolerable by the knowledge that Shishkin's friend, Viktor Nikolaich, seemed to know what he was about.

The Polish Embassy stood well back from the street. About one hundred yards away was the West German Embassy, or more accurately, embassies. The Soviets held grudges and the West German diplomats had been consigned to two ageing red-brick buildings connected by an open-air courtyard. Shuttling from one building to the other during the winter months was a sure way to shake off the drowsiness induced by sitting in an overheated room. Younger Germans at the embassy, born since the war, referred to the courtyard as the Battle of Stalingrad; when overheard, they were reprimanded. By contrast, the Polish Embassy was visually striking from the outside: built in the early Seventies, its white aluminium siding caught whatever rays of light the feeble November sun threw its way. Its boxy squatness seemed designed to advertise the serious, efficient work that went on inside.

The Rabbi had no trouble making his way past the militia guards; Soviet citizens were unlikely to claim political asylum on Polish soil. Instead, he was challenged at the foot of a staircase in the entry foyer by a stout receptionist, her dyed blond hair gathered on top of her head by a blue rubber band.

"Yes, grandpa, what is it?" The words were rudely informal but the tone of voice and her curious accent made them seem relaxed and chatty.

"I, I'd like to see Mr Gortowski. About a visa matter."

"I'm glad it's not another paternity suit, both his wives would be terribly upset." She picked up the receiver of a yellow telephone on her desk but did not dial. Instead she shouted over her shoulder, "Malgosia, is Gortowski working today?"

From the top of the stairs came a thin reply: "Who would notice? Wait, I'll look."

The whole building seemed to rattle as first feet, then legs, then a torso attached to a blond head bounded down the steps. This boy is a diplomat? thought the Rabbi. Looks more like an ambassador's son on his way to school.

"You did wanting to see me?" The voice was deep and raspy, as though Gortowski had been smoking too many cigarettes for many years. His Russian was uncertain, that much was obvious. He was thin, but not healthily so. It was hard to decide whether he was trying to grow a beard or had forgotten to shave. His eyes were pink and his hands fluttered.

"Yes, Comrade Gortowski, thank you for taking time to see me." The Rabbi tried to follow exactly the script and advice that Viktor had given him: "Remember, if you talk to him in front of his co-workers, be exceedingly polite and respectful. He'll remember that." Without saying anything else, the Rabbi mounted the stairs. Gortowski, looking more confused than annoyed, followed.

His office was three times the size of the Rabbi's dining room. But it had no furniture. There was no desk, no bookcase, no books, no phone.

The embroidered rug in the middle of the room looked miniscule. One rickety chair was in the corner by the window. Neither of them made any move to occupy it.

"I was told I should come to you," the Rabbi said, fumbling at his pocket. "I shall be making an offical trip to your country, at the invitation of the Chief Rabbi of Warsaw."

"Chief what?"

"Rabbi. Excuse me, I seem to have something in my throat." He coughed loudly, cursed silently. He had momentarily forgotten Viktor's cardinal rule: "Speak slowly, and use easy words. Otherwise he might call someone else."

"Ah, a rabbi. So you're Jewish. How did you get permission to leave the Soviet Union?" At least one of them thought this question humorous.

"I'm not leaving, Mr Gortowski. Merely visiting Poland for a few days."

"Visiting Poland for what? Excuse me, I no hear you."

"For, one, or, two, days."

"Oh, yes, all right. Where's your passport?"

He snapped it across. ("Have everything ready for him, don't cause any delays," Viktor had said.)

"Uh-huh. Good, good. And your exit permission?"

He hoped his hand would not shake. He handed over a green piece of paper, embossed with the seal of the Soviet Office of Passport Control. Beneath the seal were seventeen typed lines, and at the bottom of the paper, a signature.

Gortowski frowned. He stared. His lips moved slowly. "I thought these things must to be yellow."

("Under no circumstances are you to argue with him. Blame our government, your mother, or Shishkin here, but don't suggest that he is wrong in any way," Viktor had stressed.) He shrugged. "I really don't know, comrade. As you can see from my passport, I have never been out of the country before. I'm sure you know better than I do."

"Ah well, they maybe changed forms. What's this about death though?"

Rabbinical students are trained to analyze carefully, not to think on their feet. The Rabbi was, momentarily, stunned. His vacant eyes met those of Gortowski. And, slowly, he let a smile spread across his face.

"It only says that in the event of my death while on this trip, I should be transported back to the Soviet Union. I am old, Comrade Gortowski. It could happen anytime."

Gortowski took the passport and the green sheet of paper and walked across the room to the wide window. The Rabbi, to his surprise, felt no fear. It was beyond his control now.

"You die in my country, your government, no mine, pay for you come back."

His mind traversed the Pole's bad grammar. It was going to work. Gortowski bent over, and flipped aside one of the floor-length curtains. Behind it, he kept an ink pad, a rubber stamp, and a jar of instant coffee. He opened the ink pad, but thought better of it. He inspected the stamp, breathed hot air on it, and brought it crashing down on the upper right corner of the green page. He examined his work, smiled, and handed the paper to the Rabbi. "Ink much expensive to waste."

The Rabbi manufactured a simple sentence of gratitude, shook Gortowski's hand, and got out of the bare office. It was not until he was off the grounds of the embassy, walking down the street, that he opened the sheet of paper to look at it. The seal, set in purple ink, displaying the Polish eagle inside a circle of Latin writing that he could not understand. What he could read, and now pored over, was the lines of Russian underneath, that said the crate to which the paper was attached contained the body of a Soviet citizen who had died and whose family had been given permission to bury it out of the country. The crate, it said, should be allowed to cross the Soviet border and, due to the nature of its contents, need not be opened, except at the discretion of the examining officer.

Armed with an official form bearing the seals of not one but two government bureaucracies, the Rabbi had no trouble purchasing a railroad cargo ticket at the Kiev Station. He was even given the benefit of the ticket vendor's long experience. "Have it here five hours before the train pulls out, or without doubt, it will find its way on to the Trans-Siberian Express. Everything here has to be done three times, and it's only on the last try that they get anything right!"

Viktor, huddled in the Rabbi's small anteroom in the back of the synagogue, took small joy in their victory. "It only shows why this country doesn't work." The Rabbi was offended. "Not our country. Poland!"

"And who imposed that system on Poland?"

"I still don't understand," said the Rabbi. "Why not Israel directly?"

Both Shishkin and Viktor looked at him long enough to make him uncomfortable.

"You think they'd put the body of a Jew, who died in the hands of the KGB, on an airplane? Or on the speediest train heading south? Or maybe attach a note to the box: 'Next week in Jerusalem. Spare no expense. Send all bills to the Central Committee.' For all we know, they'll use that box to heat seven homes in Kuibyshev for a week. It would take a minimum of six weeks. No, we have to control the route, as best we can." The Rabbi noticed a difference in Shishkin as he spoke. In the past he had always used the word "We" loosely, to denote the Jewish people: "We have our rights," or "We are the victims of Soviet oppression". Since he and Viktor had materialized and helped uncover the KGB's perfidy, Shishkin used the word "we" more carefully, and in less sweeping terms. His scope and focus had been reduced. He was fighting now for himself and his friend. Viktor was more puzzling. He had been less shocked than Shishkin to see Pronsky's half-incinerated corpse, but no less sad. The difference was that while Shishkin mourned, Viktor set his mind to planning. When the Rabbi had returned that night with food for them, Viktor had quietly begun telling them about the inept Polish diplomat. Yet, considering that he was, at the moment, an outlaw and fugitive from Soviet justice, there was in him a broad streak of patriotism.

His capacity for detail was awe-inspiring. When he heard that the train would pull out of Kiev Station at three a.m., he frowned. "Five hours before that will be ten o'clock. The cargo taxis stop running at seven. That means we'd have to be there eight hours in advance, which is too early. It gives too much time to some nosy little bastard in a uniform to go poking around. The ticket-seller was right. In five hours, they'll manage to put it on the wrong train, discover their error, leave it sitting on a platform while they go get drunk, and finally get it right. I only hope it doesn't rain." There was no way for the average citizen to know. Meteorological forecasts were never printed or broadcast.

Shishkin was nearly ready to concede defeat. "Even if we had enough money, I don't think we could buy another tank. The one we had was, uh, borrowed."

Viktor understood. "Who stole it?"

"It was Pronsky. One of the foolish black diplomats he worked for had brought it with him from Africa. Although where he thought he'd go diving in Moscow is beyond me."

"I'll bet they left it there." Viktor sounded more certain than he was.

"So what? We have no way of getting back out there." Shishkin sounded like a loser.

Viktor had planned many difficult projects, alone and with others. He preferred to work alone, but this time there was no choice.

"Could you excuse us, Mark Davidovich?"

"Certainly, where are you going?"

"No, uh, what I meant was . . ."

"Oh! Oh, I see! You want to talk to Shishkin alone. Yes, yes, certainly. I'll be next door. I'll bring you more food tonight."

Shishkin watched the retreating figure. "He's really not a bad old fart."

"Shishkin," Viktor said. "The woman who brought Anna to see me. I never asked about her."

"With good reason. I wouldn't have told you anything."

"Yes, but now it's important."

"All the more reason to keep her clear of it."

"She must be someone you trust."

"Oh, she is. Discreet, trustworthy, competent."

"Good. I want you to get in contact with her. She can help us."

"No way."

"Why not?"

"Because I don't want to give her the satisfaction."

"You talk about her like an enemy."

"In a way, she is."

"Who is she then?"

"My wife."

"Your – "

"You think it's so amazing that I should have won a woman's heart?"

"Or any of her other parts," Viktor said.

"Actually, all I ever possessed was her mind. And she mine. It was a long time ago, and it was quickly over. Once we no longer thought alike, it wasn't worth it to keep up the formalities."

"Why did she help you bring Anna to me?"

"Oh, she owed me a favor. And it was the kind of thing I knew she could pull off."

"What I have in mind won't be any more difficult. The car that she brought Anna in. Is it hers?"

"Oh, yes. You have some plan?"

Viktor's speech slowed, he was no longer addressing Shishkin. "As long as the people that I think I know are really who I think they are."

When she was home, Nina Sokolova answered the phone on the first ring, just as she did in the office. What was the use of making people wait? And any corner of the one-room apartment she had occupied since her divorce was within a few strides of the other side.

"You don't know me, but please don't hang up. I want to read you something."

The voice was not muffled but Nina could not tell if it was a man's or woman's. She was not tempted to hang up. Few enough people knew her home number and of course there was no telephone directory. So either she had been called entirely at random, in which case there was no danger, or the caller really did want to speak to her.

"Go ahead, I'm listening."

> "Folk sleep in their houses, blinking; at home
> My darling blissfully slumbers. The train
> Sweeps on; while I dash along the platforms
> Each carriage door strews my heart on the plain."

Nina had read some of Pasternak's poetry as a student. It was the kind of pranksterish defiance in which even Party members could indulge if they chose. The banning of his works only made their discovery sweeter. But she had not appreciated the power of his verse until Viktor had begun reciting it, quietly, at work. And of course she had chided him and of course he did it more often then. The beauty of their friendship was that both could deny any wrongdoing: she had told him to stop and he had only been mumbling to himself. He had repeated that particular quartet, from "My Sister Life," dozens of times because she never pretended that it did not please her. It was so supremely Russian and sounded all the more so because of him.

"Very nice. What about it?" she said into the phone.

"Do you know where it was written?" How could she not? Viktor had exulted for a week about his daughter's delight when he took her to Pasternak's home.

"I know."

"As soon as possible, please." It was the way the voice said "please" that made Nina guess she was talking to a woman.

It was dark when she arrived. She had taken two buses and with more than a mile still to walk, been picked up by a slightly drunken motorist with trysting in mind. She was polite, but discouraging and after a few minutes of driving she removed his hand decisively from her lap. He let her out almost exactly where she would have turned off the road anyway.

The unlit, rutted streets caught at her ankles; fallen branches licked at her shins. By the time she saw the house she was walking in pain. Three cars approached from behind her, their growing headlights seemed to her to be in pursuit. The fourth car came toward her from the village of Peredelkino. Its lights confronting her straight on made her turn her head, so she did not see it stop next to her.

"Each carriage door strews my heart on the plain."

Without the telephone's distortion, the voice was definitely a woman's, though not feminine. Nina got in without a word. She had made up her mind as she was pushing away the amorous driver's hand, not to show fear, to do whatever needed to be done. She had no idea why Viktor was contacting her, but she would not abandon him.

The car made a series of turns that she did not try to follow and pulled up at the foot of a hillside. The driver was dark-haired, and wore a coat darker than the night that separated her from Nina. "He didn't want to involve you, but he has absolutely no choice."

"That doesn't make it any less flattering. How can I help him?"

"Walk up to the cabin on top of the hill. He spent some time there, after he disappeared. There shouldn't be too much left inside. Look around quickly, and if you see a metal canister, bring it down here. It's very important for him and – and his plan, to get it."

"You've seen Viktor?"

"I don't even know Viktor. Please don't ask me any more questions. I'm only doing this because I hate them so much."

"Hate?"

"Them. The bastards, the filth, the Nazis who run our country." The dark-haired woman turned to Nina. "Don't you hate them? Doesn't it make you sick to think of what has happened? It was supposed to be such a great experiment; to see if men's better instincts could prevail. It never got the chance. Doesn't it make you sick?"

Nina had gone stiff at the beginning of the outburst. She was not interested in arguing politics. "I'll try to get what you want."

It took some looking. She had to use the flashlight that the woman had given her instead of turning on lights. The squalidness of the room did not bother her; she knew country people who thought themselves progressive for having windows. She tried not to touch anything. She opened the door of the wardrobe with her foot. None of the clothes looked like those Viktor had worn to work. She realized she was thinking of him in intimate terms. His things, his welfare. There was a two-door cabinet beneath the sink in the toilet. She put the handle of the flashlight behind one of the half-open doors to pull it open.

Nina's drain had stopped up and overflowed a few months earlier and she had spent a difficult few hours before the plumber arrived. (She remembered now that Viktor had found the plumber and convinced him to visit Nina at the end of his official working day.) She had wrapped rags around the U-pipe beneath the sink because dirty water was oozing out of it where the joint was not properly sealed. She thought at first that this sink was of a different sort. A much-thicker pipe led from the sink to the floor. Thinking of her own predicament, she wondered how a plumber would repair this pipe if the sink stopped up, and then realized why it looked different. She gave the pipe a delicate kick and heard metal scrape the floor. She kicked it again. It tilted and fell on its side. It was the air tank.

"You'll be seeing Viktor? To take this to him?"

"Please, I already begged you not to ask me anything. I don't even know your last name. It's better, you can see that." The road they were travelling was dark, but ahead they could see the streetlights at the beginning of Moscow.

"Tell Viktor that there is a rumor about him. That he and Ludmilla were working for spies in the American Embassy. I called his wife three days ago, but a man answered and insisted that I give him my name. I did, because I am not ashamed to call the wife of my friend. And tell him that he does have friends. Many."

The woman pulled the car over to the side just before they reached the first street lights. "Forgive me, but you'll have to get out here. It would be very dangerous if you were seen with me."

"I don't mind."

"This Viktor. You love him, don't you?"

"It's almost impossible not to."

Shishkin was taking the chance of being seen on the street. There was an arrest order out for him and he had more than the average number of enemies. He decided to use Soviet progress to his advantage. There was one underground parking garage in Moscow, located on the western edge of the city, near the Olympic Village. He wondered what he would do if he were challenged; he did not possess a driver's license. Under artificial lights, the brown Zhiguli looked even dirtier than it had in Peredelkino.

He did not bother with salutations. "You're going to be fined one of these days."

"Oh, fuck your mother, you think I worry about that when I'm abetting whatever stunt you're involved in this time?"

He raised the trunk, hefted the object, which she had wrapped in brown packing paper. "This should make it easy to be unobtrusive. I just look like a regular fellow, right?"

She had to smile. "Yevgeny, if you shaved, washed, dressed like someone who walks on two legs instead of four, and never opened your mouth, you still wouldn't pass for normal."

"Sly-tongued vixen."

She told him about Nina and passed on her warning. "You know, she loves your friend."

"He's an easy person to love."

She wondered what kind of person could inspire such feelings.

Shishkin had to pretend that his last words were an afterthought, said them, quietly, over his shoulder as he was walking away. "Thank you for helping. It's not as though I wanted to create any more complications for you."

"I always told you, Yeshka, that just because we were a disaster as man and wife, we could still help each other through this awful life."

Shishkin used the metro. It was as packed at midday as at any other time, and four out of five passengers were also carrying packages, most wrapped in the ubiquitous brown paper. Walking the last five hundred yards, down Pskov Street, he felt everyone was looking at him. A militiaman dawdling near the synagogue fixed him with a stare. He put his head behind the brown paper parcel and tried to look as though he were dead. That was how to stay alive.

He found Viktor studying the crate, and looking grim. "Shishkin, I've made a decision. I'm going to go talk to them. I'm certain I can square things. I'm not involved in any of this – your police killing, whatever it was that poor Ludmilla got herself wrapped up in. I'll admit taking the letter to her, apologize for hiding for a week, take whatever's coming to me. I think I can be out in ten years. And at least Marya and Anna will be safe."

"It's too late for that." Shishkin made a point of not looking him in the face. "I didn't want to have to tell you this. Hard news, friend. I made contact with the people in the apartment that overlooks yours."

Viktor felt the air in his lungs go sour.

"I suppose they ran out of patience. There were three of them. Two held Marya down while the third one . . . did what he wanted. Then they switched. They took her away then, without even letting her get new clothes. I imagine she's being held at the women's detention cells."

Viktor simply stopped breathing. Ten seconds, twenty, half a minute. His face went red, his eyes defocused. Then came the sobbing. Finally it stopped. "And Anna?"

Shishkin was quick. "Completely all right. It happened before she got back from school. When she did get home, a woman agent was waiting for her and put her in a car. She's sure to be with your wife." He had kept this story in reserve for just such a crisis of confidence. He had not expected the complete silence that fell over the room. The man who was easy to love sat on the cold stone floor, looking at nothing, seeing the two people he most loved.

Forty-seven minutes later, Viktor rose, looked into the wooden crate, and told Shishkin: "You take the right side. I'll take the left."

*

The Rabbi had become fearless. He muttered his instructions to himself, and offered improvements, all of which were rejected. The cargo taxi, which had been ordered for six, arrived forty-five minutes late. It was not such a coincidence that the same driver pulled up, there were only a dozen or so for the city of nine million. Polite and greedy as ever, the driver strode into the synagogue, pocketing the two rubles, and bent over the crate. He jerked it up, then gave a nasal grunt of pain.

"Christ! Oh, excuse me, just an expression. Is this the same crate I brought in here yesterday?"

"Doesn't it look the same?"

"Yes, but – . Never mind. It's been a long day. Guess I'm more tired than I realize."

The Rabbi let him drag it outside without offering to help. At the back of the panel truck, the driver let the end of the crate smack down to the concrete pavement. He lifted one end until it was poised over the cargo galley and let it drop again. The crate was at a forty-five degree angle to the pavement. He squatted down and pushed the lower end until gravity brought it slamming down inside the truck.

"Listen, grandpa, I'm sorry but it's going to cost you more than two lousy rubles if you want me to unload this for you."

"Fine, comrade, I appreciate your help."

"Yeah, well, I must be getting old."

"You have a long way to go, believe me." The Rabbi was staring absently at the crate as he spoke.

They drove to a parade of open-air stands, directly across the street from Kiev Station, that sold fruit, vegetables and flowers. The driver, impatient to go home, pulled the crate out of the truck so quickly that his eyes bulged. He left it sitting upright. The Rabbi found the stocky flower-dealer that Viktor had told him about, and struck a quick deal. The man closed his stand fifteen minutes early, and pushed a long two-wheeled handcart over to the roadside.

"A relative?"

"No, just a – " He found himself unable to find the right word.

It was all over in another hour. The flower-vendor stopped traffic twice to push the overloaded cart across streets and around to the tracks behind the train station. He pocketed his money without thanks or expression. In all, the Rabbi paid out thirty-three rubles in fees and bribes. When he had asked where the money came from, Shishkin was embarrassed and Viktor concluded he had begged it from his wife. The trainmaster made jokes about leaving the crate at Oswiecem, the Polish town near Krakow that the rest of the world knew as Auschwitz. The Rabbi forced himself to smile. His time for punishment was not far off, he suspected. He went home to pray and wait, and dispose of Pronsky's body.

It took three livery men to lift it on to the baggage car, a tribute to the taxi-driver's determination. When the train pulled out, eleven minutes late, Viktor nudged Shishkin in the midsection. There was a loud groan in response, a groan of relief as much as acknowledgement. The first time the taxi-driver had dropped the crate, Shishkin's face slammed against the wood and his nose was shattered. Viktor, his face only three inches away from Shishkin's, could smell the rich flow of blood and feel it underneath his own head.

"Home," Viktor whispered.

"Home?"

"Yes, home. Where we came from, where we're going."

The train picked up speed, heading west.

I I

From the beginning, Karushkin knew the Jews who had been arrested would be trouble. The unexpected death of the fat one, Rudolph, should have served as a warning. In the old days, a body coming out of KGB custody could have disappeared – that is, it would have been driven in an unmarked truck to a remote area many miles from Moscow and buried, or drowned. Karushkin knew first-hand that young agents in a hurry to advance their careers were often used for that purpose. Knew because he had volunteered his services many times. Immoral? No more than a junior business executive who helps cover his superior's infidelities by lying to his wife.

There was nothing warped about Alexander Alfredovich Karushkin. He had never married, and was not overly fond of children. But the same is true of many important men and women worldwide, who preferred to concentrate on doing one thing well and made a conscious decision to keep sentiment in its place.

No one would suggest that Karushkin had not done well. When it had been important, he had bent his scruples, sold his beliefs and acted in the consciously pragmatic manner that characterizes determinedly successful people. Karushkin had decided when still young that he would master the secret world of the KGB, because, he was convinced, it was the one Soviet institution that would withstand change. And change, he knew from unpleasant experience, was the one real threat to the world as he conceived it.

The phone buzzed in Karushkin's apartment, and he reached across the desk where he was sitting. There was very little chance of it being a wrong number. Like other members of the small group of apparatchiks, Karushkin's home had an eight-digit number instead of the normal seven. On top of that, only about one hundred people – mostly KGB – had his number. A computer had calculated that the likelihood of someone dialling those eight digits by pure chance was in the area of

925,000 to 1. In thirteen years in this apartment, the odds had been with Karushkin.

"Yes?" On the phone, Karushkin's voice was only a fraction above a whisper. Like most things about him, this was a conscious choice. People are disconcerted by a low, purring voice on the phone. They compensate for it by speaking louder than they might ordinarily. And that can lead to misstatements and mistakes. It all worked in Karushkin's favour, gave him an extra edge. Which, he would have said, is what life is all about.

The caller was the Chairman's secretary. This always put Karushkin in a bad temper. Andropov had made his own calls, at least to deputies. Chebrikov, his successor, had brought in a male secretary who sounded as though he was running the organization by himself. He disappeared with Chebrikov, to be replaced by the woman to whom Karushkin now spoke. He had never met her, was not even sure if she occupied an office near the Chairman's. That was not how things were done at the Committee.

The secretary reminded him that the Chairman would like to see him the next morning at eight. As though it might have slipped his mind. Nothing slipped Karushkin's mind, because he had trained himself not to permit such lapses. He curtly told the secretary that he would be there.

Silence, again.

Did he like the absolute stillness of solitude? Yes and no. Karushkin was not devoid of the normal human frailties – loneliness, insecurity, craving for companionship. He had learned, however, to sublimate them, putting in their place the one certainty that mattered more than anything else in this country: no one could hurt him.

The early appointment was a bad sign. The Chairman usually dispensed with unpleasantness early in the day, while his energy level was high. Since Karushkin's life was more or less devoted to visiting unpleasantness on others, he had little sympathy.

He already knew the purpose of the meeting. He would be asked to report his progress on the militia killings and the disappearances from the US Embassy. He would have to say that he had taken three suspects in for interrogation and expected another to be captured soon. He would then have to say that all three of the prisoners had died in custody. No one would like that, not these days.

It all used to be so much easier. He kept telling himself not to think that way. The past was unimportant. But it was better, he kept answering himself. Better in all ways. Well, not for those who ran afoul of the system, of course. But he had never had much sympathy for them, anyway.

Andropov who would have changed the face of the Soviet Union had stayed in power no longer than 15 months. Before he died, though, he had given the power structure a good scare. The structure — in Russian the nomenklatura or apparatchiki — is almost impossible to identify. Like any group of powerful men that meets on the same day each week at the same bar or club without formal arrangement, so the members of the structure come into regular contact, by phone, in person, through mutual acquaintances, to exchange views, point out problems that they saw in the country, and propose solutions. In Stalin's era, any such group would quickly have been rounded up and shot. But these were different times.

It had not been generally known that Andropov was Gorbachev's mentor. The two spent much private time together, and, according to defectors who were at one time part of the Party apparatus, they voted the same way on 100 per cent of the issues brought before the Politburo. Of course, Gorbachev's remarkable and revolutionary actions in his first years of leadership are well documented. Could anyone living in the late 1980s in a country that had radio and television not know the words glasnost and perestroika? What is not understood is that, within the Soviet hierarchy, Gorbachev is not regarded with universal affection. There are two reasons: first, he is a tinkerer. He does not know exactly how to fix what ails the country, so he is trying different remedies, without much of a pattern. Second, Gorbachev is overtly trying to change things that he knows will make some people unhappy and he does not care. That might be acceptable if he was a religious missionary trying to curb abuses of the peasants in some Latin American dictatorship. But in the Soviet Union, where unanimity is built upon unspoken consensus, it is an attitude so indelicate as to be suicidal.

Karushkin arrived punctually for the meeting next morning, was kept waiting only a few minutes, then, via an inter-office buzz, was notified that he could go into the Chairman's office.

"Alexander Alfredovich, how good of you to come. I know you're very busy." The Chairman affected a modest heartiness that Karushkin found detestable. He kept up a patter of idiocies for longer than Karushkin would have thought possible. In the old days, extraneous comments at a meeting of this level were perceived as personal weakness.

"Alexander Alfredovich, I have to tell you that there's a certain amount of concern about the way you've handled the investigation of these, uh, irregular occurrences."

"Concern?"

"Well, put more bluntly, dissatisfaction."

"I see." He was not the least bit worried. He had wilfully kept the pace of the investigation slow. To produce conclusions too quickly was in no one's best interest.

"I'm not sure you do. A member of the custodial staff over at the Dzerzhinsky lodged a complaint about the condition in which you left one of the rooms."

"Custodial staff."

"Yes, the clean-up crew. Seems this fellow said that the room reeked of everything imaginable – burnt flesh, feces, vomit."

"The janitor didn't like the stink?"

"Let me finish, Alexander Alfredovich. You see, of all the bad luck, the fellow happens to be Armenian, one of the few we've got working with us."

"And, I hope, the highest-ranking one."

The Chairman squeezed his eyes shut. "I knew this was going to be difficult to explain. The custo– all right, the janitor, didn't complain to his supervisor as he should have. That way, it could have been kept in perspective. Instead, he told another Armenian, who told another. Well, one way and other, it got to the head of the Armenian Nationalities Council. They went to the Central Committee Secretary for Nationalities, demanding to know if it was an Armenian who'd been done in that room."

Karushkin pressed his lips together, willed himself not to speak.

"Now this may seem the height of absurdity, but I assure you, it's serious. The Secretary mentioned it to Raisa Maximovna at a social function and she brought it up with her husband. So yesterday, I got a call from Mikhail Sergeyivich, asking what had happened? I felt like a fool not even knowing what he was talking about."

You are a fool, Karushkin said to himself.

"Well, I found out, of course. I even saw the videotape. Did you have to do that?"

"No, I could have tickled his feet with a feather until he told me what I wanted to know."

"But that's the problem, Alexander Alfredovich. You didn't want to know anything. You just put him on that chair and let him fry!"

"What about the militiamen who were fried in their own car?"

"I know, I know. We're all unhappy about it. But, Karushkin, don't you understand? I'm saying Gorbachev himself called about this one."

"About a Jew, and a criminal one at that?"

"That doesn't matter, as you know. What are we going to do, tell him to mind his own business while we carry on as we always have?"

"I can think of more elegant phrasing, but, yes."

The Chairman had been waiting for that. "Yes, Alexander Alfredovich, that's the problem you see. Far too little concern about the political realities and far too much about petty pride."

"Petty pride?" The words felt like a jar of honey that had been dumped down his throat.

"You're more interested in keeping your own admittedly impressive success story going. You don't understand that things are changing in this country. We're trying to improve the image of the KGB, not just in the West but with our own people as well."

Karushkin had to apply pressure on his jaws to keep from answering back. After a lengthy silence, he said: "Chairman, as you know, I was assigned to the case of the militia attacks, I did not volunteer for it. However, now that . . ."

"Yes, you want to see it through or else it will seem you've been bested. That's exactly what I'm talking about. No comprehension of the greater good. You're a dinosaur." The Chairman, only a few years younger than Karushkin, was enjoying this. "Gorbachev's wife is upset, so he doesn't sleep well. He comes in grouchy, I catch hell. All because of your antiquated ideas, Alexander Alfredovich." The Chairman's smile was absolutely beatific. "You're suspended until further notice. You may continue to use your office, but you're not to make further inquiries about the matter. That's all."

It happened so fast that Karushkin did not immediately digest it. When he did, it seemed undignified to ask the Chairman to repeat it, or to argue. So he stood, turned sharply on his heel, and went out to try to pick up the pieces of his life. For almost fifty years, he had learned how to adapt and overcome. But he was an old dog now, and these newest tricks held no appeal.

The next day, several members of the structure just happened to be at the same restaurant, the Ohotnek, on Gorky Street. They gestured pleasantly to each other from their various tables. And, after lunch, they agreed to walk together down the street, as far as Pushkin Square. It had taken twelve hours for word to get around about Karushkin's meeting with the Chairman. In that time, another guard at the American Embassy disappeared.

Twelve hours is a long time.

12

Twelve hours is half a day only when there are other things to think about. Surrounded by darkness, breathing air soaked with the smells of blood and decay, stuffed into a box with inadequate space for one living person, let alone two, time is marked in groups of seconds. Twelve hours is as incomprehensible as the distance to Saturn. The motion of the train did not help, as Viktor had supposed. Instead of a lulling, back-and-forth rhythm, the freight car, linked next to last in the string of wagons, was snapped like a whip's tip by curves in the track. Every few seconds his head bumped into Shishkin's. It was simply unavoidable. Their faces were no more than two inches apart at any time. When they first tried out the box together, their heads were at opposite ends. But Shishkin argued that if the box was tipped on its end, one of them would be standing on his head for who knew how long. Better to take a chance either both or neither of them would be in such a painful position.

When the taxi-driver started to slam the crate down in front of the flower-vendor's stall, Viktor felt the box shifting and whispered fiercely to Shishkin: "Brace yourself." At the same moment that Viktor spread his hands, and tried to cling to the inside of the box to minimize his slide, Shishkin was asking: "What did you say?" and turning his head to hear better. His face was completely unprotected when it crunched into the wooden wall. His nose had been broken before, by a KGB goon, so he knew the feeling. There was absolutely nothing they could do for him and he was denied even the release of screaming out his pain.

Nothing worked the way he had expected. The first time he turned the valve of the air tank, it made such a loud hiss that he was afraid to use it again until they began to move. Breathing became an exercise, not an instinct. Once the train pulled out, he released more air from the tank. He heard the same splutter and hiss, but it lasted for only a few seconds. The tank for which Nina had risked her safety had been nearly empty. It was useless. They tried to talk, but Shishkin began coughing blood and had to spit it into Viktor's face. Viktor waited until the warm red eruptions stopped, then said: "I have an idea. I'll talk and you keep quiet. Agreed?"

"Uhh."

"Bet this is the first time you've been in that position."

He decided that the sharp exhalation from Shishkin was meant as an affirmative. His own situation, he thought, was particularly ridiculous: shoved face to face against a man who always had something to say, he nevertheless felt as lonely as he could ever imagine being.

What went through Viktor's mind during the dark escape from the country he loved? Thoughts of Marya and Anna of course. He had decided to flee until he could come back and avenge them. The unquenchable misery he felt when he thought of Marya made him feel that he too might retch. Even more he dwelled on Anna and of how she had hugged him in the car, when, three days ago?

"You know, Shishkin, I hate to complain, but the hours I spent in that box with your friends didn't prepare me for this ride."

"You want your money back, perhaps?" The voice was strained with suffering, but the sarcastic tone was intact.

"I don't hold out much hope for the Rabbi when they find out what he's done. Or for Comrade Gortowski when they realize he stamped the papers for Rudolph."

Shishkin could not remain silent. "He knew."

"Gortowski? I don't believe it."

"The Rabbi." Shishkin's words were slurred like a sleepy drunk's. Viktor did not know whether a constant patter or dark silence would be more soothing to Shishkin. For his own relief, he decided to fill the air between them with the unedited contents of his mind.

"I'm surprised we haven't suffocated in this box yet. But we seem to be getting enough air, don't we?"

"I told you. As long as the box isn't sealed airtight, oxygen will get in. The problem is that the air that's left over doesn't smell very good." Viktor thought the box smelled like Shishkin's apartment.

"I wonder what Poland will be like. If Gortowski is any indication, then no wonder the country is such a mess. I don't imagine you'll care much for the place, Shishkin. After all, you're headed into the country that was home to Auschwitz and Treblinka. Do you know, I read somewhere that, during the Middle Ages, 80 per cent of the world's Jews lived in the territory that is now Poland?"

The silence was broken only by heavy breathing. Viktor thought Shishkin might have been lucky enough to drift into sleep. The man had hardly shut his eyes since they had set out on their fortunate walk around

Peredelkino three days earlier. Viktor decided to stop talking and hope for drowsiness, too, when he heard the voice, half-strangled but an unmistakable counterthrust, saying: "And you are about to visit a country whose people have never forgotten what happened at Katyn. You are expecting flowers?"

"Well, Shishkin, even if they accuse me of being personally responsible, I won't understand what they're saying, will I?"

There was no reply. Viktor whispered the other man's name several times. This time, he really had found sleep.

The position into which he had twisted his body was becoming unbearable. He wanted to scratch his nose, put his hands above his head and stretch, bend his knees, do jumping jacks. The more he thought about the freedom of movement, the less discipline his limbs displayed. He began to fidget, kicking at the top of the box, flexing his elbows until they banged the back, twisting his neck so he felt Shishkin's face against his hair. It occurred to him that even if he kicked with all his might and shouted as loudly as he could, no one could possibly notice. Viktor knew how much noise trains made. Even in the first class, or "soft" passenger compartments, conversations were conducted at battlefield pitch.

He tried to settle himself into tranquility by concentrating. What would become of him? He was deserting – no other word for it – the country that had given him a home, work, a wife and daughter, a land so beauteous and complex that if he could live two lifetimes consecutively, he would only know a fraction of its secrets.

Yes, it was controlled by barbarians now, by short-sighted little men who had managed to turn Marxist theory into the eponym of tyranny. What other Europeans and Americans, especially, did not understand was that Russians do not expect their leaders to be merciful and good. They need only be strong to gain the admiration of the people. Where the Communists had gone wrong was in expanding their empire beyond the old duchies of Muscovy and Kiev. Go too far south of Russian heartland and you encounter treacherous Georgians, scurrilous Armenians. Too far north west and the frail, cerebral Baltic people become a smirking liability. And to the east, where tsars and commissars have always been attracted, the land where the sun rises; there live the unlovable Asian tribes: Azerbaijanis, Kazhaks, Eskimos. They have nothing more to do with Russia's destiny than the Polynesians. Yet the Communists, knowing that they seized power without justification, feel compelled to neutralize any race and region that borders their stronghold.

It was into such a neutered zone that Viktor was riding. He felt true Russian sentiments toward the Poles: contempt and distrust. They were Slavic, too, but there was nothing else to testify to their ethnic bonds. Their soldiers were brave bloodspillers, undaunted by death as long as it contributed to the freedom of the nation. The irony was that, during the clusters of years when Poland was not under foreign dominion, it was always near the brink of self-destruction, usually due either to famine or disastrous government decisions. The Polish nation that rose up against the tsar in 1863 was nothing more than a collection of greedy noblemen and wild-eyed sheep who were persuaded to follow them into waiting bayonets. The wrecked nation that survived Hitler's fury was no more capable of making decisions for its own future than was Germany herself.

In 1980, when Solidarity had sprung up, the Poles deluded themselves that it was the path to freedom from Russia. When word circulated that Polish meat was being shipped to Moscow for use during the Summer Olympics, workers at Lublin dumped telephone poles, car tires, sacks of sand and wet cement on the train tracks to prevent any cargo from crossing the border. When the government, faced with an ultimatum from Moscow, declared martial law, and squashed the union, its members cried foul. Viktor felt no sympathy for them. Had he been the leader of Solidarity, he would have guaranteed that Poland had a steady stream of foreign union leaders and politicians as visitors. Let the Russians invade, or the army take control of the country with the Prime Minister of Sweden in Warsaw. When he committed stupid mental lapses, he would berate himself for "thinking like a Pole". It was not racism, it was history.

And their language; what to make of it? Russian was the novelist's ink, the poet's rhyme. Its words could be strong but subtle, its outlook sweeping and its scrutiny minute. For Viktor, Russian was not just a way of speaking, it was an outline for life. When he and Anna had taken their vacation to Georgia and he heard how those swarthy people mangled his language, he was offended. They need not speak it fluently, but they should at least obey its rules of grammar. How would he communicate with the Poles, whose language sounded as though it had been devised by gossiping old women?

He decided that he had made a mistake. He had gone to Shishkin looking for help. But Marya had paid the price for him following the Jew's advice. Prison in Russia was preferable to a life on the run in Poland. At least he would understand what his jailers were saying. He would go back, explain it to Karushkin, he was pure Russian after all. With luck he might receive only twenty years. Marya would get over the scars, could send parcels every six months and visit him alternate years; when he got out they would be pensioners, together again, with Anna grown tall and married. What was wrong with that plan? I want to go back home. "Hachoo vozvrashatz umenye." He was crying, but silently, and in the darkness Shishkin would never know.

He knew his lips were moving but was unaware that he was talking out loud until he felt Shishkin's fingers tighten around his leg. The grip was strong, his sleep had given him strength, but the voice still bespoke pain: "My brother, our home has rejected us. Now we must build a new house." The sound of metal wheels on metal rails already seemed eternal.

At first Viktor thought he had fallen asleep, but then he concluded his brain was tardy in picking up the message: the train was slowing. How long had they been in the box? All his body signals gave the same answer: a long time. His muscles ached, his lungs demanded clean air, his stomach reminded him that it was empty while his bladder and bowels threatened to release their irritating overload.

Other noises replaced the grinding sound of distance. Viktor imagined it was the rumble of his stomach, or Shishkin's, and he wondered how intestines could growl with such cadence. Then he heard it again and he wanted to jump; it was someone talking. He opened his hand to prod Shishkin. His fingers met the other outstretched fingers.

"Yes, I hear it too. But it's not Russian they're speaking."

Shishkin was right. They had no difficulty hearing through the box. It was like listening to a far-off station on an old radio. They picked up individual words but never whole sentences.

"It's Ukrainian," Shishkin whispered.

"Shhhh. If we can hear them, can't they hear us?"

"Do you often put your ear to wooden boxes that you think are carrying dead bodies?"

"Where do you think we are, Shishkin?"

"I know where I am; I'm streched out in a coffin with the noisiest son of a bitch I've ever heard. Quiet down so I can listen."

The fuzzy radio program went on, with the volume going up and down each few seconds. Then there was silence.

"Shish—"

"Shhh."

A thud that might have started in heaven shook the box. Viktor felt his legs stiffen, instinctively getting ready to run. He forced himself to smoothe out his muscles. He was as helpless as a metro passenger during a blackout. He heard Shishkin sucking air through his mouth, so his broken nose would not make noise.

"Stanislaw, come here." This voice was different, high-pitched, the emphasis on the words was misplaced. The command was in Russian, but it was not the speaker's native language.

"Yes, is what?"

"Look at this." A stick, or a boot, tapped the top of the crate twice.

"Is box?" The second voice, closer now, was even less skilled in Russian, Viktor decided.

"Of course box is. Read sign."

"No do read. To tell?" Just as he had listened to the Rabbi and Shishkin arguing in the synagogue, Viktor found himself forgetting his own situation, and becoming fascinated with the voices on the other side of the box. It was like listening to a tape-recording of two-year-olds.

"In here is body say. Go to Poland, then Israel."

"Why Poland go?"

"Say no why. Call man carry box out. New train take."

"Man work not. Russian holiday."

"When work?"

"Day after work if not bad head have."

"We take box leave. Day after man find. New train put."

"Do what box now? Grodno not."

"Hmmmm."

The voices moved off, arguing still.

"Viktor. Did you understand?" Though it was whispering, Shishkin's clean Russian sounded bell-like in comparison to the nonsense they had just overheard.

"No. Did you?"

"I think so. One was Ukrainian. The other I'm sure was Polish. We're at Grodno, on the border."

"Then – "

"Yes. A few more miles and we'll be out of the Soviet Union." Shishkin's excitement had overcome the pain of his injuries. Viktor too felt the electricity of emotion and, for a second, did not think about Marya.

"What were they chattering about?"

"I think they were customs agents. They must have been reading, or trying to read, the label that said there was a body in this box, bound for Israel. I think they're trying to decide whether to leave it on the train, or take it off to put on another train."

"Why were they speaking Russian? If that's what that was."

"That I can answer," Shishkin said. "At all borders of the Soviet Union, our government insists that all official conversations be carried on in Russian."

"But if one was Ukrainian, and the other Polish, they could easily have spoken in one of their languages. Why make them both speak Russian?"

"You tell me, Viktor. You're the one who weeps over beet soup." Viktor felt, for the first time in his life, like an outsider regarding his own country. And then another thought came to him. "If we're at the border, they'll open the crate to inspect the contents, won't they?"

"You're right. Good customs agents would inspect thoroughly, even if it meant opening a crate that contained a corpse on a national holiday. I'll make you a wager that these two aren't quite that devoted. In fact, I'm betting my life on it. And so are you."

The train moved for a few more minutes, then came to a dead stop. They heard no more talk, no motion in the world outside their fetal enclosure. Viktor developed a way to measure time in the coffin. He tensed his right foot, then dug the heel of his left shoe into the instep of the right foot and began counting. The pain became too much to endure,by the time he reached thirty. He alternated feet and shoes, assuming each took thirty seconds to become unbearable. So passed the minutes.

Shishkin decided he would rather talk with a broken nose than remain silent. He nattered away while Viktor ticked off the seconds and waited for pain. He kept track of one hundred and twenty twinges, then started over.

They both heard the footsteps at the same time. Shishkin became silent, Viktor released the pressure on his instep. The voices that approached were different from the customs inspectors. Both belonged to men. Neither Viktor nor Shishkin could understand what was being said. They heard a tap on top of the crate, and Viktor thought he heard the word "umyer" – dead. The other man said "Tak-tak-tak" like a woodpecker. Viktor knew it was Polish for "Yes" or "Okay". There were shouts, curses, and the word "Moscow". Then silence. Fifteen minutes later, the end of the crate where they had their heads was elevated. Their feet slid on the incline, and thumped against the other end at the same second. There was a heavy, shared laugh on the outside. The crate was being dragged with one end still on the ground.

Viktor put his lips to Shishkin's ear: "Must be Poles. They're trying to lift just one end."

Shishkin said nothing.

The top end of the crate was being lowered, slowly, until it was flat. Then they felt their heads sliding toward the end. Their feet were higher than their faces. Shishkin let out a soft moan in anticipation of more pain, but the crate suddenly leveled out. They felt unsteady. Viktor figured the crate was being carried on several pairs of shoulders.

Outside, six men were struggling under the weight of the crate. Four of them were very drunk, the result of sharing three liters of bimber, a clear homemade liquor made from potato peelings. Drinking bimber was the sole nightime diversion in Suchowola. The men had sixty yards more to carry the box, and two of them were hunching their shoulders so that they were bearing almost none of the load.

"Blessed Virgin, this stiff must have put on weight since he died," said one, who had been recruited for the job from an alleyway where the police had rousted him.

"Keep going, the truck's just ahead," said one of the two sober pallbearers.

One of the drunks bent his knees. "I'll open the truck doors." The crate was unsteady for a split second, then the others redistributed the increased weight. The drunk lumbered ahead, pulled open the back door of the panel truck, and passed out.

"Knew it," said another of the inebriates. "Moved too fast, blood went to his brain. Bad thing when blood hits the brain."

"You're in no danger then, Wladyslaw."

"Why are they taking the stiff to Bialystok?" someone asked.

"Put it in the freezer until there's a train back to Moscow."

"Why not just leave it here until the next train passes through?"

"The stationmaster is superstitious. Says he's not spending the night with a corpse."

"Huh. You ever seen his wife?"

"Why does it have to go back?"

"Because something is wrong with the stamp on the shipping certificate. One of our boys caught it when the train pulled into Suchowola."

"So why didn't they catch it in Grodno?"

"Because they're Ukrainians. They only think with their pants down."

They put the crate in the back of the truck, and put a plastic cover over it. The plastic created, crudely but effectively, a perfect seal against water and air.

The drive took forty-five minutes. By the time they lifted the crate out of the truck, and took it up to the second floor of the Forensics Institute, Shishkin had passed out and Viktor was gasping wildly for air.

Dr Stefan Byrdy had dissected, by his own count, eleven thousand two hundred and seventy cadavers over a medical career that by any standards had lasted far too long. Dr Byrdy was eighty-seven years old. The last attempt to force Byrdy to retire, six weeks earlier, had failed because the chairman of the medical review board judging his case stuttered. So did Dr Byrdy. When the time came for Byrdy to demonstrate his grasp of modern forensic science, the two other members of the board peppered him with staccato questions.

"Dr Byrdy, what is the least disruptive incision for exploring decay of the stomach lining?"

"Uh-uh-uh . . ."

"That's r-r-right, an umbilical level c-c-c-cut," said the chairman.

"How would you identify traces of arsenic, Doctor Byrdy?"

"I-I-I-I. . . ."

"Y-Y-you m-m-mean iod-d-d-ine analysis. G-g-good enough."

The next chance to force Byrdy to retire was two years away. Until then, he was put on the overnight shift at the Institute, where it was thought he would be unlikely to receive any candidates for immediate autopsies.

Byrdy was delighted when the truck pulled up at the back entrance at 3.45 a.m. He heard the familiar sounds of wood scraping on to the metal gurney, rubber wheels navigating the gravel parking lot, doors creaking open, cracking shut.

"Good day to you gentlemen!" Byrdy was nearly blind. To his eyes, all hours were a sandy gray. "An accident victim?"

"No, no, just a corpse from Russia that shouldn't have been allowed to cross the border. The customs agents in Grodno will wish they'd done their job more carefully. This crate has to go back, and get another signature before we can transport it any further. We just want to store it here tonight in one of your vaults."

An eighty-seven-year-old face cannot mask disappointment. Byrdy mumbled directions, pointed vaguely to the left, trudged back to the office, where he kept a portable heater running. He had never worked on a Russian before, though he assumed that they had the same equipment as Poles. A thought occurred to him. If they found out, they would make him stop practicing. But how would they know? By the time it got back to Moscow, it would be impossible to tell the precise time of the incisions.

He put on his heaviest sweater, walked quietly down the unlit hall, and slipped soundlessly through the door. The cold of the storage vault reached his bones quicker these days, perhaps they were right, he should retire. But he had learned so much, it seemed a shame to waste it. He was annoyed to find the crate was on an operating table in the middle of the room, the lazy bastards had not even bothered to slip it into a vault.

Because of a space shortage, the surgeon's tools were hung from racks on a wall. Byrdy took down a surgical saw, a rawhide mallet used, rarely, to check for possible reflexes, and a pair of sutures. He fit the sutures into the end of the crate like a chisel and tapped with the mallet. The wood creaked. He prised with the sutures until he felt them bend. No matter. He would put them in the bottom of the garbage and say he had no idea what had happened to them. He found another crack in the crate, and applied more pressure. The end of the crate was coming off more easily than he expected.

Ten minutes later, Byrdy was working on the inner wooden box, tapping with the mallet, prying with the sutures, anticipating the joy of working inside a real Russian ribcage.

The first time he heard an answer to the tapping of his mallet, he paused. There was silence. He tapped twice, heard three knocks against the wood. He was utterly unafraid. A lifetime of working with the dead had ruined ghost stories for Dr Byrdy. Usually, when something unexpected happened, it was because he had made a mistake. He worked at the wood until he could get his fingers into a crack at the end of the inside box. He put the face of the mallet inside the box and twisted it. The wood creaked. He took the mallet out and walked over to the wall to find a larger tool. The end of the box fell to the floor. A hand reached out of the box. At that instant, Dr Byrdy did what he had never done before: promised the Blessed Virgin to retire before Christmas. The hand curled around the edge of the box, reached over the edge of the crate. A head of dark hair slid out of the box. The face beneath the hair was streaked with blood and mucous. Dr Byrdy dropped to his knees.

The bloody apparition continued to slide out of the box like a monstrous wounded snake. Its head slid down the length of the table. It was wearing shoes. It bent at the middle, just as if it were a man. It groaned, loudly. Dr Byrdy, still kneeling, put his head on the floor, and closed his eyes. When he opened them, the dead man was reaching inside the box, pulling something out. It was another creature, just like him. But this one looked truly dead. He was repeating a word that Byrdy did not understand. It sounded like a father comforting a crying child: "Shush-shush."

The ghost turned and noticed Byrdy for the first time. It pointed and spoke in something like a human voice. Byrdy did not understand the first words, but the last was clearly "doctor". Byrdy pointed to his own chest, which he could see through the heavy sweater, was pounding furiously. He nodded.

Before the old man could rise from his knees or run, the bloody monster had grabbed him and was pulling him toward the wooden crate. Byrdy wanted to protest but could not find his voice. Roughly, he was shoved

133

against the box. He looked up. The second creature was sprawled on the operating table, not moving, and no wonder. On its face and chest was enough blood to drown in. Byrdy felt strong hands on his shoulders. The first ghoul was shaking him, uttering sounds that every now and then, contained what seemed to be Polish words. He thought he heard "heart", "breathe", and "live". He saw the bloody face peering at him as though waiting for a response. Byrdy's aging mind still worked, he was beginning to understand.

"You want me to tell you if he is still alive?"

"Breathe–(unintelligible)–air–(unintelligible)–live?"

"You want me to examine your friend?"

"Friend! Friend!" The animated one clutched at the mutually intelligible word, pointed excitedly to the stone-still creature caked with blood.

Byrdy's hands were half a century of medical devotion. His touch was shaky, his eye uncertain, but he knew a heartbeat when he felt one. Weak, but there. He was old but he was a doctor, and had work to do.

He ignored the demented thing behind him, concentrated on saving the life that fluttered within the other chest. He knew only one thing to do. He took a syringe, stabbed the rubber top of a near-empty bottle of medicinal nitroglycerine, and watched as the liquid reached 15 cc. He had to spit on the patient to loosen the blood that covered his neck. When he thought he had found the right vein, he jabbed the needle into the neck, snapped the plunger home. The body jerked, the legs began to twitch, the eyelids flickered like a bad electric bulb.

Byrdy began massaging the chest. His hands cracked the patina of dried blood. He turned, motioned to the other intruder, tried to make him understand that he should rub the body, stimulate the circulation. He thought he understood.

Byrdy hurried back to his office. He had not saved a life since the end of the Second World War. He found a bottle of cognac in his desk, rushed – despite his age – back to the vault. The change was astounding. The dead man had opened his eyes and was talking.

"May-may-may-may-make him drink this!" Byrdy said.

"What did he say?" Shishkin asked.

"I think he wants to propose a toast," Viktor answered, still rubbing his friend's chest.

"Tell him I don't drink."

"Me tell him? Shishkin, I don't speak Polish!"

Byrdy was so stunned by what he saw that he put the bottle to his own mouth, filled it with cognac, swallowed.

"To your health!" Viktor said heartily. The words are the same in Russian and Polish.

"To-to-to-to your health," Byrdy responded automatically.

"Thanks to you!" Viktor boomed.

Byrdy had no idea what the blood-caked being had just said.

All three stared at each other. One second there was no language barrier, the next there was an unbridgeable chasm.

Viktor began to laugh. "Where the devil are we?"

Byrdy heard and understood the word "devil". He paled. He took another drink. "You say you're the de-de-de-devil? Of course. I should have known. Blessed Mary, protect me from my enemies!"

"Is he praying?" Shishkin asked.

"How are you feeling, Shishkin? We have to get out of here."

Shishkin laughed. "Out of where? And to where? We have no idea where we are!"

"What city is this?" Again the words were identical in both languages.

"If you're the devil, you should know where you are!" Byrdy said. "What kind of de-de-de-devil are you?"

"I think he's getting angry, Viktor. He keeps cursing at us. Maybe you're right. We should get out."

"I'll ask him again: What city are we in?"

"Bialystok, you're in the Fo-fo-fo-forensic Institute in Bialystok."

"What the devil are we doing in Bialystok? That's nearly twenty miles over the border." Shishkin seemed outraged that they had been transported so far off their planned course.

"It doesn't matter. Can you move? We have to get out." Viktor turned to Byrdy, and tried a friendly smile. "Thank you, doctor. Thank you very much. You saved his life."

"I am a do-do-do-doctor," said Byrdy, picking up just the one word.

The two bloodstained fugitives bowed politely and scuttled out of the room. They saw no one else until they were out of the Institute, and hurrying along the dark back streets.

Byrdy considered what to do. He carefully replaced the ends of the inside box and the crate, went back to his heated office, and with the bottle in one hand and a rosary in the other, alternately sipped and prayed, promising to keep his vow to the Blessed Virgin.

Viktor, in Poland only a few hours, had already rendered the country an invaluable service.

13

The streets began to look alike, and they argued over which was a more promising route for escape to they knew not where. To those afraid, the night conceals all things good, and tars over possibilities of deliverance with a black veil of despair. For Viktor and Shishkin, bold gestures were done with, and human realities had taken over: a broken nose, insufficient nourishment, angry lungs still smarting from air deprivation inside the box, a rasping thirst. Shishkin saw a dark store window behind which stood a pyramid of bottled water.

"How much noise could it make? One shot with my shoe, we grab as many as we can and we're gone before anyone can lift a phone to report the noise. I swear, I'll open the bottlecaps with my teeth, yours too, I'm too thirsty to keep trying to convince you, even."

Viktor kept walking. He had seen a light shining in the upstairs window of the building next to the store. It could be an insomniac, but equally the light could have been illuminating a surveillance camera focused on the doorway. This was new territory and he did not pretend to know its customs. Brash, irreverent, unpredictable Shishkin grumbled, then accepted the decision and trudged on. His experience with the law had been from a loser's end. Without Viktor, he would have given up three times already – once when they realized they needed to retrieve the air tank, again at the moment he had pulverized his nose, and most recently when they burst out of the Forensics Institute into the Polish night, and sensed that, although they were loose, they were also lost.

There is no center to Bialystok, no point where roads converge to give travellers a feeling of attainment. Streets swerve and cross, lights wink on at night because the only alternative is to be extinguished, and buildings stand erect more out of habit than purpose. The city is, by design, an outpost for the Soviet army. At midnight even ritual drunkards know it is time to hide, lest they be picked up by a patrol van. Until 1980, the Russians allowed Polish police to keep the town secure. There were scuffles, but more in the spirit of college fraternity dust-ups than hateful exchanges. Then Solidarity's message swept east from Gdansk and Warsaw, and Bialystok reacted like heated helium constrained too long by rubber. Rail lines to Moscow were blocked, and youths began to sport T-shirts that read, "Support NATO." In the surrounding countryside, dairy farmers poured their milk into the fields rather than sell it to the state cooperative. Word of these outrages reached Moscow, which responded with alacrity. A Soviet army barracks outside Bialystok had its staff doubled. Jeeps filled with snub-nosed young Siberians patrolled the city hourly. In three days, nine hundred persons were arrested on various charges of disorderliness and anti-Soviet provocations, although there is no law specifically forbidding them in Poland. That, of course, was the point that the Russians were making. Cleave to the unspoken understanding that your land is ours and our laws are yours, or we will spell out the terms more clearly. The imposition of martial law in December 1981 made further dialogue unnecessary. Since then Bialystok, subdued on the surface, had shown it could be most inhospitable to its *de facto* marshals. The arrogant teenage soldiers still prowled in jeeps, but they were warned at the beginning of their tour of duty not to go into Bialystok at night or in groups of less than four. There were rumors about Russian boys in uniform being set upon by bands of Polish no-goods. Soviet citizens are not so insulated from reality as to think that their soldiers are immune to the temptations of liquor and local girls. They heard the tales of trouble and assumed there had been minor problems, possibly some name-calling and fistfights. The spirit of Katyn lives on.

Shishkin was still calculating the chances of being caught while breaking into a store to steal water bottles. There were no public drinking fountains, and, being Russians, they would not have recognized one had they seen it. They had no money, they did not know how to ask for water at a house or a bar (none were open anyway) and Shishkin's flattened nose and the blood that was soaking their clothes marked them as undesirable and possibly dangerous characters. They were creeping through a warren of unlit streets that a city with self-respect would describe as a changing neighborhood. People in Bialystok called Warnashow a slum and tried to avoid it.

"Charming," Shishkin whispered, pointing to the body stretched across half the street. "Either he should drink less, or do it in pedestrian zones."

Viktor, whose business was knowing cars, heard one coming from behind them. "Move, fast," he said, but the motor was working quicker than his tongue. Headlights caught their silhouettes trying to melt into a fence on the right hand side of the street. "Uwaga," said a voice that seemed designed to split the night.

They were trapped on a narrow street between a corrugated iron fence and a brick building with a three-step stoop whose door was tightly closed. Viktor knew that there was no place to run, and no chance of losing the snow-white light that took away his vision.

"My friend," said Shishkin, "we gave it our best try. We have nothing to be ashamed of."

"What was that?" bawled a voice from behind the jeep's penetrating light. "Did I hear you two filthy Pollacks speaking Russian?"

Two thoughts occurred to Viktor simultaneously: first, that the patrol which had spotted them was Russian, not Polish, and second, that it was hard to believe that some people doubted the existence of a God. How could one otherwise explain the miraculous intervention that saves us from our own foolishness?

"Is possible, you Russians is?" Viktor said. "Oh, lucky I!"

"Drunks, I imagine," said the voice, which was moving out of the center of the light shaft. "Alexander Omarovich, we'll take these two in for the night."

"No, no," Viktor shouted. He was committed now; he had to go through with the hastily thought-out charade. "You no see. We friends your. All good now." He looked at Shishkin, who stared back blankly. He had not picked up the thread of the brain-scramble.

The voice, Viktor saw, belonged to a young man dressed in the olive drab of a Russian army officer, no more than in his late twenties. The single red band on his cap told Viktor he was misspeaking to a sergeant.

"I speak you true. We Poles but like much Soviet Union. We tell at work that Soviet good. Others no like Soviet. Tonight, after work, they take us, hurt plenty, look at nose my friend. They break. Then throw us out car in street. Now find us our friends." He was trying to commit enough errors to sound like a foreigner, while making sufficient sense to be understood. It was more difficult than talking to the doctor in the Forensics Institute. At least there, the incomprehension was for real.

The sergeant curled his neck back toward the jeep. "Did any of you understand that?"

"I think he was saying they were beat up because they're pro-Soviet. He sounds . . ."

"He sounds like a fucking idiot," said the sergeant, completing the thought. But he was looking with a fraction more compassion at Viktor and Shishkin, whose bloodied nose showed especially gory in the harsh car light. The sergeant was thinking that these two unfortunate Poles might be his redemption. He was twenty-two years old, in the second week of his Poland tour, and already in trouble. A few days earlier, his patrol had come upon a teenage girl walking alone. When they honked the jeep's horn, she gave them the finger. The sergeant had stopped them before they raped her, but most of her clothes were ripped beyond repair. Still defiant, the girl had reported the incident to her parish priest, who had angrily confronted the local Polish Party secretary, who had passed on the report to the Soviet barracks commander, who had given the sergeant hell and advised him that he was a hair's breadth from being sent to the Chinese border to complete his service. It all clicked over in the sergeant's mind in a few seconds and he made a command decision.

"Make room in the back of the jeep," he told his fellow soldiers. "You're coming with us," he told Viktor and Shishkin, and was amused by the looks of terror the words elicited. They understood that, all right.

"Yes, with glad, we come." It was Shishkin, finally up to speed, who barked out the broken reply. Shishkin knew there was no room for a wrong footing. The slightest hesitation would be correctly interpreted by the Soviet soldiers as meaning that these two had something to hide. Viktor, whose method was to think things through, to come to a conclusion and follow its course, had frozen for a second, and his friend had taken up the slack. They squeezed into the back seat of the jeep, ignoring the looks of distaste on the faces of the soldiers, who tried to prevent their uniforms from touching any of the blood or gore that coated Shishkin's face and hands.

It was easy to understand why the army patrol had picked them up. They encountered no other sign of human life on the ten-minute drive through the night-blackened streets. The roads became bumpier, and it seemed that they were passing trees. Neither Viktor nor Shishkin dared to speak, for fear of arousing the soldiers' suspicions that their Russian was more proficient than they made it seem. Instead, they stared at each other. Shishkin shrugged. The motion said: "What the hell, we gave it a good try. Let's see what's ahead."

The jeep's driver knew the route well. He went from thirty miles an hour in complete darkness to a full halt in two seconds.

The sergeant was supremely self-confident. "Follow me," he told them, without looking back over his shoulder to make sure they complied. Viktor and Shishkin tried to look confused, then tentatively fell into step. They were in what looked like a wooded area, but it lacked the smell of country freshness. Instead, the scent of gasoline hung over everything. Ahead, Viktor saw what in the darkness looked like the outlines of dozens of haystacks. It was not until the sergeant headed for one of them that they realized what they were. The Soviet army lived in tents when it was visiting other countries.

For the first time, the youthful Russian officer turned to them. "In there," he said, pointing firmly to ensure they understood. They hunched under the tent flap, and were immediately assaulted by new smells, which Viktor found even more unbearable than the gasoline. It was the smell of disinfectants, sterilization, rubber-topped sealed bottles, the smell of pain.

"I know just the right person to take care of you," said the sergeant, and it seemed that his eyes glinted evil madness. Viktor wondered if they could escape; his muscles tensed, then sagged with the realization that still was hard to accept: that in fleeing from the Soviet Union they had become permanent fugitives. Escape for them was an unending job.

"Ignacy Fedorovich, come here please," the sergeant's smile was a U-shaped threat. There was a rustle and a moan from the other side of the tent. A crew-cut head appeared over a row of canvas bags, and began to rise. "I figured you'd be taking your nap," said the sergeant. "Can't you stay awake for the few hours a week you're on duty? You're a complete incompetent. Fix this asshole's nose, he managed to get it broken in a fight." The sergeant was using idioms and slang. He turned and said, slowly, "This is a doctor. He will help you. When he is done, come and find me. I want to know your names, so I can make my report on how we found you and took care of you. Good-bye for now." And waving as if to two children, he left the tent, already planning how he would record his kind gesture to two Polish comrades.

Ignacy Fedorovich appeared to be the sergeant's junior by a year or two. But his epaulet bore a cadusis and, once awake, his manner was professional. Without a word, he plugged a stethoscope into his ears, and checked both their heartbeats. "Good, good," he mumbled reassuringly as he listened to Viktor's chest. After examining Shishkin, however, he frowned and grunted: "A bit faint." He extended both arms straight out, and pointed his hands at a chair near the pile of canvas bags where he had been sleeping. He said something to Shishkin and smiled. Shishkin looked at him as though the doctor had commented on weather conditions on Venus. With sudden alarm, Viktor realized what was happening: the doctor was trying to speak Polish. He nearly laughed at the idiocy of it. Was this what Poland was about: a series of doctors jabbering meaninglessly at them while they gaped in stupefaction?

"Dear comrade doctor, my friend was beaten up because we are friends of the Soviet Union. The least we can do is continue to speak Russian while you treat his injuries." Damn, he thought, even before he was done speaking; that was much too difficult a sentence for non-native speakers, and much better than I spoke to the sergeant.

The doctor looked at him suspiciously. "Yes, all right. It's easier for me, of course. I must say, you do speak Russian very well. I'd been told that most Poles take the obligatory six years of Russian language in school, then do their best to forget it."

Shishkin, unable to stay silent any longer, cut in: "My friend and I believe that learning in itself is never wrong; it is only important that it be put to the proper use." That sounded pompous even to Viktor, who looked at Shishkin as if he had just displayed a mouthful of masticated peas.

The doctor, too, was flustered, or else still sleepy. "Well, as I was saying, sit down here and we'll see what can be done for that face."

Shishkin looked like a boy in the dentist's chair for his first filling. In his experience, the job of men wearing uniforms was to inflict pain. He shied from the doctor's touch, grimaced at the application of alcohol to clean his face of caked blood, and grabbed the doctor's wrist when he saw a silver-colored implement being guided toward his injured nose.

"Please, friend, I can't help you if you won't let me touch you." The doctor seemed quite accustomed to squeamish patients and Viktor wondered if this was confirmation of the sergeant's opinion of his medical talent. But whether or not he knew his art, the doctor possessed a quality that was probably more important: he made his patient believe everything was going fine. "A very good sign," he exclaimed, when he inserted the tiny gauze-covered nasal spatula nearly three inches. "No problem here," he commented as he performed the first of several painful twists of the spatula handle. "Excellent," he enthused when he applied balsa wood splints to each side of the nose with the spatula still inside to prevent the cartilage from collapsing.

"That wasn't too bad, was it?" he said, tearing off the adhesive tape that held the splints in place.

Shishkin, smarting intensely from the procedure, was ready to spit out: "Fuck your mother, you oaf, it was awful," but managed to keep his lips clenched during the second of temptation. Instead he replied: "May I have some water?"

"I suppose so. You'll have to go to the mess tent and ask for it, though."

"Oh, never mind then." Viktor struck like a rattlesnake. "We can wait until we're home." He felt Shishkin's hot glare but kept his eyes on the doctor, who was replacing his instruments.

"I've put some gauze in the nasal lining to staunch any further bleeding. Come back tomorrow and I'll change it. Otherwise it might become infected."

"Thank you, thank you, we certainly will," said Viktor. "Good bye."

"Uh, didn't the sergeant say he wanted to see you? I'll take you over to his tent."

"No, that's not necessary," Viktor said quickly. "You must be very tired, doctor, just tell us where it is."

A sheepish smile spread over the medical man's face. "To tell the truth, I'm bushed. I've found a little side action while I'm here. Blonde, still in her teens, and ready to do anything. Wow, if the Pope had met this one, he'd have never become a priest. Turn left, go down three tents, and the guard will stop you. The sergeant will probably send you home in one of our jeeps. And make sure you come back to see me tomorrow."

They carefully replaced the doctor's tent flap so he could not follow their movements. Without a word or a glance passing between them they both turned right and walked as fast as possible.

"You blew it," Shishkin hissed. His voice contained a new honking timbre, no doubt the result of having gauze stuffed up his nose. Viktor hoped it was mildly painful and would make him think before speaking.

"I know, Shishkin."

"The doctor's going to tell the sergeant about us and . . ."

"I know, Shishkin."

". . . they'll track us down."

"First of all, keep walking. We have to get away from here. Second, you sound like a goose. Third, if you say one more word to me, I'm going to push that cloth the rest of the way up your nose with my shoes."

"Wasn't that what Doctor Lothario was using?"

The morning was dawning before their eyes. Viktor had seen many sun-ups, usually because he had worked through the night, sometimes because those hours had been spent carousing. He had watched some days that were born to brilliant light, others that rose from a grave of mist and rain, a few that were indistinguishable from the night, so hard was the snowfall. But never, thought Viktor, had he seen a dawn like this one: a dawn that spilled over the borders of the Union of Soviet Socialist Republics.

"So it really does shine here too." The words matched Viktor's thoughts precisely, but it was Shishkin who had spoken them. The Soviet camp was, as they had suspected, shrouded deep in pine woods, whose trees divided the sunrise into thousands of vertical spines. If the trees robbed the dawn of some of its majesty they added at least as much in their multiplication of it. Through every pair of trees, Viktor and Shishkin saw red-orange fire as they picked a path through the woods.

Viktor knew that because the sun was directly in front of them they were walking east, back toward the Soviet Union. But that threat (for the first time ever the prospect of being in his own country was a threat) seemed to Viktor less menacing than the hive of Russian infantrymen that they were abandoning.

It took Shishkin longer to remember where the sun rises and where it sets, and he took the news badly. "For Christ's sake, man, let's turn around while there's still time. If we get too close to the border, we'll be stopped, maybe by our own kind."

"Who do you think we're walking away from. Fijians?"

"I know, I know, but when someone's had his elbow up your nose you think of him as family. And of his friends as yours."

"Either you're stupid from loss of blood, or just stupid. Either way, we're not going back."

"Well, I'm not going any further east. I've been through too much to get here, Viktor."

"Yes, so I've heard. I'm certainly glad I rented a car and drove here to meet you."

"I tell you, I'm not going any further. You can do what you want. And another thing I just remembered; who the hell are you to decide I don't need water?" The voice had taken on an edge of abrasion.

Because he too was exhausted, dehydrated and scared, Viktor forgot what a complicated piece of mental machinery Shishkin was, and spoke as he might have to Anna during one of her rare displays of bad temper.

"I think there's been enough discussion. It's important to think things out before doing them. I've thought this out. I don't think you have. Now let's get going."

Shishkin looked as though he'd been spat upon. "You son of a bitch. You're no better than any of the others. All smiles and jokes as long as you're getting your way. But the minute someone disagrees with you, it's bullying and commands. That won't work with me, comrade." His mouth locked tight and his arms crossed, Shishkin sank, majestically, on to the pine-needle carpet of the woods, and crossed his arms.

Gogol might have authored the scene. In a stage whisper Viktor asked: "Don't you want to be free? We can't just sit here and wait for the Polish boy scouts to guide us. We've got to keep moving." Shishkin turned his face away; away from Viktor, away from the steadily bulging sunrise, away from the east. Viktor looked at the peaceful rustic scene around them, and felt as though some unseen predator was gaining ground on them. He was feeling stronger instincts than he had in years, and those senses told him: run.

"Yevgeny Moisovich, what are we quarreling about? Not principles, only method. You object to getting any closer to the border than we have to, and I understand that."

"Really? Then you were doing an excellent parody of ignorance."

"Let me finish. I understand, but we're exposed here far too much to justify the precaution you want to take. As soon as we figure out where we are, and our chances are greater of getting help from someone versus being arrested again, I promise you, we'll turn our backs to the east. Yevgeny, we're friends."

Shishkin's face was turned at such an angle that Viktor could not see his expression. But there was no missing the shudder that radiated from his spine across both shoulders. "I thought we were, too," he said in a small, hurt voice.

It was a moment of decision. Was friendship or freedom what he had come here for? Both of course, but which would he sacrifice, now that the choice was upon him? He told himself that he had not made a choice between freedom and family, that both were still possible, that his escape from Russia was a tactical retreat in order to rescue his beloved Marya and even more beloved Anna. And it was the thought of them, finally, that gave him the physical will to take the first step away from Shishkin. The steps did not become easier, but once he had set his direction, he was able to continue by momentum.

"Yevgeny, come with me!"

The obstinate head did not even acknowledge the noise.

"Then, let me tell you this. You are my friend, and nothing can change that. God go with you, Yevgeny."

In two minutes of walking he could no longer see Shishkin. Here, at last, was what he had always feared most; he was out of Russia, away from Russians. Is there any better definition of alone? Poland, that blighted little neighbor of which he had heard so much now seemed immense, and insensitively open-spaced. He reached a dirt road leavened with the occasional scrap of macadam and wondered whether to turn left or right. Left seemed to lead uphill; right sloped downward. Enough of taking the easy way out, he told himself and began the ascent.

Forty minutes later, he had no better idea of where he was going. Is the rest of the world like this, or only Poland? Blank stretches of passive mystery, of boring conundrum? He sat down by the road, not over-worried whether or not he might be seen. What would be harmful in a little cross-cultural chat? He remembered the frustrating conversation he had not had with Dr Byrdy, and answered his own question. He did not want to talk to Poles. He desired Shishkin's company. Tetchy as he was, he was Russian and at that moment Viktor could think of no higher compliment.

He turned his back to the hills, toward the open road and lonely travel. He wanted company, even if it smelled bad.

Perhaps it was going downhill, but he felt lighter of foot returning. He wondered if Shishkin would still be pouting and tried to decide how stern to be.

Within a few hundred feet of where they had parted an hour earlier, Viktor paused, like a retriever, with one foot poised in the air. He had heard something. Animal? No. Shishkin? Same thing. A second later he was diving out of the pathway, grasping at the loose earth and looking for cover. The noise was that of a motor. He heard the engine growl closer, then suddenly, it idled. When he saw birds flying overhead, he decided it was safe to come out. He ran back to where he had left Shishkin. The path was still surrounded by verdant living things, but it had been stripped clean of friends.

It was impossible to tell that a stubborn Russian Jew with a broken nose had ever sat there. The pine needles had made a respectful circle around a bare spot where he had plopped down in peevish disagreement, but there were no signs of the struggle he must have put up when they took him. That was it, then. It would not have taken them long to work out what had happened once they discovered that the Rabbi's exit permission had been used to ship a coffin to Poland. He was beginning to feel sorry for the old man again, when it occurred to him there was a better object for his sympathy.

About one thing, Viktor was beginning to think that Shishkin had been right: his mouth and throat were so dry that the mere intake of breath felt like heavy-grade sandpaper being stroked against his lungs. He did not think he could walk any further without water. All these trees and weeds look perfectly happy with the moisture they've been given, he told himself. What makes you so delicate? He remembered idly how in the Moscow Zoo (it was on another trip with Anna) he noticed that the animals whose natural habitat was in the woods had no water troughs. Instead, they were given bunches of leaves, which they chewed as contentedly as a Peruvian shepherd munched on coca. His body acted on its own without asking the brain to send a command. He grabbed the lowest branch of the greenest tree he could reach, a birch, and stripped its young fresh leaves in a single motion. Most fell to the ground but the ones he held on to he jammed into his mouth. Whatever moisture the leaves contained was negligible compared to the unexpectedly strong rush of chlorophyll that made him gag and spit more saliva than he thought he had in his body at the moment. The taste was so vile that he wondered for a moment how such a substance could be the basis of life for the entire plant world. Had Viktor known what chewing-gum was (it is not sold in the Soviet Union) he would have realized that the leaves had had a similar effect on his body's digestive system. By stimulating his mouth with any new taste, he had created saliva and so felt refreshed, albeit also slightly sickened.

He forgot how he felt when the woods behind him came to life. This is not a nature outing, he told himself (although how wonderful it would be for Anna to see this, and for Marya to breathe deeply and smell nothing of the factory where she worked). He showed the animal's evasive tactics that hunted men learn. He moved slowly at first, directly away from what he thought was the source of the noise. But as he moved, he was aware that since his unusual welcome to Poland in the Bialystok Forensics Institute, he had reacted slower to each succeeding crisis: the Soviet patrol had managed to pick them up, the sergeant and the doctor had momentarily confused him, and, most seriously just a few minutes earlier, he had failed to save Shishkin from whoever was bearing down on them. His reaction time was becoming longer as his sleep-, food- and water-starved body protested, and his mind became weaker and more primitive. I am regressing, Viktor told himself as he moved faster. I am becoming a woods creature, that claws and bites, that clings to shadows for protection and skitters away from noises that might bring unwanted intrusions by man.

The sound came closer, but in an uneven sort of rhythm: a clump, a treading upon grass and leaves, pause, another clump. It was an unusual enough sound for Viktor to want to know what it was. Also, it did not sound as dangerous as he had first believed. He suspected that the Soviet army, in pursuit of a wanted enemy of the state, would not sound like this. He sought cover behind a thick pine tree. It was amazing, he thought to himself, how many places there are to hide; all that is really needed is sufficient determination not to be caught and fear of what will happen if you are. Then, in the flash it took to fashion that profound formulation, he knew what he was hiding from. So we've exported that as well, he thought.

The man seemed to have a solid idea of where he wanted to go, it was only that his legs refused to cooperate. He was guiding himself by leaning to one side or another, then trying to adjust for any excess by lurching back in the other direction. He clutched the bottle in the way a high-wire artist uses a balance pole. The vodka that he swigged was the best kind: purloined, and even better, it came from his place of employment. Piotr Kolewicz was of the firm conviction that the directors of an organization that tried to enforce a rule against drinking on the job should set an example by donating their personal stores of alcohol. When he found out that the chairman of the Eastern Regional headquarters of the Polish United Workers Party had secreted several crates of Wyborowa Premium in his office, Kolewicz undertook a personal crusade to help that gentleman avoid an embarrassing situation. Imagine the scandal, he told himself foggily, if someone other than I should find that vodka. He veered to the left too far and thrust the bottle to his right just in time to avoid a head-on meeting with a shivering conifer.

PRON was an acronym in Polish, a language which delights in creating new words by turning old ones inside out. Officially it stood for the Patriotic Council for National Salvation, and was intended to unite Poles who belonged to the Communist Party with those who did not in the job of making the country work. Unfortunately for its founders, PRON required the alteration of only one letter to spell out a particularly vulgar Polish expression meaning limp prick. It took only about two weeks for that variation to become the standard way of referring to PRON. Kolewicz was the janitor in the Bialystok office, a branch of PRON that had received an especially tepid response from the surrounding community. Because of this failure to attract support, its funding by the government had been cut severely, and Kolewicz was told that he need not report to work the next week. He therefore believed, correctly, that he had little to lose by pilfering as much from the director's office as he could. Those vodka bottles he could not carry, he had lined up neatly in a path from the director's office to the front door. He was fairly certain his message would be understood. He had drunk one liter as he walked out of Bialystok during the apogee of the wind-chilled night. In six hours he had covered ten miles and convinced himself that he was a national hero on the order of Marshal Pilsudski. It had, after all, been damned daring of him not only to steal the vodka that he was carrying both in his pockets and his bladder, but also to implicate the director. Because any act that embarrassed PRON reflected badly on the Polish government, which in turn, would not please the Russians. Like nearly every Pole, Kolewicz wanted to shame and enrage the bastards that had their grip on his country's throat. Beyond that swipe at authority and the inebriation he was now enjoying as a reward, he had not planned. What was the worst that could happen? He might be forced to return to work.

He heard the movement of the hand before it gripped his neck and in almost the same instant that he felt its force, he smelled its odor: a combination of old sweat and crushed grass or leaves. Another hand swooped down and covered his mouth, which, inconveniently, he had just filled. He gagged, but there was no exit for the vodka and bile that now competed for space in his throat. Panicky as a claustrophobic in a sauna, Kolewicz began twisting his body in different directions with erratic force, but the hands only closed tighter. He heard what at first sounded like a forest animal's warning call, but by the fifth repetition he realized that it was a human voice that was urging him: "Tikha, tikha." He had lived in Bialystok all his life, on the border of the Soviet Union and knew enough Russian to understand the word for "quiet" when he heard it. His heart pulsed hard enough against his ribcage for him to feel it. He wondered, like a man before the firing-squad, two things simultaneously: how they had caught him so quickly and how much what they were going to do to him would hurt. The hand over his mouth loosened for an instant. A stream of alcohol and stomach acid jetted past the fingers, followed by Kolewicz's violent voice: "Bloodsuckers, filth of the earth. Do whatever you want to me! I'm not afraid!" He punctuated the declaration by trembling from his shoulders down and vomiting again.

Viktor had no idea what the man was saying, not only because it was in Polish, but also because Kolewicz was slapping each word into the next as though they were eggs for an omelette. It did not sound friendly, but that was not surprising considering that Viktor had leapt upon an apparently innocent hiker as if he were an opponent in a sumo wrestling match. He waited respectfully until the heaving stopped, then composed his face in as friendly a pattern as he could and said, slowly: "I am sorry I surprised you but I am in trouble. I need help, friend."

Kolewicz understood the last two words, which were the same in Polish: "pomesh" and "droog". He looked blankly, meanwhile thinking, how and why would this son of Stalin think he can help me? Viktor did not appear to be in a position of much influence. His face was streaked red (blood), brown (dirt and dried sweat) and green (leaves). He was shivering convulsively, having spent a chilly night in the Polish countryside without a coat. His eyes had a glazed-over patina, as if hot sugar had been dripped on them. Most telling to Kolewicz was the fact that his attacker had not only loosened his grip but was now standing two respectful steps away and had stretched both his rock-hard hands in front of him, palms up, a sign of supplication. Without considering why, he burst out laughing. "By the Virgin, first I steal the boss's vodka, make a fool out of him and the rest of those slugs, and by morning, I've got a dirty-faced Russian offering me assistance. Now that's comradeship!"

Viktor began to laugh too. The man was drunk, he knew, and probably as befuddled as he himself was, but at least he was acting amiably, and that made a change. "You know, friend, yours is the first smiling face I've

seen in Poland, at least the first smiling Polish face. It's a pleasant sight."
Neither understood more than ten per cent of what the other was saying,
of course; a common word, the familiar ring of a country or nationality
penetrated the barrier. But it did not matter. Like a suspected criminal
with police rifles trained on him, Viktor reached out slowly, tentatively,
and ranged his arm over Kolewicz's shoulders. The Pole never stopped
talking thereafter. Twice he decided to test Viktor by constructing
complicated sentences that called into question his mother's chastity on
her wedding night. Viktor grinned as though someone had just compli-
mented his singing voice and genially explained that Poland was every bit
as awful as he had suspected. He did not, however, volunteer the reason
for his being there; would not have, had his listener been only three
months old. They began walking.

"Do you know which way we are going, Piotr?"

"Ha-ha, yes, yes, I agree."

"You do? Good, because I don't."

"Ha-ha, yes."

"If you were in Moscow and were lost, I'd be able to help you.
Otherwise, I'm not much use anywhere in the world."

"I like your voice, Viktor. It sounds as though you've done a few
criminal things in your time, but not been caught at them. That bespeaks
character in my opinion."

"I'm scared to death. Not so much for myself but for my family. I have a
wife and daughter. They're in trouble too. Are you married?"

"You can't possibly understand how much we hate you Russians. You
know how your government is always lamenting over the twenty million
people you lost in the last Great War? Do you know the toll that was
taken in Poland? On a per capita basis, our losses were three times as great
as yours. And many of them were caused by the Russians. My father, an
uncle and his entire family were wiped out during the great so-called
liberation of Warsaw. You look too young to have fought in that war, and
I was only a kid when it ended, but hatred can be passed from one
generation to the next, like a watch. And both measure the passage of
time."

"You look like a factory worker, Piotr, not just the way you're dressed
but the lines in your face say you've never been in a good restaurant. But
there's something flowing about the way you talk. Not that I understand
it, of course, but there's a fluency about you that I like. What a shame we
can't communicate."

"Yes, indeed. And I bet you do unnatural things with dogs, don't you?"

By the time they had reached the end of the forest, they liked each other genuinely. The bond was sealed when they were walking along the road for ten minutes and a truck lumbered up from behind. Viktor, walking on the left, looked over his right shoulder; Kolewicz fired a glance over his left. Their fields of vision intersected; each saw in the other the momentary sense of panic, replaced by steeled resistance. Viktor made for the culvert on the side of the road, a place he had hoped it would not be necessary to fling himself. It smelled. With a spare motion of his head quicker than a nod, Kolewicz indicated that he understood and approved of Viktor's hiding, and that he was going to find out who was driving the truck.

The culvert smelled like an overflowed toilet. Viktor realized why when he saw a small pyramid of feces near where he had pitched himself. Animal or Pole? he asked himself, trying to imagine Shishkin's response, or poor Pronsky's, envisioning instead The Blob's sagging incomprehension of the difference.

The truck's motor was criminally inefficient, its pistons missed every third time. Viktor knew this without seeing it, while his nose, a few inches from the turd pile, was already picking up whiffs of the truck's wasted diesel, raw as a slattern's scent. He winced when he heard the brake shoes scraping against bare metal pads, one of the signs of neglect that identified a state-owned vehicle as surely as its registration. Before he could ask himself why the truck was stopping, he heard Kolewicz shouting something in greeting. Viktor forgot the odor of both the excrement and the diesel. What was Kolewicz saying to the driver of the truck? Once again he was entrusting his fate, and more important, his freedom, to someone he scarcely knew. What qualified Kolewicz as trustworthy? He had no idea what the man's happy chatter was about, would not have known what PRON was if it had been explained to him (what does it matter what non-Party members think about the situation in a Communist country?), and once it had been, would hardly have been cheered to hear that someone just fired (and presumably looking for a way to win back his job) had the capacity now to turn in a renegade Russian. Viktor was forgetting, temporarily, that Kolewicz could not understand him either, but that would not make it any easier to explain his presence in Poland if he was apprehended.

The questions that people examine thoroughly in their minds are either meaningless or those things beyond remedy: which overcoat to buy, whether another person might have made a better spouse. Decisions that should be analyzed are often made in the flash that it takes a message from the brain to reach a nerve ending and initiate a response by the muscles. Kolewicz shouted Viktor's name as though he hoped to hear it echo back;

Viktor was on his feet and trotting toward the truck before he thought to ask himself if this might be his last minute of freedom.

Kolewicz was wearing a smile, but it was not reassuring. Viktor thought that the Pole looked like a man who has just heard a mousetrap snap shut in his attic. His left hand traced rapid circles in the air that moved toward his chest. Viktor pretended for a second not to understand, while he asked himself: should I run? I've always relied on myself, not others. The answer was discouraging: that may be why you are faced with a choice between trusting strangers or flailing about blindly on your own. He knew he was making the right decision because he had none to make. He put a sudden smile of comprehension on his face and jogged toward Kolewicz who was climbing into the rumbling truck.

If a snake could take human form, Viktor imagined it would resemble the driver of the truck. His eyes were liquid poured into slits, the skin on his cheeks looked as though it would make crinkling noises when he chewed. Kolewicz, seated in the middle of the truck's cabin, was going through the pointless ritual of making introductions. Viktor was sure he heard his own name being badly pronounced, but had no idea if he had been told the driver's identity (he had, but he did not recognize Slowomir as a name). Before he had to decide whether to extend his hand, the driver had jammed the truck into first gear so noisily that Viktor wondered whether he had first depressed the clutch. The vehicle lurched about two yards before the engine died. Kolewicz smiled and lifted his shoulders apologetically, as if it were his wife at the wheel. The driver hissed something so vulgar that Kolewicz's brows wrinkled while his mouth made an "O" of distaste and reproach. The man flicked the key, back and forth, the engine burped and died twice. Viktor had seen this kind of driver before: if the machinery under the hood failed, he punished it, as though he were strapping a child with a belt. On the third try, he allowed enough diesel into the carburetor to bring the truck to life. They jolted forward again.

Kolewicz was excited, as if they'd been fortunate enough to be picked up by one of his relatives. But Viktor noticed that the two remaining bottles of vodka were now wedged between the driver and the truck's left door. In return for two bottles of good vodka, some Moscow taxi-drivers would travel to Leningrad in the winter; he wondered how far Kolewicz had managed to bargain their passage.

The answer was quick in coming. At first, Kolewicz tried to make small talk with the driver, who ignored him. When they had been rumbling along for about twenty minutes, Viktor saw a point of white in the middle distance, jutting up from over a rise in the road. As they approached, it loomed higher. It took him two full minutes to realize that it was a church steeple. That was not surprising, since the few churches that he had seen in Russia were Orthodox, and anyway were not inclined to advertise that they were in the deity-worshipping business.

"Suchowola," Kolewicz said. Viktor wondered if he should say something in response, like "I hope not," or "Bless you." They passed a dirty white sign with one word printed on it. Viktor, of course, could not read its Latin letters. "Suchowola," Kolewicz said again, pointing. Viktor imagined that that was the Polish word for sign and nodded matter-of-factly. He had no desire to learn Polish at all, much less word by word. On both sides of the truck, houses began to sprout, lashed black by airborne dirt. When they passed the church at last, Viktor was impressed. It was twice the size of any he had seen in his own country, not counting, of course, the Patriarch's cathedral or the three former churches that stood behind the Kremlin Wall and were now used to pry dollars out of tourists. This church was built not only to inspire, but to last. Viktor took in the building's solid gray stone front, and noted with instant appreciation the spacious yard that ran from the church to a wrought-iron fence some thirty yards away. He could not imagine that a church had been permitted to keep actual property, especially in fertile farmland like this. Kolewicz saw the look in Viktor's eyes. "Saint Peter's and Paul's," he announced. The names were the same in Russian, and Viktor knew that churches were named after saints. This was nothing like the majestic cathedral of St Peter and Paul in Leningrad, of course, but he could easily believe it was used more often to worship God.

The driver knew his way around. He made turns with the careless confidence of a resident, never once bothering to use his directional signal. He drove, Viktor decided, like a Soviet apparatchik, or at least someone who had enough blat – influence – to ignore traffic regulations. Viktor looked over at the snake eyes with reinforced antipathy.

They never completed the final turn. The truck's tires squealed and it veered to the right so that its cab was at a forty-five-degree angle to both the street they had been on and the one on to which they were pointed. The brakes were slammed on so hard the engine died. Kolewicz jabbed Viktor in the left side and flicked his hand toward the door. "Out." It was the tone of warder to inmate, the tone the Russian lieutenant had used (was that only a few hours ago?). Everything coalesced in Viktor's brain: the chance encounter, the coincidental approach of the truck, the driver's eyes and nonchalant driving, the new bark in Kolewicz's voice. He had been taken in by it all, like some rube from a Ukrainian farm family visiting Moscow for the first time.

As soon as he touched the pavement, he began to run back down the street from which the truck had last turned. He heard Kolewicz shout a long word, or maybe words, and in the next second, he saw a broom handle dart from a doorway in front of his knees. He barely had time to get his hands up to break his sprawl. The air whooshed out of him as his chest and stomach made violent contact with the pavement and he was left feeling strangely at peace. He did not think he had been hurt, but there was no point in getting up. He heard two sets of feet running up to him. Kolewicz grabbed his right arm, the snake hefted him from the left. All the length of the street, Kolewicz kept up an angry, loud harangue. Viktor thought he heard the word "zloty". Why would the secret police talk about money, least of all worthless Polish currency? Why, for that matter, would secret police talk at all?

In no time at all they were rounding the corner again. As soon as they were out of view of the main street, Kolewicz slapped the back of Viktor's head, hard. He shoved his face to within two inches of Viktor's and hissed something, at the same time tapping the right side of his own head with his index finger. The snake was several paces ahead of them, and when his head stopped smarting, Viktor saw that he was opening a door on the left side of the street with a set of keys. He was becoming more confused. The secret police normally do not have to let themselves into their own headquarters with keys. But when Kolewicz shoved him through the door, it felt exactly as it had when he was sent sprawling into the interrogation room at Lubyanka. This time he kept his footing, but that was about the only difference. He had no doubt that he was once again a prisoner.

The room had a few chairs, a folding cot on which were piled some blankets. In one corner was a noisy refrigerator whose motor needed cleaning. The sink next to it dripped. Kolewicz stood between him and the door, arms folded, shaking his head. He and the snake conferred for several moments, and Viktor suddenly felt an awful urge to do something, sweep the floor, adjust the points of the truck, to be of use somehow. He wanted this over with. The snake nodded and went out the door, and Viktor could hear him locking it again from the outside. Viktor dashed for a drink of water at the sink.

"Look," he started to tell Kolewicz, "if you're in the secret police, you probably speak Russian. Stop pretending that you don't." But Kolewicz fixed him with the kind of look he might have given a dog yapping excitedly about something it smelled in the air. He looked weary, and Viktor remembered how drunk he had been (could that have been playacting?). Kolewicz went to the cot, threw one of the blankets at

Viktor, took another one himself and went back to the door. He pointed to the cot meaningfully. Viktor stared back. With the exasperation of a pantomimist reduced to giving clues, Kolewicz slapped the palms of his hands together parallel to the floor, put his left cheek on to the knuckles of his right hand, closed his eyes and snored.

"Sleep?" Viktor asked.

Whether or not he understood, Kolewicz nodded heavily, then pointed to his chest. He stretched out in front of the door, put the blanket over him carelessly and within seconds was breathing deeply and rhythmically.

Nothing computed. What kind of captor went to sleep a few steps away from his unbound prisoner? Should he stave in Kolewicz's head with one of the chairs, batter down the door, and try again to escape? The question "To where?" kept rattling through his mind until it became an answer. Viktor took the blanket that had been tossed at him, lay down on the floor, covered himself and, within a minute, he too was deep into black slumber.

As soon as he heard the metallic scratching at the door, Viktor crossed the room and gently poked Kolewicz. The Pole came awake loudly, but instantly. Viktor winked, trying to recreate whatever bonds of trust there had been between them. Kolewicz was standing up, and had tossed the blanket into a corner when the door grudgingly gave way. Light swept through the room and it occurred to Viktor simultaneously that the one window had been heavily curtained and that outside, the rest of the world was probably halfway through this day.

The man who came in was short – no more than five feet six inches – and had a huge dark brown mustache that curled down both sides of his mouth and under his chin. The mustache jiggled on its own as he spoke in a low voice to Kolewicz for a moment.

"Viktor what?" he said. Viktor stared back.

"Your first name is Viktor. What is your patronymic?" He was speaking Russian, fast and fluently.

"Nikolaich."

"All right, Viktor Nikolaich. Let's get one thing straight right off. You did a stupid thing trying to run away. Don't do it again. Got it?"

"Yes."

"Did you think Piotr and Slawomir were with the SB?"

"Is that the secret police?"

"Yes. Didn't you know that?"

"No."

"Then you're obviously not from the KGB."

"Me, from the KGB?" Viktor let out his first genuine laugh since getting into the casket. "That's a safe assumption. Why do you speak Russian so well?"

This was ignored. "Second thing. If I catch you lying to me, we're going to throw you out and let you find your own way. That should be proof enough that we're not SB."

"Who are you then?"

"Jesus, you Russians are thick. Sometimes I find it impossible to believe that you actually control half this continent."

"I can understand that feeling, since your country happens to be part of our half." Viktor worried that once again he had spoken without thinking, but the heavy mustache bounced up and down, framing a laugh.

"Well said. And perceptive. Please feel free to be equally entertaining for the rest of our chat."

"With due respect, friend" – he was careful not to use comrade – "I think I'd like to know a bit about you, and your friends."

"Then you'd be in good company."

"Where am I?"

The mustache dropped into vertical pillars on each side of the mouth. "You really don't know?"

For one second, Viktor grew very tense. "I'm not back in the Soviet Union, am I?"

"By Christ's cross, I hope not. Because if you are, Piotr, Slowomir and I are in for a bad time of it. No, Viktor Nikolaich, you're in Suchowola, about twelve miles from the Soviet border. But still, thanks be to our maker, Poland."

Viktor let out his breath slowly. "Good."

"I believe you. It's my weakness, putting faith in first impressions and emotions. But it's too late to change. So I'll tell you, Viktor Nikolaich, something that may ease your mind, or may scare the hell out of you. My name is Mikhail. I speak Russian because my mother was Ukrainian and wanted me to learn Russian as well as Polish and her native tongue. I'm very smart. Which is why I was elected Suchowola chairman of Solidarity back in 1980. You've heard of Solidarity, I hope."

"Yes. But it no longer exists."

Mikhail laughed again. "And there's no unemployment in your country, right?"

"You're saying Solidarity does exist?"

"Since the bastards found out they needed us."

"I didn't know. What do you mean?"

"Viktor Nikolaich, you were very lucky to have – if I understand it correctly – attacked Piotr. He decided that you might be exactly what you are – a Russian trying to escape from your own country. Correct me if I'm wrong, please."

"It's more complicated than that."

"Yes, I'm sure, it always is. You think you're the first Russian who realized Poland was smack in the way of his progress to the West?"

"But what started this was – "

"You can tell me that later."

"If I skip that part, then nothing else makes sense."

"Nothing makes sense anyway, Viktor. Didn't you know that?"

"I'm learning quickly."

They talked easily. Mikhail brought Viktor up-to-date on Solidarity's amazing return from near obliteration, when martial law was declared in 1981, its relegalization and new starring role as sponsor of any and all opponents of Communism in the elections of 1989. Solidarity, said Mikhail with more than a touch of immodesty, was the future of Poland. Things would change now that it had a role in governing. Viktor remembered hearing much the same when Gorbachev came to power.

Viktor spoke carefully about Gorbachev and what he was doing in the Soviet Union. He could tell Mikhail had hoped for a more optimistic appraisal. He explained how he had been caught in the sticky web of militia attacks and KGB counter-measures. It brought the first interruption from Mikhail.

"Describe the man who passed you the note inside the embassy."

"I can't. I hardly saw him."

"Would you recognize him again?"

"You mean if someone came up from behind me, pushed something into my hand, muttered for a second and disappeared? Oh yes. How could I make a mistake about such a thing?"

Mikhail ignored the testiness. But his questions thereafter were more pointed, more like interrogation than conversation.

"How well do you know this Shishkin? Any chance that, if he has been taken, he would betray you?"

Viktor had to think and that made him ashamed. More in hope than certainty he said no.

"Ah-me, oh-my, you Russians! You think you're the only people on earth who understand loyalty. Your poets write about the Russian spirit as though they'd actually seen one." Mikhail was talking more to himself than to Viktor.

"My friend," Mikhail began, and Viktor, as always, was less than happy to hear someone else use his favorite form of salutation. "Either you are being used, or you are using me, or someone is using us both. And right now, Solidarity can't afford that kind of problem. Do you understand what I am saying?"

"Do you understand what you are saying?" Viktor did not know what was going to come out of his mouth, but he trusted the inner instincts that had seen him this far. "Put me back out on the streets, Mikhail, and I will somehow find my way to safety. I didn't ask for your help. I'm not even sure I want it. But don't get in my way, please."

"Spoken like a true, crazy-ass Russian. All right, Viktor, you've made your point. But you're wrong about one thing. You do need help. I can't get you out of Poland, but I sure as hell can help you escape from Suchowola. We'll have dinner first, Viktor. And then I'll take you to a wonderful place, the very best place on earth."

"Thanks, no. I just came from Moscow."

"The very best place, I said. Warsaw, Viktor, Warsaw."

14

He was Mikhail only until Viktor began telling stories. Then he quickly became Misha and the miles to Warsaw melted. He had not worked hard to convince Misha he was telling the truth. The look in his eyes when he explained what had happened to Marya made his listener reach out a supportive arm. When he described Shishkin's disappearance, Misha shook his head and muttered: "Damn obstinate people."

"Jews?" Viktor asked, ready to defend his friend.

"Russians." To this there was no answer.

The five hours from Bialystok were filled with tales that illustrated the pettiness of Party rule, the meaningless regulations that turned a hard-enough life into an existence tinged with resentment and fear. The stories sounded familiar enough: bribes and bravado, insincere smiles and impotent rage. Viktor recognized the scenarios, only the characters and their odd-sounding names were foreign to him. But, by the time they could see the pall of smog over Warsaw, Viktor had discerned another difference. His stories inevitably ended with a wan smile, a shoulder shrug and the barked "Shto dyelets?" – What can you do? – that substitutes for an outright admission of the futility of resistance. Misha's anecdotes followed the same trail of illogic and bureaucratic buffoonery. His epilogues, however, were grim-faced declarations that, with Solidarity again legal and functioning, things would change. At first, Viktor, thinking that he was expected to respond, used formula phrases like: "Sure, the same year winter ends in March," or "That's as obvious as the dimple on Lenin's chin." As Misha's litany of lament went on, he realized that his companion was in earnest.

"You don't really believe you're going to make things different, do you?"

Misha's silence shouted his answer.

He had vaguely hoped that Warsaw might resemble Moscow enough to remedy his feeling of total displacement. As in his own city, the outskirts of the Polish capital were little more than farmland, occasionally interrupted by clumps of houses. But when they began winding through the curving streets, he found no comfort. Wola, the industrial section in the east through which they passed, looked like a crazyquilt of merging and diverging alleyways. Factory noises emanated from the high buildings on either side of the car; pedestrians moved in herds, clattering over the crosswalks like bison, daring oncoming traffic to exercise its right to thoroughfare.

"Where are the militia?"

"The ones around here are probably busy shaking down the black market tsars."

"The what?"

Misha smiled into the middle-distance. "People who sell car parts, small appliances, things stolen from the factories."

"The police know about it and let it go on?"

"The ones who want to make some extra dollars do."

"The police take dollars?"

"Ah, Viktor, talking to you is like taking my daughter to the circus and watching her eyes go wide every thirty seconds." Misha was working the traffic, did not see the wince his words caused.

He concentrated on the scenes in front of him. The names of the public squares, which Misha pointed out, fascinated him: Three Crosses, Holy Redeemer, Mary Queen of Poland. Where were the futuristic statues of the New Socialist Man? Where they might have stood if this were Moscow, instead were cast-iron images of Jesus and his Mother, of St Stanislaw Kostka and Marshal Pilsudski, who had defended the land against Russian encroachment.

"Now there's something that should make you feel like you've never left Kutuzovsky Prospekt," Misha said, accompanying himself with a laugh. Viktor had to wedge his head between the dashboard and windshield to take in what he was being shown. Warsaw's Palace of Culture was a near copy of the Soviet Foreign Ministry, the Hotel Ukrainia, the Moscow State University.

"Get used to it," Misha advised, at the same moment whipping the car, front fender first, into a parking space Viktor would never have attempted. As they walked along the rutted sidewalk, Viktor kept waiting for the shrill whistle blast, the vigilant shout of "There he is! Grab him!", that would signal the end of his odyssey. The Palace, three blocks away, loomed over buildings that looked not so much uninhabitable as abandoned.

He knew which door Misha would turn into a fraction of a second before the Pole said, "This one". To Viktor it looked like a place where wanted men would hide, as if at night a neon sign spelled out the name of its refugee inhabitants. They crossed the entry foyer, and went out through a back door which gave on to a concrete courtyard.

"Second to your right," said Misha, and Viktor realized that since they had entered Warsaw his companion had become moody and monosyllabic.

The room into which they stepped was actually quite large, though it did not appear so. That was due to the hundreds of wall posters, Polish flags, placards and portraits that lined not only the four walls but the surface of one small window, and the swingspace of the door as well. Ninety of them contained one or more words written in red in a sprawling backhand script that arrested Viktor's attention.

"So that's what the word looks like."

"That's it," said Misha, as if displaying the Pope's triple tiara. "Solidarnosc."

"Mikhail, there you are!" The voice was furry, Viktor thought, even before he saw the face of its owner, which was dominated by the bushiest red mustache the visitor from Moscow had ever seen.

"Andrzej, good to see you." Misha switched to Russian. "Meet Viktor Nikolaich, from our neighbor to the east."

"Strasvuyte, Viktor. Welcome to this troubled place."

"Thank you. Your name is Andrei?"

"Close enough. It's one of the most common names in Polish, but it's spelled so as to make it almost impossible to pronounce. Even I get it wrong occasionally." He punctuated the admission with three laughing barks. Viktor decided to be wary of him.

"Andrzej spent a few years at the Frunze Military Academy as an exchange student, which accounts for his excellent Russian."

"Best years of my life, and I don't care who knows it. The Soviets spare no expense for their future generals." A smile split the mustache into above and below lip-length hairs.

"When he returned to Poland he joined the Foreign Ministry and worked his way up. In his last assignment he was second in command of the Embassy in Gabon." Misha was reciting as if from a text.

Viktor hoped his voice would not crack. "And you are still with the Ministry?"

"Have no fear, Viktor Nikolaich. My sister saw to it that my diplomatic career came to an abrupt end. Defected to the West with a German tourist."

"The government takes a dim view of such conduct, even when it's by relatives of its employees."

"Actually, the Party made the decision that I was no longer capable of raising the consciousness of Gabonites."

Viktor could see no place for himself to partake in the conversation, so he listened until Misha said, unexpectedly, "Well, I must be off. You'll take care of our friend, eh, Andrzej?"

"Don't I always?"

"Except when you don't." But this was in Polish.

"You've come a long way, haven't you Viktor? Can I get you a drink?"

"Thank you, no."

"Ah, gave it up, did you? Good thinking. I myself drink only in my own house. Dangerous enough out there without falling all over yourself." He made it sound more like state policy than personal choice. When he returned from the corner of the room where there was a cupboard and sink, Andrzej was carrying a tumbler of vodka. When Viktor saw the dent he made in it with his first sip, he became even more uneasy.

"Why did Misha bring me here?"

"Oh, it's Misha, is it? Let's just say he may think I can help you."

"And can you?"

"Sit down." He had already claimed one of the room's two identical chairs. Viktor was less than enthusiastic about sitting in a chair made of some animal's skin stretched over straw and topped by what appeared to be a human skull.

"They let me bring back my personal belongings from Gabon, but don't you know I had to pay import duty on them. I had to decide which things were most important to me."

This told Viktor a great deal, but he said nothing.

"You know, I'm what the Americans would call an entrepreneur. An idea comes to me, I find people who respect my judgment, and who will back me with their money, and I'm . . . I'm out of vodka, damn it. Be right back." Draining the glass had taken about three minutes.

"I'm into a variety of ventures." He paused and compressed his lips so that the mustache covered fully half his face.

"I had a few sidelines going in Guinea. Nothing illegal . . . well, yes I suppose a few, well, most, were. But no one got hurt. Except the rhinos. That was the best. Do you know that a lot of people think powdered rhinoceros horn is an aphrodisiac? Paid the hunters with this," he lifted his glass, "and collected about fifty dollars per set. In dollars."

"You killed the animals for their horns?"

"No." A pause. "They did." Andrzej let loose an enormous cackle. "That's what made it so perfect. If the hunters got caught, they could say whatever they liked. No one was going to arrest the first secretary of the Polish Embassy on the word of a poacher. The only risk I ran was not charging enough. And believe me, I covered myself on that score.

"So you can imagine how it affected me; having to give up the diplomatic privileges, the extra income, and move back to glorious Poland, right in the middle of an insurrection. All idealism and no ideas, that's what Solidarity was."

"But it's legal again, isn't it?"

"Legal yes. But will it be any smarter than in 1980? I doubt it. The people then pushed too hard, too fast. They don't want to make the same mistake this time around. So I'm – what should we call it – advising them."

"You have experience with unions?"

"With Communists!" The force of the statement caused vodka to slosh from his glass. His gestures were becoming vaguer, less controlled. "These Solidarity people . . ." He trailed off, but Viktor got a clear impression that Andrzej was not completely enamored of the group. "They never know how your government will react to something they try. So I float balloons for them. I still know some people at the Ministry, those that didn't turn tail as soon as they heard my sister had become a Nazi. I know one, for instance, who likes the occasional boy who's just started shaving. That bastard, some of them are younger than his own son. So he's willing to help me in my sideshows."

"And what are the sideshows?" Viktor asked.

"Well, being Russian, you probably don't know, but in Poland, it's almost impossible to buy things like washing-machines, dryers, refrigerators, sewing-machines, that kind of stuff."

Recently, Viktor and Marya had calculated that they were within five years of owning a sewing-machine.

"So, what I've done is organize some old-age pensioners. I try to find war veterans or gimps, you know, one leg, blind, that kind of thing. They get priority on new appliances. When they hear a rumor that some store might be getting a shipment of something, they go there immediately and get in line. Sometimes the rumor just isn't true, in which case, all they've wasted is their time. Let me get a refill." Thirty seconds passed. "Ahhh. That's better. But if their tip is right, they pitch camp outside the store. Within a few hours, every housewife in town has heard the same rumor and is standing in the street. But my people are there, not only first in line, but with their war decorations on their shirts, or a cripple's card in their hand. If they can hold it in their hand, that is!" Andrzej found this joke extremely funny.

"Uh, that's very interesting, Andrzej. But . . ."

"So now, I've got the Solidarity people helping me out too. I've got both sides in this fucking country working for me. And they both think I work for them. Shit, even the Americans . . ." His face clouded over quickly. He had gone too far.

"Want to know how many zloty the dollar can fetch on the black market these days?"

In fact, this question, or a variation of it, had occurred to Viktor. He had no money, no way of buying things, not even a toothbrush, which his garbage-tasting mouth told him was becoming a serious want.

"Take my advice. Stay away from the sharpies on Targowa Street. Half of them are secret police. The other half are shysters. Yids, you know. Who was it that wrote a play about Yid moneylenders? Wasn't he Russian?"

Viktor wondered if Shakespeare would appreciate being confused with Chekhov. Trading sunshine for starlight, gold for platinum.

"Anyway, I can give you as good a rate as they do, and no risk involved. But only dollars. Don't bring me Lenin's face."

"Rubles?"

"Yeech. Got enough of them." Again his furry face went sidelong and Viktor could see him wondering if he had made a mistake. There are, Viktor thought, some very good reasons not to drink.

"Anyway, when I tell my friend about you, you'll be worth lots of money."

"What friend?"

"This one, here." He slapped his pants pocket. Viktor wondered if this was some kind of rude Polish sexual inuendo.

"Andrzej, what happens to me?"

"Uhhh?"

"What will you do with me? Misha said you would help me."

"Help you, sure. Take you to day. . . ." He was passing out, Viktor knew.

"Take me what?"

"Daaaaaaa. . . ." It merged into a snore.

"Andrzej, I want to talk to Misha. Can you call him for me?"

Silence. Then snoring.

"Misha, the one who brought me here. Where does he live?"

"Nie zamich." In the last stage of consciousness, Andrzej was reverting to Polish.

"Andrzej! Wake up! Misha owes you money. Where will you go to get your money?"

"U Mikhail."

That was enough like Russian to understand. "Yes. Tell me about Mikhail's house."

"Zoo." Another universal word. But was this a direction to, or a description of the place?

"Is it near the zoo?"

"Uhhhh." Snores were breaking through the web of mustache, eyes squinted against the intrusion of wakefulness.

Viktor gently prised the glass out of Andrzej's inert hand, at the same time slipped his fingers into the pocket of his pants. He felt paper and tugged. Some filthy blue notes came free. Like a holdup-man counting his heist, he added up the numbers: 10,050 whatever-they-weres. Zlotys, but what value did a zloty have against real money, like the ruble? He reached into the pocket again. More paper. Pull. Andrzej muttered something sodden, and curled his cheek into his shoulder. Viktor looked at the paper. It was more money, but not zlotys. They were dollar bills, five of them, and each one said "100" on the front. There was also a white page of paper bearing three lines of handwriting, which Viktor could not understand. He left the door open behind him.

"Zoo," he told the driver, and scowled to discourage further conversation.

"Gzie wzizod?"

"Zoo!"

The driver muttered and the taxi spat forward like a musket blast. Although he was not quite sure what day it was (when had he and ill-starred Shishkin climbed into that pinebox?), the glinting sun told him that it was mid-afternoon. As the driver continued to imprecate him, Viktor sat back and smiled. Warsaw, he decided, was not big enough to stop him. He felt as though a balloon was being inflated inside his chest. He was, for the moment anyway, free, and testing himself against the power of a government that believed it had the right to ruin whosoever's life it touched. He had defied their power to confine him within borders and he had found that the act of resistance in itself gave him strength to continue. He was thinking of himself as an individual for the first time since his marriage.

The taxi made a hairpin turn and blended into a four-lane road that ran parallel to the Vistula River. In a quick succession of blocks, Viktor saw the spires and turrets of the Old Town, the statue of the mermaid Syrina, Warsaw's traditional protector, a cluster of blue militia vans, an enormous cross-topped stone church, and the rampway to a bridge which the driver followed.

"Zoo?" Viktor asked with a shade less confidence than before.

"Tak, tak, zoo, zoo."

Even before they stopped, he could see the polar bear standing on a manmade island of concrete, separated from the road by a chasm of some thirty feet. If the bear could somehow bridge that gap, he would be standing on the sidewalk of a street packed with cars and pedestrians. Viktor wondered how far bears could jump.

"Zoo, Pan. Shust-teschjesc." It was a moment he had been dreading. Clearly the man was telling him the fare, but the taxi had no meter to provide visual backup. What if ten thousand zloty was not even a respectable tip? Viktor handed over the bills and sat still. With no expression, the driver handed back four one thousand zloty notes. Viktor took them in his right hand, chose one of them with his left, passed it back to the driver, who smiled, bowed his head and began to say something. Viktor got out and began walking.

It was all so illogical. A foreigner and a fugitive, he appeared to those who saw him to be nothing more than a somewhat grubby citizen enjoying a placid stroll. He thought he must not only look, but smell and sound, illegal.

A middle-aged woman wearing a cloth coat and a sour expression veered directly at him from a forty-five-degree angle, her scowling attention directed at a cage to her right. To prevent a collision, Viktor grabbed her shoulders. She reacted as though swatted with a dripping broom.

"What's going on? How dare you touch me? Police! Militia!"

Had the zoo been crowded or the police more interested in preventing crime than profiting from it, the game would have ended there. A young pork-chop of an officer whose hair hung over the collar of his gray uniform was fifty yards from them. But after a one-second analysis of what he was seeing — a heavy-hipped woman playing hard-to-get — he concentrated his attention on the barking seals sliding into a pool of greasy water.

Viktor recovered first. No way to bluff this. With what he hoped was a sufficiently hopeless expression, he reached into his pocket for the piece of paper he had taken from Andrzej and offered it to her. When he saw her eyes widen even further, he looked at his hand; he was holding the four thousand zlotys in change the taxi driver had just given him.

"I . . . I . . ." Even if I knew what to say in Polish, he thought, how would I explain why I have accosted a stranger, then brazenly thrust money at her.

The widened eyes became amused slits. "Oh, so it's like that, is it? The straightforward approach. Well, all right, although I'd planned to rest today. But let's get one thing straight. For four thousand zloty I don't even take my shoes off."

Viktor could not imagine what good fortune had made her smile, but he was not about to question it. He smiled back and nodded.

"Quiet, aren't you? And, if you'll excuse me mentioning it, your clothes could use a washing too. Now, come on, pony up. How do you plan to pay? Marks, schillings, dollars?"

He recognized the last word. But how did she know he had any? His face registered incomprehension.

The grin disappeared. "You do have some more money, don't you? Come on, speak up."

That she was losing her good humor petrified him. It was worth anything to appease her. He slowly reached into his pocket and extracted one of the hundred-dollar bills.

"Christ Jesus! For that much I'll wash your clothes myself in between times and serve you your meals in bed. Are you serious?"

Money is a language of its own, Viktor thought. If she wanted the hundred in order not to make trouble, what did it matter to him? He had stolen it, not earned it. He nodded vigorously and handed over the bill. It was his turn to look wide-eyed when she gaily slipped her arm into the crook of his shoulder and tugged.

"Let's go, lover. I live just a block away."

Viktor was a foreigner, not a fool. By the time his new friend was ushering him up the fourth flight of stairs in her building and eagerly scratching at the lock, he had a good idea of who she was and what she thought was going to happen. She had evidently accepted his refusal to speak; after a few awkward pauses which he realized he should be filling with conversation, the woman started jabbering for both of them.

The apartment was modest: one room, dominated by a double bed with imitation brass posters, a bathroom the width of an average coffee table, a refrigerator whose motor growled constantly for lubrication. But Viktor's most recent chances for comparison had been Shishkin's madhouse, Andrzej's monument to African bad taste and the inside of a coffin.

A second after the door clicked shut behind him, she slipped her arms around his waist, and tickled his zipper. Gently, he disentangled himself, turned to face her.

"Do you speak Russian?" He spoke slowly, a word at a time.

She curled her mouth, shook her head. "Now that is kinky," she said to herself. Then: "Da, I speak Russian. Does that get you excited?"

He laughed, flooded with relief. It was going to be all right. "Not in the way you mean. Now what is your name?"

"Victoria."

"Then destiny has a sense of humor. Please, let me sleep for an hour, and then you will understand why this is a fortunate day for both of us."

He managed to incorporate the odor of frying bacon into his dream, which seemed to consist largely of the colors red, purple and black. It was the rough caress of his cheek that woke him, and helped him realize where he was; Marya would never have done such a thing.

"All right, lover, I've given you an hour and a half. Time to face the world." He heard her clicking a few steps across the room, then returning to the bed. When he investigated the scene through defensive slits of sight, he saw her sitting on the edge of the mattress, holding a plate and a cup.

"Coffee for my millionaire. Eggs and bacon too. So what if it's nearly dark outside?"

"Thank you. You didn't have to do that."

It was as though she had never before heard the words. Her mouth softened into an O-shape, and her hands trembled slightly as he took the ceramic mug from her. "You're really very handsome, you know." She was inching toward the center of the bed, using her hips like tire treads. Viktor became aware that the clothes he had shucked off and strewn across the bottom of the bed before collapsing into exhaustion were no longer there.

"Where are my pants?"

"Where every strong man's pants should be. Off." She was advancing across the bed on hands and knees, like a cheetah on a doe.

He laughed. It was all he could do, and it stopped her.

"What's so funny? Now look, for a hundred dollars, I'll do some pretty disgusting things, but being mocked isn't one of them. What's your problem, anyway?"

"My clothes, please."

"They're soaking in soapy water, millionaire. And in case no one's told you, it wouldn't hurt you to do the same. Hey!"

He sprang from the bed, dressed in underpants and shirt that had been on him for – five days? It took only two bounding steps to reach the bathroom, where he saw his pants, shirt and socks, blackened and inert in water that looked like clay. He was trying to find the pants' right front pocket when Victoria appeared in the doorway.

"Ought to be more careful where you leave things. Warsaw's a big city with lots of crime." She was holding four one hundred dollar bills, the crumpled zlotys and the piece of paper he had extracted from Andrzej. The brassy smile was back in place, frightening in its intensity.

"Uh, Victoria, may I please . . ."

"Sure you can have it back. I'm a whore, not a thief. Otherwise I'd have brought a rolling-pin down on your head when you were asleep, and told the police you tried to kill me when I brought you here. I'd be four hundred dollars richer and you'd be in a little bit of trouble."

"Well, I certainly wouldn't want to get into trouble."

"You're a Soviet, aren't you?"

There was no point in denying it.

"And you're in Poland without permission, aren't you?"

"Without whose permission? Everyone I've met here has been most welcoming."

"I can understand that. You're quite a charmer, whoever you are. I imagine if you were stranded in Lapland, you could talk the reindeer into sharing their fur. Don't worry, friend, I'm not going to take your little treasures. But tell me this, if you know someone in this neighborhood anyhow, why pay me a hundred dollars to provide room and board." She gave him a look. "And reject the services I normally provide?"

"What makes you think I know anyone else?"

"This address that's written down. It's only about three blocks away."

To him, the Latin writing might as well have been the recipe for gingerbread.

"Will you show me where that address is?"

"Now I know what a guide dog feels like. Yes, yes, I'll take you there, when your clothes dry. On one condition, that is." A grin crossed her face.

"What's that?"

She was giggling now. "Christ, I can't remember how long it's been since I actually wanted to do it. But there's something about you . . ." She crossed to the bath tub, flipped on the hot water tap, sloshed his clothes, and wrung the suds from them. When she had hung them on the shower curtain rod, she turned to him. "Now, it's your turn to tidy up, my big Russian bear. And when I judge that you're clean enough, I'm going to dry you off. With my tongue."

"Now look, Victoria. I'm really not here . . ."

"And I'm not selling anything. Didn't I say I wanted it? For a change it's going to be me who selects the merchandise. If you want to find out where that address is, and what this garble means, comrade, you'll climb out of those filthy togs."

As a younger man he might have fantasized just such a scenario. Now the reality struck him as ludicrous, more than lascivious. He saw her taking off her dress with a practiced economy of motion. New water was running into the tub and its rising steam felt like an embrace. If he thought of Marya for a second, it was because he thought she would understand the situation, even, perhaps, see its essential humor. He peeled off the shirt as though it was skin. Removing the underpants was like feeling a fresh spring breeze.

"Ho, ho," she said. "I may end up paying you." The water sizzled around his ankles as he stepped into the tub. "Wake me in an hour," he told her. They both laughed.

15

They found they liked each other. The contact was unexpectedly fierce and intense, but they were both too wise – or was it just too old – to be much impressed by that. He pondered the realization that lovemaking was the one natural human activity that, in order to be enjoyed, requires total concentration. He had not forgotten who or where he was, but for those minutes he was freed from worry about mere facts. When an image of Marya came into his mind, he intentionally shooed it away.

Lolling diagonally across the mattress, Victoria guessed she had known a thousand men. "I suppose I should be ashamed."

"Is that how you feel?"

"Not really. I have morals but no one else seems to. Being a whore is only a symptom of helplessness. The Communists were already in power when I was born, what hope is there for anything better? I've heard older people – men, as you might expect – talk about Poland before the war, then cry over how wonderful it was and how awful it is now. Wonderful, awful, now, then; they're all just words. Me, I've never found anything worth crying over. Have you?"

"Pain is pure. The trick to pain is to be strengthened by it, but to avoid letting anyone know how good it hurts." It occurred to him that he had always known the truth of this statement. So why had he never shared it with Marya? Because it sounded bumptious?

Viktor wondered if this conversation was being overheard and, if so, how embarrassing the transcript would be to read. Yet it sounded not the least pretentious as they spoke the words.

Just before they slept, she reached under the bed, and pulled out his four hundred dollars. "Take it and put it somewhere safe."

"It's safe," he said, rolling over.

His clothes never fully dried. Parallel sections of his pants that had been draped over the apartment's one radiator seemed to hiss when he slid them over his legs. The other parts were cold and clammy. She gave him a fruity-smelling man's oversized sweater to wear and he climbed into it without asking anything. Victoria wore the same clothes as when she bumped into him at the zoo. It really was an accident, she said. She had been appalled at the conditions in the monkey cage and could not take her eyes off it. She liked animals because they accepted nature's rules without quibbling and because they coupled without shame. Then, with no apparent intention of juxtaposition, she said, "I like you, Viktor. I think you are for real. And I am going to try to help you."

They walked through the still early morning. She told him some taxis kept logs of their pickups, and that at least one murder had been solved thanks to that evidence. Viktor said he doubted that most taxi-drivers in Moscow were sober enough to keep track of their passengers. The eggs and bacon he had eaten felt heavy but solid. To that, she had added a slice of poppy cake and three of the worst cups of coffee he had ever experienced. But it was the first real nutrition he had had in nearly two weeks and even the coffee seemed vitamin-laced. For the first time since Ludmilla's death, Viktor felt, not happy, but temporarily serene. Like the good whore she was Victoria picked up his mood. As she led the way, she dared a question about his life in the Soviet Union. She cursed herself as she saw the lines set around his mouth. "How much further?" he asked.

They stopped at a roundabout, in the center of which stood a concrete island. The island was nothing more than a pedestal for an immense and rusty steel statue of a Slavic-looking soldier holding a machine-gun at his side. The soldier's other hand rested on the shoulder of a child who gazed adoringly into the warrior's face. A bronze inscription at the soldier's feet said that the statue had been constructed by the people of Warsaw in gratitude to the Soviet army who had liberated the city from Nazi occupation. Victoria explained that locals referred to the location as "Pedophile Square". Directly across one of the streets stood a squat red-brick building that took up an entire block in each direction. It was rimmed with barbed wire and a squad of twelve armed Polish militiamen stood outside.

"The Soviet diplomatic residence compound. They all live in there, every goddamned Russian in Warsaw, for fear that they'll be murdered in their beds."

"Every one except me."

They walked halfway around the intersection. "This is your street," she told him. "Let's see; odd numbers on the left, so . . ."

He enjoyed watching – literally – her mind work. She squinted her eyes, and concentrated with such intensity that he could see the veins in her temples thumping. He reminded himself not to get to know her too well, then went back to admiring her.

He thought for a minute they had somehow returned to Andrzej's building. It was exactly the same architectural plan. The front door was unlocked, and he saw through its glass that the foyer led to two back doors, and a courtyard.

"Well, is this it? Is this what you wanted?"

"I have no idea what I want. For all I know this could be where Andrzej's girlfriend lives, and the other numbers her measurements." He had told her nearly everything that had happened to him since arriving in Warsaw (he had not said with whom) but had kept the rest of the story from her. She decided immediately not to like Andrzej because, "Anyone who has skulls on his chairs must be an awful person."

Clearly the building was residential. But whose residence was it? They went into the foyer. Concrete walls painted green, floor unswept for weeks at least. There were twenty-four apartments in the building, and Victoria read out the unfamiliar, impossible-sounding names of each tenant above grimy bronze-colored mailboxes. That did not mean that Mikhail did not live here, Viktor told himself. But even if he did, what would it matter. Andrzej would be nursing a hangover by now, but he was unlikely to overlook the loss of five hundred dollars. With a self-pitying bitterness, Viktor told himself that he had managed to become a fugitive once again, this time from people who professed to want to help him.

He was peering into the courtyard (he had been right about that) when the front door opened. Viktor whipped around so quickly that the old woman coming into the foyer gasped and put a hand to her sunken chest. "Who are you? What are you doing here?"

"Relax, grandma. We're looking for a friend, who doesn't seem to be at home." Victoria carried off the slightly irritable act with ease. The old woman, recognizing the tone of voice as belonging to yet another aggrieved Pole, shrugged and began mounting the steps.

"Which apartment do you live in?" Victoria demanded.

"The one next door to my neighbor." She had not even stopped climbing.

Viktor, of course, had kept silent, content for a change to let someone who knew the language help him. He was wondering about two things simultaneously: how to decipher the rest of the information on the piece of paper, and Victoria's ability to contract her internal muscles during lovemaking. He had found fidelity to Marya a small enough burden for nearly a decade. What had turned him into a satyr in twenty-four hours? The air of Poland? The excitement of life on the run? Bacon and eggs? He recognized the mental processes that meant he was kidding himself. Whatever it was, was in Victoria herself. But to acknowledge that meant admitting something for which he was completely unprepared. And besides, his inner self said, you're not likely to be around long enough to contemplate the problem.

She had said nothing. He felt her eyes, heard her hands, smelled her curiosity. And that described his predicament. Sensually confused. But sensual. He looked across the foyer and felt as though he was an iron filing suddenly within magnet range.

"There's nothing more you can do here, is there?" The voice was low; he felt sexual tension even in the question.

"I suppose not."

"Then why don't we get away from here? It may be a good thing that you didn't find anything or anyone. What would you do, here in the nowhere of a building where even grandmas have smart answers to straightforward questions. Let's go."

Of course he had not understood the grandma remark. But it was already becoming their way not to hold up decisions, action, with stale questions. It was her eyes, not her words that made him say, "You're right."

Warsaw on a Sunday is the kind of city all its residents wish for the other six days. Breezes free of exhaust fumes sweep through the streets like a promise of redemption. The traffic, lighter to begin with, moves more forgivingly and horns are used for salutation, rather than a staccato signal of impatience. Most stores were closed, but those that one might wish were open, were. A flower stall offered bunches of freesias in cellophane cones; by pointing, Viktor bought one with a handful of remarkably dirty zloty Victoria had given him. It was the first purchase he had made since haggling for the turkey at the Moscow customs house. When he saw Victoria radiate pleasure like a just-kissed teenager, he decided that money was like the flowers' roots: unimportant, worthy of nothing better than burial, except that without them, there would be no pretty blooms for women to enjoy.

They spoke in the street only when there was no one else around. The sound of Russian would not brighten any Warsavite's Sunday, she said.

At the corner of the street where she lived, a gray-coated militiaman passed by and Victoria paused for a moment longer than necessary.

"What?" he asked. "Trying to decide whether to turn me over to the law?"

"No. Whether to turn myself over to you."

"Have no fear. I'm still exhausted."

"That's not what I mean. What is it about you? What makes me care? Why does it matter?"

He was beginning to understand that she was not vamping. "Look, Victoria, I, I . . ."

She caught the discomfort in his voice, allowed him to escape. "Nope, never mind. Well, what'll it be? Sight-see or see me?"

It was, he thought, one of the lamest jobs of acting he had ever witnessed. But, if this was artifice, was the other emotion he was seeing real? He concocted several answers, none pleasing.

In the apartment, he stared out of the window, aware that, on the bed, Victoria was also turning things over in her mind. He wondered what thinking sounded like in Polish. This was the other side of the existence he was leading: the long silences, the fear, the emptiness of hours not devoted directly to survival. He did not, he decided, regret anything that he had done. But if that were true, why was he guiltily skulking around in a foreign country, afraid not only of his own country's retribution, but unwilling as well to face the woman who had given him sanctuary and temporary peace of mind?

The only antidote was boldness. "I'm going back to that address to see why it's important."

"Do you want me to come with you?" She spoke, Viktor thought, like the nurse of an invalid who had said he needed to relieve himself.

"Don't you have work to do?" He immediately wished he had not said it. What was the matter with him?

The street no longer seemed so much lively as annoyingly active. At Pedophile Square, he felt, sequentially, pride in his Russianness, a self-admiring disbelief that he had gotten this far, resentment of his situation, guilt at having left Marya and Anna behind, a towering need for revenge against Karushkin and the others who had done this to him, longing for Shishkin, confusion about what, if anything, Victoria meant to him, and an overwhelming fatigue with the whole business. Like a good social scientist (a term he would not have recognized in any language), Viktor was more concerned with trying to recognize the things that were happening to him than with immediately explaining them. He knew, for instance, that he had become inordinately attached to Victoria, whom he had known for two days. He was also telling himself that he had not abandoned his family, which until two weeks ago had been a sufficient explanation for the creation of the universe. He had gone to Shishkin in despair, been bewitched by his loud talk of defying the system, and, like a little boy playing a villain, had donned the characteristics of Outlaw On The Run.

And Russia, Russia. The country that he loved so fiercely had turned against him and now he had done the same to her. But was not the motherland's cruelty a part of her allure? Was she not treating him like a child she favored, and so could torment, abuse, sadden? Now, Viktor knew, he had forfeited all claim to his heritage. He was Russian, yes, but he was no longer Russia. He remembered a line from a Yevtushenko poem, "Kamikaze", that asked: "So what if we get busted up and crushed?" That was it, the essence of Russia; the uncaring, unfeeling mother, whose omniscient heartlessness makes us love her more.

He was close to the apartment building now. In the middle of a straight stretch of street, he saw a sight unthinkable in Moscow: a man sitting on the sidewalk, with his hand extended. Beggars in a Communist country?

The apartment building was just as he had left it. He stood in front of the door like a supplicant, unable to screw up the courage to demand anything. How many times in Moscow had he brazened his way past doormen, guards, police and other agents designed to keep him from doing something that was not allowed? What made this different? The fact that he was acting outside the law? Hardly. His regard for the law in his mother country was negligible. It was the country itself, not its governance, that held his affection. Even as he stood unprotected on the unsparing sidewalk of a city he knew almost nothing about, Viktor admitted that he was taking a certain pleasure in constantly walking blindfolded along the edge of disaster. Again he revelled in the simple fact that he had not yet been found, arrested, returned to the Soviet Union for some incalculable punishment.

"You shouldn't walk the streets alone, Viktor Nikolaich. Very foolish." The voice, speaking Russian, was enough to paralyze him. The claw-like grip from behind was extraneous.

So now it was over, Viktor told himself. A good try, but not good enough. In a way, this restored his faith in the system. It was too powerful to be trifled with, yet efficient enough to exact vengeance even on piddling nuisances like him.

He turned, and for the first time in his life, felt his mouth drop open involuntarily. Recognition was instant, followed by deep, searing shock.

"Strasvuyte, moy droog," said the man from the American Embassy in Moscow. "I never got to thank you for delivering my letter to Ludmilla."

Knees require the coordination of sixteen muscles to remain locked in place; it is no wonder they buckle under stress. As Viktor sank toward the pavement, the hand that had been on his shoulder kept him from falling completely.

"Walk, Viktor. It'll clear your head."

They moved further down the street, and Viktor's legs recalled how to operate.

"Let go of me."

"Only if I know you won't try to run, or shout, or otherwise make a scene."

"All right." He had no idea what he planned to do. By contrast, his companion seemed in perfect control of the situation. They crossed the street to a park, and began to follow its rutted concrete pathways.

"Let's get the small talk out of the way first. You can call me Dave, since that's not my name. I still work in the Embassy in Moscow, where what I do is none of your business."

Viktor looked at him for the first time. He was an inch or two taller than Viktor, with a face best described as expressionless. His Russian was stunningly perfect, though now, under observation, it was clear that he was not a native. His hair was dark and curly, his complexion more olive than the usual Slavic milk-paste. Although their first meeting seemed years ago, Viktor believed he was wearing the same clothes as then: white shirt, black pants, unshined black shoes. The shock was gone, taking with it both the physical clumsiness and mental paralysis it had brought on.

"What are you doing here? Were you waiting for me?"

"Let's each do half the work. You answer the first question. I'll handle the second. I'll even go first. No. I was waiting for someone else."

"Andrzej."

"You still have to answer your question." The look in his face gave Viktor the answer.

"I'm here because I . . . left Moscow."

"Oh. Got the LOT special excursion weekend fare, did you?"

"Did you know the letter I gave to Ludmilla would cause her to kill herself?"

"What a strange question. Of course not. I don't even know what it said."

"Who wrote it then?"

"Someone who had something to say to Ludmilla."

"Who are you? You're not Russian. Why do you speak it so well?"

His reward was a cold stare and a long silence. Then: "This is the only gratuitous question I'm going to allow you. The answer is because I've trained for the past ten, no, eleven years now, to speak and think exclusively in Russian. For me to slip up could cost me my life."

"Gratuitous."

Dave smiled. "Viktor, what do you think of Gorbachev?"

"What is this? A public opinion survey?"

"Do you understand what he's doing in your country?"

"Well, of course. He's reforming." As soon as he said them, the words sounded unbelievably stupid.

"Yes, he is that. And do you approve of that?"

"I . . . I suppose so. It doesn't matter much to me. I have my own life."

"In that respect, Viktor, you are like most of your countrymen. You just want to be left alone, to live your lives, right?"

"Something like that."

"That's a very reasonable attitude. And it's one that Gorbachev, by and large, is counting on. But you know, Viktor, not everyone is as flexible as you. There are some people who don't like what Gorbachev is doing. In fact they're determined to stop him, one way or another."

"But wasn't that all settled at the Party conference in '88? Gorbachev won all the votes, all his programs were approved." Viktor realized that although he had read about the conference in the newspaper, he had never said a word about it to anyone, even Marya.

"The conference. Yes, he seemed to have the upper hand there. But, take my word for it, a lot of people still think it's not over."

"What does any of this have to do with me?"

"Patience, Viktor. Another question: do you know about the guards who've gone missing at the American Embassy?"

"Everyone knows about that."

A smile flickered across Dave's face. "Yes, it's the buzz of Moscow, isn't it?" He paused. "How do you think that makes Gorbachev feel?"

"Probably not too happy."

"And how do you think it goes down with the other members of the Politburo, the ones who think he's gone too far already?"

"And what's your role in all this?"

He was treated to another smile. "Well, even old enemies like us and the Russians occasionally extend professional courtesies, you know?"

"Meaning you're helping them to do this?"

"Gorbachev's the first real leader you've had in the Soviet Union with enough intelligence to be dangerous. Lenin just tried to keep the revolution alive. Stalin butchered everyone, and Khrushchev and Brezhnev were really just peasants. Andropov might have shaken things up, if he had lived long enough."

"So why would you want to embarrass him like this?"

Dave squinted at him, and cocked his head slightly, like a dog hearing a far-off noise. "I've just told you, Viktor. Gorbachev has the potential to make the Soviet Union a first-class power."

"We are a first-class power." The answer was automatic, inbred.

"Sure you are. Right down to the cute horse-drawn carts that do most of your farmwork."

"All right. We have a way to go."

"Yes, you do. And the longer it takes you, the happier we'll be."

"Meaning that if Gorbachev is embarrassed, he won't be able to follow through on his reforms. But why would any Soviet want to help in a plan like that?" The question was genuine. He did not understand.

"Viktor, you're too young to remember, but perhaps you've heard about it: during the worst of the Stalin purges, the joke that was whispered around when people were arrested, and their families insisted they were innocent. People used to say, 'Innocent? How can he be innocent . . . ?"

". . . He's already been charged.' I've heard about it. So what?"

"The people we're talking about, Viktor, don't want to wait to see what Gorbachev does next. They're action types."

It was like hearing the facts of life. Viktor listened to the American's explanation of how his Russia was once again trying to destroy itself.

They were in front of the apartment building again. Dave planted one foot on the sidewalk, the other on the step that led to the lobby door.

"How did you find me?" Viktor asked suddenly.

It was the first time he saw the American startled. "Me find you?"

For just a second, Viktor knew what it must feel like when an explorer stumbles upon an unknown land. The address of the building where they stood had come from Andrzej's pocket. Dave had not found him. He had chanced upon Dave. As if on cue, the American stared up for just a second at the building.

"I have to go now Viktor. You'd better tell me where I can find you. We'll need to talk some more."

"Who is up there?" Viktor gestured indistinctly to the building.

"Friends. Friends in need."

"I think it would be best, friend Dave, if we meet here again tomorrow."

"No. Tell me where you'll be."

Viktor laughed. "I don't want to. And I don't think that you're in a position to do much about it."

He tried intentionally to lose himself in the streets. Twice when he saw open doors to apartment buildings, he went in and climbed a flight of stairs to see if anyone was following him. When he heard no footsteps behind his, he descended and began searching for another wrong turn to take. By the time he arrived at the street where Victoria lived, he had decided that Dave was too dangerous to resist. Besides, he could not gamble with the possibility that Dave actually knew something about Marya and Anna. He would put himself in the hands of someone who understood this dirty business.

He buzzed Victoria's apartment and, almost immediately, heard the answering electric buzz that allowed him to open the foyer door.

He climbed the stairs quickly, feeling lighter for the decision he had made. This time, when he heard another pair of footsteps behind him, he did not worry. Just another tenant.

Suddenly, the footfalls from below were faster. Whoever it was wanted to catch up with him. He began taking the stairs two, three at a time. The sensation of lightness vanished. He felt awkward, immediately winded. Two flights to Victoria's floor. From above, he heard a door open, heard her voice say his name. He knew not to answer, not in Russian. On the first step of the final flight, the tip of his shoe failed to clear the metal edge of the step. In an instant, he felt it all at once: the loss of breath, the pain as his chin, then his forehead hit separate steps, the grinding hurt in his knees. From above, Victoria repeated his name, this time with evident concern. From below, the footsteps hurried closer. Viktor could feel his pursuer turn at the flight landing, then stop when he saw Viktor prone and helpless.

A man's chuckle, but it sounded genuinely amused, not grimly pleased. "So, moy droog, could you use, perhaps, a helping hand?"

Unbelieving, he let Shishkin raise him from defeat.

16

Victoria did not pretend pleasure that Shishkin was sitting on her bed. She watched the two friends hug, listened to them laugh, and then, like an aggrieved wife, asked Viktor to join her in the bathroom.

"My God, he's filthy. I could smell him before he got into the apartment. And neither he, nor you, have bothered to explain who he is. You just lumber in and start pounding each other on the shoulders."

He had to admit she was right. His introductions had been, at best, incomplete. Now he saw the makings of shrill anger in Victoria and wondered why it delighted him. Marya had seldom objected to anything; in extremis, she would level a skeptical glance and a lopsided grin.

"I knew conditions in Poland were bad, but doubling up on trips to the toilet – well, I'm going to contribute my Party dues next month to the Warsaw sanitation department." Shishkin's smile was intact under his skunk beard, but Viktor noticed the eyes were focused intently. He had years of experience at being disliked.

"Yevgeny Moisovich, I think we need to get a few things straight before we go any further."

"Further? You mean like to Berlin or London? And what kind of things? For instance, why am I here imposing my odious self on this lovely Polish lady, instead of rotting in a boxcar on my way to a labor camp in the Arctic Circle?"

"God, he's got a mouth on him." Victoria was preparing tea, but had put out only two cups.

Viktor had no intention of discussing specific events in front of her. "The first thing you can tell me is how you found me here."

Over the whistle of the kettle, Victoria said, "And after he's told you, you can tell me." She slopped water into the teapot, grabbed an imitation leather purse, and slammed the door behind her.

Viktor poured, gestured to the ceiling. "As far as I know, we're alone."

"Then why not just say there are no microphones. Besides, it hardly matters. I imagine she's on her way to the police. A bit of a temper, that one."

"Strong heart, hard head."

Shishkin accepted the tea, fingered the sleeve of the sweater Viktor was wearing. "You've settled in nicely, I see."

"Never mind that, Shishkin. Start talking."

The dissident gulped tea, exhaled steam. "All right. But before I begin, let's agree that no matter what happens, we'll remain friends."

"That certainly sounds like a man at peace with himself."

"Oh, Viktor, Viktor, why couldn't you be Jewish? You'd find it all so much easier to understand."

"Save the theology, Shishkin, and concentrate on telling the truth. I'll wait to hear how you found this place. What happened after we were separated out their in the wilds?"

"What happened? Why, just what I had expected. I walked until I thought I would drop. It took me much longer to reach the village than I had anticipated."

Now it was Viktor's turn to breathe slowly. "The village? Tell me about it, Yevgeny."

"That's why it would help if you were Jewish. You'd understand why I had to do as I did."

"I'll just have to muddle through as the lesser being that I am."

"All right. Presuming you haven't forgotten about your life before arriving here – " he cast an amused glance at the door through which Victoria had left– "you will remember that it was thanks to the Rabbi's exit permission that we were able to cross the border in our wooden lovenest."

"Don't try making me feel guilty. It won't work. The Rabbi did a brave, generous thing."

"I agree. And I'm sure that, if asked his opinion, so would he. Nevertheless, after resolving to let us use the exit permission, the Rabbi asked a small favor in return."

"Which you decided not to tell me about. . . ."

"You had so many other things on your mind."

". . . because you thought I'd refuse."

"There was also that, yes."

"And what, if I may ask now, was that favor? Console a sick relative? Do some matchmaking for his niece?"

Shishkin shook his head like the straight man in a comedy team. "You see, the Rabbi knew that there is a small group of Jews living in Eastern Poland, who, despite much persecution and hardship . . . ."

"Get to the point, Shishkin."

" . . . and hardship, had managed to print a number of books in Russian containing portions of the Torah."

"Oh, Jesus, Shishkin."

"Nope. Not a mention of either him or me."

"You were going to see if the books could be smuggled into the Soviet Union?"

"I just wanted to get an idea of the chance of success."

"And that's why you pretended to have a tantrum there in the middle of the forest? So I'd leave you alone and you could go to this village? What was its name?"

"Suchowola."

Viktor was almost certain that was the name of the place where he had been taken in the truck by Kolewicz, where he had tried to escape, been wrestled to the ground by The Snake, and where, finally and against his will, he had been introduced to Misha.

"Anyway, I get there and bumble around until someone understands me when I speak Yiddish. That's only a stew made from Russian, Polish and German, so it's not surprising someone on the border of Poland and Russia understands it, right?"

Viktor sipped tea silently. He knew from experience that Shishkin would get to the point. When was not worth contemplating.

"So the linguist takes me to one house, and someone there takes me to another, and finally, I'm in the presence of the great Polish criminals and Jewish freedom fighters, the Ruthensteins. Incredible! He must have been a hundred years old on a good day. She was much younger – say eighty. But he does all the talking for them, traditional couple that they are. He also insists on taking me down into the cellar to see the great stock of Russian Torahs they've been getting ready to overthrow Communism with. I tell you, Viktor, I nearly cried. Maybe there were thirty of them. And how had the cunning Ruthensteins been copying them? On a photostat machine at the local library. Each time they'd go in, they copied one or two pages, never more. Usually the machine was broken. Besides, they wouldn't want to raise anyone's suspicions, would they? At that rate it took them about a year to make a single copy. The medieval monks worked faster! And the first of these quality products had been done six or seven years ago. Ever see a seven-year-old photostat? It looks like someone threw last night's leftovers on a piece of gray paper that had glue on it. And it was this collection of illegible mold spores that the Rabbi had heard about, seventh-hand, after some major embellishment. Why, he talked as though there were thousands of perfectly printed Torahs, sealed in airtight packets, ready to start a revolution. Ah, the Russian gift for exaggeration."

Viktor knew a cry of despair when he heard it. Shishkin did not wail easily, at least not with him.

"I'm sorry Yevgeny."

"Why?" asked the Jew miserably. "Why should I deserve any better for betraying your trust?"

"Well." He did not want Shishkin to suffer any more, but neither did he want to comfort him. Comfort restored Shishkin's audacity.

"So, after being shown, one by one, their pitiful little supply of subversion, complete with descriptions of how they'd gone out in a snowstorm to copy page 26 of this copy, and almost been caught by the librarian while duplicating page 99 of that one, I was ready to go. But no! The ruthless Ruthensteins of Suchowola must fête the master criminal from Moscow. I've never eaten so much bad food in my life. I think the old man poured from a bottle of copying fluid, although he called it kosher wine. But I was thirsty enough to drink it and ask for more. When I finally got over my indigestion, and asked them who their contacts were in Warsaw, they just looked at me. I might as well have said in Washington."

Viktor wondered what there was to say. Did Shishkin, the uncompromising nonconformist, the militant defender of impossible causes, expect happy endings? Did he think those that shared his beliefs were, as a reward, magically endowed?

"So you found yourself with two fierce new friends, who had no idea of what dissent was all about."

Shishkin's face showed the disappointment he had endured. "I can tell you, my friend, I'd rather be with you, uninformed Gentile that you are, than any of these great protectors of my own race." He put down his teacup and moved to Viktor with the stately pace of a good man humbling himself. They embraced again, and rasped each other with rough cheeks.

"I shouldn't be so hard on them, I suppose. They gave me some money, dollars even. And after a lot of muttering to each other and into the phone, someone came to their house and arranged for me to get to Warsaw." A bitter smile. "A goy, wouldn't you know it. Spoke good Russian though."

"What was his name?"

"Who can remember? Don't all these Polish names sound alike to you, with their -wiczes, and -skis at the end? I remember his first name, though. Mikhail."

Suchowola was too small and the circumstances too unique for there to be two. But Viktor's experience was that Shishkin gave straighter, faster answers when he did not understand the significance of his words.

"And this person, Mikhail, brought you to Warsaw?"

"No, he said he wished he could, but he was busy with something very important. He had some unpleasant weaselly-looking type drive me here."

That would have been The Snake. "When was this, Shishkin?"

"What's today, Sunday? This was Friday, I suppose. Early, very early."

"And when you got to Warsaw?"

"That's the only good part. Mr Personality, who didn't speak a word of anything intelligible, dumped me in front of some apartment building. Well, waiting to greet me was a strange-looking fellow, all hair and shining eyes, but he's been to Russia to study. Clever fellow, he is. Right off, he let me know that he'd help me to get out of Poland, for a price. That's what I liked about him, Viktor: no pretensions to great ideals, just an honest respect for money. I like to think I can tell when a man is made of mush, and when he means what he says. I put my faith in this man. But, like I said, he's strange. You should see the furniture in his apartment . . . Hey, what's the matter?"

Viktor was holding up his hand as though to fend off blows. "I wonder what the odds on two people being this stupid might be. A million to one?"

"Which two?"

"And getting better every minute," Viktor said, more to himself than his baffled friend. "The man you met was named Andrzej, he had a bushy mustache and his flat is furnished with African atrocities."

"I liked them. But how did you know?"

"That can wait. Tell me, right now Yevgeny, with no messing around, how you found me here."

"I was coming to that."

"Tell me!"

"You sound like a Soviet. Calm down. Andrzej said I couldn't stay at his place because it was dangerous. I gave him the money I'd gotten from the Ruthensteins. He gave me some tins of food and took me to the flat across town."

"What do you mean: the flat across town?"

"The one where I saw you. Talking with that undertaker or whoever he is."

"Where were you that you could see me?"

"I was up in the flat on the fifth floor. I was waiting for you to come up, we all were. But then you started to slink away. So I followed."

"'We all were'? Who 'we all', Shishkin?"

"What a strange way to talk. Is that proper Russian?"

"WHO?"

"Us, we, the boys upstairs, them."

"Shishkin, are the people in that apartment Russian?"

"Why would a Russian come to a hole like this? Unfriendliest place I've been since I was in jail. I nodded to them when Andrzej took me in, and he shushed me, told me not to say a word. I was put in a separate room. They slept together on the floor. They weren't talkative, I can tell you. Playing cards, chess, they hardly even looked up when I went out."

"No one tried to stop you from leaving?"

"Who's to stop me? Most of them are just kids. No, I walked right out."

Dave was down on the street with me, thought Viktor, and Andrzej was just waking up to his hangover and discovering his lost money. Could they carry this off, by themselves, without local cooperation? He had to go back, he knew that much.

Why had Andrzej taken Shishkin to such a sensitive location? The answer was achingly obvious: Andrezj, the money-vacuum, would trade on anyone who had the dollars to keep him in vodka.

Viktor could hardly get the words out, so awful was the prospect of their being realized. "You will have to stay here."

"With Poland's answer to a geisha girl due back any minute? Where will you be?"

"I'll be off doing something stupid."

The street was even more depressing without Victoria. What would he do if Dave was there? What if Andrzej intercepted him? Even worse, he could be picked up on the street. He couldn't even hold a conversation with another pedestrian.

He waited in the park across the street worrying that, five floors above, Dave was watching and deciding how best to destroy him. There was heavy traffic through the building's front door. Most appeared to be residents, lugging food, or toilet paper or whatever they had been lucky enough to cadge. Each time one went in or out, the door settled shut with an authoritative thump. Now or never, he told himself, and moved across the street like a man with much on his mind.

Where's grandma when I need her, he asked himself. As he reached the top step in front of the building's door, it opened and he expected to see the same withered woman who had met him and Victoria. But it was a little boy, who smiled at Viktor and said something like: "Shuchvartasvgia."

Viktor smiled in return, nodded yes, and caught the door before it shut.

The little boy looked at him quizzically through the glass. Please don't let me be undone by an eight-year-old. He went up the stairs. The lift would be too hard on his nerves.

Second door to the left of the stairs Shishkin had said. It was metal gray like the others. Before he could talk himself out of it, Viktor knocked.

Nothing.

All right, Viktor told himself. You did what you could. Now get the hell out of here.

The door swung back a crack and Viktor heard what he knew he would.

"Da?"

It was a hollow monosyllable, not a challenge, the kind of half-dead tone that represents the Soviet spirit. It was the sound of a bored secretary at a government office, of an incompetent clerk at a bread store, an unwilling neighbor roused from a comfortable chair.

And Viktor knew what to do.

"Strasvuyte, moy droog," he said carefully into the inch of air between the door and the jamb. "May I have a word with you?"

Eyes that were not quite dead, rather in suspended animation. He could have been a naked woman, a ticking nuclear device, or an abandoned baby, the look would have been the same.

Viktor, however, went through the full range of human emotion. The face behind the crack in the door was thin, and a few days' stubble obscured the cheeks. But the nose was bent at an improbable angle and the chin curved up like the bottom of a teacup.

"Borislav Nemetz? Surely that's you?"

The same gaze was fastened to the face in front of him. But now, having put a name to it, Viktor saw him in context: the gray uniform, the blue-banded hat, the superior smirk of a guard in front of the US Embassy. As creatures of the KGB go, Nemetz was not bad. He never impeded Viktor needlessly, never made life more difficult than it already was. He accepted cigarettes and whisky which Viktor bought in the dollar stores, and in return made sure that Viktor never waited too long to pass through the embassy gates. His disappearance, now almost three months past, was the first that Viktor had noticed.

"Nemetz?"

The door opened fractionally, as much an invitation as he could expect. Viktor stepped in slowly, and saw, without doubt, that he had found the embassy guard. Russians are never suntanned, but the ivory hue of Nemetz's face made it seem he had never been in direct light. His mouth hung slightly slack so that Viktor could see the familiar steel teeth.

"Borislav? It's Viktor Nikolaich. Your friend!"

He might have been reciting the Sanskrit alphabet. Nemetz stared through him, without a blink. From deeper in the apartment, Viktor heard a noise, something like a grunt. He stepped past Nemetz gently, as though trying to avoid knocking down a paper house. Past the foyer was a room. He looked in.

They were all there, just as he had suspected. The faces were as familiar as those of his closest friends. Viktor had seen them nearly every day when he dropped off mail, or picked up packages at the embassy. Ivan Ivanovich, who liked a good joke, Mikhail Golosovich, whose liver should have given out long ago, Vyachaslav Dorogomilovich, who confided how he longed to have an American woman – any American woman – someday. Viktor saw their empty faces, but could not divorce them from their personalities, now so strangely absent. They sat on the floor, or on chairs, stared out of the window on to the street where Viktor had met with Dave. Some sat on opposite sides of a chessboard, as Shishkin had told him. But no moves were made, no strategies were plotted here.

"Do you know me? I am Viktor Nikolaich Melanov." The chesspieces were no less responsive. Their faces looked at his, then away. He was the only thinking being in the room.

Russian newspapers, and a few books were tossed around the sitting room. He walked past Vyachaslav Dorogomilovich, who, before he got to know Viktor, had once threatened to report him to the KGB. Prematurely gray, he sat now placidly, looking at two eights and a Queen of Hearts. He was not playing with anyone else. When he had disappeared from his post, Viktor asked the new guard if anything could be done for Vyachaslav's family. He knew he had a son a year younger than Anna.

There was one bedroom, the one in which Shishkin must have spent a night. No sheets or blankets on the much-spotted mattress; the window was covered but not by a curtain. Instead a piece of rough fabric was nailed into the wall. Viktor thought he knew what he was looking for. Where would it be?

The kitchen was dirty, the refrigerator unplugged. Roaches scrabbled along the greasy electric stovetop.

Viktor reached above the dusty sink, opened a shoddily built cabinet. There they were. Row after row of white cardboard boxes, each the size of a packet of cigarettes. The writing on the boxes was in Latin letters; he had no idea what it said. He opened one: the syringe, its needlepoint capped by a plastic teat, spilled out on to the floor. The vial with it was sealed in a tiny plastic bag.

"It keeps them quiet, you have to admit."

Viktor's shout of fear was involuntary. He dropped the box, spun around.

Dave stood by the door, keys in his hand. At his knees, Borislav Nemetz squatted and pondered a fleck of wall paint.

"Personally, I think we should give this stuff to all the KGB. Even those who don't want to defect." His laugh was thin, hard.

"What is it?" Viktor made no move to pick up the vial he had dropped.

"An experiment. Strong muscle relaxant, artificial metabolic brake, memory block, depressant."

"Soviet?"

"What? Do you think we would use 'mind-altering drugs' like the criminal Soviet medical establishment? Everyone knows the Russian doctors are in league with the secret police." Dave was speaking as though reading the words from a book. "Actually, our boys came up with this. Works wonders."

"So none of these men really defected?"

"I don't know. They look defective to me, don't you think?"

"You gave them something to knock them out."

"No. Just subdue them, like these fellows here. And then, as you can clearly see, we brought them to freedom."

"Here?"

"Viktor, they don't know where they are. They're so zonked they might think they're still guarding the embassy."

"So how do you get them out of the Soviet Union?"

"I told you. We had some help."

"The help of people who don't like Gorbachev."

"The very same."

"But in Moscow, people think they've defected. Gone to you Americans for asylum."

"The first one did."

"The first one? Who was that? When was that?"

"About three months ago. Poshtats was his name."

"Was?"

"Was. Doesn't that sound familiar?"

"Why should it?"

"Do you know anyone of that name?"

"I knew – " It all came together in a mental slam-flash. "Ludmilla's name was Poshtats before she married. She was . . . you gave me . . ."

"She was his sister."

"And he tried to defect?"

187

"Tried. Said he had information about how our own Marine guards were letting Russian whores in at night, letting them see the restricted areas of the embassy. Complete bullshit, of course."

"And so you – "

"Handed him right over to Karushkin. You know Colonel Karushkin, I understand."

"And the letter you gave me for Ludmilla . . ."

"Told her that her brother was a traitor and would be judged that way."

"And she killed herself."

"An overreaction, in my opinion."

"You're a dirty bastard."

"Ah, to hear real insults in good Russian. It's a wonderful language for berating someone, isn't it? And now, Viktor, if you don't mind telling me, how did you find this place and how did you get in?"

Viktor took an instinctive step toward the door. Dave huffed a chuckle and said, "Don't be alarmed, my friend. I have no intention of trying to keep you here against your will. You're in enough trouble as it is."

"You're letting me go?"

"Of course. What harm can you do me? Think the Polish police will come storming in here because a Russian desperado tells them some crazy-sounding story? You'd be the one arrested."

Viktor pondered a moment. It was true. To whom would he go? The Soviet Embassy? The Americans? He was a man without a movement.

"And how do you get them here?"

"Amazing what fits in a diplomatic pouch. Especially when the KGB have orders not to inspect it."

Viktor knew that Dave was right. The size of the shipments that embassies sent into and out of Moscow was scandalous. And the Americans were the worst offenders.

"Why do you bring them here? Why not take them to America?"

Dave snapped his fingers. "Now why didn't I think of that? What a good idea. It's just that I think our friend, Colonel Karushkin, might not agree to that plan."

"But they're out of his reach anyway."

"Are they?"

"What do you mean?"

"Go, Viktor, run. Run fast. You know, I like you. There's something about you. It gives me hope for the miserable country you come from."

"On behalf of my miserable country, thank you."

"You should know one other thing, friend." Dave tossed the apartment key up with his left hand, caught it in his right. "Karushkin is coming for you."

Victoria was waiting for him at the door. "He's not staying here," she said. Her arms were folded across her body.

"Just for a while."

"No! The whole apartment already smells."

"Of what?"

"Jews."

"May I come in, please?"

Shishkin was sitting cross-legged on the floor. He looked at Viktor and said, "I didn't want to touch anything that would absorb my malodorous religion. Also, I think I can smell pork frying, or maybe it's just passion for salt."

"Shut up, Christ-killer." Shishkin put on a scholarly expression and shot back, "Not true! He was convicted by a Roman tribunal and connected to that wooden character builder by pagan nails. The Jews were just there to take bets on how many times he would stumble, and there was probably a Yid lawyer on the hill to help him with his will. For a commission, of course."

The whore's face puffed up as if slapped.

"Stop it, you two." Viktor had no idea of what he was going to say. So he sighed. "Victoria, under normal circumstances, I would speak to you alone, in private, to ask your permission for and opinion of what I am going to do. But these circumstances are very far from common. I have been honest with you. You know I am in trouble in Russia. It is Shishkin who gave me the courage to leave. I owe him much. And he is my friend." He could think of nothing more powerful or convincing.

Shishkin turned to Victoria. "And may I say, lovely lady, that staying in your house" – he ignored Viktor's wince – "will be nearly as great an honor for me as it will for you."

"Stay in my house. My house?"

"I was coming to that," said Viktor.

"Coming, nothing. You are going. Away from here. Now. With your loud kike friend."

"Victoria, we are going. But please let us stay for two days."

Blood fled her face as if her throat had been cut. "Going? Going away?" A most uncharacteristic tremor had crept into her voice.

"So we've got to get away. From the Russians, the Poles, the Americans."

"And from me!" The tears actually popped from her eyes. Both men watched in awed silence, as though observing a live birth. Victoria collapsed on to her bed and spat out a torrent of violent Polish. After two full minutes of sobbing, she stilled. Wiping her eyes carefully on the bedspread, she raised herself on her elbows. "Don't you understand, Viktor? You're the first good break I've ever had. Until I met you, I was special. A whore, and a good one. Now I'm just another woman in love. I have just two questions for you."

"Victoria, I'll answer — "

"When do we leave and do I need to bring high heels? I hate high heels when I'm travelling."

From the bathtub, Shishkin snored. Victoria breathed sleep-softened air in Viktor's ear as he lay awake on his back, trying to picture Czechoslovakia. Shishkin said he had heard it embodied the worst national flaws of Germany and Russia. Viktor knew that their smoked meats were highly prized in Moscow, on the few occasions when they were not snapped up by the Party shops. The word was that living standards in Prague shamed the rest of Eastern Europe. But it was Victoria who had managed to capture the essence of the place, though none of them knew it since none of them had been there. She accomplished this with the dog joke: A Polish dog crossing into Czechoslovakia meets a Czechoslovak dog sneaking into Poland across the border. Each is amazed to see the other doing this and they ask simultaneously, "Why are you going to my country?" The Polish dog recovers first. "I am going to Czechoslovakia so I can eat. And you?" "I am going to Poland so I can bark."

They made him shave the next morning. He howled and moaned and called them anti-Semites, to which Victoria replied, "What else?" But, in the end, he agreed that some things came above religious scruples. And that, since his religious convictions were really only the manifestation of an overall protest against Soviet rule, they could be sacrificed if there was a chance to do some real damage.

He claimed to have forgotten how to shave, but quickly remembered when Victoria stepped forward to perform the service for him with the cut-throat razor she kept in her kitchen drawer for defensive purposes. It was the razor Viktor had been using, with bloody results, since moving in.

When he stepped out of the bathroom, grumbling, Shishkin was momentarily stopped by the look Viktor had given him. "What is it? Have I cut my ear off?"

"Who would have guessed? You're actually not bad-looking!"

"And you actually are."

The morning hours were easy to kill. It was the afternoon, as he finally decided what to do, that made him fidget. He repaired a leak in the kitchen sink, although Victoria pointed out that she had lived with the constant dripping for years. The faucet was silent. So were they, except when Victoria tried to coax conversation from him. "So all it needed was another of those pieces of rubber around it?"

"A washer, yes."

"Well, I don't see why I should be expected to have those in stock."

"Never mind, the other thing worked just as well."

"Are you angry that I had those?"

"Why should I be angry?"

"I mean, some of the scum I've had to do business with. Who knows what germs they had?"

"And now we know they always work as washers."

He never talked with Marya about what he was going to do, only about things already accomplished. Was it possible that she had receded this much, from reality to recollection? He hated to think it, but it was true.

17

He thought about it all morning. By mid-afternoon he knew what he should do. By early evening, he had worked up the courage to say he would do it.

"You are crazed," offered Shishkin when he heard. "What makes you think you can get in again? It sounds like that American wasn't too pleased to find you there. Besides, he tells you Karushkin is coming after you. And you still want to try this?"

But Viktor was in the silent stage of reflection that only those with no second thoughts can achieve. He hummed back at Shishkin, stroked the side of his own face, turned away.

Victoria lay on the bed, listening. Viktor was waiting for her to speak, wanted to hear her judgment. He knew that while Shishkin could not stop his mouth from moving, he probably had nothing to suggest. He wished to know what Victoria, whose silence he had come to regard as inspirational, would tell him to do.

She rose, moved to him with an intentionally overdone sway in her hips, and said: "I'm hungry. Let's go out."

She took them to a quasi-French place called Napoleon, located seven kilometers outside Warsaw on the road to Gdansk. Throw them off the track, she told Viktor while they nuzzled in the back seat. She won the taxi-driver's promise to return by 9.15.

They were all surprised to be met at the door by a tuxedoed maître d' who said: "Bonsoir. Vous avez reservé?"

"What?" Victoria's response uncannily resembled a parrot squawk. "Don't you speak Polish?"

"Of course I do, madame. I merely assumed that the gentlemen with you were foreigners and so I spoke the international language." The oiliness in the voice was choking.

"And what made you think they were foreigners?"

"Their, uh, attire is, uh, unusual."

It was true. Viktor wore the fruity-smelling sweater that Victoria had given him, and the trousers that had been steam-dried on the radiator. Shishkin was still wearing the suit of clothes in which he had been buffeted around the coffin. Victoria had never considered that Viktor might own, or what he would look like in, different clothes. And she could not have cared less about Shishkin's appearance.

Victoria was not fast on her feet. She relied on her own temerity. "And what about it, cupcake? In fact, they are foreign. They're Bulgarian . . . filmmakers. Here at the invitation of the Minister of Culture, whom I know. Shall I tell the Minister that you turned his guests away because you have no fashion sense? What's your name anyway, sunshine?" Victoria hadn't the slightest idea of the name of the Minister of Culture. But, more importantly, she was certain that the monkey-suited waiter did not, either. In Poland, being equal to an adversary and knowing it is the same as winning.

"I'll, uh, find you a table. Fortunately, we are not fully booked this evening."

"Don't make me laugh. I've been here before. Some of the chairs in this place have never had anything but dust sitting on them. We'll wait in the bar." The two Russians moved behind her as though in a minefield, planting their feet exactly where hers had been. The bar was located through two swinging glass doors, off to the left from the main eating room. Two couples, fashionably dressed, sat at one table, consuming the kind of cocktails that Poles think indicate civilization: a bluish Curaçao-based suspension laced with whisky.

"Set 'em up," ordered Victoria, when she caught the bartender's eye. The tone and volume of her voice were impossible to ignore. "Vodka for everyone, including yourself." Again, habits. In other days, Victoria had trolled barrooms, and in the kind into which she was admitted, such suggestions were common.

The bartender, who had been selected for the job because he looked as though he had been everywhere in the world at least once, had never before been invited to partake of his own stock. His skill was in keeping the bar orderly, while at the same time ensuring that the clientèle drank steadily. This was a delicate task: being Slavs, most Poles are unable to gauge the effect of the alcohol they are drinking until they are foundering.

Victoria had the gleaming eyes of a hell-raiser. Moreover, by ordering vodka, she was proclaiming that she was here to drink, not to be seen doing it. And her two dirty companions looked as though they had just sold their yearly harvests at the peasants' market and were looking for a quick way to spend the proceeds.

"I'm sure you and your" – the barman could think of no word to describe Viktor and Shishkin that did not carry a sexual inuendo, at least in his own mind. He stopped, gulped, his brain scrambling wildly, then came up with – "accompaniment would prefer some water or soda with the vodka, would you not?"

Victoria leaned over the wooden bar, with what she thought was Marlene Dietrich-like allure, and said: "You just give us the vodka, which you've probably already watered, and leave the rest to us, sugar." This was followed by a ghastly smile.

As they sat at the round covered table for six which Victoria had appropriated, Viktor hissed: "Why don't you just call the police and tell them we're here. It will save them paying overtime to the men who come to arrest us."

"Easy, my grizzly. You're not intimidated by a couple of dishwashers in fancy clothes, are you?"

"Intimidation has nothing to do with it. We came here for a quiet meal. Fine. Let's not draw attention to ourselves." He saw Shishkin smiling. "What's so amusing?"

"I was just trying to imagine the scene if Karushkin decided to use his first night in Warsaw to have a couple of stiff drinks and a good dinner, and was told to come here. What do you think his face would look like if he came through the door and saw us, spilling vodka down our necks?"

The waiter carried over a liter bottle of Wyborowa, plunged up to its neck in a glass ice-bucket. Three glasses, about the size of a spool of cotton thread, were arranged around it. "That will be sixteen thousand zloty, please."

Victoria had been about to pick up one of the glasses. She drew back her hand. "Are you out of whatever small mind you possess? For sixteen thousand zloty I can buy a partnership in the liquor store near where I live. A liter of export-grade Wyborowa sells for six thousand, and this isn't export grade."

"I'm sorry, madame, but that is the price charged here."

"Let me see your price list."

"Price list? Whatever for? Everyone who works here knows the prices, as do our more regular customers." There was more than one knife's edge in the voice.

"I happen to know that Polish law requires all restaurants – and I presume this dump qualifies – to post their prices somewhere. Bars usually have theirs taped to the back of the cash register, or some other place where no one ever thinks to look. Now either show me where yours is, or admit that you're in violation of the law."

The barman had grown very red. He was raising his hands, and Viktor and Shishkin thought he might pounce on them, or Victoria, any minute. "Very well, madame. In this case, I shall make an exception, and charge you only eight thousand zloty. But you and your gentlemen must promise not to create any further disturbance."

"By which you mean not to tell the manager you're a thief? I'll think about it. Now leave us alone." Victoria was beaming as she turned away from the slinking barman and said, discreetly, in Russian: "Now here's to us, a pretty odd assortment of people."

Viktor, who after ten years' abstinence had convinced himself he no longer liked the taste of vodka, drank deeply.

The bottle no longer contained enough to fill up all three glasses when the tuxedoed maître d' told them their table was ready. He might have been telling the truth earlier; all the other tables were occupied. Theirs was in the middle of the large room, exposed, as it were, to all sides. The menus they were given had large black fake-leather covers with a red string running down the spine and attached to a tassel of the same color. The maître d' was all slick attention and unctuous service now; working for his tip. Viktor recognized the man as the type he least liked to work with. As soon as the minimum amount of work was done, and payment guaranteed, all effort ceased.

They were surprised to see the menus in both Latin and Cyrillic letters. The waiter simpered. "I regret that we do not have our carte de jour in Bulgarian, but I trust the gentlemen will be able to read Russian."

"We'll do just fine, thank you." Victoria might have been swiping at a mosquito. "Tell your waiters to set up the champagne trick for us." She slammed a handful of zloty bills on to the table.

With frigid dignity, the maître d' said: "You are referring to the bubbling fountain. It will be our pleasure, madame."

As he left, Victoria made a scooping motion with her index and middle fingers. "Pretentious prick." Viktor winced and looked around him to see who else might have heard.

Three young waiters bounced out of the kitchen. One pushed a rectangular butler's table on wheels. On the table was a cardboard carton, bearing red lettering which said, in Russian: "Fragile. Soviet champagne. No hooks."

"Does that mean you're not permitted to stay?" Shishkin asked Victoria. It took a few seconds for her to reach the high crimson glow that meant she had understood the taunt. Around the carton were twenty-one hollow-stemmed champagne glasses, the kind into which it used to be said a woman's breast should fit. With practiced rhythm, one of the waiters unloaded the carton of champagne while the other two constructed a pyramid of glasses, six on the bottom row, then five, four, three, two and at a top, a single glass.

"Now watch this, you two." Victoria's tone of voice seemed to imply that what was to follow would put an end to any anti-Polish thoughts the two Russians might ever have again. The sound of the first cork popping attracted the attention of any of the diners who were not already looking at the spectacle. The waiter carelessly upended the bottle, and a gush of effervescent wine spilled into the mouth of the top glass, rolled into the stem, and quickly filled the bowl. It reached the top of the glass less than a second later, and coursed over the side.

As the last drop left the ninth bottle, the pourer turned it right side up like a magician waving his top hat once the rabbit has disappeared. A bark of applause broke out among the diners, eclipsed by Victoria's shrill whistle of approval. The waiter, with great dignity, began disassembling the pyramid and distributing the champagne glasses. The last three were laid before Viktor, Shishkin and Victoria.

Their dinners had been ready for quite a while, delayed by the epic champagne-fall. In the interim, the plates had been placed on the floor by the door leading to the kitchen. Victoria had ordered the same for all of them – beef en brochette, served with the vegetable of the day, which today like all other days was saffron rice. But the delay had allowed the plates to grow cold. When they arrived, the beef looked like chunks of dirt or worse, the rice was glued resiliently together.

"Well, at least my champagne is warm." Shishkin never allowed a knife to go unplunged.

The maître d' approached, along with an elderly man in a black suit and a shirt that Viktor could have sworn had detachable collars and cuffs. He bowed formally before Victoria before planting a chaste kiss on her hand.

"Dear lady, how kind of you to share with us your happiness at having two guests from a foreign land. And for me, what a happy coincidence. I am Zbigniew Mankiewicz."

The maître d' smiled. "Professor Mankiewicz is chairman of modern languages at Warsaw University. I told him your companions were from Bulgaria."

The professor assumed a cheerful smile. "Please don't think that I've come here to inflict my own poor Bulgarian on your guests. I would never think of such a thing. It's true I just returned from a trip there, an exchange with the University at Varna. But I'm afraid the Bulgarian tongue is too subtle for me. Do these two gentlemen, perchance, speak Polish?"

"No, I'm afraid they don't. That's why they need me. Need me to translate for them, that is."

"Ah, but might I assume that they speak Russian, since their own language is inevitably bound up with the mother of Slavic expression?" The tiny professor had said this last in Russian, and had turned to face Shishkin, for some reason taking him to be the leader of the two.

"Da, da, you most certainly can assume that," Shishkin said, nodding. "We speak Russian because it would be too much to expect people to know our own language which, you may know, contributed the Cyrillic alphabet to the world. It was not the Russians, as they would have you believe."

"Yes, I'm sure." Mankiewicz swallowed hard, then said something that sounded like Russian, except that every third word was wrong or unintelligible.

They stared at him as if he had just sneezed while chewing a mouthful of caviar.

"What did you say professor?" Victoria alone had not picked up the violent change in mood. "I speak Russian but I'm afraid I didn't catch that last."

He said in Polish: "Neither did your friends, who, I must tell you madame, are not Bulgarian. They did not understand the very simple sentence I just spoke to them. But it is even simpler to tell they are not from Bulgaria. The Bulgarian way of saying yes is to shake one's head from side to side, the way most other people of Europe say no. To say no, they do this – " and the elderly man proceeded to move his head as though he had water in his ears, bounding his left ear on his left shoulder, then his right ear on right shoulder. "I am sorry to tell you this, madame, but these men have lied to you if they said they were from Bulgaria. I should guess them to be native-born Russians, though this one – " he poked a finger at Shishkin – "might possibly be a Jew." Mankiewicz tottered back to his table, from which he glared several times at Shishkin.

Victoria pulled from her purse a stack of paper that could have contained a novella. She began counting the zloty, calling simultaneously for the check. Shishkin asked insistently, "What's wrong, what's happened?" but Viktor had already put the situation together in his mind. "The game's up, let's get going." She screwed the top on to the last, still-nearly full bottle of vodka that they had ordered, mumbling, "I paid for it." Shishkin lifted an unopened champagne bottle from its ice bucket.

The taxi-driver who had brought them to Napoleon's was waiting out front. "Came for what he thinks I promised him," she hissed to Viktor, her hand inside his sweater. "You'll have to follow my lead."

"What's this?" protested the driver. "I thought you'd be alone."

"I will be as soon as you drop these two off. Then you can drive me to my place."

The grumbling driver, under Victoria's instructions, took them to within a block of the apartment building.

"Wait here," she told him.

"What is going on?" Viktor asked as soon as they had all gotten out of the cab. "You told me taxis make records of their passengers. Why have this one return, and let him put us down here, so close?"

"Don't worry, my lion," said Victoria. The liquor had brightened her eyes and enlivened her speech. "By the time this one recovers, we'll be long gone. Now go do what you have to do. But remember: the Krakowski Station at five before midnight, outside the eastern entrance." She puffed a kiss at him, stuck her tongue out at Shishkin and got back into the taxi, this time in the front seat. They could hear her giggling with the driver as he pulled away.

They looked at each others, then down the street toward the building. Shishkin sighed for dramatic effect. "How do I merit such misery?"

"Easily, Yevgeny. You're Russian and you know me."

"Yes, both things I may regret someday."

"But not now."

"No, not now."

This time the door of the building had not closed securely; they had no trouble getting in. "Why are there no guards, why don't the Americans have someone watching?" Shishkin asked no one in particular. Viktor recognized it as worry-talk. Up the five flights, two of them still unlit.

"Think about it. Wouldn't it be unusual for Americans to be posted here? In Poland. A Soviet ally?"

"Then why aren't there Polish police, or Soviets? Someone. You can't just keep KGB militiamen prisoners without taking precautions. Can you?"

"They don't even know they're in Poland. You saw them. So did I. They're drugged beyond caring."

"So how do you expect them to fend for themselves?"

"I don't. That's the point."

Viktor knocked boldly on the door. He wanted to go in with confidence so that what he was planning to do would not arouse any anxiety among the drugged Russians.

He was wrong. There was a sentry, of sorts.

"So," slurred Andrzej, opening the door wide, "have you come back to give me my money?"

Both Russians were caught flatfooted. "I've heard a bit more about that money," said Viktor. "Sounds to me as if you overcharged my friend here for his hotel room. Especially," he tried to stare over Andrzej's shoulder, "since it's already got quite a few occupants."

Andrzej moved to block Viktor's view, and Viktor got a whiff of him. He was three-quarters drunk, at least. Viktor, unused to the effect of alcohol, was also feeling slightly woozy from the vodka and champagne at the restaurant. But he was alert enough to act. He breathed intentionally into Andrzej's face, made sure the fumes registered. "I think I like Polish vodka better than Russian," he said, making the words flow together. From behind his back he produced the bottle Victoria had insisted on taking from the restaurant. "Tell me what you think."

"Sure," said Andrzej, happy to be diverted by free booze. He flicked off the cap with a single swipe of his middle finger. The top danced into the darkness of the stairwell. Andrzej tilted the bottle and his neck at the same time, and brought his arm up.

Thwack! He never saw the champagne bottle that Shishkin brought over the back of his skull. It did not crack, but the force of the blow popped the cork. Silver fizz covered Shishkin, then quickly mixed with Andrzej's blood.

"Let's go," Viktor said, feeling slightly sick.

Most were asleep, a few meandered around without purpose, oblivious of the hour.

"Borislav, where are you?" called Viktor. He found him spread-eagled across a piece of carpeting in the bedroom. The bed was empty.

"Borislav, Nemetz, do you hear me?" Drugged, he came alert faster than a drunk, but his look was one of total incomprehension. "Borislav, it's Viktor Nikolaich, you remember me, don't you? I was here yesterday."

"Where are my cigarettes?" It was something dredged up from the past purely by face association.

"I have them for you downstairs. You must go with my friend to get them."

Unwillingly, Nemetz came to his feet. Even more reluctantly, he let Shishkin lead him to the door, down the stairs.

"Petrov, Vassily Ignativich, are you here?"

Three minutes later, Viktor had convinced him that a copy of *Playboy* awaited him at street level. Shishkin led him down to his reward.

Andrzej moved several times during this exodus, but neither worried about him. After almost an hour, it was finished. Andrzej was tied, compassionately but securely, with sheets from the bed.

"Where did they go?" Viktor asked as they closed the door behind them.

"Different directions. I told the one who wanted to see a porno movie to go down to the next building and ask the first woman he met. Be a pity if she didn't understand him, wouldn't it?"

On the street again, Viktor saw one of the KGB guards a hundred yards away, placidly inspecting trash cans like an abused hound. They went to the corner, and after only thirty seconds, hailed a taxi.

Viktor knew what to say. "Krakowski vauxhall." The driver, himself a taciturn fellow, nodded and made a U-turn. At least these two weren't drunk, he told himself.

Krakowski station was very like Soviet train terminals: vast, unheated, unwashed, jam-packed. Shishkin waited outside, which he explained was "the place of choice for cowards".

Viktor remembered how it felt to be drunk. And with a fair share of a bottle of vodka and a glass of champagne inside him for the first time in almost ten years, it was not entirely acting when he swaggered up to the bend of a long line at the first ticket window and bellowed: "Who here speaks Russian?"

This caused more of a stir than, say, a Frenchman, demanding that someone speak his language in London. Most Poles remember enough Russian from their compulsory schooling in it to understand such a question. Viktor was greeted with hostile glares among those whom he was trying to nudge out of line, and by a helpless look on the part of the ticket clerk whose window he had chosen: the woman did not remember any Russian at all. It took several minutes of shouting and awkward silence before a thin, blond young man quite obviously, to Viktor anyway, a homosexual, addressed him. "They say you speak only Russian. What do you want?"

"At last, someone in this damn village who's had an education," Viktor roared. "I want a ticket to West Berlin."

"West Berlin? For that you need an exit permission. Do you have one?"

"Exit permission my ass! I've gotten this far, I'm not about to be stopped now."

"May I assume you're not Polish?"

"You can assume it. I can rejoice in it. Of course not. I'm Russian, and not bound by your pissante laws."

"I'm afraid everyone who wants to leave Poland is bound by our, uh, pissante laws. May I see your passport?"

"I don't have to justify anything to you or any other puny Pole. After all I've been through, I don't have to justify anything to anyone."

"So you won't show me your passport?"

"I'll show you what you really want to see, cuty. But we'd better go in the men's room, where you'll be more comfortable."

The young man's face stiffened; the mildly patronizing tone left his voice. "What's your name?"

"Melanov, Viktor Nikolaich. A name you'll be hearing more about soon."

"Well, Mr soon-to-be-famous, for the moment, you've got two problems. Without a passport and an exit permission, you can't get to West Berlin. And even if you had both, you couldn't get to it from here. This station handles only southbound trains."

"Dammit, the other faggot who brought me here in his taxi said this was the station for Berlin."

"I'm afraid not. You want the Poznan station. Any taxi outside will know how to get there."

"Poznan stadon, Ponzan sadon, podzor sazon . . ." Each meaningless pair of words dribbled away less distinctly as Viktor weaved toward the door.

The young man smiled bitterly to himself. He would remember the name Melanov.

Twenty minutes later, Victoria arrived at the station, pushed to the front of the line and bought three tickets to Prague for herself, Mr Wladyslaw Riebek, 47, a steel-mill hand and Mr Zbigniew Kolchowski, 49, taxi-driver. Riebek had left his passport in her sheets years ago. Kolchowski, with luck, would not miss his for days.

The train left exactly on time.

18

Viktor had entered Poland in a box. Now he was leaving in another one, larger it is true, but only slightly more comfortable. He was jammed between a fat man and a larger woman, each of whom seemed intent on establishing primacy on the backless steel bench. Third-class train travel in Poland makes certain social assumptions, chief among them that anyone so straitened as to use it will not have the temerity to complain. The boxcar – no other term fit – was a windowless, unheated enclosure of wood and steel. To convert it into a freight carrying box, it would be necessary only to remove the three steel benches, each about twelve feet long. Two had been bolted lengthwise on either side, the third ran down the middle of the car. Naturally, the two side benches were more coveted, since they afforded the wall of the car to lean against. Shishkin had outmaneuvered a Polish soldier on leave to get the last sliver of space on one end bench, thus earning himself yet another enemy. Victoria had switched on her charm and convinced a spry middle-aged fellow to give up his seat on the other side bench.

Viktor was compressed in the middle, wondering if internal organs could explode when kept under constant pressure for seven hours. He envied Shishkin, who had availed himself of the toilet while Viktor was carrying out the tickets-to-Berlin dodge. And Victoria had refused to answer all questions about what she had done once she and the taxi-driver were headed back to her apartment. Opportunity for talk was limited. As soon as she bought the tickets, they had sprinted for the train, boarded and sat separately. To avoid possible conversation and the revelation that he could not speak Polish, Viktor had tried to feign sleep. He soon realized that no one could sleep in the position his body had been molded into, and that anyone who was pretending to doze peacefully looked even more suspicious than a person who refused to speak. Besides, neither of his immediate neighbors looked like the kind to initiate time-killing banter.

From time to time, he and Shishkin heard wisps of conversation in a language that sounded too much like Russian to be Polish, yet not enough like it for them to understand. Though they could not discuss it, each assumed correctly that Czech was being spoken. It seemed to consist mostly of the roots of Russian words couched between beginnings and ends made up of sounds like "schwo", "schnee" and "schnwa". These, Viktor thought, would be the dogs who had had their bark returning home for a solid meal.

He no longer pretended that there was a plan. Enough things had gone awry in Poland to shatter any illusion that he was locked in a game of tactics and strategy with Karushkin. He was just living through more months of the same life under Communism that he had always known: confusion, false words, fear.

Something else had changed too. He realized as he thought it through that he no longer cared what happened. He wanted Marya safe and well and alive and Anna happy and with a future. Beyond that, there seemed little difference in what fate he, Shishkin or Victoria was dealt. He recognized this as a variation of the zombie syndrome, but felt helpless to defend against it. He knew his mistake: he had congratulated himself too early. Because secretly Viktor never believed that he and Shishkin could escape the Soviet Union, their success had made him feel that he had accomplished more than was the case. No breath feels so good as the first one drawn after winning a race. If the happy runner suddenly realizes that he has run only the first lap, and that he has many more to complete, it is almost impossible to recover the spirit of competition and the zest for victory.

Seven hours without conversation, without water, without sleep and without a place to rest his back. The only things he had, he had in plenty: the sour smell of human flesh, a pressing bladder and a headache. He had fooled himself into thinking that his years of abstinence from alcohol provided him with immunity against its effects. Their rapid consumption of a bottle in the restaurant, capped by the silly champagne, brought him back to the realities of a hangover: the feeling that there was jagged glass just in front of and around his eyes; an agonizing battle against the bubbles trying to escape through each passage of his body; the suspicion, verging on certainty, that he would never feel well again.

Whenever he looked at Victoria, on the side bench, two directly conflicting emotions seared through Viktor like voltage: admiration for her courage and anger at her recklessness. There was no doubt of the courage, both the kind that had sustained her through years of a life that

203

Viktor did not want to imagine, and the kind that endowed her with the nerve to throw her lot in with two on-the-run Russians.

But his sense of survival was outraged by her need to show off. He realized that even when he met her, she was playing the edge, walking some line that threatened to hurt her, and at best could satisfy her only momentarily. Why insist on going to a restaurant? Why flirt with the taxi-driver? Simply because he had a passport? Could she have been scheming even then to use it for their escape? He doubted she had so much forethought. The surly behavior with the waiter and bartender, and the lies about their nationality, so easily revealed by tiny Professor Mankiewicz. Viktor, who had survived in Moscow by mixing constant caution with occasional risks, was sure that Mankiewicz would eventually be located by the KGB and tell his story. That was why Viktor had decided to announce his presence with the drunken act in Krakowski Station. It was just possible that his pursuers might believe Berlin was his destination. That might give them enough lead-time to reach Czechoslovakia.

And then what? For all the warmth of spring, Czechoslovakia was oppressive, rabidly pro-Soviet, filled with secret police and informers, and worst of all, unknown. The idea made sense when he and Shishkin first roughed it out; now it seemed as lunatic as leaving Moscow in a coffin.

A coffin. Karushkin chuckled as he ran his hands over the wood, gingerly touched the seam where the bottom had been prised loose. He had seen in Melanov the components of a problem, not of thoughtful opposition. But this? How could anyone – the border guards, the KGB, anyone – have anticipated this?

Karushkin made himself stop. He was thinking like a victim, not a pursuer. Making up excuses to cover ineptitude when his career had been spent rejecting all reasons for failure. It was part of the myth: that the KGB knew all, controlled all, foresaw every eventuality. This was rubbish. The KGB got its information through hard work: voluminous files kept up-to-date, the selective use of informers who were paid fairly, good communications with branch offices. Karushkin was in Warsaw now because a Polish Army intelligence officer in Bialystok had heard rumors of strange goings-on at the Forensics Center there involving a coffin that had been off-loaded from a train. Because MIV, the military intelligence unit in the army, encouraged operatives to report unverified information, the agent had made a two-line mention of the incident in a weekly briefing paper. Within twenty-four hours, the information had been computerized. The next day, the KGB central computer ran cross-checks on: Melanov, Viktor Nikolaich; Shishkin, Yevgeny Moisovich; all passengers travelling by rail and air whose names were within two letters of the suspects'; reports of missing or stolen passports and exit permissions.

The last hit paydirt. The permission slip issued to the Rabbi bore a number. That number was part of a serial used for exits by people, not objects. The inspector at Grodno did not have the authority (nor the inclination) to open the coffin, but he had noted the irregular number and reported it.

Karushkin never knew that. The computer had received more than five hundred items for which irregular exit permission slips had appeared. Without further instructions, it ordered a cross-check of every one of the items. One of them was the coffin that had left the Soviet Union from Kievsky Station. Still operating automatically, it requested a cross-check (Poland) of any mentions of coffins coming from the Soviet Union. There was only one.

When Karushkin realized that Shishkin and Viktor were together, he almost panicked. He was faced with a dilemma. Despite being suspended, he retained some influence. Because the suspension was not generally known, he was still cut in on all normal cable traffic. And thus, he learned how he had been tricked. Should he take the information to the Chairman, show him what happened when the KGB allowed politics to dictate policy? That might vindicate him and give him a free hand, which at this point was all-important. Or it might result in another tongue-lashing by the Chairman, and further restrictions on his activities, which would be fatal. Karushkin had survived and prospered during the long, dark night of Stalin, the unpredictable farce of Khrushchev, the gray and graceless Brezhnev epoch — all by following a strategy designed to avoid major errors. He decided again on the conservative approach: say nothing, let the official machinery creak along. Meanwhile, he made another, equally important choice: to get Melanov and Shishkin himself.

Without authorization, he commandeered a young agent who spoke Polish. Next, he bullied the section chief holding Marya and Anna to release them into his custody. One phone call to the Chairman's office requesting confirmation of Colonel Karushkin's authority to do this would have ended the game. But KGB operatives — even in the age of Gorbachev — are disinclined to try to override or resist a superior. Sixty years of secret killing and terror have left their mark.

Karushkin, age sixty-nine, did something for the first time in his life on that day: he bought an airplane ticket by himself, with his own money. He was outraged at the rudeness, the waiting, the uncooperative attitude at the Aeroflot counter at Sheremetyevo Airport. Did ordinary

Russians put up with this all the time? He was sorely tempted to whip out his KGB credential and savor the look on the face of the fat woman who dawdled with his tickets. "You're lucky there's space on the flight, grandpa. Now go over there and pay, get a receipt and get back in this line. If I'm still here then I'll give you your tickets."

Karushkin wondered: did Gorbachev know?

No one in Poland's secret police would know about his suspension, of that he was sure. And the unannounced appearance of a KGB colonel from Moscow would carry weight of its own. Beyond official courtesies – a car, a place to stay, a telephone – he would not have to trouble the SB overmuch. And his quarry would produce no feedback to Moscow. They were not capable of altering the balance of world power. Whether he found them the next day or week, Karushkin knew, made little difference to anyone but him. But it did make a difference. He was a man who had made a career of working the system to his own advantage. As such he was burdened by its often idiotic demands.

The coffin had been fetched from Bialystok, and so had the old coroner. As Karushkin listened to the translation of the coroner's stuttering description of Viktor and Shishkin as they slowly emerged from the coffin, he grinned.

The logic was unassailable, Viktor concluded. The Czechs would think he was Polish and the Poles would be convinced he was Czech. He had only to look bemused when anyone addressed him, and shove the taxi-driver's passport at them. No one would look; everyday people in the Soviet empire are not anxious to be seen touching other people's passports.

It worked in Radom and Kielce, in Jedrzejow and Kazimierza Wielke. By the time the train pulled into Krakow, seven and a half hours after leaving Warsaw, Viktor was confident. Krakow was the capital of the long-dead Polish empire, the city where kings had looked out of the windows of Wawel Castle on to the Vistula River. And when the brown-uniformed conductor rolled open the door to the third-class compartment and shouted: "Everyone out!", it became the place where Viktor saw the beginning of the end of his adventure and the dénouement of his life.

"Out? Why out?" said Victoria, and her voice, though a welcome sound after so long, made Viktor nervous because it betrayed defeat. "This is a direct train to Prague."

"Was a direct train to Prague," said the mouth above the uniform collar. "Got engine trouble. Have to have it looked at here. Everybody out."

There was a general clamor then. The Czechs, who numbered about a third of the compartment, looked around with startled, contemptuous expressions. In such situations, the Teutonic tendencies of Czechs often surface: demands for order and timeliness, scant patience with inefficiency. But most Czechs are intelligent enough (another national trait) to exhibit such Germanic behavior only outside the boundaries of their own homeland.

Victoria hustled to the door of the carriage, signalled for Viktor and Shishkin to follow. As they stepped down from the car, another brown uniform gave them each an orange ticket. The Russians accepted theirs wordlessly. Victoria scanned the contents, and smiled.

"It's not as bad as it might be," she said to Viktor, speaking quietly although they were in the midst of the enormous din of the Krakow train station. Because only Victoria had left with luggage, they had little trouble outpacing the other passengers in moving down the platform. Victoria walked between Viktor and Shishkin but her face was turned so that only Viktor could hear what she said. "The ticket says the train will leave at nine a.m. That's about four hours from now."

Viktor looked at her blankly, then said: "Are you telling me it's five in the morning?"

"What time did you think it was?"

He had not paid attention to time for twelve hours, since his scheduled meeting with Dave had passed. The dinner had been a haze of vodka and fear, and the time on the train had seemed endless and so, imponderable.

"Are you hungry?" Victoria asked.

Shishkin spoke for the first time. "I am so travel-sick. That fellow I was sitting next to smelled like all my garbage from last year had come back for a visit."

"It would take brave garbage to do that. If you're not," she said to Viktor, "I know a pleasant place here to pass a few hours."

"Auschwitz, no doubt. That's only a short drive from Krakow, isn't it?" Shishkin asked.

"Something you should keep in mind," the whore fired back. "It's a little club, right in the heart of the city. If I recall correctly, it would only be a fifteen-minute taxi ride. And I've still got lots of zloty."

"What kind of club would open at this time?" Viktor was using his earnest voice. "Please, Victoria, no more booze. As it is, I don't think my head will ever fit properly on top of my body again."

"Don't worry, my brave all-nighter. The only way you can get a buzz from the stuff they serve here is if air got in the canned orange juice."

"What's this place called?" They had reached a rank of taxis whose drivers were standing in a semi-circle, muttering among themselves.

"How much to Pod Baromi?" Victoria asked no one in particular.

"Never heard of it," said the oldest of the drivers, but Viktor noticed the hostility that lit up his eyes.

"Seven thousand," said a younger driver with a beard. His grin was unmistakable.

"Four thousand and I'll buy your way in."

"Nah, I was just there last week. They're going to put Kalabinski away soon if he's not careful."

"They wouldn't dare," Victoria answered.

The young man snorted. "They would, but they won't. Okay. Five thousand. Get on in."

For no reason that Viktor could discern, Victoria apparently felt free to speak to the two Russians in the back seat of the cab. "There's no place like Pod Baromi. On weekends it stays open all night. Of course, they can't serve alcohol. But you can believe that the audience gets high."

"What are we talking about?" Viktor was nervous both because she was speaking Russian, and because he did not like the way this place, whatever it was, sounded. Was Victoria about to expose them to her peculiar need for danger yet again? "And what about him?" He jerked his chin toward the front seat, where the driver, apparently oblivious of the strange language behind him, was working the near-empty streets.

"Don't worry about him. He says he's been to Pod Baromi and anyone who's been there won't do us any harm."

Viktor wondered: Does she think the secret police took an oath never to mislead their victims?

Even as he fretted, Viktor admired the little of Krakow he saw, shrouded by the last shadows of night, framed by the car's windshield.

Along the graceful curves of the Vistula banks, stately stone walls rose, but not so high as to cut off the view of the water. The taxi-driver crossed the Grunwald Bridge and cut into Luwidska Street. As though under some movie director's orders, the first feeble strand of light fell from the sky, and Viktor, totally unprepared, beheld the castle. Its turrets fairly hung over the steep embankment that plunged to the river. Its crenellated wall bespoke some past age, when no limits were placed on the whims of royalty. The tiny unglassed holes in the gray stone brought to mind the days when such fortifications were defended with spears, hot oil, and suicidal bravery. Viktor looked at Shishkin, who was also unashamedly gaping. For the first time, both of them understood why Poles were so bloody-minded in preserving what they grandly called their national identity. Now, nearing five-thirty, Viktor saw that the day was beginning to dawn. It was Shishkin who nudged him, and still wary of speaking their own language, pointed wordlessly to the scene in front of them.

They had come to the huge square Central Market, where all was chaos. Women hawked flowers in immense wicker baskets and hurled slurs at those who passed them by. Stocky men, all wearing dark blue or black workers' caps, swarmed over the cobblestones, each shouldering what Viktor at first thought might be multi-colored cannon barrels. "Bolts of cloth," said Victoria, nudging her way into the foreigners' confusion. "Krakow used to be Europe's biggest cloth market."

It was also a fruit, herb, vegetable, meat, tool, car part and souvenir market and each was revved to high pitch with the first burst of day's light. No such huge, single place of commerce existed in Moscow and, from the Russians' expressions, they might have been seeing the New York Stock Exchange in full swing.

"Is this the place you are taking us?" Viktor hoped it was. He wanted to mingle with these businessmen, bargain with them, see if he could better them in dealing.

"It's not far from here," said Victoria, and, a second later, the taxi came to a stop. The driver turned around. "You're not from Krakow, so you may not know; this is as . . ."

". . . far as you can go. Yes, I told you, I've been here. And what makes you think I'm not from here?"

"It's your accent." He folded the five thousand zloty into his shirt pocket. "Enjoy Kalabinski."

They stood on the extreme north-east corner of the market, where Mikolajska Street met Florianska. Victoria pointed to the south, where the square ended abruptly at the juncture of two tan stone buildings.

"There's no door," observed Shishkin as they reached the corner. Victoria smirked. "You, proud Jew, assume we're going some place that's at street level."

"I don't see any ladder coming down from heaven."

"Should you? Is your real name Jacob?" Victoria's cheeks were blooming pink, just as they had been at the restaurant. Viktor had recognized that as a trustworthy indication that she was feeling feisty. If so, he had to try to shut her down before something happened that was even more catastrophic than the things that had already befallen them.

Victoria never gave him a chance. As they reached the corner of the square, she stomped hard on a metal trap door set in the concrete surface. The door was the kind that shops use to have goods delivered from the street directly to underground storerooms. The clang made by Victoria's heavy footsteps was still in the air. An ugly sound came from below, something like a guard dog just before it attacks.

The sound, however, had meaning to Victoria, who stepped back and said something in Polish using a fruity tone of voice. The metal door lifted and revealed a thick-necked young man and an older woman whose hair reached her waist. Both were smiling. They were also carrying thick white clubs attached to their wrists by heavy black leather thongs.

"My God," Shishkin said. "Those are police billy clubs." The effect of this observation in Russian was immediate. The woman snarled, the man lifted his club as if to strike. For the first time, Victoria looked panicked. She swirled out a chain of poly-syllabic assurances, then waited like a defendant watching the jury return.

"Yeesh," said the woman, and it registered with Viktor that she, not the muscle-man, was in charge.

The steps dropped almost straight down. Viktor peered at each one before planting his foot on it. Behind him, Victoria folded her skirt between her legs and came down backwards, like a fireman on a ladder. Shishkin stood at the top for so long that the muscular guard tapped him on the foot with his white stick.

"Is this how you persuade people to come into your hellhole?"

The young man stared back.

The woman said something testily.

"Shishkin, get down here," Viktor ordered.

"Better yet, stay up there and be damned." Victoria, having reached the bottom of the stairs safely, was once again brave.

Viktor had expected darkness. Instead, he found himself in the midst of – what? – was there such a thing as murky brightness? He wondered: What do they do, empty all the city's furnaces down here? Never had he seen, or smelt, such a concentration of smoke in one place. Even buildings that caught fire in Moscow were suffused by the surrounding air outside. A second later, an arrow of white light swept across the space where he stood, both blinding and paralyzing him. Then he understood.

The spotlight rolled across his line of vision again and he winced. He heard a tideswell of laughter. When he opened his eyes, he saw Victoria waving both hands and trying to make herself heard above the hooting. She said something in her powerful whore's voice. The last word was the name the taxi-driver had mentioned twice: Kalabinski. There was a split second of silence, then a low mocking man's voice, followed by a cannonade of new guffaws. Another voice, amplified, rose over the crest of chuckles.

"Hurry up, you two, come with me." Victoria was abrupt. They pushed forward through the soupy air for about ten feet. A series of bobbing white lumps slowly became heads, which acquired faces, whose mouths seemed in constant motion.

Have I forgotten what people look like when they're laughing? Viktor asked himself. Laughing was an understatement. The fifty or so heads which he saw were rolling back and forth with little or no control.

There was not an empty seat in the impromptu nightclub. Victoria solved the problem the same way she had on the train. After five seconds of intense conversation, two older men seated at a round cocktail table for four obligingly stood up and offered their chairs. The two younger women, obviously not their wives, at first protested the undue courtesy, but quickly backed off when Victoria hissed something at them.

"Sit." There was nothing in the command to suggest a choice. Viktor, feeling very much like a wayward hound, dropped on to the metal folding chair closest to him. Shishkin had to squirm around the table, rubbing his buttocks against the shoulders of two patrons at the nearest table. Viktor noticed both of the men turn and sniff their jackets.

The amplified voice was again carrying through the smoke-choked room. Every ten seconds or so, there was a pause, punctuated by a burst of appreciative laughter.

"Samizdat comedy, right?"

"That's right. Things that could never be said or written or, if the bastards had their way, even thought. But here, they say everything, make fun of anyone, kick their asses. And no one does anything."

As Victoria spoke, Viktor watched the man on the stage doing a credible imitation of the Chairman of the KGB. He said a few words of bad Russian, then thrust his hand into the front of his trousers, and shook it vigorously. There was a cacophony of applause.

"Why don't the police just raid the place, arrest everyone, and be done with it?" Shishkin knew what he knew, and repression was what he knew best.

Victoria answered without sarcasm. "Because this is better for them. It provides an outlet, a pressure valve if you will. Everyone knows Pod Baromi is here, anyone can get in, if they know someone who will vouch for them. The police know who comes regularly, and what's said. The place only operates from midnight to six a.m., so no one's skipping work. And they don't serve booze, so there're no fights. It's perfect."

"Perfect madness," said Shishkin. "If Jews in the Soviet Union tried something like this, they'd burn the building down with everyone inside."

"Appropriate," replied the whore. "Anyway, if Jews tried this, it wouldn't be funny. This is."

Her claim seemed to be borne out by the audience, which at the moment was gyrating with laughter as the man on stage, now wearing sunglasses with hammers and sickles on the smoked lenses, marched around with a broomstick shoved under the back of his shirt. Viktor recognized the intended victim: the country's president.

"Kalabinski can imitate anyone, anything. He knows just how far to go to get a response, but he never goes too far. There would be no point."

The man whom Victoria was extolling pulled the broomstick from underneath his clothing and put it between his legs. "Come here, my dear comrade," he said, in Russian it seemed, since Viktor understood. Apparently the words were the same in Polish, for the room went wild with laughter.

Victoria dried her eyes. "The Foreign Minister fancies himself quite a ladies' man," she explained. "But I've heard the façade ends once the lights go out."

"What? Only heard?"

"Shishkin!" Viktor remembered that he had to keep everyone under control. Knowing where they were, he felt less secure than ever. Why would Victoria come to a place like this when they were on the run?

Kalabinski was taking a final bow; the humiliation of prominent Communists was over. Without a word, Victoria left the table, went directly to the stage, and gestured until the performer bent down and put his ear to her lips. She pointed to the table; he nodded. Whatever she said next put expression in his face. He shook his head vigorously. Victoria overrode his comments. He shrugged, she grinned. He said something, which she obviously did not catch. He bent lower, spoke carefully into her ear, then she into his. He nodded. She nodded. He began to speak again, but there was no point. Victoria was already walking briskly back to the table.

"Quick, before I forget. Remember this: Martin Hruska. Malatova 190, 391–530."

"What?" Both men spoke together.

"Martin Hruska. Malatova . . . uh . . . Dammit I forget already."

"Maltova 190," said Viktor.

391–530," said Shishkin.

"All right. Each of you remember what you just said. When we get there, we'll put it all together."

"Get where? Put what together?"

Victoria's playful smile was back in place. "Never you mind, my Russian playthings. I've done it again. Where would you yokels be without me?"

They left the Pod Baromi unnoticed. When Viktor turned around, he could just barely make out the outline of the table where they had been sitting. It was now occupied by six fresh-faced girls, laughing at the opening joke of Kalabinski's monologue. "Malatova 190," he said to himself. "Malatova 190."

When the train pulled out, only fifteen minutes late, Viktor had claimed a space on the side bench, next to Victoria. Despite the chill, she had taken off her coat and spread it across her knees. Underneath its acrylic folds, they held hands. The only border station with Czechoslovakia was at Cieszyn, where the train stopped in front of a ratty, unpainted wooden hut. From it emerged a drunken customs inspector, who came aboard and ordered everyone to have his passport ready. Victoria tripped him as he came to her. With his balance already robbed by liquor, he sprawled on top of her, open hands clutching at her ample breasts. She pushed him away with a curse. Embarrassed, he forgot to look at Viktor's documents, and left the third-class car to the sound of hoots and jeers. Shishkin, on the other side of the car, smiled and pocketed his filched passport.

Five sleepless hours later, they were in Prague.

19

Smoke-choked, rumor-rife, hate-filled Prague. They felt its anger as soon as they stepped off the bottom rung of the train's collapsible ladder, and on to concrete recently washed with rancid water.

"Hurry along," said a rough voice wearing a dark blue uniform. What the travellers actually heard was "Schevwatzen vuy", but there was no doubt of what the policeman was telling them.

The inside of Tsentraly Voksal, the main train station, was like being at the bottom of a pot whose contents were slowly being steamed into soup. Passengers and those who wished they were sidled along the train platforms, tentatively seeking confirmation that thus and such a train was already there, or soon would be, or might ever be. Viktor studied them in confusion as Victoria led them confidently toward an exit. What was it about them that made him uneasy?

"What is it about these people?" Shishkin said in a low tone. "They all look as if their rich uncle had died just before he signed his will." They were walking down a platform marked "3". The train on which they had arrived lined their view to the right. To their left was a green Soviet train whose side announced it had come from Bratsk. It was in a lane labelled "7".

"That's the first intelligent thing you've said since you came skulking in to my apartment," said Victoria. "They do all look like that. But why should they be unhappy? I've heard you can buy meat here any time you want it, no rationing at all."

Viktor was thinking that each of them had expressed the problem in the terms they best understood: Shishkin imagined more bad luck heaped on to him, Victoria saw happiness in piles of food. As he made his own first judgments about this thousand-year-old-city, he concluded that short-changed customers would look angrier. There was no anger here. The key to the city of Prague was shared sadness.

Tsentraly Voksal resembled a wagon wheel. Each track was a spoke, radiating out from a central waiting depot. They had now reached this area. Victoria led them to a bench, on which sat ten people. Regarding them from left to right, their faces looked like a psychological progression chart from Neutrality to Despair. She put her bag in the one empty space on the bench, between Obsessive and Resigned.

"Do you remember your numbers?" she said so suddenly and loudly that Viktor, Pessimism, Shishkin and Downhearted all looked at her with round eyes of surprise.

"What do you — " Shishkin began.

"Malatova 190." Viktor had no doubt.

Shishkin's shaved face could not hide guilt as well as his beard. "I, uh. I think it was . . ."

"You idiot." Victoria was incautious. Three spaces down, Self-Doubt, sensing confrontation, got up and moved to safer quarters.

Viktor soothed. "Never mind. I remember that too. It's 391–530."

"That's what I was going to say."

"You were going to, my . . ."

"Are you comrades from the Soviet Union?" asked Severely Depressed, who was sitting next to Victoria and spoke Russian as though she were reading a difficult passage: correctly, but without intonation.

"Da." "Da." "Da." The visitors sounded like three people singing the same song without knowing any of the words.

"How good," commented SD, scowling. She wore a brown cloth coat with an orange scarf wrapped around her neck. Her lusterless hair was a battlefield of dull brown and morose gray that made it difficult to tell whether she was wasting her late thirties or living out her sixties.

"For us? For Prague?" Shishkin sensed that there was no danger here. That made it safe for him to revert to form.

"You will here see many beauties. Prague has."

"Are you an example?" Shishkin's eyes danced with wicked glee.

"Please," said Victoria, "where can we get some money? We want to change money."

She might have been making a homosexual pass, so distressed was the woman's reaction. Clutching her ugly coat around her, she pulled herself out of the seat as though jet-propelled. "I do not know you," she said loudly over her shoulder. This was followed by the same announcement, in Czech, to anyone who might be listening, as she hurried away.

"What was that all about?" Victoria asked. "There's nothing illegal about changing my zloty for Czech crowns, is there?"

"Probably not," said Viktor, speaking for the first time. "But just as probably, she decided it was better not to know anything about it."

"What kind of attitude is that?"

"Soviet." Both men spoke in the same second.

Victoria muttered something in Polish and strode off.

"We've just arrived, relax. And perhaps she" – he nodded in the direction Victoria had pursued – "can make contact with Malatova 190, who- or wherever that is. Let's find out."

Victoria was marching back across the waiting room with her smarter-than-anyone-else smile. "All right comrades, I've saved us again. This way please, there's a taxi waiting."

"You seem to do a lot of business with taxi-drivers." Shishkin said it neutrally enough. Viktor said nothing – he was finding that increasingly attractive – but he too was nervous about Victoria's seemingly endless ability to make the right contact, just in time, with the only person capable of resolving whatever problem they had.

"Come on, Shishkin. We can't stay here for ever."

"Why not? The bench was just beginning to feel good."

Viktor picked up Victoria's bag. The two Russians followed her through a web of people who, like the ones on the bench, conveyed their unhappiness with every glance. A side door made of hundred-year-old wood with a frosted, colored glass pane let them out of the station and on to a steeply graded street, where a whole other world was in progress. Here there was no loitering; indecision was clearly unacceptable. Cars seemed to move too fast for the narrowness of the roadway and its inclination. The pedestrians walking uphill moved without effort, as though hydraulically driven. Those going downhill fairly flew. Two paces to their right an ugly orange car with no exterior markings choked its exhaust into the general population's lungs.

A gray presence dressed in a gray suit, with a gray snap brim hat stood by a black Skoda sedan, holding the back door open. He was probably fifty years old and might have last smiled forty years ago. "Get in, get in." Victoria acted like a mother suffering through a field trip of third graders. "This man speaks some Polish, he told me."

The car was bigger than a Zhiguli, smaller than a Volga. Other than comparing it with Soviet cars, Viktor did not know what to make of it. The dashboard was plastered with stencils: "Marlboro," "NBC", "JVC/ Technics". He could not understand them, though he knew they were Western. Nothing from his culture was so well printed or brightly colored.

"Why not a sign that says, 'I like Communism?'" said Shishkin, who had seen them too. The driver heard the word and swiveled around. He did not frown, at least no more than he always did. But he said something to Victoria in what Viktor and Shishkin assumed must be Polish.

"What?" she said to him.

He repeated what he had said and so did she.

"Do you speak Polish?" she said.

"Tak."

"What language were you speaking?"

"Polski."

"That wasn't Polish. Where did you learn it?"

"Polska."

"My ass. Say something else."

He tried. Victoria groaned. "He's useless. I can't understand a word he's saying."

"Perhaps you don't speak Polish." Shishkin was enjoying this.

"Look, can you change money for us?" Victoria asked.

He spoke for a long time, but no one understood him.

"Back to the station. Take us back! Voksal."

"Voksal. Tak."

The car took the next right and five minutes later they were back at the station's taxi queue. The driver wanted to be paid. Victoria proffered zloty. The driver reacted as if handed a diamondback rattler. "Change," said Victoria, in Polish, Russian, and Lithuanian. "Tak," said the driver. He motioned for them to wait and hurried off down the line of taxis. Two minutes later he returned accompanied by a snide-looking youth with brilliantined black hair.

"You want change money?" he said in rough Russian.

"Yes," said Victoria too quickly. Viktor saw a look in her eyes that he did not like. She was trawling.

"Have you checked to see if he has a passport?" said Shishkin.

"I am so tired right now I can't be bothered to kick your Jewish ass across this street. But fair warning: I'm going to fix you."

"Sorry, it's already been done. When I was thirteen days old."

"Stop quibbling." Viktor studied the youth: the eyes were deceptive, the smile mocking. This was a wise guy, he concluded, not to be trusted. They existed everywhere in the Soviet Union. The fellow who just happens to have something you want, turns up by chance in his car when you're stranded, knows just where to go for a favor you need. Viktor knew these people because he was one himself, a fixer, a problem-solver, a doer. But his was a service, he liked to think. He actually helped people. This was business.

"My friend," he said in a slow, even voice. "Could you tell me please where I could make a phone call, and, I am embarrassed to ask but I've just arrived, lend me the proper coins?"

"If you've just arrived, who are you going to call?" But he fished out some crown coins and handed them over. "You can use the phone over there by the entrance."

"Does it work?"

He got a look at surprise. "Of course." Viktor told himself he was in Czechoslovakia now. People expected things to function.

Pay phones are about the same all over the world. He picked up the dark-brown receiver, dropped a one-crown coin into the slot, waited until the beeping on the line turned into a purr, and dialled 391–530. Victoria would of course be angry, but he had begun to doubt her ability to deal with the situation. He never questioned his own.

The phone was lifted after one long and one short ring.

"Da." It was not a question.

"Do you speak Russian?"

"Da."

Viktor really did not know what to say. He had not planned this well, and he was afraid. Give his name, explain why he was calling, set up a meeting? All seemed equally perilous.

"A friend in Krakow gave me your number."

"I see." The voice, too calm, was anything but reassuring.

"And . . . and suggested you might be able to help me." It was the longest sentence he had attempted. The long pause made him fear it was too complicated.

But the voice on the other end was unflustered. "What does your friend in Krakow look like?"

Viktor was stunned. What did Kalabinski look like? "That depends on who he was making fun of. Do we want to be discussing this right now?"

"You're right, of course." The long pause could have meant anything.

"You haven't changed any money on the black market, have you?"

"No."

"Don't. They're all agents."

Viktor was about to speak again when he heard: "Yets-na tresitch pyit. Say that."

"Say what?"

"I'll say it one more time. Then I'm hanging up. 'Yets-na tresitch pyit.' Soon." Beep beep beep went the phone.

Try memorizing three foreign words in five seconds. Most memories depend upon rote, and some kind of phonic association on which to hang the new phrase. Viktor had none. He walked back toward Shishkin, who had already demonstrated the limits of his recollective power, and Victoria, who was chatting away with the would-be money changer.

"Yets-na tresitch pyit," he told them.

"Certainly," said Shishkin, pulling a face.

"What?" squawked Victoria.

"When?" said the Czech money-changer smoothly.

Viktor's doubts were now resolved. This man was not to be trusted. And he decided, purely on instinct, that Martin Hruska, or whoever he had just talked to, was. You have to trust someone. But the Czech's reply had so put him off that he now forgot the words.

"What did I just say?"

"Shebi-trebi-glebi." Shishkin was chuckling.

"A bunch of rubbish sounds," Victoria told him.

"You no remember?" asked the man. His smile and his hard eyes claimed victory.

"This is Jiri," said Victoria with a smile. "He's going to change money for us."

"But no here. My car we go. Go!" Jiri had already paid off the first taxi-driver. He had them to himself.

"What's wrong, Viktor?" Shishkin had picked up his worried vibration.

"Victoria, let's talk about this first."

"What's to talk, my bear cub? We need money, Jiri's got it. And I think I can convince him to help us."

Viktor wondered how Victoria could think that way. Then he answered himself: because she's a whore, stupid. He squeezed her hand and whispered. "It's not always that simple. And this isn't Poland. We don't know this country, and we have to move slowly."

"Hurry," said Jiri, walking briskly in front of them. Viktor doubted he could hear what he was saying.

"I don't like the look of this fellow. Let's thank him and ask him what those words mean that I just said."

"Where did you hear them?"

"From Martin Hruska. Or whoever answers his phone."

He felt her hand pull away. "You just called him? Kalabinski gave that number to me, not you! I wanted to call him!"

He reached for her hand again, missed, got her hip. "Look, Victoria, this isn't a game of who knows more. We're all taking a risk here. With our lives. You've been wonderful to come here with us, we'd have never gotten out of Poland without you. But you have to act sensibly.

Czechoslovakia is more dangerous, and Hruska says the money-changers are informers. Let's just get away."

Even before he was done, he knew he had failed. She looked at him with red resentment, then surged ahead.

Shishkin, who had trailed behind him in silence, put a hand on Viktor's shoulder. "Trouble, my friend. You know it. I know it. Let's hope she doesn't find out until we're gone."

The yellow Skoda purred. Viktor wanted to ask how Jiri kept it in such good repair, but Victoria's frozen expression in the front seat precluded much banter. Besides, he wanted to see what he was passing through. Gray and smoky, Prague was clearly one of those cities that held greatness. This was not a good century for it perhaps, but the pride of ages past showed through the shabbifying effects of socialism. As they cruised down Hybernska Street, Viktor saw brass poles that held working gas lamps; but attached to many of them were royal-blue trash-bins. He watched the Czechoslovak flag – a blue triangle balanced between trapezoids of red and white – flutter in the afternoon breeze; just ahead, two white uniformed militiamen were berating an old man for crossing the street against a red light. The center of the street belched white steam; underground pipes heated the buildings on either side. The shops looked well stocked; he spied a ham hanging in a window that might have caused a fistfight in poorer sections of Moscow. And Victoria was right: there were no queues, or at least none that stretched out on to the sidewalk.

He tried to take in the images outside the car just as he tried to ignore the pine-scented fumes that filled the inside.

"So, we change?" the driver wanted to know.

"Why not?" answered Victoria.

"Change what?" Shishkin demanded.

"Never mind," said the whore. "I know what I'm doing."

"You say you change zloty? How much?"

"What is the rate of exchange?"

Oh, God, Viktor told himself, she's doing a black-market swap with a perfect stranger in a foreign country and she doesn't know the rate of exchange.

"Three thousand zloty for one crown," said the driver, without taking his eyes from the road.

Viktor tried, unsuccessfully, to remember how many crowns and zloty it took to buy a ruble in Moscow. He knew the rates were posted just inside the main door in the Vneshtorgbank. But he could not read the sign in his memory.

"All right," said Victoria, as though she had just been given too much change at a store. "I have fifty thousand zloty."

"Sixteen crowns then."

"And how much is your fare?"

"Eighteen crowns."

"What kind of joke is this?" Victoria's voice betrayed her soon-to-do-something-stupid warning.

"Czech joke." There was not the slightest hint of humor in the answer. The driver concentrated on making a precise right turn on to Italska Street.

"The hotel is here."

"What hotel?"

"My friend change crowns for zloty. He work this hotel. Name Alcron."

"Why don't we just change our money at the bank?" said Shishkin. "It's not illegal, is it?"

"At bank, they ask your passport. You wish show your passport?" The driver spoke to Shishkin. But his eyes were focused on the image of Viktor that he had in the rear-view mirror. "I think you are Jew. Is right? Never mind, right, wrong. You sit in car, even better you stay in trunk. Yes?" Without waiting for Shishkin's opinion, he got out and Victoria, without looking back, went with him up five wide steps that were covered with dirty red carpeting and through a revolving door of smoked glass. Once they disappeared inside, Viktor followed.

Viktor quickly sized up the Alcron, with its dusty, once expensive wine red carpet in the middle of one reception area. Unfortunately, the carpet covered only about ten per cent of the floor. The rest was unapologetic concrete, gray as a forgotten fish. Furniture, of sorts, was arranged around the walls: a moldering brown plush divan, a series of chairs that might once have passed for imitation leather, but were now recognizable as experiments in synthetics, coffee tables that were probably not up to the job.

Straight ahead, he saw Victoria and Jiri seated on one of the divans. The Czech had his hand in Victoria's lap; she clenched her mouth in a smile and clutched her purse with both hands.

Viktor went back outside, and waited. Five minutes later, Jiri got into the car, smirking. He pulled out of the hotel parking zone, into the crash and jam of Italska Street.

"Where is the woman? Where are we going?"

Jiri said the words like song lyrics. "Yets-na tresitch pyit."

It was not that there were so many cars; rather, they seemed to take extraordinary amounts of time to do what they needed to do. The result was a parade of angry drivers with a single common weapon: the horn. It took seven minutes to negotiate the one hundred feet that separated the hotel from the corner of Wenceslas Square. The moment the car edged its way into the intersection, Viktor saw it: the 800-yard long avenue with four lanes of traffic in each direction, a line of tram tracks down the middle, and shops on either side. And at the top of the boulevard, there it stood: the 100-foot high statue of Vaclav of Bohemia, the tenth-century ruler known for his kindness and his enlightened government. Westerners had perverted his legend: he was a prince, not a king, and the Christmas carol commemorating his bountiful goodwill omits the fact that his mother killed his grandmother and that Vaclav himself was murdered by his brother.

But for Viktor, the statue, and the avenue along which Jiri now rolled, represented the way he and his people were viewed outside Russia. What did it matter that Gorbachev was now leading the chorus of platitudes about the responsibilities of freedom? It was the memory of tanks with red stars on their sides that the world remembered. Of posies stuck in gun barrels by the shy but determined-unto-death young Czechs back in 1968. He strained to see the statue from the back seat, but Jiri misunderstood.

"Yes, still holes in buildings, from your guns." He pointed. It was true. Above a shop that sold flowers, great gouges of the yellow stone façade were missing. Tank shells.

"I am sorry that it happened." The words came from Viktor's mouth, but his brain had not planned them. Their source was deeper than his skull, darker than his stomach.

A series of turns. Viktor had always been able to acclimatize himself quickly in strange cities. But the twists of this section of Prague were made indistinguishable by the overwash of gray, the dour sameness of its buildings. He had heard of the city's splendid beauty. Where was it all? He saw a riddle of back streets populated by stout, unsmiling citizens. They moved from shop to shop, in search of something, or perhaps, Viktor thought, they knew already what was and was not there, but were compelled to make the painful journeys anyway.

They came off Zitna Street, followed the low purr of traffic past Karlovo Park, its already sparse greenery dulled by the insistent gloom. A militiaman waved his white baton at them. Either Jiri decided to ignore what to Viktor seemed a clear summons to pull over, or traffic directions were given out differently in Czechoslovakia. They swept past the intersection and glided another hundred yards along Jecna Street until Jiri slid into a no parking zone on the left side of the one-way street. This smooth movement was not lost on Viktor in the back seat.

"Here house you want." Jiri might have been pointing out a good restaurant, for all the inflexion in his voice.

"How do you know we want a house?" Shishkin asked.

Jiri would not talk to him. "You say me 'Yets-na tresitch pyit.' There Jecna tresitch pyit."

"It's an address, Shishkin. What number is it in Russian, Jiri?"

"I say, tresitch pyit. Thirty-five. Your friend there." That said, he turned his head so that he looked directly out the windshield. In his mind, the back seat was already empty.

The double doors of Jecna No 35 seemed a more appropriate entry to an urban cathedral than the apartment house they served. Their great maple width stood like armored breastplates against intrusions from outside. Their windows – again, as in the train station, stained glass – began eight feet above street level. The iron latches were rusted, but they had clearly stood up to the test of time.

The man who stood at the foot of the steps was tiny. He appeared shrunken and Viktor at first made the mistake of thinking he must be old. But the face under a large gray felt hat was unlined, though not youthful. The silver wire-rim spectacles aided eyes that sparkled with intelligence. This was a middle-aged man, small-boned, perhaps, but very much a man.

"Martin Hruska, at your service," he said in the same whispery voice Viktor had heard on the phone.

It took seven minutes to give him the briefest idea of why they were in Prague. His Russian was excellent and he obviously understood every word of Viktor's hurried encapsulation. But all he said at its end was: "Quite an adventure."

"Jiri brought us here," Viktor said. Unconsciously, he had begun speaking in a whisper too. "Do you think that's safe?"

"That would depend on which Jiri it is." Hruska smiled.

"Well, he's – " Shishkin had said very little and wanted to help but Hruska cut him off.

"Half of Prague is named Jiri. Half those Jiris report to the police. And this address is not unknown to the authorities."

"Then why tell us to come here?" Shishkin demanded.

"What does it matter where we meet? The phone call was tapped."

"Why would they tap your phone? Who are you?" Viktor had been wondering and truly wanted to know.

"During that happy time of our history called the Prague Spring I was Minister for Religious Affairs," Hruska said. He saw the alarm on the Russians' faces. "Do not be afraid. I no longer serve the Communists. The

223

government of your country, specifically Comrade Brezhnev, thought I misunderstood my job. Whereas they wanted a minister to help curb Religious Affairs, I was trying to promote them. I was removed shortly before your tanks paid us their troubling visit. Since then, I have been what might be called a dissident."

"Why did that crazy Pollack in Krakow think you could help us?" Shishkin was being insulting, Viktor thought. Perhaps he thought his was the only faith that could suffer nobly.

"Kalabinski is a rare man," answered Hruska. "Intellectual, independent, comical, Catholic. He and I have never met, but we have exchanged letters, carried by mutual friends. I suppose mine was the first name that came to him when your, ah, companion, mentioned Prague."

"Can you help us?" Viktor was beginning to shake from fatigue and fear.

"I? No. But perhaps I can put you in touch with some people who can. Will you wait here please?" Without waiting for an answer, he turned and mounted the stairs.

Viktor looked outside the heavy door. Jiri's car was gone. Probably straight to the police. End of the road. Then, like a searchlight cutting through fog, he remembered he had said that before, in Poland. And before that, in Moscow. No, he told himself, we're not going to lose. We're not.

Hruska came down as quietly as he had ascended. "Go up to the third floor. Do as they tell you. They are difficult people, but good ones. God bless you."

"Aren't you coming with us? Where are you sending us?" Shishkin seemed to ask all the questions. Viktor felt a tranquility that had spread throughout him.

"It is better if I go now. As I said, this address is well known as a place where enemies of the government live. My presence here would only make things worse for them, and you." He walked quickly out through the door, and it settled shut.

Old filth smells different from new dirt. The stairs had not been washed for years and the collective abuse of thousands of footsteps had left them grimed beyond the hope of repair. The grit shifted beneath their feet, and Viktor wondered why dirt and darkness were associated with evil, light and purity with good.

No place that scares you is far enough away. The third floor was at forehead level, as Viktor, trudging a step ahead of Shishkin, saw the door open.

A woman-child was standing there, in her face the slow curving bones of classic Slavic beauty. Her brown hair, so ragged it looked to have been cut with a knife, seemed nevertheless to give off a dull glow. She wore one of the cheap acrylic flowered dresses that was as close as anything to the uniform of women in Eastern Europe. Viktor guessed she might be between twelve and fifteen. Shishkin, unaware of her presence, ploughed into Viktor's back.

"Watch where you – Oh," he said, as though caught in an embarrassing act.

The child smiled. "Hello, friends," she said in English. "May the peace of Christ be with you."

"Strasvuyte, ninuchka," said Viktor. Although he had not understood what was said to him, he knew what language it was. He wanted to set the record straight.

"Spraechen Sie Deutsch?"

"Nyet," said both men, Shishkin slightly more emphatic.

"Français non plus?"

Shishkin moved forward. "What is this, the United Nations?"

The beautiful child smiled, though it was not clear whether in appreciation of Shishkin's churlish humor, or at the irony of the situation. Finally, she beckoned him forward with her hand.

Shishkin's flat in Moscow had smelled of neglect. This one reeked of a variety of human failings: perspiration, excrement, overcrowding. As he stepped inside Viktor saw three blankets lying on the floor of the entry foyer; inside each a small child slept or fidgeted. A few feet ahead stood a plain-looking woman, dressed in a much-too-large black dress that buttoned at the top of her neck and fell, in one piece, to the floor where it dragged several inches. She wore ugly black spectacles and a pained expression.

"You are the friends of Martin Hruska," she told them in clear-cut, confident Russian.

"I wouldn't say friends," Viktor replied immediately, "since we've only known him for ten minutes."

"Here all are friends. It is as our Lord Jesus Christ wished."

"Did he also wish you to live packed together like caviar?" Even before Shishkin spoke another three heads had appeared through a doorway.

"You, my friend, speak of restrictions placed on our temporary condition. But have you forgotten the glory that the Son of God promises to all who follow his words?"

"Yes, that must have slipped my mind."

Viktor looked at the beautiful girl who had let them in, then at the older woman, and decided to take a chance. "Your daughter does not speak Russian?"

The mother registered no surprise. "We think it a dead language. As you soon will, once you are away from your country's grip."

"We didn't come here for a language lesson," Shishkin said.

"No indeed. You have come to us because our Master ordained that it come to pass. And who you are in this life is not important. We are all Children of Christ."

"Some of us more than others," Shishkin muttered.

"Remember that when he was dying in agony for our sins, Jesus took time to comfort the two criminals at his side. 'This day,' he told them, 'you will be in paradise.' It will not be today, but tomorrow, I can tell you, my friends, you will be in Austria."

They looked at her very closely, then at each other, then spoke simultaneously.

"I'll be goddamned," said Viktor, just as Shishkin announced: "Then Praise be Christ."

20

They were fanatics: Viktor realized that as soon as she led them into the main room of the flat. It was bigger than he would have guessed. Rooms shot off hallways like the branches of a tree.

"Come, brothers," said the woman, evidently unconcerned about what they might see. The first doorway they passed revealed an old man sprawled across a cardboard box, that according to its Russian lettering, had once held a television.

"Pavel is a playwright, but sometimes he falls victim to the demon of drink," said their guide and hostess.

"Mr Gorbachev has taken care of that in the Soviet Union," said Shishkin. "And in a way Communists can understand. He's added vodka to the list of things you can no longer find in the shops."

"Here it is expensive, but available. Pavel sometimes spends his entire month's pension from the Writers' Union on wine or beer, then comes here to live until the first of the new month."

"Isn't that a bit too convenient?" Viktor asked. "What incentive does he have to stop?"

"We do not judge him. We simply help him."

Viktor decided two minutes' acquaintance did not entitle him to take the questioning further.

From the next room came a keening that was both muffled and piercing. "I would put you in this room, my best, except that Karol is in there, as you can hear."

"Oh, of course, Karol. Wouldn't want to turn him out of his room." Shishkin was reaching that point at which he could no longer ignore the absurdity of their situation.

Viktor tried to forestall an explosion. "May I ask your name?"

She did not stop walking. "What are names really, except the first limitation put on us by our own mothers, who profess to love us, but whose love is as nothing compared with Him who made us?"

"Didn't your mother make you?" Shishkin cut in, ignoring Viktor's warning look.

"I tell my daughter not to think of me as her mother, but as a fellow sinner, someone who was conveniently used as the channel for her creation, and nothing more."

Viktor reflected that if Anna ever thought of him that way, he would curl up and wait for death. The Anna thought itself set his heart athump.

"Might I use the toilet?" Shishkin inquired. The way he drew out the last two words, the question sounded as offensive as "May I blow smoke in your eyes?"

She was ready with an answer. "If you could wait until you leave here, it would be better. I ask those who stay to disregard all the horrid urges pressed upon them by physical weakness. It helps us concentrate on more important things."

Shishkin was dumbstruck, a reaction that in itself made the lunacy acceptable to Viktor.

"You don't let them piss? No wonder everyone is lying as quietly as possible."

She sat, without asking them to do the same, on what once had been a dark wood coffee table; now it was a receptacle for bottles, books, butts and, evidently, bottoms. From one corner, a monotonous burr came from a badly tuned radio. Overhead, a bare bulb suspended by a wire swayed according to the movement of bodies below.

"Now, my good men, let us talk." The Russian was correct, but wildly antiquated. "My good men" was a form of address from the age of Peter, when cow-bellied gentlemen in St Petersburg bowed deeply to ladies on the other side of the boulevard.

"You are fugitives from your homeland. Your story, or at least its basic outline, is known to me."

Shishkin, finally perturbed beyond silence, reached for his beard, then remembered it was no longer there. "What are you talking about? Do you intend to help us? Help us how? When? You've said tomorrow we'll be out of here. How do you plan to do that?"

"Now I know," she said, as unruffled as tap water. "You are the Jew. No Christian would speak that way to another. Keep your tongue, serpent of Satan. You will be delivered to another life through the mercy of Holy Mother Church."

"Is she related to Old Aunt Masha? Or is she the one that Crazy Uncle Sergei has been schlepping on the sly?"

"Oh God! A sinner stands before you!" The woman's eyes were mostly white, her hands had shot above her head as if her wrists were attached to ropes dangling from the ceiling. It was unclear which direction the incantation was going to take. "He is not of the body of Christ, and yet he dares to mock our sacred Savior and rescuer."

"Isn't that redundant?" Viktor heard Shishkin speak but did not look at him as he egged the woman on. He stared out of the window, wondering where Jiri had parked his car and whether Victoria was still in it with him. He noticed there were no longer any cars parked on the near side. On the far side, all the cars sitting by the curb were white, and all had drivers inside.

"Shishkin. Shishkin, will you shut up? I think they've found us."

"Who?"

"Come here and look at the street," To the woman: "What color are police cars in Prague?"

"White. A mockery of the color of purity."

"Damn."

Shishkin needed only two seconds to come to the same conclusion. "Run for it, or hide?"

Viktor was about to opt for the first when he heard the door of the apartment implode. A loud voice in a language he did not understand gave orders. The reaction of those inside was less dramatic than he would have expected. No screams or panicked running, no curses or struggles. They accepted a police raid with the same passionless shrug as they might have munched their Eucharist biscuits.

There was no question of escape. Viktor chanced one last look out of the window, subconciously wondering about the damage a jump would inflict. He saw he would probably not even reach the ground. The sidewalk in front of the building was thick now with white-uniformed police. How odd they looked to him, like armed milkmen.

"Say nothing. Absolutely nothing." The woman's hiss had a new quality that made it less obnoxious. Viktor knew: she was scared.

The captain in charge was a beer drinker, that much was obvious as they caught a glimpse of him in the hallway. His white tunic was pulled rigid across a boulder belly and pointed nipples. He moved confidently through the maze of rooms. Obviously this was not his first visit. The woman sat on the coffee table, her eyes completely disengaged from the Russians who waited by the window. When Shishkin whispered, "Let's just both tell the whole truth" into Viktor's ear, she gave him such a hateful glare that he blushed, and became silent.

In bunches, the residents of the flat came into the main room. Some shuffled in nervously, others might have been sleep-walking. The woman's daughter stood in the farthest corner, picking at the top button of her dress.

The big-gutted captain came in last, looked around as though he was scanning a party for a dance partner. His eyes passed quickly over Viktor and Shishkin, and the two Russians wondered if it was possible the KGB had not yet distributed their photographs.

When the captain spoke, Viktor felt as though he should be able to understand at least a portion of what was being said. Some words were the same as Russian. But those that were different gauzed over the meaning of sentences so effectively, his comprehension was near zero.

The big voice was in complete command of the room, yet the intrusion seemed to be having little effect on the Czechs. They had a bleary, otherworldly look about them, as though they were watching this scene on late-night television. Viktor heard a word that was close to the Russian imperative "Come!", and saw the daughter step away from the wall and toward the captain in the center of the room. She had not yet come to a halt when he struck her with an open-handed slap on her left temple. Her head rocked back and her right hand went up in instinctive self-defense. The captain, feigning outrage at this insolence, punched the girl precisely in her solar plexus. Viktor saw the breath go out of her like air abandons a punctured balloon. He remembered from youthful fights what it felt like to come to the end of one breath and realize that no replacement air was coming in. He glanced at the mother, ready to risk all to alleviate the suffering he was sure would be on her face. But her eyes, focused squarely on the beating, registered the same emotion that reading a cookbook might cause. He felt Shishkin's hand, behind his back, attach itself firmly to the belt loop on the back of his pants. When their eyes met, Shishkin gave an imperceptible head shake. His face spelled silent reality, fierce-as-winter truth.

The captain knew about pain points. He grabbed the girl's left breast with his right hand and twisted in a gesture so hateful it could not be confused with desire. She inhaled deeply, so he repeated the solar plexus punch. With that, she was down on her knees and elbows, retching, heaving, trying to vomit, breathe and choke at the same moment. The captain's knee flashed out, caught her nose neatly, put her on her back. She was not moving.

He came to her mother then, stared down for a second and spat in her face. He had had a workout, so the saliva was thick and buttery white. It traced the path down the woman's cheek, dropped into her lap. Viktor heard them exchange a few words, among them, he was certain, the letters "KGB". The mother made a quiet declaration, which produced a ruffle of laughter in the captain. He gestured to the girl, and two of his men picked her up, hands and feet, and took her out of the flat. The mother was still seated when the door closed.

The others dreamily left the room. A few muttered words of encouragement to the mother, some patted her shoulder. None, Viktor noticed, offered to wipe the spittle from her face, so he did with his shirttail.

"Did they come here for us?" He could think of no other way to resume conversation with her.

"Of course not. Why would they come for you? They come to harass God's faithful." The woman still had not budged from the coffee table.

"Aren't you concerned about your daughter? About where they've taken her?"

"They have taken her to a police hospital, where her injuries will be treated. She will be released in time for her trial. She has never been away longer than three days."

"This has happened before?" Shishkin's voice was tremulous.

"Several times. They come here every month, in fact they were overdue by several days."

"Who are they?"

"Choose your own name. VSP, militia, secret police."

"But your daughter . . ." It was Shishkin, the non-parent, who pressed.

"They found out last year how devoted to her I am, and so have made her a special target. They come here, beat her, then take her to juvenile court and charge her with being a prostitute, abused by a dissatisfied customer. The charge has been thrown out twice for lack of evidence, but the intention is to make it impossible for her to enter the university. Background checks are as important here as academic achievement. Her chances are already nearly nil."

"Are they doing this to you because of your religion?" Shishkin asked. If so, it all made sense to him.

"She does not feel the pain. I have told her how to blank herself out at the first blow. She was asleep throughout."

"How can you say that, do you have any idea what it feels like to take a knee in the nose?"

"Our Lord was subjected to – "

"Your Lord be damned!" shouted Shishkin. He saw immediately that others had understood him. It was one of those times when Russian and Czech were too similar for convenience. There were angry stirrings within the large room. The man who had been identified as Pavel came swaying up, burbled something in the woman's ear. She burbled back.

"Pavel is right, of course. An alcoholic, but a very bright man. This raid is a blessing. You have been seen by police, and, it seems, they believe you to be part of our group. So you can come with us, openly, when we go to the Primate."

"The who?"

"Franticek Cardinal Tomasek, Archbishop of Prague and Primate of all Bohemia. You have heard of him of course."

"Of course," said Shishkin. "He's often quoted in *Pravda*'s weekly Religion column. You know, 'Socialism and the Soul.' A great favourite back home."

"He is a living saint," said the woman. "And your salvation."

Ten minutes later, they were following the woman, Pavel, Karol, and two other men down the same steps they had mounted ninety minutes earlier.

They came out on to the street and turned left. They were moving away from the section of the street where the police had parked, now emptied. Viktor craned his neck, looking for Jiri's yellow car. If he saw it, he would know what Jiri was. Had he been scared away by the police, or had he brought them? He wanted to check back at the Alcron Hotel to see if Victoria was still there. But he could hardly let Shishkin-the-Christ-killer go to see the holy man while he sought out his Polish whore. There were no easy answers, no straight paths.

Viktor knew Moscow's streets as other men knew the curve of a mistress's hip. But the winding skeleton of alleys and ways that composed downtown Prague made him nervous and insecure. The middle of Jecna Street was cobbled. They walked past one side street. Nothing. The second one, to the left, was not meant for traffic; a restraining chain that had been in place across the mouth of the street lay feebly on the ground. About twenty feet down this side street, Viktor saw Jiri's car. The motor was still but the battery-powered inside lights produced a waxy yellow glow. Shishkin had seen it too.

"Go on ahead, I'll catch up with you." Even as he moved toward the car, Viktor was wondering what to say. There were no shapes silhouetted by the light. Perhaps they were looking for him, Viktor thought, and as he did, he caught a slight movement. He moved quietly, out of natural caution, not stealth. Ten feet to go, and he saw the movement again, this time recognizing it. He moved his right foot forward, brought his left alongside. The car's windows were closed, so he was spared the sounds. Jiri's upper body, still clothed, moved steadily but without haste, up, down, up, down. From what he could see, Viktor imagined Victoria's head was lying on the passenger side of the front seat, her knees probably curled behind, or twined in, the steering wheel.

He should have known in Warsaw when the taxi-driver's passport so conveniently fell into their possession. He should have believed in Shishkin's acid but accurate judgment delivered within minutes of meeting her. He should have, but he could not, not then, perhaps not now. He felt nothing as he turned around, retraced the steps, reached Jecna Street, and turned left. It was only when he saw the woman up ahead, evidently looking for him, that he felt the knife twist in his stomach. It did not matter what Victoria did with whom, after all, what was she to him? What counted was this hissing hypocrite on whom he now had to rely.

Viktor had no real views on the Roman Catholic Church. In Moscow, there was only one place for followers of the Pope to congregate. The Church of St Louis had deteriorated over the years as a result of a nicely honed campaign of KGB intimidation. It did not embolden worshippers that the church was located on Malaya Lubyanka, near the prison for political detainees. He had never stopped inside during a service, but he once parked in front of the church and read the sign on its front door: 'Masses in Latin, sermons in Polish and Russian.' What a wonderful commingling of mutually antagonistic worlds, he thought. If he had known on the day that he read that sign how it would come to epitomize his own world turned upside-down, he would probably have released the car's brakes and hurried around to lie beneath its front wheels.

He had expected to travel in some beat-up conveyance, perhaps even horse-drawn, in keeping with the medieval ideas he had encountered. So he was surprised to find Pavel holding open the door of an orange taxi and gesturing with impatience. Drunks of course hate to be kept waiting, especially if they think a drink may come of their efforts. The driver at first refused to take them all, but had a change of heart when the woman produced a note, evidently of large denomination, and thrust it into his hand.

"It is illegal to carry more than three passengers, so we must pay more to do it," she explained quietly. Finally, thought Viktor, they were speaking a common language.

Its official name is Prague Castle, but everyone refers to it as Hradcany, a ridge of hills that overlooks the west bank of the Vlatava. The castle is wedge-shaped, and two courtyards, one built by Viennese, the other by natives, lead to the main reception room. Rising behind the castle like Blake's Red Dragon is St Vitus's Cathedral, a smaller, less noteworthy, hardly awe-inspiring structure, fittingly located behind a small entry between the castle and the cathedral. A rusty-hinged brown wooden door was all that stood between the Archbishop of Prague and the outside world. And, as the afternoon took hold, it was all that separated Viktor and Shishkin from the rest of their very confused lives.

The Russians waited in the taxi – its driver chatting to them evidently about nothing, since he never asked for a response – until the woman emerged from the brown door and beckoned.

"Didn't I see two soldiers standing just across the square?" Shishkin was looking about the cardinal's residence as though on the lookout for trap doors, revolving walls and man-eating spiders.

"Yes. They are the honor guard for the President's residence. Also they note who comes and goes here. They know me well."

"And us too, now?"

"They will presume you are two new guests in my house."

The woman's voice and face had softened since entering the house. Perhaps she felt more relaxed here, relieved of authority. The notion did not make Viktor less suspicious of her sanity.

Each stair released its own song of pain as they ascended. Viktor knew how to relieve stress on staircases: small shivs of wood inserted at the joints and glued or nailed into place. Perhaps the archbishop would let him stay here for the rest of his life, fixing up the place, in return for a promise that he would never have to face the real world again.

At the top of the stairs, a boy – could he be more than thirteen? –dressed in black shirt and pants, white socks and black shoes, rose from a chair. He extended a hand to the woman, who ignored it, made the sign of the cross instead. Did she thrive or just survive on rudeness, Viktor wondered. But the boy seemed to expect it. He turned on his heel and led them to a reddish brown door, which he opened. "The Archbishop of Prague," he intoned.

He was asleep at his desk. His head lolled to the left, his tongue hung out like a lazy dog's, and the snore was a rasp of oncoming death. His hands clutched the armrests of the gold-painted chair so that his knuckles were marblesque. The boy cleared his throat, a hopeful gesture that had no effect. Viktor felt like doing the same in sympathy for the phlegm-filled respiratory tract whose noise filled the room. "Your Eminence, uh, Your Eminence."

"Goddamn, what is it?" There was no mistaking it, the words, spoken in Czech, were identical to the Russian. Viktor smiled. Shishkin thrust out his lower lip and nodded approvingly.

The woman stepped forward. "Your Eminence! It is I. With me are the visitors you know of. The" – she had to swallow before saying it – "Russians."

Tomasek took no more than a second to come awake, the mark, thought Viktor, of a frequent catnapper. That was confirmed when the cardinal availed himself of the classic excuse: "Hmm. Hot in here. Must have dozed off. Open a window." The young man dashed to throw open a window that might have been called stained glass had it contained any color but gray. A gust of cool air completed Tomasek's public awakening, and he looked at the woman for the first time.

"Oh, you," and there was no mistaking the regret in his voice.

This time, Viktor could not follow the Czech she spoke. "Your Eminence, I have brought the two visitors who request your help. They have been guided to me by Almighty – "

"All right, I get the drift. Leave us."

"But these men speak only Russian. They are – "

"I'll manage. Tomek here can be my tongue. Good-bye."

"But Your Eminence, Karol and Pavel are here. I imagine you want – "

"Imagine what you want, not what I want. Good-bye."

The fine points of grammar were lost on Viktor and Shishkin, but both knew a brushoff when they heard one. The others had been gone only a few seconds when Tomasek motioned to the boy and gently informed him that he would not, after all, be needed as translator. The youth bowed, backed out of the room.

"Do they imagine, for God's sake, that one can hold an important position in Czechoslovakia today and not speak passable Russian?" The cardinal was smiling. Clearly his command of the language pleased him. "Besides, she gets on my nerves when she's around too long. Good heart, I suppose, but nothing to keep her ears from collapsing on one another."

He looked at them so that each could imagine he was receiving undivided attention. "Gentlemen. I am glad you are here. Probably no gladder than you, considering your alternatives. But glad enough. I imagine your presence here was noted, but it hardly matters. It takes days for the sentries' reports to be sifted through. Mostly my visitors are official delegations, occasional foreign journalists, parents who can't believe their little girl had gotten herself pregnant. You are, I am happy to see, none of those things."

Viktor felt Shishkin take in breath and could not stop him. "Sir, excuse me for not knowing your title and for speaking without an invitation, but that nutty woman told us we could, no, would be out of here by tomorrow. Can you explain that, please?"

The old man's smile, once put on display, was a cross between saintly and satanic. He was by no means handsome; though tall, his gut was too generous to describe as merely stocky. His neck overflowed his crimson cassock collar and seemed to have been cut from a redwood stump. His hands looked like they had undergone torture by the Iroquois, his nose was the size and shape of a household light bulb. But his eyes were pure life; blue and dancing, his mouth moved easily and turned naturally upward at the corners, and his gestures were those of a much younger man. Tomasek stared at Shishkin, let his smile do its work, while he decided what and how to tell the Russians.

"Friends in Christ — and I include you in that," he said with a nod to Shishkin — "you have been caught up in something that you have no experience with. You have run afoul of the system not because of your own actions, but because the system itself is in flux. Mr Gorbachev has some ideas about what he wants his country to become, but he has very little idea of how to achieve it, or at least how to achieve it without first destroying the Soviet Union.

"You see before you," Tomasek said, "a prisoner living in a gilded cage. I am eighty-nine years old and I had expected to end my life somewhat differently. Maybe as Pope, maybe in prison. But I think they have found for me an even worse fate: a man with flowing robes, a big house and a long title (by the way, Mr Shishkin, feel free to call me Frantisek if 'Your Eminence' is too large a concession) but one who can do nothing of any importance for the God I have chosen to serve." Viktor and Shishkin looked at the old man without knowing what to say. At that moment, the cardinal looked, and sounded, like an old farmer lamenting the loss of his favorite cow. Not for the first time, Viktor wondered whether they were being set up by people whom they had no choice but to trust. Neither could imagine why the churchman would unburden himself before them.

"Yes, I'm old and, frankly, not scared of much now. A lot of people, including the ones across the square, see me as a symbol of the things they fear. If I wanted to, I could have half a million people in this square, a lot of them probably armed with pitchforks and foundry hammers. Think of what it would look like on television for the Americans, and your countrymen too. But I don't because I know a lot of them would be killed. They think that as long as I'm kept happy, and therefore, quiet, they can go on murdering the soul of this country.

"I don't know you well enough to care about you as anything more than God's children," Tomasek said, again wincing in politeness to Shishkin. "Your situation, though, has become known to me because of the sorry consequences of your actions. You left the Soviet Union only with considerable help, expensive help."

"What are you talking about?" Shishkin sliced in.

"Yes, expensive help. The Chief Rabbi of Moscow may be, what you

236

would consider, 'competition' to me. But I knew him as a good man and a brave one."

"Knew?" Viktor did not delude himself that the cardinal's Russian was failing him.

"The Rabbi was called in for questioning shortly after you left. While in police custody, he had a so-called heart attack. He died three days ago."

They remembered the disheveled, irascible little man. His wisdom, his kindness, goodness. Shishkin put his hand over his stomach.

"You will remember that the Rabbi was going to go to Poland, and had obtained the exit visa that, shall we say, came to be used for another purpose." The farmer was gone, replaced by a shrewd prince of the Church. "We, who try to keep open the path to our various gods, also keep track of each other's visits rather jealously, you know. Too many Russian Jews travel and the Polish Catholics become anxious. If the Baptists in Romania have foreign visitors, then the Lutherans in Berlin are antsy. It makes life very difficult for the Ministers of Culture. But that is their problem."

His voice became hard. "A few months ago, I asked for permission to travel to Austria, to celebrate, with the Archbishop of Vienna, the feast of the Ascension. For the past three years, he has made it a point to visit one of the countries of the socialist sphere on this day, to remind us that we are all brothers. I was told no, that I could not go because the Rabbi of Moscow would be in Poland. Yesterday, I was told that the decision has been reconsidered, and that I could go after all. Today I was also told to be vigilant for any information about two Soviet citizens who are, and I quote, 'of special concern' to a KGB colonel named Karushkin."

He laughed at the look on their faces. "Did you think you could avoid them forever? I, of course, told them I would be delighted to inform them of anything I learn."

"Now look you old – " Shishkin was ready to fight his way out.

"And I shall. I'm going to let them know where you are. I'm also to ask them if they plan to take you back by force."

"What's wrong with you? Do you think they're like vampires, afraid of that cross you're wearing?" Viktor's adrenaline was pumping.

"No. But I don't think they're ready for the spectacle of beating an old man, especially this old man, senseless, and dragging you off the helicopter that will take us to Austria."

"And just why not?" Shishkin, seething, asked.

"Because it's being sent by another friend of mine who knows how things work in this part of the world. A Pole. Once his name was Wojtyla. Now it's His Holiness, the Pope."

21

"The Pope? The Pope?" Karushkin hoped that if he repeated it enough the answer might change. He was standing in the office of the Deputy Director of the STP, the Czech secret police, holding a useless copy of the report on the latest known activities of Melanov, Viktor Nikolaich, and Shishkin, Yevgeny Moisovich. Useless not only because it was in Czech, and because, having been prepared by Czechs it would come nowhere near meeting the KGB standards to which he was accustomed. Useless also because he could think of no way to stop the damned Pope from sending his own aircraft to Prague if he wanted to.

There were ways of course, such as the use of a Hind-24 attack helicopter, but none which Karushkin wanted to consider. He kicked the front of the desk of the Deputy Director, a middle-aged and earnest man whom Karushkin knew. "What else do we know about the damned Pope?"

"Nothing, that in the opinion of the Director of STP, would be of interest to the comrade colonel."

Karushkin's mouth dropped open. Was he hearing an unwillingness to cooperate? He was about to begin an angry response when a thought struck him: Could STP know he was acting on his own? In more than forty years of service, the one attitude he had never encountered was insolence. Was he going to tolerate it now? He looked again at the Deputy Director, who sat in his metal and vinyl chair with incredibly good posture. The look he gave Karushkin was not quite insolent, but it was far from the respect usually shown to a KGB colonel. Yes, thought Karushkin, I imagine I am going to tolerate it.

He turned to go. The Deputy Director saluted, but he didn't bother to get out of his chair. Karushkin knew where things stood.

Normally, the Soviet Embassy in whatever country he was in would have provided him with a car and driver. But upon checking in with the Deputy Chief of Mission (he noticed himself dealing with far too many deputies), he had been told that the entire five-car motor pool was in use.

When he asked about accommodations, he was told the Ambassador had guests staying at the residence, but that a room would be reserved for him at one of the city's better hotels. He should have understood from those initial slights that his visit was not being viewed favorably in Moscow. But it was too late now to change course. Too many people had been questioned, his prestige, as in the old days, was again on the line with each decision.

Certainly, he had been lucky while in Warsaw to find Professor Mankiewicz. The little man had no desire to help the KGB. But the restaurant head waiter had reported the incident to the police, and had included the fact that Mankiewicz, a regular customer, had talked to a suspicious party of diners. Mankiewicz told them everything that he knew, all the while salving his conscience by asserting that he would not say anything to endanger the people he was discussing. The descriptions of the two Russians left no doubt that Karushkin had found his quarry.

The SB, the Polish secret police, had received Karushkin like Communist royalty, and quickly assigned him a fulltime adjutant whose Russian was better than that of some of Karushkin's own flunkies in Moscow. Together, they made the rounds in Warsaw: checking computer logs of suspicious incidents and unusual arrivals and departures, running over the latest tapes of telephone conversations involving foreign diplomats and correspondents (the adjutant valiantly insisting that Russians living in Warsaw were never under surveillance. Karushkin harrumphed once and let it go at that).

When he heard about the rash of Russian-speaking zombies walking the streets, Karushkin was genuinely amused. Melanov had a real talent for the symbolic defensive thrust. Hunted by the KGB, he had turned loose KGB guards. Having stumbled into the midst of an internecine war, he proceeded to internationalize it. He hated Melanov, but he had to admire him.

On the second day he made contact with Dave. Their conversation was to the point; they were both practiced professionals.

"Why didn't you finish him off in Moscow?" Dave wanted to know.

"Because I had no reason to think he would run. What kind of man would leave his family like that?" Then: "For that matter, why didn't you take care of him here?"

"He's not part of my job, Colonel. I just get your guards out of Moscow and hold them here."

"How much information have you gotten from them?" Karushkin's question was more academic than patriotic; he hoped the guards would provide the Americans with enough embarrassing information to force Gorbachev into action. Or retirement.

Karushkin said nothing to Dave about Shishkin. He was not willing to cross the two equally risky operations in which he was engaged.

The interview with Andrzej was even less enjoyable. Warriors do not like turncoats, even those who help them to victory. The minute he met Andrzej, Karushkin smelled scum. When, toward the end of the conversation, Andrzej asked when the KGB would reimburse him the $500 that Viktor had stolen, Karushkin smiled and said he would be happy to pay the money back — in rubles. Andrzej's protests were meaningless; he had already told Karushkin everything that he knew.

"Why would men like that help you?" Karushkin asked the SB agent once Andrzej had obeyed the order to get the hell out.

"What choice do they have, Comrade Colonel?"

"Choice? Why, in the Soviet Union, men like that would have a dozen ways of flouting laws, cutting corners and thumbing their noses at the authorities, all without ever cooperating for a second." He was thinking specifically of Viktor while he said this.

The Pole eyed him, deciding whether to speak. "With all respect, Comrade, I think you're making the mistake of thinking that what can go on in your country must also be tolerated here."

That is, in fact, precisely what Karushkin thought; but here, in this confining SB office, still filled with the stench of Andrzej, he feared it sounded a trifle naïve. So he said: "Explain what you mean."

"Are we talking off the main street, sir?" The Russian expression meant off the record, and also carried a hint of something not entirely proper.

"Go on."

"Well, how the hell can I say it, sir, without giving offense? I know who you are, and that you are part of the establishment in the Soviet Union. And now that I've met you, well, I like you, sir, and I don't want you to misunderstand me."

"Get on with it son. I imagine I'll survive."

"Well, then, here it is, sir. Comrade Gorbachev has changed a lot of things in your country, in a very short time, and although I am not a student of political thought, well, as a neighbor of the Soviet Union, I'd like to say I think the things he's done have been for the better."

Karushkin said nothing.

"But the things that he's changed have a lot to do with problems that really haven't been problems here."

"For instance?"

"For instance, he's stopped persecuting the churches, hasn't he? He even let the American President visit some monks in a monastery during his visit. Well, here, sir, that's never been a problem, you see. The Church is important, we all know it, and everyone respects everyone else's right to have a little say in how things are run."

"That doesn't enlighten me as to why walking garbage like Andrzej is helping the SB."

"It's like I said, sir, what choice have they? You see, the other thing Comrade Gorbachev has done is try to create conditions where people can make some decisions about their lives. You don't want to work hard? Fine, but resign yourself to being a low-grade nobody. You want to put your cock into your work, well, then, you might just get somewhere, get promoted, see? Become a boss, like you?"

Both men realized that the implication of this speech was that Karushkin, a product of the pre-Gorbachev era, had not "put his cock" into his work. The SB agent blushed.

"I'm only telling you the way it looks to me sir."

"Never mind, go on. I'm interested."

"Here, sir, you see, no one's told us to try harder if we want to succeed. Not officially anyway. The bosses here are scared shitless, excuse me, sir, but that's the truth. Scared shitless that Gorbachev, I mean, comrade – "

"You don't have to canonize him every time."

"Fine. Scared that Gorbachev will either change his mind, or not last long enough to follow through on what he's started."

"Why should anyone be interested in what you useless Poles want or think?"

"Because if your Saint Gorbachev trips up, we'll be at the front of the army that comes into Moscow to show how it's done."

"I realize there is very little affection for us in the hearts of most Poles," Karushkin said gently.

"It's not a question of affection. It's instinct. Like a dog that's been beaten all its life, since it was a puppy, by its owner. Sure, the owner also feeds it. But if that dog gets a chance, it's not going to thank the owner for the food. It's going to attack him for the cruelty it's endured. Do you see?"

Karushkin noticed the young man had dropped the 'sir'. He didn't mind, but thought it was just as well to end the conversation. Familiarity breeds contempt.

The key that unlocked the mystery came on the third day. Professor Mankiewicz's description of the Polish woman with Viktor and Shishkin had puzzled them all. Had Melanov had help from the beginning? Contacts in Poland? Had the whole thing been part of an international scheme?

Karushkin asked for an SB investigation. He was impressed with the results. Working on the Leninist principle that anyone who would help an anti-socialist element like Melanov was probably also a misguided individual, the SB produced a list of women aged 25 to 50, living in Warsaw, who had been arrested during the last year. There were 766, not counting female detainees during illegal demonstrations of the Solidarity union.

"Why not include them?" Karushkin asked.

"Because that would make the number 10,980," said the adjutant. "Oh," said Karushkin. Enjoy it, son, he thought. Reality tramples hard on illusions.

The computers needed for cross-checking names with physical characteristics (eye color, height and weight, according to Mankiewicz's description) would be busy for sixteen hours, Karushkin was told. He briefly considered making a scene, then decided against it. He was in no position to ruffle feathers.

Prostitution is not, strictly speaking, illegal in Poland. There is no law against it, but it is frowned upon first because it violates the Leninist dictum that one citizen should never be hired directly by another, and second, because it is hard for the state to get its cut of such transactions. The girls who trawl the entrances of the tourist hotels report to the police, who are primarily interested in snaring foreigners who can later be subjected to pressure, and, in some fortunate cases, turned into sources of information.

But the workaday whores plying Marshalkowska Street, the bus terminals and the zoo are regarded officially more as self-sufficient if unofficial laborers, who, like everyone else, are doing a job, supplying a product, filling a need.

Victoria had never been arrested for hustling. There had been. an incident, several months before she met Viktor, as she made her daily walk through the zoo. Her name was on the computer: she had been in an affray with a client in a public place.

"You have whores working the zoo?" The adjutant nodded in a "Yeah, so what?" way as the Russian flipped through Victoria's short police record. The 766 names had finally been delivered, after an all-day wait. Karushkin realized he sounded like a wide-eyed child or a country bumpkin, but he was amazed every time he learned something new about Poland. The place was completely out of control. Inmates running the prison, although he would not have used that expression out loud. And Gorbachev wanted to loosen things up even more? He was glad he would not live to see the new century.

A thought occurred to him as he sat at the adjutant's desk, leafing through more dossiers. "How many of these women speak Russian?"

The young man grimaced. "Comrade Colonel, you told me to be frank with you, so I will. We all have to take six years of Russian in school. Most people without political ambitions try to forget it as soon as possible."

"Why didn't you?"

"I have ambition."

It was tempting, but Karushkin decided not to pursue that line of conversation. In a personal sense, he was interested in what the young man might want to do with his life, and how he thought knowing Russian would aid him. But an open show of curiosity might imply some willingness to help him achieve his goals. Karushkin was having enough trouble saving his own reputation.

"The Professor said the woman sitting with Melanov and Shishkin was speaking Russian. Go see him and ask him how well was she speaking it. Also, isn't the Soviet Diplomatic Residence located near the zoo?" He knew it was. He had gone there to present himself to the Ambassador and ask for lodging. Instead he had been put up in a second-rate hotel, the Warszawa, near the main studios of Polish television.

Was it not logical to presume that even the fine Soviet men posted to fraternal Poland occasionally sought relief from boredom and loneliness? And is it not likely that they would prefer that relief be be delivered in their mother tongue?

"And find out if this zoo whore speaks Russian." You want original thinking, Mr Gorbachev, unfettered by old-style Marxist taboos? Fine. Let's see how much truth you can take.

It had all been so easy. Mankiewicz, dragged from his home, sat like a brain-dead patient at the desk as photographs were shown him. Twice the wizened face lit up, then dimmed as he said: "No. Not her." When he saw Victoria's picture, he raised his eyes slowly, as though praying. "Yes. This one." Karushkin never doubted him.

Names. Schools. Old addresses. Teachers and neighbors. Foreign languages spoken: Russian. Jobs held and lost. Last known address. Like water bursting from a weakened pipe the information streamed out of invisible data banks and on to poor quality, Soviet-made computer paper. Only then, in Karushkin's sixty-nine-year-old mind, did it become real and believable. He liked touching knowledge; the smell of a book never before opened, or not opened in years; the dust that rose from recumbent filing-cabinets. It was not until he saw Victoria's name in black ink that she became real to him. Former factory worker, expelled twenty years ago from a Party study group for demonstrating an improper attitude. Hadn't voted since then, changed addresses three times, always after confrontations with the landlord or other tenants. Believed to work as a prostitute at the zoo. The altercations with the militia officer and the old woman. Nothing more.

Karushkin thought: the perfect soulmate for Melanov.

To most snoopers, her apartment, the last one mentioned in the file, would have looked appallingly ordinary. To Karushkin, it was a monument to Melanov's recent presence. Hairs in the bathtub determined to belong to a male, and of Melanov's color and blood type. Scraps of partially-burned paper which contained Cyrillic handwriting. No way to determine what had been written because the SB analysts had no expertise in Russian. Damn Poles! And of course, sending the paper to Moscow was out of the question.

In the margin of a women's magazine, in Victoria's writing, was a series of letters connected by arrows: "V,V,S › Cz › V, V (S?) › Aus?" Karushkin let the analysts have it, but only after he had studied it for the better part of an hour. He thought he knew what it meant. He wondered if Viktor and Shishkin did.

He was offered an SB car and driver to Prague. Instead, he chose to board a CSA flight leaving Warsaw the next morning at five-thirty. This time his tickets were purchased for him. He arrived at four-thirty without sleep and of course began checking to see by how much the flight would be delayed. He was lucky; it left by eight a.m. and he was at the STP office by eleven, having had only once to flash his credential – at the airport, where a blue-uniformed, snub-nosed woman tried to rifle through his small hand-carried suitcase. When she saw the blue leather case that revealed his identity, the woman tried to snatch it away, while at the same time loudly calling her colleagues to come over and see a real Russian spy's card. Karushkin gently but insistently held on to the case, and made sure to remember the name of this incredibly ignorant cow. It was his contention that, although the powerful could not manage every detail of existence to their satisfaction, and indeed should not try to, that blatant situations should be handled by whoever stumbled upon them, whether it was a KGB colonel, the director of airport security or Mr Gorbachev himself. New thinking.

Karushkin had been in STP headquarters only once before, after the 1968 unpleasantness. Then, his arrival had been greeted by long and pendulous silence. He had been specifically asked by Brezhnev to assess the state of morale, fraternal spirit and loyalty of the Czech secret police. At the time he was happy to note that there were relatively few suspicious figures; half a dozen with relatives involved in the uprising; a few who had unwisely expressed their support for the Dubcek government when that had seemed a safe thing to do. Karushkin did not think that his report had caused anyone's death, and only in a few cases might it have resulted in prison terms. He preferred to think that he had been dispatched as a corrective measure, a shot of penicillin into a sick body politic.

Now, more than twenty years later, the doctor was back, but the patient, claiming as always to know what was best, wanted no more treatment. Karushkin had little time for imagery, but he would have sworn that even the air in the STP office he was entering smelled different; not only gasoline and fume-laden, that was as much a part of Prague as the Vlatava. But there was a current of hostility, or worse, indifference, to his presence that seemed to attack him at the door and follow him into the office of the Deputy Director, the Director himself being mysteriously unavailable. After almost fifty years of service, Karushkin was unaccustomed to closed doors. He was used to doing what he wanted, using whatever and whose ever facilities he decided he needed.

It seemed to him that eyes followed him as he walked into the nest of offices that were used by the top STP officers. The Deputy Director was named Turpin, and Karushkin had first met him in 1968 when Turpin was a young officer ready to do big things. The Prague Spring had provided exactly the opportunity he sought and he had eagerly found and exposed suspected Dubcek sympathizers. His rise was steady and predictable, based in part on the very favorable mention of him contained in Karushkin's report upon returning to Moscow.

But their earlier affiliation was as much in the past as the spirit of Prague. Turpin shook Karushkin's hand, bade him sit, did so himself, behind a metal desk with many scratch marks and few papers, and then said nothing. Karushkin felt, and knew he was meant to feel, uncomfortable. He asked if Turpin knew why he was here.

"I believe so, Comrade Colonel."

"And you have been given instructions to assist me?"

"No, Comrade Colonel. I have been told to evaluate your situation and report to the Director."

"Turpin, I am seeking the STP's help in the search for two Russian criminals. I demand your cooperation. I think it is the very least you owe me."

Turpin's broad-cheeked face softened from its official pose. "Comrade Colonel, I of course remember our previous efforts together. I know that you wrote favorably of me. And I have occasionally thought of you. Fondly, I should add." The mask of propriety returned. "But I must tell you that the mission you have chosen to engage in has not been viewed entirely sympathetically, in your organization or mine. Your search for these criminals is a personal vendetta. We know – because you insisted that our Polish comrades contact us," Karushkin thought he heard disapproval in the voice – " – that this man, Melanov, and his partner, the Jew, have entered our country. We know they are travelling with a woman. We know they made contact with a taxi-driver, named Jiri, who is one of our informants. And today, we learned where they are."

"Where?"

"They are in the residence of the Catholic Primate, Cardinal Tomasek."

"How do you know that?"

"The cardinal informed us."

Karushkin thought that humorous. He could hardly contain his excitement. "Look, Turpin, can we talk off the main street?" He remembered, and was embarrassed, that he was using the same phrase the Polish adjutant had meekly employed to speak freely. He disliked the position in which he found himself, but saw no alternative.

"Go right ahead." Hardly an encouraging response.

"It's true that I am here, uh, unofficially. And that you are under no obligation to help me. But I think, in a few months' time, you'll be glad to have your name mentioned by me again."

He had chosen the right words. That much was clear from the look on Turpin's face. The Deputy Director had been on the fast track for the first part of his career, but now was wondering if the best had already been, what the rest of his life would be like. The truth was, that since Gorbachev had come to power, the Party establishment in Czechoslovakia had been in turmoil; those identified as too dogmatic had found themselves suddenly unpopular. Gustav Husak, who had become Party Chairman after the 1968 invasion, had been retired in an unseemly way. Within the STP, no one who had played an active role in putting down the uprising had been promoted since Gorbachev's rise. Turpin had been passively worried about this for the last few months, since a job that he had hoped to get had gone to someone of less seniority, someone thought to sympathize with the liberal wing of the Party. But, he thought, as Karushkin sat silently in front of him, if I could help solve a conspiracy that has Moscow connections. . . . And then, there is Karushkin, who helped get me where I am now, and look at him, reduced to begging. . . .

"All right, Colonel." The dropping of the "Comrade", both men knew, was significant. They were off the main street now. Loyalty usually stands little chance against ambition.

"You're staying at the residence?"

The pause said everything. "No. A hotel. The Alcron."

"I see. Very convenient." Turpin knew now precisely where Karushkin stood. "By the way, Colonel, you do know what's happening here tomorrow, don't you? The Pope's helicopter?"

"The what?"

"Yes, the Pope is sending his helicopter to pick up our beloved Primate," the adjective was drawn out to emphasize its irony, "and take him to Vienna for some Catholic feast day. It's caused a bit of a problem for us, both because, technically, it violates our airspace, and also because it sets a precedent."

"I can see that it does. Why is it being allowed?"

"Orders, Colonel. The new philosophy is: Don't make enemies."

"Idiots. You're going to lose control of everything. You watch." Then it all came together.

"The Pope? The Pope?" So he knew now why Viktor was there. And so he had kicked the desk, and demanded roughly: "What else do we know about the damned Pope?"

"Nothing that, in the opinion of the Director of STP, would be of interest to the Comrade Colonel."

Damn, thought Karushkin. He was going to have to do this himself. He wished he had friends.

22

The young man, Tomek, knocked softly on the door and, when Viktor answered it, spoke in the tones of one used to long periods of silence. "There is a woman downstairs who says she knows you." The way he pronounced the word "woman" made Viktor wonder when he had last used it.

"Not much mystery in that, unless you've been spreading your boundless charm by remote control." Shishkin was sitting in the puffy upholstered chair that, it appeared, the cardinal seldom punished with his weight.

"Tell her to come up," Viktor said quietly.

"I'm sorry, Pan Melanov, but His Eminence has certain rules about the admission of women. . . ." Viktor could not get used to the honorific "Pan", but the boy would call him nothing else.

"He let that raving bitch come into his office." Shishkin had not forgotten the nameless woman's bigotry and overbearing attitude.

"Shall I tell her you will come down?" said the boy, diplomatically cutting off further debate.

"Yes, of course."

Closing the door, he saw Shishkin shaking his head in exaggerated disgust. "She's bad news, friend, and if you don't watch it, she'll be the death of you. She's had a disagreement over her fee with this latest taxi-driver, and decided that since I'm not available, she'll settle for you."

"Or perhaps she's come to shoot for the moon, Yevgeny. You are, by your own admission, God's gift."

"I'll settle for his messenger's loan of a helicopter, if you don't mind. Can you believe it, Viktor?" There was none of Shishkin's usual sarcasm in the question.

"Can I? Sure. Do I? Let's discuss it the day after tomorrow over wiesswurst."

He and Shishkin had been directed from their interview in the cardinal's office to a bathroom, where young Tomek delicately suggested they might wish to freshen up. While Shishkin bathed, Viktor shaved, using, he presumed, the cardinal's Polish-made razor. When Viktor had succeeded in dislodging Shishkin's grime from the tub, he rather wastefully let the hot water run until it was painful to the touch, then eased in and lay spread-eagled. Still tingling from the radiant heat, they were led to a small room on the same floor as the bath, and told to make themselves comfortable. Clothes, of course, were a moot question. They put on their own much abused shirts and pants. Within minutes, both had fallen heavily asleep. The accumulated tension and lack of rest ever since they had left Moscow were showing. Viktor's last conscious thought was that he must hold on for one more day. Sunrise is just around the corner, he told himself.

He might have run a comb through his hair, but the thought of listening to any more Shishkin babble evaporated his vanity. Besides, he thought, what did it matter how he looked? He had already made up his mind about Victoria. The physical aspects of her betrayal mattered not at all; what possible claim on her sexual fidelity did he have? It was her wildness that left him chilled. The woman had no self-control, and that, to a man like Viktor, was a far more serious failing than promiscuity.

In his near-boiling bath, Viktor had taken the time to think, a luxury denied him during the days he had just lived through. He saw his too-large belly, the hair sprouting from his shoulders, the ungainly sprawl of his legs; he made himself ask the question: who do you think you are? You have been led on by one phony after another: Shishkin, Victoria, Hruska, the woman and now Cardinal Tomasek. Each one with inflated promises and plans, each one sucking you in deeper. And because you are at heart no better, you have thrilled to their tunes. Viktor the world traveller, Viktor the spy, Viktor the brave, the cunning. What has happened to you, that you believe you can run from the KGB, saunter through foreign countries and pop out like an effervescent drink somewhere in the West?

And so he could not provide Shishkin a straight answer when asked "Do you believe it?"; and so he would have to tell Victoria the truth now, as he clumped heavily down the carpeted steps of the derelict mansion.

His wife stood at the bottom of the steps, looking at him without expression.

"Well, I was wondering when you'd come looking for me. Out of grocery money, is that it?" The words just came out, he was too wonderstruck and scared to stop the flow of babble that was part of his nature.

"Viktor Nikolaich." She never called him that. Marya was dressed in one of her better suits, a brown hundred per cent wool outfit from Finland for which he had redeemed considerable favors due. Her eyes had the vacant cast about them that can come after reading a book for too long. The voice was one so full of exhaustion that he felt a pull behind his knees, a guilty pain in his scrotum.

"Anna?" The two syllables of his daughter's name broke from him before he could descend another step. If anything is wrong, if she is not. . . .

"She's all right." Marya released the briefest sliver of a smile when she saw her husband's relief. She had thought she knew him so well. Then, with no regard for the steps or their ragged angle, Viktor was churning down and had his arms around her, making Russian noises, and smelling the travel on her body. He felt no return hug and expected none. He had an idea what it would be like. But Marya was here and Anna was all right, and Viktor Nikolaich Melanov, who had begun to walk down the steps to give the brush-off to a whore, now clung to his brown-suited, tired-faced wife, with the ardor of a man who has just been given a chance to relive an error-filled life.

This was the next best thing.

"Why are you here? How did you get here? Oh, Marya, you have no idea. . . ."

"No, I didn't." She was trying to remain icy, but a tremor in her voice betrayed what swirled beneath her breath.

Clearly, some explaining was in order. "My cabbage head" – the endearment had not been in his consciousness since the last time they had made love, weeks before, but popped out without notice at the sight of her. "Listen to me. You need to know . . ."

"I need to know many things, Vik-trushka" – the diminutive was a good sign he thought, until she said, "But you need to know this: I'm here and Anna is here because that man, Karushkin, brought us. His men are outside now. I didn't come to you, I have been sent."

The joy of seeing her, the sound of his daughter's name on her lips fell apart like an overripe rose.

"What does he want? How did he know I was here? Has he known all along?" His wife's short declaration contained too much raw information for him to word his questions in order of importance or distress. He pulled in air, then asked what he knew should have been his first question: "Marya, are you all right?"

"All right, Viktor?" Had her voice changed, he asked himself. Was it possible that his reliable, mousy Marya, was tinting her tones with sarcasm? "Yes, I'm all right, I guess."

"Marya, in Moscow, I saw you in our home, through a window. There was a man there. And then I heard . . ."

"What did you hear, Viktor? Whatever it was was probably true. It hasn't been much fun since you left us."

"Left you? You can't think that I left on purpose."

"You mean you were on your way home and someone stopped you and made you leave the country in a casket?"

"Tell me exactly what happened, Marya. When did they come to our home? When did you come here?"

"I don't know how long it's been. I just make sure that Anna has two meals each day and doesn't catch cold sleeping wherever they put us. But if I had to guess, I'd say I've been under arrest in my own house for a few weeks and taken to Poland and now here. This is Prague, isn't it, Viktor?"

"Yes, Prague," He felt as though he was expected to tell her something about it. The simple sentences about caring for Anna had reached him in a way that nothing had since he and Shishkin had escaped. Or had they ever escaped? Had they moved along on Karushkin's chessboard as he wished? One country forward, now one to the right.

"Marya, come upstairs. We have to talk."

"I'm not allowed to go upstairs."

"Oh, the hell with the boy and the old man. I'll take care of them."

"What boy? What are you talking about? Karushkin told me to stay right at the bottom of the steps. He has Anna, Viktor. I'm not about to do anything to make him angry."

It was peasant wisdom, the certainty of consequences, a sure knowledge of human cruelty. I knew these things once, Viktor thought. Just last month, I lived my life by these rules, too. He held her arms at the elbows, made sure she was looking nowhere but in his eyes. "Marya, we've each been through some very difficult times. All because of me. I've done some things that weren't very intelligent" – he saw a flash, then, of the Marya who called him a "durak", a fool, for forgetting to buy bread – "but you must believe that none of this was my idea."

"Must believe? Viktor, you sound like them." 'Them', the leaders, the rulers, the Party. Everyone who was not 'them' used it. "Here's what's to be believed. Karushkin has Anna, and, for what it's worth, me, under his thumb. He's moved us around like baggage, and from what I can see, he's been looking for you. He knew where you were by the time we left Poland, because that was only yesterday. But I don't think he knows what to do with you now that he's found you."

"I sympathize with his problem."

"He wants to see you, Viktor."

"He'll have to take a number."

"Stop this! Stop this immediately, do you hear me?" The sudden volume of her voice in this quiet misused mansion was like an unexpected cry in the night. Viktor flinched, then settled.

"I just told you he has Anna. He has found you, and that is that." There was a trembling fury about her that forbade response. "I love you, Viktor, I think you know that. But whatever you have done has caused Anna to be taken by these people. Now you must go and pay whatever price they ask to have her released, unharmed. Do you understand?"

The peasant wisdom spread over him like a mid-morning dusting of snow in December. He swallowed, resigned.

"Yes, of course, Marya. You're right. Where is Karushkin?"

"Outside." She sounded as impartial as a theater usher.

"I have to go upstairs first."

"They tell me you have a Polish woman now. Is she up there?"

"They tell you wrong. It's just Shishkin."

He saw her reaction. "I remember the night you brought him to our house. I remember how proud you were to do something like that. All I wanted was for him to get out."

"Things haven't changed much." He went upstairs without looking back at her.

"Well, Viktor, it's been a good run." Shishkin let the back of his head rest against the wall. "Do you remember back in Poland? I was ready to give up on you then, ready to go back. And when that bastard dentist went to to to work on me . . ."

"Yes." He said it too fast, exactly the thing he wanted to avoid. "Yevgeny, there's something you can tell me, something I have to know before I see Karushkin."

"Oh very well. The next plane for New York leaves tomorrow morning."

"Don't fool around, friend. Marya and Anna are in his grip."

"What can I tell you, comrade?" Shishkin had his wiseass smile in place.

"You can tell me about the police who were killed in Moscow."

The smile did not so much fade as collapse. Good, thought Viktor, he is scared, so more inclined to tell the truth.

"We're quite a ways from Moscow now, Viktor. And I'm not sure you're interested in the details. . . ."

"Let me decide what I'm interested in, Yevgeny." Viktor forgot all the things he had reminded himself to be – offhand, casual, friendly, unassuming. He wanted his daughter back safely, and Shishkin could help. That was all that mattered. "What did you know about them?"

Shishkin drew a large breath, as though preparing a long answer. "I've told you that already. We Jews have suffered long enough under the commissars. We had to . . ."

"I don't want your views. I want to know how you knew where the police would be. How you knew when and where to strike at them. The truth, Yevgeny."

"The truth. Not a thing that comes easily to these lips. Well, anyway, most of what I told you in Moscow was true. The few Jews with any nerve who live there decided that we had to at least bloody the Party a bit. Gorbachev's ideas about Jews aren't as revolutionary as his notions of private farms and profit-sharing. He sees us as a problem. And he's right. Jews and Russians were never really meant to mix. It's just a trick of geography."

"Hurry, Yevgeny. I don't have much time."

"I know. But if you don't at least understand our point of view, you won't see why the things that happened, happened.

"Pronsky, Bessmyrtinkh and a few others wanted to do something big, loud, important, to get the commissars' attention. I was more in favor of quietly trying to come to terms with . . . Don't look at me that way, I was!

"I made it known that I thought we'd just make things more difficult for ourselves trying to hurt them. Naturally nobody listened to me. But then, one of the KGB goons who'd beaten me up – you remember, Viktor, that's when we met and you took me home to your place – one of those guys came to my apartment. I figured he wanted to rearrange my bones again. But he said he was bringing a message from the people he worked for. Those kinds of people don't change employers, so I knew who he was talking about. The message – I've never forgotten it – was: 'No one ever got anywhere without a weapon.' Well, I had no idea what he was gabbling about, but then he produced a little notebook. Inside were the assignments for the Moscow militia for the next six weeks. Names, hours to be worked, locations where cars would be patroling."

"And you started hitting them," Viktor said.

"Of course not! Would you take something like that and just assume it was being given to you for your personal use? No. But I let Pronsky and Bessmyrtinkh have it. And they found people who watched to see if the list was right. And it was. So, a few weeks later, my bonebreaking friend is back. Another list, another six weeks' schedule. And this time, Pronsky decided to try a little experiment."

"And that was the first attack?"

"Yes, I only found out about it after the fact." Shishkin sounded like he was already in an interrogation chamber.

"Shishkin, I don't care what you did or why. Just tell me: did you ever find out who was behind the idea to give you that information?"

"Viktor, when you're doing things that cost people – even militiamen – their lives, you don't ask those kinds of questions."

He was right, of course. Viktor knew that, put in the same situation, he would never want to know. He said nothing for a full minute. Then:

"Yevgeny, I'm going down to see them now. I don't know what will happen to me. But I want you to know I won't do anything that will put you in more trouble. Much as I love my daughter and wife, I won't turn on you."

Shishkin looked at Viktor as though he had just declared his undying love for him.

Which, of course, he had.

"Go Viktor. May my God and yours put their bearded heads together and find some way to save us all."

Viktor closed the door softly, so as not to cause the Primate undue disturbance.

Marya sat in the back seat of the car, next to Karushkin. Viktor had hoped Anna would be there too, but knew better.

Karushkin appeared to have aged dramatically since Viktor had last seen him in Dzerzinsky Square. He wore a fine gray overcoat, and a maroon tie peeped through the top. But there was something caved-in about his face, especially at the jaws. Something to be put to good use?

"You look terrible," Karushkin said, with a polite smile. "No." That was in response to Viktor's move to open the back door, get in with him and Marya. "You drive, please. I want the advantage of seeing you without having to crook my head."

He noticed for the first time that the seat behind the wheel was empty. Why make me drive, he wondered.

Karushkin, ever aware, said: "You're a driver, right? I thought you might like to compare Prague with our home. Your former home."

Viktor was sure the amendment to the sentence had a purpose besides clarity.

"Since it's my wife in the back seat, why don't you drive, Colonel?"

Karushkin took it well. "Yes, I can understand your desire to be with her. After all, it's been a while."

In the rear-view mirror, he could see Marya's strained face, anxious eyes, knotted brow. He decided to quit playing for points.

"Where to?"

"Turn around and go down the street on the right."

The car was a Skoda, heavier than a Russian Zhiguli, but the steering was as loose as a go-cart's. Viktor felt it buck as soon as he turned on to the street. Cobblestones.

"Right over there", Karushkin was saying, "was where Kafka was born." He was pointing like a setter out the right window. It was unclear if he was addressing Viktor or Marya, neither of whom replied. "Well, anyway, now your trip to Prague has taught you something."

"That there's no place like home?"

"Viktor!" Marya's voice was urgent. It occurred to him that his wife seldom saw and heard him when he was playing the role of provocative clown. He wondered if she would like him better if she knew that side of him.

A series of rapid decisions overtook him then. He pulled over to the curb, barely allowing space for a car coming in the opposite direction to get past. He cut the motor. He turned around as much as the seat would permit. And he looked directly at Karushkin.

"Colonel, we all know that you've got me and that I'll do whatever you say, because you have my wife and my daughter. But you will not toy with me in this sadistic way. If you plan to kill us, do it here and now – "

"Viktor!"

" – but if you want something from me, stop screwing around and tell me what it is."

Karushkin looked suitably impressed. He nodded. "All right. I'll do as you insist. I was going to tell you that you could all come back to Moscow and that your wife and child would be allowed to live normal lives while you serve your prison term. But I can see you're not a man to be trifled with. So I'm canceling that offer. Now start the car and drive."

Viktor began to regret the grandstanding. He revved the uncertain motor, pulled away.

"I don't think, Melanov, that you quite understand the position I'm in. Your escape was extremely embarrassing to a man in my position."

"Why? You weren't responsible for that. You could have easily shifted the blame to someone else. You'd released me, and had every reason to think I'd be back. In fact, if I hadn't come into contact with Shishkin, I would have been."

"Yes, I imagine you would have. Nervy actions like that don't come naturally to you, do they?"

"If you mean by that, I like to think things out, yes."

Karushkin smiled faintly, settled back in the seat. "Go two more streets and turn right, then go to the end of that street."

Weirdly, Viktor found it relaxing to drive. It was something with which he was familiar in a situation where everything else seemed frightening. That was the most important thing: to keep Karushkin from knowing how frightened he was.

But Karushkin had been at his business for too long not to understand the effect he had on people. Melanov, he thought, was doing a very good job of pretending bravery, but his insides must be melting with the agony of uncertainty right now. How best to use that, to make himself master of a contest that he was not entirely certain he could win?

The house where he directed Viktor to stop was detached from the row of cheap brick houses on the street. It also had a driveway of sorts, already holding two identical black cars. Viktor recognized them: Volgas, Russian-made and the KGB car of choice. They were selected for use in Moscow because of their inconspicuousness. But in Prague, they looked, and were, badly out of place.

Karushkin said, "The STP here keeps an extensive network of informants. As you must know, Czech notions of loyalty are somewhat different from most people's."

"Like the KGB's?"

"Exactly. The STP gave me a few of their best informants' names. It was little enough trouble to track you down. Don't even consider trying to get away."

"Why lie? I know the cardinal told you where I was."

"Yes. But I've also talked with the slut."

"Victoria?"

"Is that the whore's name? Oh, yes, of course it is. How long do you think it took me to convince her to tell me everything she knew? Viktor? You have no friends."

Was he surprised? Viktor had thought Victoria might prove of tougher substance. Forget her, he told himself. Worry about your family.

Viktor was prepared for tricks, but Karushkin wanted there to be none. The front door opened as they were getting out of the car. Even before he had straightened up, Viktor saw her: she was standing behind the man who had opened the door, wearing a summer dress that he immediately thought might not be warm enough. He began to hurry toward the house, without closing the car door.

"No!" said Karushkin loudly, but not Viktor thought, with the full authority of a KGB colonel. The man at the front door stepped in front of Anna, blocked Viktor's sight of her, and quickly but quietly closed the door. In the last second, Viktor thought he saw her make a small attempt at a wave.

"All right, Viktor Nikolaich, that will be quite far enough." Karushkin appeared to be having some trouble in getting out of the car's back seat. Viktor hoped he was in pain. He also realized that he disliked Karushkin using his first name.

Karushkin came around, took Viktor gently by the elbow, ignoring Marya, who stood by the car.

"Don't be alarmed. Your daughter is in perfect health."

"She looks cold to me."

"Wait until you get inside. You'll see how well a Soviet citizen can live when someone else is paying the bill."

The two men walked to the house together. Marya never moved. When Karushkin opened the front door, Viktor felt the hush of dry heat. The house must have been heated to at least 75 degrees, which to a Russian seems more like a gymnasium than living quarters. The furniture, Viktor noticed, was cheap-looking.

"You must excuse the décor," Karushkin said immediately. "We had very little time to choose our meeting ground."

How does he do that, Viktor wondered, know exactly what I am thinking and comment on it?

"Go to your right, down the hallway."

The hallway was lit only by one weak bulb and Viktor noted mentally the contrast between Karushkin's generous attitude toward heat and his pecuniousness about light. He thought about it long enough for his common sense to tell him to stop it. This was not why he was here.

But why was he here?

In this house, there were no secrets, no surprises. "To the left," said Karushkin, and Viktor walked into a room with a table and three chairs, a sideboard loaded with everyday plates, cups and saucers, and a window cut into the wall that connected to the next room. Through the window he saw Anna sitting (back straight, good posture, he noticed) in an ugly green chair. The man who had appeared at the door with her sat opposite in a wooden dining chair that belonged to the set from Viktor's room.

"She cannot see you," Karushkin said quickly. "But do not raise your voice, because it is not soundproof, and she will know you are here and become upset. I am letting you see her to convince you that nothing bad has happened to her. Yet."

Why did Viktor think that Karushkin's voice had less authority than when he had been questioned in Moscow?

"I told you, Melanov, that your escape caused me problems. We are going to rectify those problems, you and I. So," he said with a sudden heartiness, "how do you like Prague?"

Viktor saw that Anna's head lifted at the moment Karushkin's voice was raised. So she could hear them.

"From what I have seen, it has all the advantages of Moscow, except the good fortune to be occupied by Russians."

"True, true. The Czechs are abominable people. They adored Hitler when he was strong, then welcomed us when we liberated them."

"Liberated countries can be ungrateful. Look at the Afghans."

"Yes. Thank God you did not have your coffin taken to the Kazakhstan train station in Moscow. We might be having this discussion in Kandahar."

"Unlikely that the Pope would send a helicopter there, isn't it?"

"I find it incredible that he had done so here. But then, Melanov, I am of the old school. Know thine enemy."

Viktor said nothing. Wondered if Marya had come in.

"You're taking me back, is that it?"

"You weren't listening. I told you in the car that had been my original intention, along with your wife and child. But Melanov, well, Melanov, what can I say? I have come to respect you. As an adversary – and I have dealt with many – you provided a certain challenge. And I believe that should be rewarded."

Karushkin was walking around the table slowly, talking swiftly but, Viktor thought, in disjointed fashion. Could he be drunk?

"You see, having spent time with your wife and daughter, and now having seen you in this atmosphere of, well, let's say an outpost of Marxism-Leninism, I've concluded that your actions speak volumes about you."

It was as though the man was running together a series of sentences that he had used in the past, but in no real order.

"And so I'm going to give you what your attempt to escape clearly shows that you must want."

Through the two-way mirror, Viktor saw Marya walk into the next room, put her arm around Anna, reassure her.

"You wanted to leave, and you did. You went first to Warsaw, but Poland provides no satisfactory link with the West, does it? So you came here. And you found your way to that doddering old man in red, who just happens to be going to Austria and thinks he'll take you with him, to show off like some new species of tropical fruit."

Karushkin was running his words together. This is not the same man who was in complete control in Moscow, Viktor thought.

"So I'm going to let you go, Melanov. Go with the Primate. Enjoy the fruits of Austria. Go on to the United States if you want to."

Viktor turned his full attention to what Karushkin was saying now.

"You see, if I had my way, I'd send a T–70 tank over to that old charlatan's house and blow him and everyone else in there into little bits. But that's not the way we do things now. No, now we let ourselves be made fools of, by even bigger fools like you and that Jew. Well, so be it. You don't like it in Moscow, you leave. Tired of Poland and your whore? Come here. Get an offer to fly across the border? Take it. You've lived your life to suit your own moods recently, haven't you? Haven't shown much consideration for your loved ones since you've been here, have you?"

Here it comes, Viktor thought.

"Well, I say, let each man have what he wants most. And we're going to see what you want. You want to go to the West? I'm going to let you. But you'll have to go alone, Melanov. They won't be coming with you."

Viktor saw Karushkin's hand pointing toward the glass in the wall. In the other room, Marya was still rocking Anna, talking softly to her.

"Now I suppose you think that unfair, do you Viktor?"

"Unfair? Yes. Also in keeping with you. Torturer."

Karushkin made his eyebrows go up. "What? Unhappy with my offer? Well, I can see there's no pleasing you. But all right. Rather than be accused of cruelty, I'll make it more attractive to you."

Please say I can take them with me, Viktor thought, wondering with whom he was pleading.

"You deliver the Jew to me, Melanov. He and I have a few things to discuss."

"And if I do, I can take them with me?"

"It's not a perfect world, you know. Sometimes we only get half of what we want. Give me Shishkin, and you can take one of them with you. You decide."

A twisting pain climbed through Viktor's bowels, into his stomach, began to constrict his chest.

"The other one goes back with you?"

"That's right. The other one goes with me. And the Jew. And you can spend the rest of your life wondering exactly where she is, and how much she is suffering. While you enjoy the West, comrade."

23

He sat. Sat watching his daughter and her mother have a low, serious talk about what he could only imagine was him. The trap that he had begun to spring upon himself the first time he tried to bend the rules of Soviet society was now lockjaw tight. In three weeks he had thought wonderful thoughts about himself, about freedom, about intelligence and courage. Now it came down to him, sitting in an unpleasantly straight dining chair with a scratchy artificial seat cover that made his lower back itch. While his daughter nodded sagely, absorbing some peasant wisdom from the woman he had so recently and willingly betrayed.

He had asked to be allowed to talk to Anna, to Marya. Permission refused. And Karushkin had warned him that if he attempted to communicate with Shishkin by any means except those approved, his family would be sent to a particularly little talked-about facility in Kazakhstan where radical medical experiments were conducted, mostly on life-term prisoners. Viktor wanted to think that since Gorbachev had taken charge such things were only an old KGB legacy. Things were different now, such savagery was as old-fashioned as Brezhnev's haircut. But he lacked any proof on which to pin that conclusion, especially if it meant Anna's safety.

Safety? The word that he had allowed to run through his mind came back like a bullet off a stone wall. You compromised her safety the day you first offered Western cigarettes to an embassy guard, the day you arranged for a customs official to have his brake shoes changed without charge, the day you first realized that your clown's face and facile tongue were believable to some people.

Stop now. Think about those you love and how you can undo your recent stupidity.

"I won't turn on you," he had told Shishkin. "Now you must go and pay whatever price they ask," wise Marya had said. "Moy droog." Shishkin had used it to begin a thousand silly sentences. My friend, my wife, my daughter.

Decide among them? How? Who?

He heard footsteps in the hallway and immediately looked through the window. Either his women did not hear or did not acknowledge the noise. He went to the door, opened it. The man who had stood at the front door with Anna was headed there again. Now he heard someone knocking. "Stay there. Make a wrong move and you know what happens." A tough, uneducated accent, like the doorman at a Moscow restaurant.

When the man opened the door, Viktor immediately saw the cuffs of a white jacket, and the gleaming cuffs of white pants. Czechoslovak police, possibly STP. He heard a high-pitched parade of nonsense words, then heard the man at the door answer in gutter Russian.

"Shto?"

"Shto?"

Standoff, thought Viktor. The Russian turned away, came past Viktor again, went into the room across the hall from the one where Marya and Anna sat. A few seconds later, Karushkin emerged. It was not, Viktor thought, so much that he looked old as that he was scared. He looked at Viktor for just a second, seemed about to speak, then went on.

Someone else was in the doorway when Karushkin got there, someone who spoke Russian. Viktor's view was impaired by the half-open door, but he heard them:

"You are Soviet?"

"Yes." Karushkin sounded far less sure of himself, Viktor thought.

"I am Captain Pracht, of the third division of the National Security Police. You have come from the residence of the Cardinal."

No hint of a question in that sentence, Viktor thought. Like the KGB, STP men didn't ask questions because they already knew the answers.

"What makes you think that?" Considering he was a KGB colonel, Karushkin seemed weak, fearful, incriminating.

"Your presence was reported. You were followed. Why were you there?"

"We, ah, had, a sort of business there. Done now, actually. Good to know that you're watching. Thank you."

Karushkin was trying to shut the door on the captain, who had wedged a foot across the doorway to prevent that. It was comic, Viktor thought. He would not have believed it of Karushkin. A man with his authority, acting as if he was here . . .

as if . . .

he was here . . .

without . . .

"What's going on here?" Viktor roared as he walked briskly to the door. "Who are you?" he said distinctly to the captain. "I'm certainly sorry you've been disturbed, Colonel. I told this idiot" – gesturing at Karushkin – "that you were not to be disturbed. But obviously these field agents can't follow orders."

Karushkin was staring as if he had just urinated on the rug. The doorman made a move toward Viktor, but Karushkin, with a nearly imperceptible motion of his hand, called him off.

"Colonel?" The Czech took his foot out of the doorway.

"Oh, fuck your mother, now I've done it!" Viktor slapped his forehead. "Colonel, perhaps you would like me to deal with this, this, intrusion. Please sir, go back to your work. I'll see it's handled properly."

Captive and colonel looked at each other for a long moment.

"Yes. Do that," Karushkin said slowly. He kept his eyes on Viktor. "As you know, I have some important things back there. We wouldn't want anything to happen to them, would we?"

"I haven't forgotten that."

Viktor leaned his head just a fraction toward Karushkin, said rapidly: "I know that tin rubles are worthless." It was the moral of an old tale about a man who tries to pay for a castle with tin money. He loses not only the castle, but his wife, whom he thought would love him more if he bestowed such a gift upon her.

The captain, he saw gratefully, looked bewildered.

Karushkin nodded slowly, showed a smile that, had they not been under these circumstances, might have seemed amused, even friendly.

"Yes, all right then. See to it." He turned and walked back down the hall, the slow-witted doorman trailing behind him, mouthing the word "Rubles?"

Viktor took a deep breath, hoped it was not noticeable. "Now then, captain, I'm afraid I've made an awful error. I must beg your help to avoid ending my career in disgrace. If you see my point." He put an arm over the captain's shoulder. If he knocks me away, Viktor thought, it's all over.

The captain stood still, squinted his eyes.

"What career are we talking about?" His Russian was quite good overall.

"The same line of work as you, I think, Captain. Ultimately, we all take our orders from the same people. Only we are farther from home. Can you send this man away?" He indicated the white-uniformed officer who had first knocked on the door.

The captain told him, in Czech, to wait in the car.

"You speak Russian so well, Captain," Viktor said when they were alone. Arm still slung over his shoulder, he led him toward the softer of two chairs in the house's main room. The captain was about his age, had graying hair, a slight paunch, lively eyes. "Have you spent much time in Moscow?"

"No. I applied for a special program, but was turned down."

"I wonder who makes these decisions. First they say they're looking for intelligent people, then let someone like you get away." The captain let himself be guided to the chair. Viktor saw a bottle of vodka and glasses on the sideboard.

"Care for a toothache remedy?" He hoped the captain understood the slang.

"Well, all right then. I thought drinking was no longer appreciated in Moscow."

"Oh, fuck your mother, Misha talks like he's Saint Cyril come back to save us. But I know stories about him." At that instant, Viktor could think of not a single Gorbachev joke. What irony for him to be betrayed by a swollen tongue. Then his mind clicked in. "How do you think he got that mark on his forehead? Passed out one night in a puddle of Stolichnaya Special Reserve. By the time the Tsarina found him next morning, it had burned its way through."

The captain opened his mouth as far as his lips permitted and looked at Viktor. Was the joke too dangerous to share? The explosion of laughter startled him for a second, then he relaxed.

"Oh Christ. The Tsarina!" The captain punched himself in the knee and doubled over. He was really breaking up. "I've never heard her called that before. When they visited Prague, there were more of us assigned to watch Raisa than him." He accepted the glass from Viktor and tipped it back.

"Back home, she insists on the youngest ones as her bodyguards. Her, body, guards." He winked.

"So, you're with, them?" The captain delayed for just a moment before the final word, so as to make clear his meaning.

"Yes." The captain nodded, once. Fraternity had been established.

"The colonel in there, my boss, was sent to deliver a message to the old Redbird." They both snorted, and the captain held out his glass in response to Viktor's offer. "I mean, it's bad enough he's going to Austria. But in the Pope's damn helicopter?"

"If you ask me, off the main street of course, things have gotten too loose in the past few years." The "last few years" was the universal way for critics to refer to the Gorbachev era. The captain emptied his face suddenly, and added: "But as I say, that's off the main street."

Viktor made a short backhand sweeping motion. "Let me tell you, you're not the only person who feels that way. Lots of people back home – and I don't mean the plumber and the butcher – think he's gone too far. I mean, pulling out of Afghanistan like that? We looked like fools."

"We made sure it got very little attention here," said the captain with a satisfied nod. He licked the inside rim of his glass. Viktor refilled it.

"Well, I can tell you one thing," he said. "There have been a lot of changes, but we've kept our patch pretty much the way it's always been."

"I'm glad to hear that. There's talk about things going soft in the Square."

It took Viktor a second to understand what he meant. "Don't you believe it," he said, raising his glass, but not drinking. "We're not going to let him do any lasting damage."

The captain stood up.

He's been leading me on, Viktor thought, letting me make a treasonous fool out of myself, and now he's going to take me. Well, I tried.

"Here's to common sense. May it win out in the end," said the captain.

"Na storovye."

"Na storovye."

Viktor let the vodka go down, felt it bottom out somewhere near his heart.

"What's the colonel's name?"

Viktor had been ready for the question. "Look, comrade. I'll tell you if you want. But if I do, I'll need to have your name, and make a report, and frankly, anyone associated with this trip of ours is going to get a lot of attention in a few days. The wrong kind of attention."

The captain stopped smiling. "Because of the Primate?"

Viktor nodded.

"You mean you're going to . . ."

"He had his chance. We talked with him."

"Fuck your mother." The words came out slowly, almost reverently. He sat back down.

"Now if you still want to know his name . . ."

"No! No, never mind."

"Good. Ah, Captain, there's still one thing." Can I actually do this, Viktor wondered. He stood. "About my letting slip that he was a colonel."

"Yes?" The captain's voice was flat.

Viktor reached into his pocket, at first felt nothing but pants lining. Then, yes, it was still there. "I shouldn't have said that, and now you can see why. I'll be in a jam if it leaks out here. It's all my fault, so . . ." He pulled his hand out of his pocket, fingered the hundred-dollar bill, put it on the arm of the chair where the captain sat.

"I had planned to use that while I was here. To pick up a few things, you know, for the wife. Can't take a trip without her wanting me to scour every store in the damn city. Why, once I went to Berlin . . . thought they'd charge me overweight on the plane back home."

The captain was eyeing the money.

"Where'd you get this?" Viktor couldn't tell if he was furious or envious.

"Well, there are some perks attached to the job."

"Christ. This is better identification than a red card. Who else from Moscow would have a hundred dollars?"

"Who else indeed?"

In one surprisingly graceful motion, the captain stood, palmed the money and pocketed it.

"It's been nice talking to you."

"Except that you were never here."

"Don't let things get out of control back in Moscow," he said, clapping Viktor on the shoulder.

"Don't worry," Viktor answered, crossing with him to the door. "Nothing important is going to change."

"Well done, Melanov. I can see why you've avoided trouble for so long."

Viktor said nothing as Karushkin, his previous confidence restored, approached him from the hallway.

"I didn't want to have to pull rank on that fool. Imagine! Having us followed. Your intervention was very skilful."

"You're all alone," Viktor said quietly.

"Yes, it often feels that way. A giant among pygmies."

"No one knows you're here." Viktor hoped his voice would not crack from tension.

"What exactly do you mean?"

"You're here without authorization. You're here for yourself, not for them."

"Highly unlikely, Melanov. As you can see I brought my own escort." He nodded toward the room from which he had been listening.

"Who, Brainless in there? He might be your chauffeur, but he's not KGB. He couldn't pass the written exam."

The same pallor – one that might have been old age but was actually fear – clouded Karushkin's face.

"I told you I had help from the STP in finding you."

"What you said was that you were lucky."

"You have no idea of what you're saying, Melanov."

"That's true. I don't know much about how you people operate. But I know how a man looks when he's doing something he shouldn't. He looks like you."

"That hardly matters, does it? Because you'll still never see your wife and daughter again unless I say so."

"You mean both of them?" He knew he had spoken without thinking, wished he could take the words back.

Karushkin tilted his chin up, smiled. "That's better. No, Melanov, only one or the other. To the West. Upon delivery of Shishkin. As agreed."

Viktor felt his head spin again at the thought of having to choose between his wife and daughter. "You don't need me to get Shishkin. You know where he is. Why don't you have the police storm in and take him?"

Karushkin screwed up his face. "I knew that question would emerge. Frankly, in the old days, nothing would have been easier. But, as you rightly suggested, my visit here is, let us say, unofficial." He squeezed his eyelids shut, then let them flutter open. "Those fools will ruin everything before they're finished. Coexist with the Americans. Open the churches. Allow the Jews to leave. Give the press a free hand. Make businesses show profits. It's going to ruin us!" The last words came out so loud that the doorman peered out from the room down the hall. Satisfied that Karushkin was not calling for help, he disappeared again.

The interruption gave the old man time to regain control. "And people like you and that Jew, untrustworthy, conniving. . . ."

"In other words, you had enough clout to come here and bring my wife and daughter, but not enough to break into the cardinal's house." He was just realizing something. "If you'd found us before we got there. . . ?"

"Then none of this would be necessary."

"Did Jiri tell you where we were?"

"What is a Jiri, Melanov?"

Viktor felt a small surge of gratitude to the madwoman who had insisted that they see the cardinal.

"And, if I don't help you, Yevgeny will get on that helicopter in a few hours and fly away. And you won't be able to stop him."

A thought occurred to him. "Why do you want Shishkin so badly? You've got me to make an example of. Let Marya and Anna go to the West and I'll confess to anything."

Karushkin seemed not to be listening. "They think that wanting to be strong is old-fashioned. So instead, they're giving it all away. And to the wrong people. Not to the Russians. But the Jews, the Americans, the Africans, Indians."

"You're just a dried-out old leaf, trying to stop the wind from blowing you down. This has nothing to do with our escaping. This is personal, isn't it?"

Karushkin smiled, a smile of accumulated wisdom, treachery and a long experienced life, and walked back to the room from which he came.

Viktor returned to the dining room where he had been sitting, and did some more of that. To break the monotony, he tried thinking as well. Night fell. He saw that Anna was asleep, cradled in her mother's arms in the ugly green armchair. He was afraid to try to talk to them, to disregard Karushkin. The KGB colonel seemed less in control than before, and so, more dangerous. At least his wife and daughter were in sight, and well. For the moment.

Three hours passed that way. When Karushkin opened the door of the dining room Viktor stood, as though welcoming a guest.

"Have you thought it over?" Karushkin asked.

"I've thought about it."

"And?"

"I'll deliver Shishkin. But both Anna and Marya come with me."

Karushkin shook his head. "Have you ever noticed that desperate people have no sense of fairness?"

"That's what makes them desperate."

"Yes, but they disregard rules, ignore limitations, make impossible demands."

"I suppose I don't see desperation from the same vantage point as you."

"Of course not. But that doesn't make it any fairer."

"How often does that approach win you any sympathy, Colonel?"

Karushkin smacked his hands together. "Damn, Melanov, are you crazy or courageous?"

"Define the difference." Viktor was beginning to shake inside. He hoped he could keep it from showing.

"I must say, Melanov, you are different from the rest. I knew it as soon as I saw you. Charming, arrogant, appealing in a way. But you're not going to charm me. You made the biggest mistake of your life defying me. And the Jew? Well, there's a lot more than blood between him and me. No, you're each going to pay the price for crossing me. You pay first. Who leaves with you, your wife or daughter?"

"Anna." Until the second that he said the name, he wasn't certain that he could do it. Condemn Marya to hell, while he left behind the world he knew. His first thought had been to get Anna to Austria safely, then kill himself. But where did that leave her? The misery was inescapable, because to escape it would cause more. And Karushkin knew it.

"I thought you'd say that. Very well. It's time to go. Now you may see your wife."

"Now I don't want to."

"Again you surprise me Melanov. A singular person, no doubt about it."

"Anna comes with us."

"Still trying to make your own rules? No. She comes later."

"Then we're going nowhere."

The two Russians stood only a foot apart, the older man glaring at the younger. Perhaps neither recognized how alike they were; their talents simply were harnessed to different currents. Viktor watched Karushkin thinking, saw the first flicker of defeat in his eyes and waited for the words.

"I'm going to let you have this one. But stay here, or I take both of them back with me." He walked out of the room and down the hall. A minute later, Viktor saw the doorman go into the room where Marya held Anna. There was a brief conversation, during which the girl awoke. A second later, the doorman was pulling Anna from her mother's arms, while Marya screamed. Without realizing it, Viktor was screaming too: "It's all right, Marya, let him take her. She's going with me! Let him take her. It's all right!"

He didn't know how long the clamor went on. Finally he could tell that Marya recognized his voice, understood what he was shouting. She fell back into the chair. Anna was sobbing, "Mama, Mama!" but put up no more resistance to the big man. The door opened, and Anna was in his arms.

"Daddy, Daddy, I don't want to leave Mummy. Why can't I stay with Mummy? Where are we going? Why can't she come?"

All questions to which he had no answers. He held her tightly, soothed her with strokes and nuzzles. Inside of three minutes, she had stopped whimpering. He whispered to her. She rubbed his face with her hands, which felt cold, put her nose in his neck. Viktor felt dizzy from the joy it gave him.

"Here," Karushkin said, as they prepared to get into the car. He shoved a thickly padded brown envelope, sealed shut, at Viktor. "There's a message inside for Shishkin. I think it will convince him to come out with me."

"What does it say?" Viktor wanted to know.

"Don't you think there's such a thing as knowing too much, Melanov?"

The drive seemed shorter with the doorman at the wheel. Viktor had asked to be allowed to sit with Anna in the back seat, but Karushkin refused. Instead the colonel sat next to his daughter and said nothing. Up the street where Kafka had been born, into the cobblestoned square with the Party headquarters on one side, the Primate's residence on the other. Behind the residence, behind St Vitus's Cathedral, Viktor saw that a space had been roped off. For the Pope's helicopter? For anti-aircraft gunners when the helicopter tried to land? Just as possible in this country of hidden horrors.

The doorman pulled into precisely the spot where the car had been parked when Viktor got into it. Before he could turn his head, Anna had sprung open the back door nearest her and was sprinting to the residence. Karushkin, old and surprised, tried to grab the end of her dress as she squirted out of the car, but failed.

"Get her, damn it!" The doorman lunged toward his door but Viktor was all over him. He punched and gouged and pinched and scratched without regard for manhood or propriety. The doorman gave up trying to get out of the car and set about punishing Viktor. A jab to the throat cut off his breath. A fist in the crotch made him want to vomit. But as he slumped against the car door, he saw Anna being pulled inside the Primate's house by Tomek.

"God damn you Melanov, you're a dead man." Karushkin screamed like a woman scorned. "I'll have your balls."

Viktor could even smile as he said: "I think your trained dog here got the better part of them already." Adrenaline combined with nausea made him woozy.

"She's dead, Melanov. You've killed her!"

For a second Viktor wondered what the colonel was shouting about. Then he remembered. Marya.

"Better dead than in a carryover from your sick past, Colonel."

"I promise you, she'll go slowly."

The pain from his scrotum had welded the bottom half of Viktor's body to the seat. He turned around and using only his arms and shoulders, got the colonel just by the lapel of his suit jacket and pulled him forward. He felt the doorman begin to pound on his kidneys, but the pain took second place to deeper feelings.

He hit Karushkin across the forehead with an open hand for everyone who worked in his office. He clubbed him on the nose with his fist on behalf of Marya, he gouged him in the eye for Anna. He twisted his nose between

269

two fingers in honor of Shishkin. He pulled away when he saw blood on the back of his hand, and when the doorman had chopped him for the second time behind the ear.

"You threatened my daughter, you fucking monster. You hurt my wife. I'll see you in hell, Karushkin."

The old man was slumped against the back seat, unmoving. His eyes showed only white. But his mouth was cocked in a smile. Words bubbled up to his lips, then hissed away. A minute passed.

"Melanov, what a fool you are. And yet how typical of all our people. Sudden anger, the short-term satisfaction of revenge. But what then? What has this earned you?"

"Well, for one thing, I think we can now renegotiate our bargain."

"What's that?"

"My daughter is inside the cardinal's house now. You yourself have admitted that you don't dare storm the place. So Anna's safe, or as safe as anyone can be once he's been touched by your miserable organization."

Karushkin's smile was forced. He wiped blood with a handkerchief. "I take it back. You're not typical at all. Most Russians would be cowering in fear, awaiting retaliation for such an utterly dishonorable act. Not only are you not ashamed, you're still trying to bargain with me."

"The times have changed, Colonel. You might be the last man in the Soviet Union to be finding that out."

"What change? Gorbachev? Don't worry yourself over him, Melanov. And don't put too much faith in his ability to make an entire system bend. There are still enough straight thinkers back there" – he gestured vaguely, hoping it was to the East – "to keep us on track."

"On track or in chains?"

"That all depends on which end of the chain is attached to you." The colonel heaved. He was tired, Viktor thought. "Oh, Melanov. What a bother you've proven to be. In the old days . . ."

"Have you ever noticed, Colonel, that the people who talk about 'the old days' are the ones who don't have many new ones left?"

"What do you want, Melanov?"

"My wife."

"Obviously. But that would give you everything you want before I get Shishkin."

"What's the matter, Colonel? Don't you trust me?"

Again Karushkin issued a weak laugh. "I hope your woman listened to us. We told her not to leave that house, or she'd never see her daughter again."

"Then she'll be there."

"When Shishkin comes out to us, we'll have your wife here. She can come in then."

"And you'll let her leave on the helicopter with us?"

"That's up to the Pope. Make sure Shishkin reads the message in that envelope." Karushkin's eyes defocused. He was in pain from the beating. Viktor opened the car door, took the envelope, and without looking back, hurried toward the Residence.

"Where is my daughter?" he asked Tomek, who seemed to spend his entire life at the door, waiting for visitors. The dusty foyer reminded Viktor of the dirty work he was about to do.

"She is with His Eminence, Pan Melanov. No," he said when he saw Viktor about to protest, "let her stay there. His Eminence is really good with children. And, His Eminence believes, you are not fully able to explain to her everything that has happened."

Hard to argue with that, Viktor thought. He tried to picture Anna, probably sitting next to the massive cardinal, listening as he spoke softly, soothingly to her. He liked the image that it conjured up.

"All right. You know who's in that car that we arrived in?" Tomek nodded. "It will be back in a few minutes. My wife will be in it. If there's any way of getting her in here safely, any way at all, you do it."

"Of course, Pan Melanov. I understand."

Perhaps he did at that. "Tell me, Tomek, what stops them from overrunning this place and taking us all away?"

"God works in strange ways, you know," answered the boy, his Czech eyes illuminated by some inner light.

24

"So you see, moy droog, it's probably in both our best interests to find out what they have to say. Perhaps we can work the whole thing out."

Viktor shifted from foot to foot as he stood in front of Shishkin, who did not budge. Viktor suspected he was unmoved in another sense, as well.

"Just a few hours ago, wasn't it Viktor, I said it's been a good race? We've kept a step ahead of the bastards, and I think we should be proud of ourselves. Let's not do anything to spoil that now." Shishkin could not break the habit of stroking his face, in search of his missing beard. It made him look wise. Viktor knew it meant something else.

"Look, Yevgeny, I went out and met him. You're right, he's a cruel piece of work. But not entirely insane, like some of them."

"And you think I should go out there, and take his measure, right?"

"Well, put that way, yes, I do."

It was near midnight. Shishkin had spent the entire day holed up in the house. Confinement before freedom. They talked about how they had felt cooped up in the coffin on their way to Poland. Better to fly like a hawk, they agreed. How soon would it be? A few hours? Shishkin was only half-listening. "He must have you pretty scared, eh? To talk you into being his messenger boy."

The emotions Viktor felt were many – embarrassment, shame, anger at Shishkin's condescending attitude. But he remembered that Marya would soon be outside in the car, and that even if Anna was inside the cardinal's residence, they were still a long way from safety.

"Why don't you read his letter to you? It's bound to have some kind of enticement in it. That's how these people operate, isn't it?"

"I don't know, friend. You've spent more time with them recently than I." Viktor could taste the reproach. "Well, it won't kill me to find out what he has to say." He tore open the envelope's seal with some difficulty.

"Hmmm. If I present myself . . . full and fair investigation of past grievances . . . possible clemency for violations of Soviet law . . . spirit of cooperation." He looked up. "This sounds like the kind of letter you get for going through a red light. Why did he bother?"

"Can't say. I've never been caught going through a red light." It was a weak laugh, but it was the first they had shared since arriving at the Primate's.

Shishkin opened his eyes as wide as he could make them go. They looked like imperfect birds' eggs, alabaster flecked with red.

"He wants me badly, doesn't he, Viktor?"

"Yes, Yevgeny. For some unknown reason he's chosen you."

"Well naturally. I'm one of the Chosen People. And there's a reason. There's always a reason." The one-note laugh was not a sound that made Viktor feel better.

"Viktor Nikolaich, answer me this: does he have your wife?"

There are otherwise honorable men who cheat at cards. Others steal hotel towels, dress up in women's clothes, commit adultery. Once their dark urges are satisfied, they reclaim, indeed insist upon, their membership in mainstream mankind, and live happily by its rules until temptation strikes again. Viktor's word was his wealth. He dealt fairly, if not always according to the rules, with policemen and black marketeers alike. He remembered once telling Anna, when she asked for an explanation of truth and untruth: "If people don't trust you, you will never be happy." Thinking of Anna, downstairs now, he looked at his truest friend, with whom he had shared a three-week lifetime, and, hesitating only to take a breath, said: "Yes."

Shishkin dropped his head, decided. "We can't let him hurt her. Some things are more important than survival."

Viktor moved toward Karushkin's black car with considerably more confidence this time. The doorman kept the motor idling. The KGB colonel sat in the back seat with Marya. Viktor thought he again had the look of a scared old man. Marya's fear was more basic. Through the car window, he saw her mouth the word "Anna?" He nodded decisively, gave her his soothing smile. She returned one of her own.

"Here are Shishkin's terms," Viktor began, marveling at his own gall. He thought Karushkin pursed an ironic smile with his wrinkled lips.

"The Pope's helicopter is due in about five hours. Shishkin, Anna and I get on the helicopter along with the Primate. You bring Marya to the helicopter. Shishkin gets out, she gets in. We fly away."

"No." Karushkin's voice had the finality of history.

You must do this, Viktor told himself, as he looked at Marya. Be strong, his eyes told her.

He turned around and began walking away.

"Did Shishkin read my letter?" With only a few feet separating them, Karushkin sounded weaker.

Viktor stopped. "He made several good suggestions about style and grammar."

"Once your wife gets on board, he'll come without a fight?"

"No, he specifically said he wants to have a shootout with the entire Red Army."

"Don't think it's always this easy, Melanov. It's just that I want Shishkin." The colonel consulted his watch. "Your wife will spend the rest of the night with us." He twisted his mouth and the result resembled a smile. "Don't worry, she's used to it. We'll be back at four a.m."

"I'll try to fit you into my schedule." He gave Marya a little wave, the kind they used to trade when he was just another Russian, rushing off to work.

Viktor thought the room had grown cold in the short time he was away, but Shishkin, snoozing under a blanket on the sofa, had beads of sweat on his forehead and above his lip.

"What's up, moy droog? Obviously not you."

"Well, my temperature, anyway. God, I feel awful. Must be close association with high-ranking Christians. I guess I shouldn't have gobbled those communion wafers I found in the Cardinal's room."

Viktor gave him a sidelong glance. "Pull yourself together. In a few hours we'll be trying to decide between Wiener schnitzel and Linzer torte."

"Oh God, don't mention food." And with the agility of desperation, Shishkin lunged for the bathroom. Viktor heard the sounds of vomiting, the strangling struggle for air, the long moan afterward.

"I see you're going to be as much fun to travel with as ever," he said. He got comfortable in the armchair that Shishkin had commandeered for most of the day, and closed his eyes.

He was surprised to wake up because he had thought he would be unable to sleep. Having no watch, he looked out of the window. False dawn was stealing into the sky.

"Yevgeny, rouse yourself. It's time to do great things."

He expected a grunt or a curse. The complete silence he got in response brought him fully awake. His eyes adjusted at double speed to the dim scene before him.

274

Shishkin had never made it back to the couch. He was lying face down, halfway out of the bathroom. The smell of sickness eddied out around him so strongly that Viktor gagged when he first bent over the inert form to turn him over.

Viktor put his fingers on Shishkin's wrist to find a pulse. It was then that he noticed his hands. The fingertips were blackened. He brought them closer to his face. There was a scent like singed hair. Viktor could not help inspecting his own hands. They looked normal.

The young man Tomek was the first to respond to the bellowed Russian cry for help. Either he slept in his clothes or had never gone to bed, or he was already awake for he came in the room dressed exactly as he had been hours earlier.

They lifted Shishkin to the couch and went through all the useless rigmarole they had both seen in movies: loosening the sick man's clothes, putting a cold cloth on his head.

"There's no pulse," Tomek said simply, in Czech. Viktor understood.

Tomek left and returned a few minutes later with the cardinal, who repeated the pulse test.

"Your friend is dead, I'm afraid."

"He wasn't though." Viktor was looking out of the window. "He was ready to go out and offer himself to the bastards. Look at his hands."

"Did he eat anything that you didn't? Drink something? Take any drugs?"

"Yes, drug addiction is a big problem among Jewish dissidents on the run from the KGB in Czechoslovakia."

Tomek came back. "Eminence, the Russians' car is outside. Also, the helicopter should be touching down in a few minutes."

"Thank you, Tomek." He looked at Viktor's back. "Do you still want to come?"

They heard the whupp-whupp of the helicopter at the same moment, followed by the growl of its motors as it descended into the plaza behind the Residence. Viktor turned away from the window. "How far do we have to go?" he asked.

"Only twenty steps, if it's parked where it should be. And knowing the Austrians, they'll have set it down within a millimeter of dead center."

"Dead center." Viktor forced air out of his nostrils. He walked over to Shishkin's body, knelt down, ignoring the vomit and the reek. "Well, moy droog, shall we run the last lap of this race? I just looked out the window. Sunrise is just around the corner."

This time Karushkin was standing outside the car. "You see what happens Melanov, when you start getting big ideas? People get hurt." He folded his arms across his sparrow's chest. "And you, my friend, now have nothing to trade, do you?"

He knows, Viktor thought. He was shaking, but he doubted Karushkin could see it. He tried to look past the colonel, into the car, to see that Marya was there. But the windows were rolled up tight, and cast a black reflection in the weak early morning light.

"Where is my wife, Karushkin?"

"Did he suffer long, Melanov? Give me the details. We've had different results in various experiments. Evidently he vomited. I can smell it on you."

"What are you talking about, Colonel?"

"The letter, of course. The one you delivered to him. The paper was coated with ricin. It's a derivative of a plant found in Turkey and Bulgaria. Remember Georgy Markov, the Bulgarian writer who defected? We used ricin on him, back in 1978. He was stabbed with the point of an umbrella containing a pellet of it. He took four days to die. It's much more powerful now. Last year, we also found out you don't have to be injected epidermally. It seeps through! Isn't that wonderful? So all you need do is get it in contact with the skin. It eats its way right through. Once it reaches the bloodstream, it just elevates the victim's temperature until his heart, quite literally, explodes from the heat."

"The letter?"

"Yes, Melanov. By the way, my deepest gratitude for your cooperation. We didn't know how else to get something into his hands. Then we decided to let his trusted friend do it for us." Karushkin made a face. "Why are you just staring, Melanov? He is dead, isn't he?"

The door opened and Cardinal Tomasek stepped out, dressed in crimson. He held Anna's hand. Behind them, moving oddly but clearly recognizable, was Shishkin, dressed in the white cassock, and surplice of a Catholic priest. Viktor saw Karushkin's eyes go wide, saw him swivel around as though to say something to the doorman, then back.

"But, the tests were one hundred per cent effective and fatal. He read the letter, didn't he?"

"He did indeed, Colonel. And to answer your question, yes, he was quite sick last night. Threw up all over himself. He had to borrow that sorry get-up from the cardinal. But, as you can see . . ." Viktor extended his arm, palm up.

As the cardinal had predicted, the little procession needed only twenty or so steps. There stood a helicopter that, in the first rays of dawn, looked like it was made of gold. The cockpit, of course, was clear hard plastic. But everything else was painted in pristine white and glowing gold, the Papal colors. On the tail of the whirlybird were painted two ornate, crossed keys. They had to help Shishkin into the cockpit. In fact, the cardinal only got him in by lifting him. Viktor stood impassive next to Karushkin.

"Now, Colonel, let's talk."

Karushkin was stunned. From his expression, he might have just been hit on the bridge of the nose by a low-flying canteloupe.

"I've figured a few things out in the last couple of hours, Colonel. The first of them is that you are a traitor."

"He's alive?" Karushkin had a stupid expression on his face that Viktor enjoyed immensely.

"You were the one who told Shishkin where the militia patrols would be, so that his friends could hit them. You said something yesterday in the house. 'They're going to ruin everything.' You're trying to stop all the reforms that Gorbachev has started, especially the ones that affect your, let's call it your profession. The missing guards outside the embassy, that's your work too. Dave, or whatever his name is, from the American Embassy, is helping you with that part?"

Karushkin was not focusing on Viktor's face. He seemed to be having trouble with his balance, too. He held on to the handle of the car door and Viktor saw the tension in his knuckles.

"When Shishkin and I got out, you saw an opportunity to embarrass Gorbachev. But to do that, you don't need us back in Moscow. At least not me and my family. Shishkin alone should be sufficient."

Karushkin listened to this as if he was hearing nothing more than office gossip.

"So you see, Colonel, I do have something to bargain with. You let my wife go, right now, and I won't say anything once I reach Austria."

"And Shishkin?"

"I give you my word, Shishkin won't talk either." He swallowed twice. "Now, let my wife go."

"I still want Shishkin," Karushkin said. There was a slate-hard timbre in his voice.

"You want Shishkin, and my promise to keep quiet? What else have you got to bargain with, Colonel?" The very words appalled him, but Viktor was caught up in the frenzy of the moment.

"Go to the helicopter. I'll bring my bargaining chips."

Viktor went ahead. When he got to the 'copter, he could see that its interior was very much like a car's, with a front and back seat. The Cardinal was in the back, with Shishkin. Squatting between them, trying hard to be invisible, was Tomek. He had hoisted Shishkin on to his shoulders as though giving him a piggy back ride. They had had a hard time finding a cassock that would cover both the boy and the dead man, until the cardinal remembered that he had some old ones. "I wasn't always this thin," he had said. How Tomek had managed to carry Shishkin's lifeless weight to the helicopter – with his legs intentionally buckled so that they would not look too tall – Viktor could not imagine. The strength of faith.

Anna was already in front, next to the pilot, a light-haired Austrian, with a huge mustache, who was complaining volubly in German. Neither the Primate nor the boy paid the slightest attention to him.

"Get in," said Tomasek.

"Not yet. He's bringing my wife."

"Wir koennen nicht mit einem toten fliegen," shouted the pilot.

Karushkin's car scoured over the cobblestones at about 50 mph – the doorman was trying to frighten Marya again, he thought, and probably succeeding.

The car came to a shrieking halt about ten feet from the chopper. The pilot began to complain about this too. The back door opened, and Marya came out, looking around as if it was her first day on the planet.

Viktor bellowed: "Marya for my word of silence, Karushkin."

From the far side of the car, Karushkin got out, cupped his hand to his ear.

Viktor repeated the terms. To his surprise, there was movement in the back seat of the car. Someone else was in there.

"And Shishkin?" the colonel shouted.

"What's your other bargaining chip?"

Karushkin bent over, looked into the car and said something.

I should have known it all along, Viktor thought.

Victoria got out, put her arm through Marya's and began guiding her toward the helicopter.

"Viktor?" It was Marya, resisting the other woman's grasp, and asking for guidance. "Where's Anna?"

"Hurry, get in here!" he shouted at them. "Now," he screamed at Tomek. With the cardinal's help, they lifted Shishkin's body out of the seat, and with his trunk at a hideous angle, stuck his head out the door of the cockpit. If it looked strange to Karushkin from where he stood, he would put it down to the cumbersome way one had to move in a helicopter.

"Was machen Sie?" the pilot wanted to know.

"Start this thing up!" Viktor shouted. He put his index finger in the air and made a circle. The pilot started flipping switches.

"Get out here, Shishkin!" shouted Karushkin. "Your friend has turned on you."

"Ah nyet, Yevgeny," Viktor whispered. He put his lips against the cold cheek and pressed hard. "Never, never would I have turned on you, moy droog."

They pushed Shishkin's body out on to the cobblestoned square. It rolled over once, and became still. At the same time, Viktor rushed to Marya and Victoria, and pushed them toward the helicopter, shielding their backs with his body. He could see Karushkin coming around the car, to inspect Shishkin. The doorman, he saw, had a gun in his hand.

"I had to knock him unconscious. He was going to put up a fight!" Viktor said. He was sure no one could hear him, since he could hardly hear himself over the whipping noise of the blades as they picked up speed.

He all but kicked Marya up into the cockpit, did the same with Victoria. If she had resisted in any way, he was ready to club her with his fist. He was shutting the door of the cockpit, as Karushkin came up to the body. The first thing the colonel did was look at Shishkin's fingers. He shot a look at the helicopter, pointed to the dead man, and began laughing wildly. He's mad, Viktor thought, and was about to think something else when he felt his stomach rise up into his throat. He had never been aboard an airborne helicopter before and was not used to its sudden surge on takeoff.

He realized that the cathedral, the Primate's residence, indeed all of Prague, was beneath his feet. They were flying! Flying away from Karushkin, the KGB, the part of the world that Mikhail Gorbachev thought he could change.

Already Shishkin's body was invisible. "Goodbye, moy droog," Viktor whispered, as tears that he did not control coursed down his cheeks. Then he looked up and saw his wife was crying too. So was Victoria, and the Cardinal had a happy smile just short of weepy. Anna was looking out of the cockpit, her mouth wide open, eyes trying to take in the miles of terrain she saw floating under her.

"Daddy, it's like a dream!" she squealed, but the noise of the rotors drowned her small voice.

Viktor almost knocked the pilot's headset off climbing over the seat to cradle his daughter. Once he had done that, he reached back up to his wife, squeezed her tightly, then let go. He looked at Victoria for a moment. She looked dazed. He had no idea why Karushkin had brought her along. Perhaps to offer her freedom too if Viktor would return to Moscow with him? Did Karushkin think Viktor would have trouble choosing which woman he wanted?

There was time for finding that out later.

Marya had a strange expression on her face, and Viktor knew that she knew who Victoria was. There would be quite a lot of explaining to do, he thought, and then a belly laugh boiled up within him, a laugh unlike any he had ever felt before. For the next two hours, while they flew from one country to another, out of one world and into a better one, he could neither be expected to listen to or explain anything. Thank God for the engine's roar, he thought. "Thank God," he shouted, directly into the ear of the Cardinal, who sat contentedly next to him.

"Yes, thanks be to God," said the cardinal, along with something unintelligible. Viktor wasn't sure, but he felt almost certain that the old man was saying "Our friend in time of need."

25

If this is Sulfazine, it must be Wednesday. Poshtats felt the needle being withdrawn, then the restraining strap loosened. He tried to bunch his concentration together as quickly as possible before the madness began. He hoped he could again vomit himself unconscious before the beatings. Then he saw them coming forward with the wet canvas, felt his arms being lifted, and the vest covering his chest. This was the worst, he knew. The canvas became tight, and together with the Sulfazine, it felt as if his heart was trying to explode out of his ribcage.

No one who knew him as a student would have recognized Vsevelod Poshtats. In six months, most of his hair had fallen out. His teeth were either stumps or broken points. His skin was the color of grease, and his vision was nearly gone. He knew he was in a gulag near Perm, knew there was a routine to the tortures he endured, knew he would die soon, but not soon enough.

A rubber truncheon crunched over his bare skull, adding white dots to the red field of pain that he saw constantly behind his closed eyes. He smelled a man's foul breath near his nose, and guessed they were about to put tubes into his nostrils. Ever since his septum had been shattered in the first beating, the tubes crisscrossed each other at will as they were shoved through his respiratory system.

The first rush from the Sulfazine came now, causing him to shiver. His legs began to go numb, but that, he knew, would change soon enough into a hypersensitivity to any touch, any caress, let alone the slaps and lashes they would inflict.

They lifted him off the frozen dirt floor and dragged him to a separate cell. When the drug had taken over his nervous system, they would alternately beat and question him. What he answered did not affect the amount of torture they meted out, and his pain had no relation to the questions. They were always the same: "When did Melanov convince you to work for the Americans?" "Who was your superior in the plot?" "Why did Dave turn you over to the KGB?"

He had tried telling them the truth at first. Later, he varied his answers according to what he thought they wanted to hear. Now, he offered arbitrary lies until the blackness claimed him.

He smelled someone else in the cell. The Sulfazine heightened his olfactory abilities, another kind of punishment. When he was certain the guards were gone, he slowly opened his eyes. The old man on the bench across from him was hugging his knees close to his face, sobbing. Poshtats was not strong enough to lift himself and, besides, the canvas restrained his movement.

"Who are you?" he croaked. In the past, they had put spies in with him, hoping he would betray a confidence.

The sobbing went on for a while. Poshtats closed his eyes.

He heard a reply but it meant nothing to Poshtats. He had been arrested before Karushkin's name became synonomous with treason.

First, the old man began to babble, then shout. "It is time for your interrogation to begin. Guards! Bring in the chair. Doctor! Test his blood pressure, to see how long he will last. Strap him in. Good. Now, you disgrace to all Russians, talk! Who told you how to get out? Was it the Rabbi? How did you make contact with Shishkin? Talk Melanov, talk!"

They came for the old man a few minutes – or hours – later. He was flailing away at the bench, calling it names and weeping. As two guards locked his arms behind his back and pulled him toward the door, Poshtats heard him saying: "It's not over, Melanov. I'll be back again. And you'll talk. Yes, you'll talk."

Poshtats tried to prevent the sound of the madman's screaming from worsening his pain. The canvas was already choking him.

Epilogue

The town of Ezsterbruz is slow to wake most mornings. Outsiders provide its few services: deliveries of milk, crusty brown Austrian bread, the special mail service that the Bundespost had been convinced to contribute, free of charge, by one of the Socialist members of the local landestag. The Romanians, in the habit of rising long before dawn to queue for milk and eggs, are roaming the streets, looking sullen and lost. By eight o'clock, the Poles are usually up and about, trying to explain to whoever will listen why Solidarity cannot govern any better than the Communists. The Czechs stay inside their barracks, occupying themselves with whatever it is that industrious, joyless, boring people do in the mornings. The Russians doze until the last possible minute, contemptuous of the lesser Slavic tribes among them.

Nearly the entire Austrian population of Ezsterbruz, and of the surrounding towns, is dourly employed with the insincere task of making the refugees from the East feel at home. Some deliver food. Some treat their ailments. An uncommonly large percentage offer psychiatric counseling, on the theory that anyone not blessed from birth with Austrian citizenship must need it.

Because it is a dumping ground of the unhappy and unwelcome, Ezsterbruz does not have what a Chamber of Commerce in Iowa might wishfully call "community feeling". Instead, each nationality stays very much to itself, insular and suspicious of overtures of friendship. Many things were happening in their countries, they knew, but they did not trust each other enough to discuss them.

But everyone knew Viktor. Whether he was successful in helping them get out of the ghetto and into the country of their dreams, or was merely the garrulous Russian who had brought down a KGB colonel, he rated special treatment. On this summer morning, he was trying to convince a Polish engineer to form a partnership with a Czech draftsman to build new quonset huts on the edge of the town. The grant being offered by the landestag was for one hundred thousand schillings per structure. At that rate, Viktor calculated, each man would clear almost five thousand schillings in profit. Since it was a state-ordered project, there would be none of the infernal tax that the Austrians seem to add like whipped cream to everything. The Pole was ready to commit, but the Czech insisted that he would have to be the senior partner, and receive 51 per cent of any earnings. The Pole told the Czech to do something to himself which would violate Austria's Morals Code. Viktor could see the deal melting away, as did most of the businesses he tried to create.

"My friends," he said, "we're making the mistake of thinking as though we were back home." Victoria translated for the Pole. Tomek explained to the recalcitrant Czech what was being said. "These Austrians are building inferior housing for the people coming in, and they think we should be grateful for whatever they dump on to us."

"The Poles should be grateful," said the Czech. "They don't know any better. But Czechs are used to a better life. I worked at two jobs in Brno, and I bought my parents a summer cottage in Slapy, right on the lake."

"What did he say about Poles?" asked the engineer, before Tomek had finished translating.

"He said they're hard workers," answered Viktor. "Shall I tell you a story about a Czech planner? He's been given responsibility for developing Prague's first underground parking garage, right?" Victoria knew the story so well by now that she could translate, more or less, simultaneously, without listening to Viktor. "Night after night, he comes home late, and finally his wife has had it. She screams at him that he doesn't pay any attention to her. The planner says, 'Honey you're right. I admit it. I've been sleeping with another woman.' 'Don't lie to me,' shouts his wife. 'You've been working overtime at the office!'" While the engineer was rollicking, Tomek told the Czech about the Polish defector who winds up in the Ukraine because he was holding his map upside down. In the end, the two men agreed on an even split of the profits. Viktor recommended a lawyer who would aid them in making their bid for the project. An East German, he said, who had decided to settle in Austria instead of in West Germany because he knew the Austrians weren't as smart. That was not, in truth, the reason; with or without a Berlin wall, the lawyer faced a patrimony suit if he set foot in West Germany. But it made both men laugh even harder, and they agreed to see the man the next day.

"Who's next?" said Viktor.

"That slimy Romanian who screwed the Bulgarian doctor's teenage daughter," said Victoria, who did not really find the Romanian slimy and had herself slept with him, several times, for free. But she and Viktor could no longer discuss sexual activities, even someone else's.

"Stefan will translate for the corkscrew?"

"I suppose so. The doctor speaks Russian fluently."

"Then I'll probably find for him."

He knew he sounded like a corrupt judge. Well, give a better explanation of what he did! For the first month after his arrival, Viktor had done little more than fend off various wheedling Americans who had offered him money and freedom (he found interesting the order of their inducements), if he would allow certain government officials to debrief him about his involvement with Karushkin. He told the Americans he might talk to them later; first though, he had an appointment with the Soviet Embassy to tell them everything he knew about the spy called Dave at the US Embassy in Moscow. It was the only revenge in which he felt any joy.

News of Karushkin's arrest had leaked out almost immediately, part of a disjointed story about a plot to defuse Gorbachev's reforms, attacks on militiamen, and, wildest of all, some totally unfounded allegations that some two dozen guards at the US Embassy had been induced to defect by none other than the KGB. A suave spokesman for the Soviet Foreign Ministry had spent several days patiently denying that there had been any changes in the Committee for State Security and challenging any foreign newsman to substantiate the anti-Soviet rumors they were writing. There was no organization known as the structure, he told them. In today's Soviet Union, there was only restructuring — perestroika.

The wild-sounding stories from Moscow dropped off the front pages as Eastern Europe began to unravel. Still, the refugees of Ezsterbruz realized that the Viktor Nikolaich Melanov of whom they had heard so much was among them, and besieged him for details of how he had outwitted Karushkin. He consistently denied that he knew anything about anything, which for these people, was the strongest possible affirmation that they were living with a hero.

Soon after arriving, Viktor chanced upon a dispute between a Russian chess master and a Polish professor over who was better qualified for a job as a gardener, a job that paid Austria's minimum wage. Unable to communicate adequately with the professor, he had located Victoria. It was through her that he learned that Tomek, the Primate's private secretary, had refused to return to Prague and had quit his training to become a priest. Victoria had welcomed him to the secular world in her special way. Viktor found jobs for the Russian and the Pole, and at a higher wage. The word went out: there was a Moscow magician here who could fix all problems.

Along with Victoria and Tomek, he recruited Stefan, a Romanian, and Lev, a Bulgarian, both of whom spoke excellent Russian. The Austrians objected: Viktor did not have a meldungzeitung, a permit to work in Austria. He was forbidden to act as anyone's arbiter or agent. A representative from Ezsterbruz threatened to complain to the United Nations office in Vienna that the Austrians were mistreating the refugees whom they had offered to help.

Viktor was told that it had been a misunderstanding, that of course he could form a service organization, as long as he did not profit from it personally.

He called it "Droog" – Friend – and took on another Czech who spoke good German to bargain with the Austrians. Viktor was back in business.

The problem was at home.

In the two-room flat they had been alloted, Viktor suffered Marya's unforgiving silence. They had agreed to stay together for Anna's sake. She was so excited about their new life, was doing so well in school and learning German with such ease and fervor that neither could bear the thought of destabilizing her family life. But Viktor knew that there was very little left between him and his wife. Her position was devastatingly simple: he had betrayed and abandoned her and Anna. He had been ready to leave them behind, to the KGB, while he plunged for freedom. Had Karushkin not been just as corrupt, desperate and unprincipled, they would never have seen him again. Viktor's attempts to soothe her were coldly rebuffed. His apology was unacceptable. When he tried to explain about Victoria, she wept noiselessly until he stopped. He told her that time would heal the wounds, but his heart told him it was over.

Victoria proved an excellent translator, especially with the men. She added flirtatious winks and encouraged them to do as Viktor advised, whether or not she thought it was the right thing. By mutual consent, they never allowed themselves to be alone. Once, by accident, just after she had helped him resolve the conflict between the Russian and the Pole, they met at the door to the building where the refugees received their monthly subsidy checks from the Austrian government. It was early in the morning, but he had already been awake for several hours, after trying to convince Marya to forgive him.

"Tell me, Victoria, why did you ever say you loved me? What did it mean to you?"

"Mean to me? I suppose I said what I thought you wanted to hear. You were different, Viktor. Always will be. There you were, filthy and lost in a strange, unfriendly country. And yet you had no intention of not succeeding. You knew exactly what had to be done. You were always in control. And I wanted to get out of Poland. It was that simple."

"Then why did you take off with that taxi-driver in Prague? Who, by the way, was an informer."

"Jiri? Oh I knew what he was almost as soon as we met him. He turned me over to Karushkin without blinking. But when I saw you and the Jew – I'm sorry, shouldn't hate a dead man – you and Shishkin, I realized that I didn't matter to you. So I decided you wouldn't matter to me, either."

"But you did matter to me!" He was surprised at how fiercely he said it.

"Well, maybe." She shrugged. "Anyway, we're here now. And what we had before is gone. Can't we just be, well, friends?"

"Of course, Victoria. Of course we can be friends."

"Well then, let's enjoy that."

To her it was that simple. Sleep with whoever pleased you, for as long as it pleased you, and for whatever good might come of it. Had he betrayed Marya for this woman?

No. The answer came as certainly as his love for Anna. No, he had taken her help and her body and her knowledge of Polish, and no single one had been more important than the other. She thought he knew what he was doing? He wanted to set her straight, but checked himself. She has illusions, let her keep them. Viktor the sly, the artful. It was a wonderful disguise. Until he thought of Shishkin.

The Czechoslovak government, made furiously aware of who the Primate had carried with him on the Papal plane, unleashed severe retaliation. Emigration was all but halted. No new priests could be ordained, since priesthood in Czechoslovakia requires state licensing. The Primate was told he would never again leave Czechoslovakia. Viktor had been told that the old man replied: "Leaving is no great accomplishment. It's feeling as though you're no longer here that is such a godsend. And I have that feeling." Within a few months, there would be a different government in Prague, and the Primate would be a revered figure. Finally, the Primate obtained permission for Shishkin's remains to be buried in Prague's Jewish cemetery – the oldest in Europe. Viktor felt sure his friend would have liked that.

After two months, Viktor was told that a newly arrived Russian had asked specifically to see him. He went to barracks 16, bungalow 3, bed 7 (the Austrians had the infuriating habit of putting everything in perfect, bland order) and saw an old man lying feebly on a bunk. He had no idea who it was.

"Strasvuyte, moy droog," he began. He never used the word comrade now.

"Strasvuyte, Viktor Nikolaich," the old voice croaked. The man sat up in bed, and reached down alongside it. He brought up an old brown shoe. "Do you see this?"

"Yes. Does that mean I pass the eye test?"

"These shoes were last soled at Arkady's, the shoemaker in Gorkova Street. Does that ring a bell?"

"Arkady's? Yes, I know the shop. I often recommended it."

"As you did with me Viktor. Remember one morning, on the metro, when my sole was loose?"

It was like trying to remember exactly how many cups of coffee he had drunk in his life. "I, uh, I think I . . ."

"Never mind, Viktor. I told you I was sure I would see you again. My son loved you, Viktor."

"Your son?"

"My name is Shishkin, Moises Yefremovich. Yevgeny was my boy."

"You are Shishkin's father?"

"Always was, always will be. I want to thank you Viktor. His wife told me how you got out, once it was done with and there was nothing an old man could do to ruin it for you. It's because of what you and Yevgeny managed to do that I had the courage to apply to leave. They don't mind old Jews leaving, you know. It's the young ones they want to keep."

"We just did it. It wasn't very well thought out." Viktor was in a slight trance. He remembered the old man now, or thought he did.

Shishkin's father frowned. "Don't ever say that. You and Yevgeny are already legend in Moscow. The young people know about you, and how you outfoxed Karushkin. Viktor, you are the only Russian in the world right now who has a right not to live in Russia. Because of you, the young people will keep demanding, keep insisting, and keep getting more. We will do what they have done in Romania, in Poland, Czechoslovakia." He put down the shoe.

"Now, Viktor, tell me about my son."

Viktor did not even try to hold back the tears. "Well, Moises," he began, "your son Yevgeny, my friend, was the world's biggest fool . . ."

Their story would live, after all.